TSUI

徐

Geoffrey Meikle

Published by

MELROSE
BOOKS

An Imprint of Melrose Press Limited
St Thomas Place, Ely
Cambridgeshire
CB7 4GG, UK
www.melrosebooks.com

FIRST EDITION

Cover designed by Jeremy Kay

ISBN 978 1 907040 27 6

Printed and bound in Great Britain by:
CPI Antony Rowe. Chippenham, Wiltshire

Rather light a candle
Than complain about the dark.

Chinese wisdom

I have treasures I guard and cherish.
The first is love,
The second is contentment,
The third is humility.
Only the loving are courageous.
Only the contented are magnanimous.
Only the humble are capable of command.

Lao-Tse

There is a tide in the affairs of men
Which, taken at the flood, leads on to fortune;
Omitted, all the voyage of their life
Is bound in shallows and in miseries.
On such a full sea are we now afloat;
And we must take the current when it serves,
Or lose our ventures.

Shakespeare

There are many kinds of violence and non-violence,
but one cannot distinguish them from external factors alone.
If one's motivation is negative, the action it produces is,
in the deepest sense, violent, even though it may appear
to be smooth and gentle. Conversely, if one's motivation
is sincere and positive but the circumstances require
harsh behaviour, essentially one is practising non-violence.
No matter what the case may be, I feel that a compassionate
concern for the benefits of others, not simply for one's self,
is the sole justification for the use of force.

Dalai Lama

I have no time for fashionable philanthropy; saving lives to put them back in misery.

Tsui

Dedicated to the future

CONTENTS

Hong Kong unless otherwise indicated

South China Sea
2005

The three men sat in the stern of the yacht, drinks in hand, quietly talking where the crewmen could not hear them above the sound of the chattering sails and the distant helicopter.

The young expat spoke, in nearly perfect Mandarin.

"We don't have the authority."

The older man turned slowly, cigar in hand. Slightly greying, slim and fit. A handsome Eurasian, whom the girls still loved. The money helped.

"We are the authority."

Though he spoke softly there was no mistaking the cold steely severity of his tone, or the intensity behind his eyes.

The second young man stood up and went to the rail. Tall and athletic, he moved with assured grace across the moving deck. A striking likeness to the older man. He did not speak but stared across the water in the evening light to Hong Kong Island, to Central, with The Peak behind. The crew were expertly lowering sail, starting engines and mounting the lights as they came into the Hong Kong harbour proper, jostling hard-working ferries and a few other privately owned cruisers and yachts as the neon ads came on.

His father was a well respected and, to most, an awe-inspiring shipping, property and media tycoon – one of the new breed of Chinese taipan: ruthless, power hungry and single minded, his 'hong' almost equalling Jardine, though Jardine didn't really count any more, being domiciled in Bermuda and listed in Singapore. In China his contacts were legendary. His time with the military, British and Taiwanese, had been interesting and essential. Cambridge, and a golf blue playing in the pines of Royal Worlington, had been good for networking. The planning had taken more than thirty years. The time was now. If ever it was.

Their unmarked helicopter escort swung away to Kai Tak as the company launch came alongside.

Melrose, Scotland
1988

The gravel crunched under their feet as they walked, disorientated by the first thick autumn fog, up the drive from their boarding house to the main building at Melrose College. They had no hope of seeing the intimidating Scottish baronial building, a cross between a house and a castle, set in the Border Hills. They stopped in what they imagined was a corner of the large forecourt, their hair wet from walking through the fog. They could only see a few yards ahead. There were six of them: new boys, new fags, in Carnoustie House, each boarding house being named after a famous Scottish golf course.

They had endured afternoon tea in house with the housemaster and his wife, and their parents, who had been sent on their way. Now, alone in their new environment, they had little to say to one another. They talked about their prep schools and whether or not they had been boarders. Bruce had surprised them by saying he'd been a boarder since he was five.

"My dad is in rubber in Malaysia." It seemed an odd explanation.

The other fathers were a physicist, a doctor, a confectionery manufacturer in Glasgow, and a lawyer. The last of the six was part Chinese, walking a bit apart, hands behind back.

"What about your old man, Tsui?" said Bruce. They always used surnames at College.

"Oh, he's in business in Hong Kong," Tsui replied.

Bruce was interested. They'd have a bit in common. He'd found that Far East people stuck together.

"What are you doing for holidays? I'm going to stay in school for long weekends, then I'm going to an aunt in Brighton for the short holidays, and home for the long summer holidays."

"I'm not sure," said Tsui. "Father is coming over for the first long weekend."

Bruce said nothing. A bit far to come for four days, he thought.

"What do you think about Tiananmen Square?" Bruce asked.

Tsui looked across at him, taken aback. "Bad. Father says it will touch everything for the next twenty years or more."

Murray shouted at Bruce, through the fog, "With a family name like Bruce, what's your Christian name?"

Here we go again, thought Bruce, cursing his parents.

"Given name. It's Bruce."

"What!" laughed Macrae, "Bruce Bruce. Certainly Scots!"

Then it was Thomson's turn.

"Lucky you're not in a James Bond film. 'The name's Bruce, Bruce Bruce'!"

KAOHSIUNG, TAIWAN 1989

He strode across the great lobby, marble floors covered with thick Chinese dragon rugs, huge round pillars supporting ornate crossbeams all painted bright red with gold trimmings. He reached the massive reception desk with its marble top and plush leather fixtures. Elegant girls in black-and-red silk cheongsams waited for him, smiling.

"Good morning, Mr Li," she said, still smiling. "Your suite is ready." And she pushed a completed registration form towards him for his signature. Looked about right, he thought as he read: Li Kai Sing, Minister of National Defence. No address. His security would bring the bags.

* * *

The plump, energetic Minister looked out of his lounge room window overlooking Cheng Ching Lake, Crystal Clear Lake. Some tourists were out in the rowing boats already. He always had to stay at the Grand Hotels as they were government owned and run. At least this one was a lot smaller than the one in Taipei. Friendlier too, and up in the hills, away from the pollution.

"Is that everything, Sir?"

"Yes thanks, Ng. I'll want you to take me down to the village later. I don't want the department car. I'll be at the meeting room in thirty minutes."

He was down from Taipei for the quarterly, supposedly covert, meeting with the Americans to brief them on Taiwanese defence strategy. Should only take three hours or so, and his deputy would do the talking. When the Americans had gone, he'd hit some balls at the driving range and then go down to the house. The Chinese were making an 'incident' of Diaoyu Island again. He smiled to himself. Clever people. And the Yanks always worried about the manpower, our three hundred thousand against their two million. Let them! All we needed was the firepower and the commissions.

* * *

He was with Ng, driving down the unsealed road towards the village. The trees were hung as usual with a few dead and bloating cats tied round the neck to free the evil spirits.

In the village a travelling opera was playing nightly this week. He had always been fascinated by the bamboo theatre which was built within hours of the troupe's arrival. As a boy he had run around inside, watching its creation from the first vertical bamboo pole, scaled by a young trouper like an agile monkey. All this ingenious activity was more interesting to him than the opera itself.

The typhoon had unexpectedly turned back in the Taiwan Straits and was heading straight for Kaohsiung.

He had phoned the girls and they were waiting for him as Ng parked the car and let him out. One of the girls, he had helped through immigration.

"Wait here, Ng," he said.

Ng nodded and went back to the car.

His two favourite girls smiled at him gently and lead him to one of the two upstairs rooms with its circular revolving bed, and mirrors on the ceiling. They gave him a shower, and then a sauna, with a large brandy. Sinatra was playing in the background. They laughed and talked nonsense as he relaxed. They were massaging him when he first heard the gale on the windows and felt the house judder.

"Look at the trees swaying," said Solange, the Indian-Malay, as she walked across the room, looking tall in her white full-length bathrobe.

He heard the bathroom window pop inwards and shatter, pressure created as the eye of the typhoon approached. The storm tore in.

"Get away from the window, Solange!" Li shouted. Too late. With a crack like a rifle it shattered from floor to ceiling. Glass flew with terrifying speed, lacerating the girl. She fell screaming to the floor, her blood spurting from her severed throat. They could do nothing for her. Ng rushed him out of the brothel down towards the village.

Dazed and bemused, he was amazed to see the theatre still standing, the bamboo bending to the wind.

Trees blocked the road now. When the typhoon died down, they'd walk back to the hotel. The Grand would have its phones back on first and he'd call Tsui's man. He'd sort it.

LAIRD HOUSE, THE PEAK 1989

Looking out over Victoria Harbour and all the office and apartment blocks below him, he picked out the cranes on the half-completed Tsui Centre in Wanchai: shopping malls, cinema complex, office space and the new OSM head office. Suzy Wong was at last moving out of Wanchai as other business moved in, squeezed out of Central by the physical land shortage and soaring prices. When they had bought the land the price had been very good; few people realised then that Wanchai was changing.

His gaze moved further away to Lion Rock and the other dragon hills covered by the rays of the setting sun. He smiled as he remembered his governess saying that Kowloon meant Nine Dragons, and that the Emperor himself, Golden Dragon, was the ninth dragon. The hills surrounded the Fragrant Harbour, one of the best deep-water ports in the world. Out of sight, beyond Lion Rock, was the temple the family traditionally used.

Deep in thought, he took his whisky off the side table and drank. Grant's twelve-year malt; smooth as silk. They had bought some shares years ago, and were now thinking of taking a controlling interest. Sales and prices were rocketing, and the Japanese were deserting Suntory for the real thing. The Scottish board of directors would make it an interesting fight, but he had some people on the inside.

A discreet cough interrupted his thoughts. One of the elderly Chinese white-coated houseboys stood beside him, a large brown string-tied envelope on a silver salver held out towards him. The envelope was sealed twice with their coded tape, the code changing every twelve hours at noon and midnight.

"A company messenger brought this, Sir."

For 'company messenger' read 'company spy'. Tsui took it without speaking, breaking the seal.

"Will there be any reply, Sir?"

"No. You can go."

He had given this project to hand-picked workers in his research department, with the final overview by their boss. They were always told to be brief. Even so, this one ran to more than twenty pages. He flipped to the Executive Summary at the back.

> *There is one remaining clandestine NINJA academy in Japan's Shiga Prefecture in the foothills of the Alps. Training is from five years old, not from birth, as in former times. Still, NINJUTSU is at the heart – the Art of Stealth, the Way of Invisibility. They remain mercenary assassins for hire. As well as their black stealth at night, operating in the dark quietly, unseen and unnoticed, they are still experts in disguise and poison and in their own way of martial arts. In our opinion there are no better commandos.*

Turning back to the first page of the report he smiled as he read:

> *A little known fact: the culture of the NINJAS began in China two thousand years ago as presented in Sun Tzu's The Art of War, chapter thirteen. As Sun Tsu says, all war (business) is based on deception...*

Sipping his whisky, he remembered his time at Shanghai University, where he had spent six months of the Business Studies course on Sun Tzu. His lecturer had been a fan, almost a disciple. The essence of Sun's work, he had told them, was in the quotation thirteen/eighteen: 'Be Subtle! Be subtle! And use your spies of every kind in every business' and in his quotation 'if you wish peace prepare for war.'

* * *

Vimana was in the drawing room; a tall and lovely Indian Goan in a fashionable sarong, gazing at herself in the full-length gilt-framed mirror. She smoothed the side of her hair and flicked an imaginary spec of food from the corner of her lips. Laird House was getting ready for the evening, quiet and peaceful, with the kids away at school. She was used to big hotels where the hustle and bustle never ceased. Tomorrow would be different, with cocktails for the governor. As head housekeeper she was already finished for the day but, as she was provided with a small flat within walking distance, it was easy to come in to make random checks. The older Chinese staff didn't like her, or her random checks, but pretended to accept that she was the boss.

The ornamental Chinese brass dinner gong in the anteroom would be struck at eight o'clock for dinner, twenty minutes from now. Her two-way radio crackled into life.

"Vimana? This is Sebastian. I've got an hour off. Can I meet you? Usual place."

She didn't hesitate. "OK. Ten minutes."

Sebastian was a handsome, dark Maori, built like an All Black flanker, and head of house security. His company from South Auckland had the contract for all the family members, wherever they were, and for the house. The two managers were good friends. She had taken him after six days, nearly three months ago. Apart from information, she decided it was about time he began to pay personally. A trip back to see the rest of the family in Goa would be a start. She left the drawing room, to freshen up in the cloakroom next door.

They met by the upstairs linen cupboard. Sebastian had put a small snib on the inside of the door.

* * *

Tsui stood up and walked across the patio to the balustrade. Cicadas were in full chorus in the warm, still evening. The lights had come on around the harbour below, the advertising on Kowloonside blazing towards him. He watched the Peak tram taking its load of customers to the revolving restaurant at the top. He felt good, always relaxed when he was back at the big house. When his eldest son Iain got married in a few years he'd move in and Tsui would move to the apartment in the grounds, assuming they ever got out of China. In the meantime the house would be kept busy with visiting nieces, nephews and cousins using the house as a base, like Antonia, his eldest brother's daughter, who was coming from the Visayas to study law at the Chinese University.

He looked at his watch. Seven twenty-five. Soon the the Comprador would be here. It was a habit, almost a tradition that, whenever they were both in town, they would meet at seven thirty for a drink. Many of the big 'hongs' had dispensed with the function of a comprador, to their considerable loss, he thought. Their comprador was highly effective as a go-between, a facilitator. He was expected to know all that was going on, and be able to negotiate whatever was asked of him, often by simply calling upon his myriad contacts – a network that now went around the world and deep into China. His company, K. K. Chen Ltd, really a company working within Tsui's company, took a cut on every deal. Last year his company had gone public on the local exchange, though the Comprador had kept seventy per cent for himself and his family.

At the same time, Tsui was taking his company private again, at considerable risk and cost. But it had to be done. He had to have control to do as he wished without being bound by rules of disclosure, and interfering and intrusive shareholders. He thought of Shelagh, his Scottish wife. What would she think? He missed her strong personality and valued opinions: a devil's advocate par excellence.

She had been killed four years ago in a car accident late at night on the winding, misty road up to The Peak. The Comprador had rushed the driver away over the border to the mainland, away from himself and the police.

He thought Shelagh would have said something like "Have a go, if you must, but it's probably impracticable."

"Good evening, Taipan."

He was the only one who still called him that. He and his kin had worked as the comprador for Tsui and his relatives uninterrupted since eighteen fifty-one. If Taipan was good enough then, it was good enough now.

Tonight the Comprador was not wearing his mandarin gown but an elegant high-quality locally-made suit, equal to any Armani. He was tall for a Chinese and as thin as a bamboo. A wispy long beard hung from his chin. His dark eyes were sparkling and energetic, always questioning. He was about ten years older than Tsui, though it was hard to tell.

"Good evening, Comprador."

They turned together and walked towards the table and chairs. The houseboy stopped hovering and left them alone.

"Cognac?"

The Chinese had made Hong Kong's consumption of cognac the highest per capita in the world.

"Thank you." The Comprador bowed.

He refilled his Grant's and they settled into their chairs, no servants looking after them, no one in earshot.

"No challenges, I think, Comprador?" asked Tsui.

"Nothing of magnitude, Taipan. But we must soon finalise our cover for Sinbad Fuel Systems. It's a little devious, but we are in the business of making money, *n'est pas*?" The Comprador smiled slightly.

"Indeed, I agree." Tsui always enjoyed his talks with the the Comprador. Intellectually astute, he kept him on his toes, alert. He wished he didn't have to go to The Lodge later. The networking had been weak. For him, an agnostic, it had become a pompous waste of time. Yet there were some lodges in China, so he would keep paying his dues.

Taipei, Taiwan
1989

Tsui Wai Kwok, Tsui's younger brother and legal counsel for the company, was doing the 'milk run' to Taipei – three meetings in two days, then back to Hong Kong. Sebastian sat beside him, his commanding presence and Island features causing chatter amongst the cabin crew.

The government people they dealt with were pleased that they always flew China Airlines. It scored them a few points, Wai Kwok supposed. He'd much rather be on Cathay. China Airlines were flown by military pilots, who thought of their planes before the comfort of their passengers. Anyway, it shouldn't be China Airlines, he thought. Misleading. Should be Taiwan Airlines. The KMT still held on to the idea that the seat of government for all of China was in Taipei.

They began their descent as the turbulence got much worse.

"Better tighten your seat belt, Sir," said Sebastian, fastening his own vigorously as he spoke.

Wai Kwok did so without speaking, trying to release the tension in his body. He didn't like flying even though he did so much, and in first class. He could see the airfield now and how the plane was crabbing its way towards the runway in the high crosswind.

"He should abort," he muttered under his breath.

The pilot slammed the plane into the tarmac. Wai Kwok heard one of the tires go and the food trolleys jump up in the air, breaking loose. Some overhead lockers sprung open, scattering luggage on the passengers. The oxygen masks fell down. Someone screamed. To his credit the pilot kept the plane straight, pulled up before the end of the runway, and started taxiing in.

"That's it!"' he said, turning, pale, to Sebastian. "No more China Airlines! We'll change the return tickets."

Sebastian was smiling and nodding in agreement.

"Let's get a drink," he said, swinging the strap of his overnight bag over his shoulder. They stopped at the nearest bar.

"Two brandies, please."

* * *

Wai Kwok looked out of the old taxi, rattling as they hit the potholes, feeling two brandies better and back on the ground. They had recently bought the apartment off Jenai Road near the business district, fed up with the erratic supply of decent hotel rooms and the Hilton always being booked out. The traffic was jam-packed with cars and motorbikes even at the tail end of rush hour. Motorbikes were everywhere in Taipei. They were the best way to get around: cheaper to run and better for dodging in and out of traffic. The pollution always seemed heavier than Hong Kong but with so many two-stroke engines he guessed the carbon monoxide would be less.

"We'll go to the apartment first," Wai Kwok said, turning to Sebastian, "and get into something casual before we go to Sogo. About ten minutes more to go." The maids would have a meal ready for them and the rooms made up.

"What time are we meeting him?" Sebastian asked.

"About eight. I'll phone him from a pay phone when we get there."

* * *

Sebastian didn't talk much. He was a cheerful enough person who could laugh and drink and party along with the best of them, but not on duty. He had learnt over the years that reticence with employers was usually appreciated. They were inside Sogo now, going up the escalator in the bright, high atrium. They got off at the first floor at the 'café' style coffee shop.

"Where are the phones?" Wai Kwok spoke abruptly, all business now.

"There are some over there," said Sebastian, pointing to the back of the coffee shop. Wai Kwok started walking over to them, leaving his briefcase with Sebastian and searching in his pocket for the right coins. Sebastian knew he preferred using public phones on trips like this. He watched him go, small steps with his short legs. He was very different from his tall, Eurasian-looking brothers. Wai Kwok looked very Chinese, conservative, a lawyer, a 'suit'.

"He'll be about twenty minutes," he said, returning. "Let's have a coffee and some of that Black Forest cake."

Always the sweet tooth, Sebastian thought. Carrying too much weight already.

* * *

He came towards them, nodding in recognition. His ill-fitting blue suit was crumpled. He looked dishevelled and a little nervous as he sat down with them.

"Coffee?" Wai Kwok watched him.

"Thanks. Black, please." He looked around him at the evening crowd, after-work shopping.

"Everything all right?" Sebastian asked calmly, in his deep Maori voice.

"Yes thanks…. Well no, actually. I thought I was being followed—"

Wai Kwok interrupted sharply, "Is everything sorted at the house?"

"Yes. The Def—" he began to say, as Wai Kwok interrupted again, holding up his hand.

"No names, Kite." He still felt stupid using the codenames his brother had introduced six months ago; no names at all had worked fine before. "You know better than that! Is everything fixed, and how much does the company owe you?"

"Yes, it's all cleared up now. It was a mess. The police got there too quickly—"

"Never mind the details. How much?"

"Ten thousand US dollars."

"OK." Wai Kwok sounded on edge too. "The usual place in Austria?" Austrian accounts were even better than Swiss: no need for any addresses, just the numbered account.

"Yes thanks." He looked defensive and weary.

"Right. You are a sleeper now, effective immediately, please. You'd better leave us now," said Wai Kwok: an order, not a request.

Kite left without speaking, as keen to leave as they were to see him go, still checking the crowd and pretending to window shop as he went towards the escalator. Sebastian saw them first: two agents waiting at the bottom. He sat up, alert, muscles tense. Kite saw them and turned on the escalator to go up, only to see two more coming down. He went with them without a struggle. No point.

Wai Kwok was on his feet now, casually making his way towards the same escalator Kite had used, to the ground level for a taxi dropping shoppers off, rather than to the official taxi rank one floor up. Good move, thought Sebastian, catching up with him. As they walked Sebastian started thinking over his country briefing prepared by the OSM research department: 'Only two years after martial law, the country is still under quasi-military rule, and the agents of the NSB act just as before. Known colloquially as the Taiwan KGB or TKGB, and feared as much as the Japanese police during the occupation, they still operate from Mystical 110, Yang Ming Mountain.' He wondered why they made themselves so obvious in white shirts, grey trousers, black shoes and a military haircut. He had changed into Giordano, Levis and sneakers. Perhaps they wanted to be noticed.

Before they reached the taxi rank Wai Kwok reached into his jacket pocket to switch off his Chinese Whistle. Recently designed by the technicians of the PLA, once switched it would immobilize any hostile bugging device within two hundred feet. Yet, conversely, it could also act as a listening device for the user, and record conversations.

* * *

They had arrived at their morning appointment, Li and Leung, the second-largest law firm in Taiwan and the biggest in patent law, and with enough wooden panelling and leather furniture to prove it. Sebastian was waiting in reception, reading *The Economist*. Mr Li was shepherding Wai Kwok into his office.

"Good morning, Mr Tsui. Have a seat. Cup of tea?" The secretary left. "How's your brother? And the trip over?" Always in a hurry, thought Wai Kwok, as if *he* was paying the fees. "What can we do for you this morning?"

"It's about Sinbad Fuel Systems."

"Ah yes," said Mr Li, reaching for one of the files scattered about, amongst countless 'Post-its', on his large mahogany desk. "As you are aware, our patent law states that if you want to register your invention in Taiwan you must do so within thirty days of the original overseas application. Sinbad Fuel Systems has not done so. So, as far as we are concerned, you can go ahead. Here's the copy of their US application you asked for."

Wai Kwok took the papers and glanced through them as he spoke.

"Thank you. We should proceed at once." He could have done all this from Hong Kong, but his brother had insisted on using Li and Leung face to face.

* * *

They were in the Blue Diamond coffee shop, a block away from Li and Leung. Mr Li's assistant was meeting them for lunch around one, depending on when he could get away. The coffee shop had live music with gracious girls singing in Mandarin and wearing the same azure full-length dresses as the waitresses. The waitress girls gave courteous service with sweet smiles, and men stayed longer than they had intended, encouraged also by the all-day liquor licence. Even the cups for coffee and Chinese tea were preheated.

Wai Kwok was reviewing the patent application whilst drinking the brandy the girl had sold him with his coffee. Sebastian was reading again, this time the *Taipei Times* and watching, more exposed here than at the office.

"You know," Wai Kwok spoke, "one of the big three car manufacturers bought the SFS patent worldwide – well nearly worldwide. They plan to sit on the idea, not use it, because they are committed to ten years' forward orders of conventional carburettors.

Pity, because the new carburettors and attachments cost only one hundred and fifty dollars per car, cut fuel consumption by twenty-five per cent, and emissions by eighty per cent."

"Sounds good," said Sebastian, standing up and putting his paper back in the rack before the girls could do it for him. He had seen Li's assistant at the entrance. As the assistant sat down with them he ordered.

Without preamble he started talking. "What Mr Li did not tell you is that the Paris convention countries are getting cross with Taiwan. They will try to ban exports from Taiwan of previously patented goods. And don't forget, China joined in nineteen eighty-five, though I don't think that counts for much."

Their food arrived without interrupting their conversation. Useful information, Wai Kwok thought. But the lawyers did not know the depths of the Comprador's *guanxi* – contacts and relations – and that some of them were only interested in a particular part of the Chinese market, and the influence they could buy.

* * *

Sebastian woke, fully alert. It was just after five on his alarm. Carefully he pulled the curtain aside at ground level. An army patrol in full battle order was moving through the apartments' garden. Surprised, he let the curtain drop. A nation on military alert? Or something more personal than that?

Their Cathay flight was at nine. Might as well get up now, he decided.

HEAD OFFICE, CENTRAL 1990

He walked across to the bank of elevators, through the throng of people, towards his own private elevator direct to his office suite on the seventh floor. The uniformed security guard pressed the button on the wall, opening the doors for him.

"Good Morning, Tsui," he said, touching his cap.

Tsui nodded as he went into the lift, the doors closing behind him. Everyone in the organisation called him only by his family name. He liked the custom, reminding him of his army days. It also helped him be less pompous and more humble, as Lao-Tse admonished. As he came out of the lift into the anteroom he heard Chopin on the sound system; it must be Wednesday. Monday was Bo Ya, Tuesday was Beethoven, Thursday Tchaikovsky and Friday his favourite, Vivaldi. For those people who came in over the weekend there was Air Supply. Quite a United Nations, he smiled to himself. Yet none of the listeners except himself, the Comprador, and his number one nephew knew that the music came with a subliminal message instilling company loyalty. It was the nephew who had procured the system in the Mid West; and he had installed it.

Coming into the office was for him like putting on a pair of comfortable old slippers. He enjoyed his work, the power and the perks that came with it, and the environment he had created for himself. He crossed the book-lined foyer to his executive conference room. A tea girl was laying out elegant cups and saucers for the meeting this morning. She did not speak, and he let her carry on working. She wore a uniform in the company colours: blue and gold. Her trousers were tight, accentuated as she leant across the large table.

His father had moved in first and made this room a man's room. He had brought some company relics from the old godown on what had then been the waterfront, cold and damp in the winter, hot and humid in summer. His father's pieces fitted in well. Quality always did. The old, solid fireplace made of oak, not working now, but a focal point, with an antique mirror above. The large conference table made of Norfolk pine taken from their last clipper, the *Bellatrix*. The framed company ensign in gold and blue horizontal bars, the blue taking up two thirds of the flag. The Venetian mirror that used to hang on the opposite wall had been removed by the Feng Shui master.

The only thing he had added was the model naval gun on the mantelpiece – an exact replica of Jardine's noonday gun. But, unlike the noonday gun which Jardine's uniformed staff were required to fire at noon, Tsui's gun fired its cap when any meeting ran for an hour. He agreed with old Henry Ford – one hour was long enough for any decisions.

He went through the door in the far corner of the conference room, to his own office. This he had changed with the help of Hong Kong's best designer, Charles Fung. Modern and minimal. A bronze glass desk, with its cleverly hidden files for his personal documents. A large table in similar fashion standing against the right-hand wall next to the door to his washroom, covered with company prospectuses, business magazines, the day's papers, and a large cutglass vase full of fresh flowers, which his wife Shelagh used to arrange. On the other side of the desk he had two Nordic Falcon armchairs in brown leather, matching his opulent swivelling deskchair. To balance the modern he had historic Chinese warriors as ornaments, with his sheaved samurai swords hanging above them. There was an antique hand-painted Go table cleared for play, the white clamshell and the black slate stones in two polished wooden bowls. He had a life-sized oil painting of Shelagh on the wall in front of him.

Looking out of the floor-to-ceiling windows, his view of the harbour and Star ferries going back and forth was interrupted by the new buildings on the more recently reclaimed land, particularly the skyscraper directly in front with the large round porthole style windows: the 'Swiss Cheese' building, Jardine House. The Chinese, no friends of Jardine, had another nickname for it: 'The House of a Thousand Arseholes'. Jardine House had been a main reason for going to Wanchai and insisting on a waterfront site on the outside edge of the final reclamation.

Under his feet he could feel the retractable cover of the spiral staircase going down to the accounts department and the trading floor. He had heard on the BBC World Service at breakfast this morning that the pound had been volatile. George Soros again, maybe. He'd check it out later.

In accounts they kept the company's walk-in fireproof safe for securities, bonds and any other critical active documents they were required to keep by law, though Hong Kong law was less demanding than most. And in that safe another, Chubb's best, cemented to the floor, where his gold bullion was secretly secured.

Walking over to his desk, he looked at his watch. Thirty-five minutes until the meeting. He'd read the mail, which his secretaries had opened and censored, selecting a few for his perusal and putting those on his desk in a leather folder. Cheng Cheng had put on top of the pile the memo and Japanese brochures from their travel company.

* * *

He went into the conference room. They were all there, and they all had their papers, files and briefcases, with the exception of the Comprador, who never appeared to carry around anything save a small note-pad and a silver pencil in what appeared to be an old-fashioned silver cigarette case.

"Good morning," Tsui said.

They acknowledged him and sat down with their cups of tea and coffee – five of them plus Tsui. His tea was waiting for him at the top end of the table, in a fine-quality traditional Chinese cup with a lid to keep it warm, and to keep the dirt out if you were a peasant farmer or a worker on a building site. His brother continued speaking.

"You see, Mr Ross, the company gets about fifty business plans, proposals, a week. At this meeting we look at a selected one each month, and we actually go with about one in two thousand. Of course, we are telling you we are very interested in your project by meeting with you this morning."

Tsui was watching Ian Ross, currently head of the flagging 'Uncle Sam's Donuts' chain in London. He was a cocky thirty-five, but not arrogant, just sure of himself. He would be putting in quarter of a million US of his own money. Not much, but it showed a certain commitment. Yet Ross wouldn't be sitting here at this conference table at all if it were not for his girlfriend and partner. She sat beside him, now quiet and determined, from Shanghai via London. One of the Diaspora. The Shanghainese were exceptional, outstanding in business. Their supremacy was in growing a business.

Wai Kwok spoke again, quietly but strongly, with intent and authority, touching all bases with his preamble.

"We have all seen the proposal," he said, looking around the table, "and Simon and his people have seen the video." He turned to the man on his right, the head of hospitality.

"Very professional. Yes. Good." Simon had learnt not to talk too much when Tsui was around.

Wai Kwok was keen to draw the girl into the meeting, and Ross sensed that he did. That had been their plan anyway. He'd back her up with the figures if necessary.

"So you see, Ms Tang, Mr Ross, we are all fairly well briefed. Perhaps you can give us a thumbnail sketch of the business?" Maybe he shouldn't use that phrase these days.

* * *

"In summation…" – Ian Ross was on his feet, taking over easily from his partner – "… we plan to open Chinese fast food restaurants similar to MacDonalds, starting with three company-owned outlets, then to franchise fifty in the first five years, and five hundred in the first ten years. We may do better than this.

"We will be different from MacDonalds, apart from the obvious, in that we will snap freeze dishes in central kitchens – about twenty outlets to a kitchen. The food will be reconstituted at each outlet. There are many advantages to this, but the main benefit is requiring fewer – expensive – chefs. Also, their pay rates will be less, as they will be working normal day hours. And there will be no need for a chef at each outlet.

"Assuming we go ahead, we will take up the offer of help in menu development, thank you, Simon." He turned to smile and nod at him. "We already have a celebrity Asian chef on board. They can work together. Your point about a children's menu is well made. MacDonald's get around sixty per cent of their sales from children.

"The outlets will of course be branded. Colours, staff, frontage etc. There will be first-rate transparencies of the food by a leading commercial photographer in London. Each tray will show the national flag of the country originating that particular dish. There will be Chinese music throughout, and, on the same sound track, the background noises of an Asian kitchen, with the sound of cooking in a wok and so forth. The microwaves will have their bells removed, be silent.

"And finally, gentlemen, Madam…" – he turned to smile at his partner – "…we will, in one way, be similar to MacDonalds. You know that MacDonalds are not in the business of selling hamburgers. They are in the property business. And very successful too. It is rumoured that they are the biggest property owners in the world, after the Catholic Church. We, like them, will buy the land under every outlet and lease it back to the franchisees. Their rent will pay for our mortgages. Like MacDonalds, they will also pay their monthly royalty of six per cent, and their two-per-cent advertising co-op, both of audited turnover.

"Last but not least. The business will be called 'Asiaway'."

He sat down, sweating a bit, but not too much. Nobody spoke. Tsui checked the time. Five to eleven. He looked at his brother, and at the Comprador. A 'Yes' with them. He began to speak.

"Thank you, Ian." Given names now; that's good, thought the young Jew. Tsui knew from experience that he was a good judge of character, probably his best asset. He felt this meeting had good karma. He continued:

"This is what I propose. If you agree, my brother Wai Kwok will draw up the papers. The ownership of the company Asiaway will be fifty-fifty. We will incorporate in the BVI. We start in London, then other UK cities, then the US. Don't get distracted by other countries asking for a master franchise. We will register the mark in the usual places. We will have joint CEOs – Ms Tang and you, Ian. There will be no cross-funding to 'Uncle Sam's Donuts'. We will put in a first tranche of five million US, and a second tranche of twenty million, subject to hitting agreed targets. It should be self-funding by then, with our lines of credit for the land."

He stood up as Ross came over to shake hands. Susan Tang smiled. Wai Kwok was talking again.

"We should meet for dinner. I'll bring my wife. Can your wife come, Simon? Will you organise it? We'll meet at your hotel, Ian, if that's OK. Say, eight o'clock at the Mandarin?"

They began walking their guests to the lift as he spoke. Unexpectedly the one-hour gun went off. Startled, the visitors looked towards the sound and the smoking barrel.

"It's OK!" said Simon, laughing. "I'll explain on the way down."

They shook hands again, smiling. The doors closed. The Comprador, Wai Kwok and Tsui were staying together for an early lunch.

* * *

"Let's go through to the office," Tsui said, leading the way. They settled down, at ease, equals amongst equals, or nearly so. The Comprador spoke first.

"An international restaurant chain – wonderful network for drug distribution, don't you think?" He smiled towards Wai Kwok.

"Maybe. But, you know as well as we do, we got out of the opium trade in spectacular fashion in eighteen seventy-one, a year after Jardine, supposedly because of crazy competition," he said. "The margins were too small. We didn't need it. We were branching out into other things. We still don't need it, and now the risks are too high anyway. But you know all that!"

"Yes," said the Comprador, stroking his long beard. "Of course. It is interesting, though. We have our reasons but we still don't condemn it on moral grounds."

Tsui spoke. "Antonia is coming to lunch with us. Our big brother…" – and he glanced at Wai Kwok – "…has sent her up to get herself organised for Uni. Let's cover any agenda we have before she arrives."

"My Taipei trip. All is satisfactory." Wai Kwok put on his legal voice. "And yes, we were right; those Harvard patent attorneys for Sinbad Fuel Systems forgot to register in Taiwan. So we can manufacture there, for export to China through the PLA."

"Comprador, do the PLA have enough clout to make the car manufacturers, including the foreign joint ventures, build in the SFS?" asked Tsui, cutting incisively to the essence of the matter.

"Yes, Tsui," replied the Comprador, without pause. He spoke softly and with authority.

"Also I have arranged with SAS – South Auckland Security, not the other lot – to debug our offices and homes on a daily basis," continued Wai Kwok, "and I've given CWs to those who need them. That is already in place."

"Good," said Tsui. "Next, about the company name change. We've been considering it for ages. Even had a call from that PR bloke, with Walter Thompson asking about the rumour. So I've decided, and I know both of you don't agree, to stick with Great-grandfather's name, One Sun Moon Ltd. But to highlight the initials – OSM. We'll develop OSM as a brand throughout the group."

The Comprador made no comment, starting to talk on his own account.

"I have been researching IRA cells as a means of control. For them it works, but for us it will not be necessary to go to that level of security."

Tsui nodded, but kept his own counsel. He did not entirely agree.

"We will continue on a need-to-know basis. As to the lodges," continued the Comprador, now looking directly at Tsui, "we will wind down our sect within a sect. Simply said, it is far too loose, badly organised. And once we have all our contacts in place, we will sever all connection with, how do you call it? This mason – ey." He still held Tsui's eye, as he had all the time he spoke.

"Agreed," said Tsui, though for his own reasons he personally would remain a mason. There was tension in the room. Much as he did not like it, he had to agree. When he had gone, the Comprador and Wai Kwok would have to keep OSM moving forward. They had to know that he would back their decisions, right or wrong.

"Anything else?" he continued, and then answering his own question, "We'll keep using code-names for anyone in on the 'China Deal'."

"Oh! God," exclaimed his younger brother, "I feel ridiculous using them! All those Scottish birds. None of the men want to be known as 'Grouse', and of course the girls won't use 'Thrush'! At least Grandmother would approve their country of origin!" Their maternal grandmother was Scots, proud and forceful. In her time she had been responsible for making the company strong and for pushing for expansion more than her husband thought possible.

"Get used to it," was all Tsui said.

"I have the Arabs coming in," said the Comprador. "They want to talk about the stud in New Zealand. If they offer much more, we should sell."

The Comprador didn't think horses were a wise investment, and they all knew it. Yet they were a real passion of Tsui's, a passion which gave him great satisfaction. In breeding it took years to make money, but in the end, with careful planning and the right people, you would. Or at least he thought so. It wasn't from the racing and the betting, but from the stud. And the money you made from the socialising – *guanxi*. But the Comprador was against. They'd probably have to be let go. He said nothing.

"Have you got some young girls organised, Comprador? They were quite taken last time, weren't they?" said Wai Kwok.

The Comprador looked at him disparagingly, implying that such details should not be spoken of here.

"Yes."

Tsui was looking at the Post-it his secretary had left on his desk. It was the simple menu for lunch.

Clear Seaweed Soup
Noodles with Tofu and Vegetables
Fresh Fruit Bowl
Chinese Tea..

Her secret message was in the two full stops at the end. Tsui smiled. He spoke again.

"While I think of it. *The Art of War*. Comprador, will you please see that all the Asian managers have read it, and you for the expats, Wai Kwok? Those who haven't given you a critique, have them do so. Then hand them on to me. We can learn a lot about our people from knowing what they think of Sun Tzu."

He stood up, and the others did likewise. Their meeting was over.

Tsui picked up the phone.

"Has Antonia arrived yet?" He paused. "Bring her in, please."

Waiting, the Comprador gently picked up one of the Chinese warriors, looked at it for long time, and then put it back, without speaking. Wai Kwok was standing, looking out of the window at Jardine House.

"You remember FILTH – Failed in London, Try Hong Kong," he remarked. "Well, now that there are more *guilos* in Shanghai, there's a new one. FISHTAIL – Failed in Shanghai, Try Again in London!" As he laughed at his own joke, the Comprador smiled. He wasn't at all sure about *guilos*: the years had made him wary.

The office door opened and Cheng Cheng, as his personal secretary, escorted in his niece. Antonia was good looking: a striking mixture of China and the Philippines, with a touch of Scots. She had escaped the heavy Teutonic features of many Eurasians. She skipped across the carpet to hug her uncles, Tsui and Wai Kwok, and turned, with a swirl of her skirt, to smile at the Comprador.

"Good morning, Comprador." She was always nervous in front of him.

Cheng Cheng smiled at Tsui, and left the room.

Macdonnell Road, Mid-levels 1990

Tsui sat on the cane settee with the thick cotton-filled cushions on the small veranda looking down again at the Star ferries and the harbour, but this time from Mid-levels, nine hundred feet below Laird House. The view was nearer, as if he had foreshortened it with a telephoto lens. He could hear Cheng Cheng fixing their early-evening drinks. Chinese New Year was over, so it was quieter now that the neighbour's mah-jong tables had been stored away and the rattling of the tiles at the end of each hand had stopped, until next weekend.

It had started six months after Shelagh was killed. In the office she had touched his hand by mistake, handing him a file, or so it seemed. He had held on to her, brought her to him, and she did not resist.

They had gone together to Macau that weekend and had tried to stay incognito at Stanley Ho's garish Lisboa Hotel. They had talked in their room, between making love and ordering room service. They had only gone out once, on Sunday, going across the bridge to Taipa for a simple seafood lunch on the beach.

She had lived up to her birth name Cheng Cheng, 'free, uninhibited, flourishing'. He knew her well after seven years working together. Her loyalty, her diligence, her independence. He also knew she had been married before, with two sons. One of them now ran their travel firm, promoted for birth and loyalty, not merit. But Tsui had not known her free spirit, her uninhibited self, and he was happy for it. It was there in their loving and in her conversation.

"If we are to be lovers, I don't want any 'hide and seek'. Let our affair be an open book for the world to read." And later. "And I will carry on as your secretary – we can still work together? I love my work." And all this to the taipan, he thought, smiling to himself at the recollection.

Two years later he had bought her this modest, compact, but cleverly designed flat. The location was perfect, halfway between the house and the office, and she had been thrilled. No protests, just enthusiasm.

Then eighteen months ago they decided they deserved a 'honeymoon'. He had organised it – a week in Paris at the Prince de Galles. When he told her she said jokingly, "I always dreamt of a honeymoon in Macau. Never mind, Paris will do!"

Tsui thought that the Prince de Galles was one of the world's outstanding hotels, awash as it was with old-world luxury in the public rooms and in the suites. The bathrooms were almost half the size of this flat, he thought, fitted out with the original brass taps and old-fashioned marble, and with a bath obviously made for two. She had loved the Hotel's rich cotton and crested bath robes and breakfast in bed each day: croissants that melted in your mouth, real butter, hotel-made cherry jams and strong black coffee.

They had been to lunch at the La Tour d'Argent, overlooking the Seine with the tourist barges going by, and with the Notre Dame behind, for their numbered pressed duck, which she had requested from the ladies' menu without prices. They had done the Arc de Triomphe, the Eiffel Tower, and the Left Bank to buy a picture. But a lot of the time they had just wandered about in the beautiful late-May weather. It was when they had stopped for a mid-morning coffee in a café on the Champs-Elysees, soaking up the spring sunshine and watching the cosmopolitan crowd go by, that he had learnt more about her. Cheng Cheng had started talking about all the girls' fashions and the girls.

"They're so young and vibrant," she had said. He watched her, dark eyes sparkling, stroking her hair. The question was in his eyes.

"What? Oh! Yes, I like girls!" Again, her free spirit. He had asked if she was bisexual. She had looked at him apprehensively, and, smiling, had said, "Yes, do you mind?"

He didn't, so long as there were no secrets and no one got hurt. In fact he rather liked the idea and he told her so. "Shelagh had been too," he had said, and she had replied, simply and pleasantly, "I know, Tsui."

* * *

To make the trip a business trip he had their man from London over for the day. They had taken a small hotel meeting room in the morning and had gone on the Seine in the afternoon. There wasn't much business to talk over, except for the fight with Grant's board and the takeover bid, which the man was heading and winning.

Then on the Saturday he had flown over to Edinburgh and driven down to Melrose College to see his number one son play in a junior rugby match against his school's great rival. He had been invited to sit in the headmaster's stand, and they had won. Iain, playing at centre, had scored two key tries. All that mud, he had thought. He preferred their other major sport, the only school in Scotland to make it so – golf. Much more useful in international business. They had two eighteen-hole full-length courses, three nine-hole pitch and putt, and extensive practice areas, along with three teaching pros. One of the end-of-term night-time 'dares' was to hit a nine iron over the main school building.

He had arranged for a shopping escort to go out for the day with Cheng Cheng. He didn't do shopping. When he got back Cheng Cheng seemed in a good mood, contented and relaxed. "We didn't do an awful lot of shopping," she had said. "All those spring showers!" She had grinned at him, handing him his drink. "How was Iain?" He had smiled back. "Good. Thanks."

It had been on that last evening after a good meal and the best part of two bottles of champagne in the quiet and opulent restaurant off the lobby that she started talking of the one thing that worried him about their relationship. She had started by saying, "You never ask about my parents, my grandparents." But, he reflected, I do know about your parents. His people had checked her out years ago when she joined the company. She had come to him after being the secretary and personal assistant in America to the taipan of a conglomerate he had bought out. Wonderful references, but the taipan, Patrick Fitzgibbon, had been furious to see her 'poached'.

"Stolen," he had said. Fitzgibbon had started another hong, becoming an irritating rival.

Her father had come south from Shanghai, and had a business exporting duck down from the New Territories and selling the ducks to restaurants in Kowloon. That had put her through Maryknoll Convent School to become an executive secretary. Her mother had died in childbirth at the age of fifteen. But there was nothing to be found about her maternal grandparents, almost certainly because the records had been lost during the Japanese occupation.

STANLEY, STANLEY POINT 1941

The Australian nurse turned to the young kitchen orderly. Their artillery guns on the ridge at Wong Nai Chung Gap had gone silent. It wouldn't be long now. The Red Cross hospital at St Stephen's was in the direct line of march to Stanley Fort.

"You'd better get out of the wards now. Let's see.... Maybe hide in the larder."

The orderly's childlike eyes were dilated with terror, like a cornered wild animal. The nurse could see that she didn't really understand, so she took her firmly by the hand and lead her through the kitchen to the larder door. She took the key off her key ring and opened the door.

"Go in here and lock the door," she said, motioning with her hands and putting the key on the inside of the lock. The girl faintly smiled her thanks. Alone now, she closed the door and climbed up behind the bags of rice. On the back wall they had made a peephole into Ward Three so that in the evenings they could watch the foreign nurses playing with some of the stronger patients. She had a look now. In the ward it was calm. Some of the nurses busied themselves going around their patients. Outside the small arms fire was getting nearer.

The first soldier smashed the front door open with his rifle butt. She could not see them, but she could hear them screaming and shouting in Japanese, and the crashing of their boots as they ran through the hospital from ward to ward. Then there was a different kind of screaming. She looked again through the spyhole. Their tortured faces and demented actions made her vomit and shiver. She began uncontrollably urinating. She was transfixed watching the murder in the ward, biting her hand till it bled. The

Japanese soldiers were going from bed to bed, bayoneting the patients where they lay, with sickening thuds on flesh and bone. Two of the nurses who had tried to stop them lay unconscious on the floor. With all the patients dead or dying, the invaders turned, grinning, to the nurses who, with no possible escape, were standing together in a corner of the ward.

The first nurse struggled frantically, only to be pistol-whipped and stripped. Four soldiers pinned her down, laughing with glee like monkeys, a frenzy of animal lust, as the fifth one raped her. The other girls talked quickly to each other, and began taking their clothes off. It made no difference. They were all bayoneted after rape, as she watched in terror, biting, shaking and whimpering softly.

Later someone tried the door handle, then kicked their way in as she sank to the floor behind the sacks. They found her when they started to clear out the food. Six young soldiers took her out to the kitchen, slapped her about and spreadeagled her on the serving table. Being twelve years old, she was small and tight. She began to bleed; too much pain to cry out. She passed out when the fourth one was on her.

She came to in the dark. Why hadn't they killed her? Maybe they thought she was dead? Or too young? In agony, she crawled out through the hospital vegetable garden to the small farm next door, and hid through the night with the pigs.

Despite the fact that the local population was being treated as sub-human and the terrible risks involved, the next day the farmer and his wife brought her in. The wife tore off her foul-smelling, blood- and manure-stained orderly's uniform. She burnt it in the cooking fire. She bathed her and dressed her in some of her daughter's clothes. After she had eaten a little ginger congee, and asking no questions, they smuggled her back to her family shack by the beach.

* * *

It was four months later when she discovered that she was pregnant, her periods erratic with malnutrition. Because of the occupation, there were no Chinese herbs to terminate her pregnancy. Anyway, it was almost certainly too late. Her favourite cousin had agreed to say he was the father, until a baby girl was born, so obviously half Japanese. It had been very hard for her, ostracised, no nuns to turn to. They had been interned.

Macdonnell Road, Mid-levels 1990

Cheng Cheng came out onto the veranda with their two Grant's and wearing one of the yukatas Tsui had brought back from the hotel in Tokyo. Her black, shoulder-length hair shone in the lights, the see-through yukata accentuating her slender figure, still a size ten, sometimes a twelve. The scent of Chanel came to him as she leant across him with his drink.

"You know," Tsui started as Cheng Cheng settled beside him on the small sofa, "It's time you had your own maid. It's going to get a lot busier at work." He paused. He couldn't tell her yet; maybe never. "Antonia called in the other day. Some distant cousin desperate for work overseas. I told Antonia to do the paperwork. If you don't like her, we can use her up at the house. She's sixteen, though her passport shows nineteen. Antonia says she's a good worker and very loyal. She was working out on the coconut plantation, but they brought her into the house."

Cheng Cheng said nothing and continued gazing at the view, immersed in her own personal thoughts. Tsui drank.

When Cheng Cheng had moved in, the company had bought the five other flats on this floor. It had been an excellent investment, and they could make sure the other tenants were properly screened. They would move one of the tenants out, and the maid could move in. That way they could still have their privacy. He'd sort out the details when they were at the office. Now he wanted to talk about her former husband, Peter Maynard, an expat police officer, as many of them were, with the Hong Kong police.

"Peter's getting expensive. He says the new man at ICAC is causing trouble. Will you talk to him next time you see him?"

"I think we should cut him loose," Cheng Cheng said with conviction.

"Not yet," said Tsui. "We might still need him."

North Island, New Zealand 1990

Antonia, buckled up, sat beside her father as they came in on final approach at Auckland airport.

"Do your belt up, Dad," she said. He always waited till the last possible minute, disliking any authority, anyone telling him what to do. She smiled to herself, thankful that he was like that. It was part of family history now. She had learnt he had rebelled against being the eldest son with all the responsibility and obligations that entailed. He had never wanted to be a taipan. To the dismay of his father, when challenged by him he had renounced his birthright and had gone to live on the coconut plantation the company owned in the Visayas. That was the story she'd been told since childhood.

Occasionally Alexander would help Tsui out with the horses. Like his brother, he had a passion for them, mainly for breeding thoroughbreds. He was helping now as Tsui was again on a long trip to China. They were on their way to their Kawhia stud to pick up three horses that had been spending the last few months away from the Hong Kong summer heat in the relatively cool and verdant paddocks of the Waikato.

Antonia turned away from looking out of the window, to her father. He was a large man, cramped even in business-class seats. He always appeared calm and confident, in control. The children on the plantation called him 'Man Mountain'. She smiled at the memory.

The plane's tyres touched the tarmac for a perfect landing.

"I love Auckland airport," she said. "Surrounded by green fields, the sea in the distance. That isthmus with that long row of Lombardy poplars. So beautiful! What vision the person who planted them must have had."

"All those long words!" her father replied. "Must be pending university. But you're right, it is lovely. And relaxing. Not like the hustle and hassle of Kai Tak; or the stampede, through a maze of metal fencing like a cattle yard, off the honeymoon seven-four-sevens in Okinawa. More like the peace and tranquility of Devonport, where the people wander out onto the apron to meet the passengers."

They checked through quickly and picked up the hire car, heading south to Hamilton and then on to Cambridge and the stud. It was a glorious autumn day, locals in shirtsleeves.

"Let's stop for lunch," Antonia said. "Afterwards I want to browse in the antique shops. There's nothing like them in the Philippines, and I want to find something special for Tsui for letting me stay at Laird House while I'm starting at university."

She parked without waiting for his answer. Just like her mother, he thought.

* * *

They drove out of Cambridge over the Victoria Bridge and the Waikato River towards Kawhia Stud, about ten minutes away.

"What did you get Tsui?" Alexander said.

"I found it in a tiny shop up a lane, only room for about three customers at a time! I got Uncle a green stone Te Toki. The shopkeeper told me they're getting very rare," she replied, not taking her eyes off the road.

"All right, I'll bite. What is a Te Toki?" her father asked.

She grinned. "It's an adze – an emblem of rank and authority for Maori chiefs."

"Very appropriate," he said. "He can hang it next to his samurai sword. Good choice though. He'll love it. Make sure it isn't broken on the trip."

That's right, she thought. She would wrap it in hay and bubble pack and put it in the overhead locker, well away from the horses and their gear.

* * *

They turned in to the tree-lined stud driveway. There was a new bold sign: OSM STUD.

"What the hell's that?" he said. "What happened to 'Kawhia'?"

"Oh! I heard them talking when I was in Hong Kong. They're going to OSM everything. A new corporate brand," Antonia said quietly.

"Bugger! I suppose they'll try and do the coconut farm as well. Well, they can get stuffed. Sorry, excuse the French."

In the courtyard in front of the big ranch style homestead Gavin Mcleod, the stud manager, stood waiting to welcome them. He had seen them turn in a half-mile away down the drive from his office window. He was always happy to have Alexander to stay – a real friend, and never a 'boss'. Not like when Tsui came on his whirlwind tours, all faxes and e-mails and urgent overseas calls. With Alexander everyone relaxed, even the horses. He was a better horseman than his brother. And Antonia lit up the scenery. Never the prima donna, always sweet and polite, vivacious.

"Hullo, Gavin. How are you?" said Alexander, stiffly getting out of the small car. The two men shook hands.

"Hullo, Alex. How're things?" replied Gavin, and then, "Good afternoon, Miss Antonia."

Antonia smiled and waved from the other side of the car. Gavin was all right: a gentle giant of a man like her father, both genuine and honest. Like most people who worked with horses, well, in breeding, anyway.

"Let's go down to the horses," Alexander was saying. "The bags can wait."

"They've been boxed most of the time for a couple of weeks or so to get them a bit acclimatised, ready for the racing stable routine, and they've been on a low-protein diet for the trip, I'll give you some saline drenches, in case they become dehydrated." Gavin's long sentences and Scottish accent were hard to follow sometimes. But what he said made sense.

"Has Micky O'Brien arrived yet?" asked Alexander. Micky O'Brien was their Irish jockey who rode the big races for them. He mainly rode in Australia and had been third in the jockey championship last year. Brought up on the back of a horse, he had immigrated with his family to Australia when he was six. The Australian government was giving away ten-pound tickets for passage. He was a 'rough diamond', hungry for money.

"He got in yesterday," replied Gavin. "Disappeared after lunch today. I've a feeling he might be 'riding another winner' up in the hay barn, if you know what I mean. Sorry, Antonia." And he chuckled deeply, embarrassed.

"Damn man! He's impossible. Is he helping load the horses, and travelling with us tomorrow?" said Alexander.

"Oh sure," said Gavin, surprised at Alexander's brusque tone.

* * *

They were on the wide veranda, having coffee and brandy in the cool evening air. The rolling paddocks of the property were dotted with brood mares and yearlings. In the distance Mount Maungatautari stood, dominating the horizon. Antonia wandered to the end of the veranda away from the two men talking of horses and horse-racing, daydreaming of home and comparing the two. She was surprised to hear Micky talk quietly behind her.

"Beaut, isn't it? So lush and green. Not like Honkers or Oz, is it?"

She didn't speak so he continued, as he glanced towards Alexander and Gavin still talking animatedly. "Enough horse talk for one evening, don't you think?" Then, almost whispering in her ear, "Antonia, would you like to sleep with me tonight?"

She was flustered, which annoyed her. And she was beginning to blush. If she made a fuss her father would be out of control. She turned to O'Brien. "No thank you," she said, sounding rather strained and formal.

"No offence? Nothing ventured… and you are very beautiful, you know."

She didn't reply. She saw Gavin coming towards them across the veranda, towering over the jockey.

"More brandy, anyone?" he said. "Are you warm enough, Antonia? The evenings are still chilly. Everything all right?" glancing down meaningfully at Micky O'Brien.

"Yes, thanks, Gavin. Lovely, thank you," she said, regaining her composure. That could mean anything, he thought. Anyway, she seemed in control.

* * *

They were back at Auckland airport going to 'International Freight'. The journey had been smooth in the carefully padded, spacious and airy stud box. The three horses and the pony had settled well. The Highland pony, James, a nice-looking dun, barely fourteen hands, was the constant companion of the flighty Bellatrix, their top horse in training. She had won the Hong Kong Invitational last year by a couple of lengths. Tsui was thinking of sending her down to Australia for the double: the Caufield and Melbourne Cups, if the quarantinc wasn't too much of a palaver. Of course, James would go too.

The plane stood waiting on the tarmac, the new company OSM logo emblazoned on the tail. Now it was a flying stable, on lease as such to anyone who could pay. Afterwards it would convert back to the corporate jet. The horse box backed up slowly towards the wide coconut matting covered ramp at the back of the plane.

"You take the pony in first. I'll follow with Bella," Alexander said. Already Gavin and the stablehand were untying the other horses. James went steadily down and up the ramps, ears pricked, with Bellatrix following sideways, like a crab, tossing her head and snorting, eyes wide. Quietly and firmly they were put in their stalls. They sniffed and pulled at their hay nets, moving restlessly.

Immigration and customs checked them out. The bags were put in the hold, the groom's and jockey's stuff with the horses, and Antonia's Te Toki above her seat with the hand luggage. They had to be seated for take off and landing. The rest of the time they could be with the horses.

"Bon Journey. Give my regards to Hong Kong," said Gavin, shaking hands with Alexander and kissing Antonia on the cheek. Never mind, he'd known her since she was a kid.

Kai Tak Airport, Hong Kong 1990

They were coming in round the back of Hong Kong Island. Antonia had been invited to sit behind the second officer so that she could be more involved in the exhilarating landing. In a few minutes they were over Kowloon. She noticed they were flying to the left of the markers, but said nothing.

As if reading her thoughts the captain said, "If we hold out just a little bit left we get an easier turn to the runway."

All concentration now, no more chitchat. Moments before the chequered board they took a sharp sixty-degree turn to starboard. She saw the right-hand markers on the tops of buildings now, as the runway loomed large ahead. They were steadily losing height to about two hundred feet above the last two-storey buildings in Nga Tsin Wai Street. You'd think the wheels would collect the laundry off the rooftops, thought Antonia. Then they were over the airport security fence and touching down smoothly on the tarmac. These pilots flew in to Hong Kong three or four times a week. They swung off the runway and began to taxi in to the freight terminal. Antonia looked back at the horses. Micky O'Brien and the groom were with them. They seemed settled enough.

When their plane stopped, the doors opened and the passenger steps were pushed into place. Hong Kong Immigration and Customs came on board. At the back came a young Chinese policeman with an Alsatian. The dog seemed excited and began to bark. They were checking the overhead lockers.

"What's this?" questioned the customs officer, taking down Antonia's gift.

The dog sniffed it all over, then moved on down the aisle, still barking and pulling on its leash. The policeman seemed to be losing control.

"It's a greenstone Maori artefact. It's a present for my uncle, Mr Tsui."

"I'd better have a quick look anyway." He took out his knife and ripped through the packing. He pulled at the hay she had wrapped it in until he could see some greenstone.

"That's fine," he said, turning to see what the dog was making such a fuss about. It was barking, standing on its two hind legs, straining forward on his leash. The horses were becoming restless.

"Keep that bloody dog away! Get it out!" yelled Micky.

The policeman stumbled on the slatted floor. The dog broke free, snapping and snarling towards the equipment and holdalls. It was too much for the thoroughbreds. One reared up, breaking its halter rope. As it came down its off fore slipped outside the stall rails. It snapped like a dry twig and swung uselessly around as the horse still struggled on three legs. The Kiwi stablehand reacted instantly, diving in his bags for the stun gun. Straight into the neck, and in five seconds the horse slumped to the ground in a heap, its broken leg sticking out at a crazy angle.

The young policeman had at last pulled the dog back, still barking, into the passenger area, and the other three began to settle, snorting and stamping their feet. Alexander was first to speak.

"Jesus Christ! You damned idiot with the dog. This is going to cost someone."

"Excuse me, Sir," the immigration officer was talking decisively. "We'll have to sort that out later. Right now we have to decide what to do. This slot is needed for DHL inbound from Tokyo."

"The hell with your DHL! I think that horse has to be put down."

"Can you do that?" asked the officer.

"No! I'm not licensed here. And anyway we're not allowed to carry the equipment. We need a vet. And we'll need the low loader and pulley from the racecourse," said Alexander.

"No, there's no time for that. We'll use a fork-lift," said the officer, leaving the plane, talking earnestly on his walkie-talkie.

"Let's unload the others and get them in the horse box. They've still got to get to Happy Valley."

The groom looked pale and shocked, anxious to do something. The horses were organised and loaded with the help of the trainer; the bags put in the limo; the equipment and the jockey's gear in the front of the horse box, above the cab. Peter Maynard had appeared from nowhere.

"A rum do, eh?" he said. "The vet won't be long. You don't have to hang about. Alexander, your brother wants you to call him from the car."

Alexander didn't reply, but turned to the groom. "Are the other horses OK, Jim?"

"Yes," he replied, looking over to Micky O'Brien chatting to Antonia. "Can you have a look at the pony, though, Mr Alexander?" They walked up the ramp.

"What's up with James?"

"No, he's fine," he said, patting him on the neck. "It's the jockey. In his racing boots there's some sealed packets."

"Shit! Drugs. No wonder…. Shit!"

The vet had arrived quickly. O'Brien had gone with him into the plane. Minutes later they heard the shot. The fork-lift was standing by, carrying an empty wooden pallet. As Antonia and Alexander left, they saw through the rear window the fork-lift backing slowly down the ramp. The horse's head lolled over one side, its tongue hanging out, and the useless leg under its body. On the other side, its hind legs were dragging on the ground.

* * *

They were leaving the airport, heading for XHT, the Cross-Harbour Tunnel. With no rush hour yet, they were making good time. He'd call Tsui on the scrambled phone.

"Hullo, Tsui. How was China? You're back early."

"Hullo, Alexander. Which horse was it?" Tsui asked.

"One of the two-year-olds," replied Alexander.

He's insured, thought Tsui.

"Is Bellatrix all right?"

"Yes.... Is this phone OK?"

"Yes, they're checked daily these days. What happened?"

"The police dog spooked the horses.... We had to put one down."

"Yes, I heard that. Maynard was there."

"There's something else.... Micky O'Brien was bringing in some cocaine. Jim saw it in his gear. That's what started the dog off..." There was no response. "...We're coming up to the tunnel. I'll have to go."

Turning to his daughter he said, "Not a word, OK?"

* * *

Tsui was furious. Micky O'Brien was headstrong, wilful, too full of himself. He had thought he could control him with money. He had misjudged him and that made him more angry. Yet he was the only one to get the best out of Bellatrix.

He'd have to call the Lizard, his principal Mainland contact. Jovial, rotund and gregarious when he wanted to be, his real persona was made of iron, totally ruthless. His cover was in manufacturing plastic and material flowers. He exported to the United States, which meant lots of travel overseas. Tsui took his coffee to the window and relaxed, watching a Star ferry make its crossing.

He dialled Lizard's private line.

"Hullo."

"Hullo, Lizard. This is Osprey. Can we talk?"

"What a cock-up. What does O'Brien think he's doing? He's your man. Sounds like a loose cannon," said the Lizard, in quick-fire succession.

"I agree," replied Tsui. "His proposed role as one of our international couriers is dead."

"Indeed so," hissed the Lizard. "If it weren't for your need to have him for your inconvenient horse-racing, which by the way I don't understand, we'd have to say goodbye to him."

"You mean, terminate him?"

For Tsui the trouble was that O'Brien thought he'd been so clever, thought he'd got away with it this afternoon. Yet he couldn't tell the Lizard about Maynard. Maynard would be expensive this time. Never mind, they would more than recover their costs by acquiring the cocaine, by stealth. The process was already underway.

NASSAU, THE BAHAMAS 1991

He put Cheng Cheng's cases on the luggage rack, and she tipped him in US dollars.

"Thank you, Ma'am, have a good evening."

The phone rang. It was Sebastian.

"Everything all right, Ms Sa?" he asked.

"Yes, fine thanks, Sebastian. That was a long flight! I think I'll have room service and call it a day," she said.

"Fine. I'll be at reception at nine. You've got my room number, just in case?"

"Yes, thanks. Seven five two. At the end of the corridor."

"That's right. OK, Ms Sa, sleep well."

She hung up the phone and looked out of the hotel window. Her view was over the hotel swimming pools and palms to the two high cruise ships moored in sparkling blue water, and beyond them to the beautiful white beaches of Paradise Island. She had booked them into junior executive suites – Hilton hotel's answer to serviced offices around the world, with a large desk, two phone lines, a computer port and a full-service business centre available twenty-four hours a day.

Yet an overflowing bowl of tropical fruit and the half-bottle of champagne on ice did not encourage office work. The British Colonial had all the feel of a resort hotel, relaxing and laid back, with guests bringing sand into the lobby from the hotel's private beach.

Tsui had called the head office from China to ask her to take the Bahamas trip for him. The Bahamas were the home base of the inventor of the Sinbad Fuel Systems, no doubt for tax reasons. Tsui had made her a director of the OSM Company handling the SFS project, saying that it was a well-earned promotion. They had decided to take the Hong Kong licence, which the Americans had not troubled with, so that they would have insider information for the Taiwan/China project.

Darkness was drawing in. The carnival lights on the cruise ships looked like Christmas trees. She switched on her room lights, pulled the curtains, then remembered, annoyed with herself, that it should have been the other way round. She rang room service and ordered a Malaysian omelette. A small strip light lit up a heavily framed picture on the opposite wall. It looked like a seventeenth-century pirate. She crossed the room to read the discreet notice beside the picture.

A privateer not a pirate.
Sir Henry Morgan
1663–1674
A privateer carried a 'letter of marque'
in this case from the government of Jamaica
to fight the Spaniards on behalf of England.

She smiled to herself. One of their merchant bankers in the Landmark back in Hong Kong was part of the of the J. P. Morgan group. She wondered if this pirate was one of their forefathers. More than likely. Just last week the Hong Kong stock exchange had asked again for Morgan's to strengthen their Chinese walls. She had noticed in reception that some bankers were holding a convention in the hotel. They would feel at home in these waters.

Room Service came quickly, the food attractively presented. She ate, watching American television, had a shower and got ready for bed. She wasn't tired now so she took out her well-thumbed copy of *The Art of War*, thinking about Tsui and why he was always delayed in China and how well he fitted Sun Tzu on 'Commanders'. *Wisdom, Sincerity, Benevolence, Courage, Strictness. The general who harkens to my counsel, and acts upon it, will succeed.*

* * *

Sebastian was waiting for her when she arrived at reception at nine sharp. He smiled broadly, his big Maori frame rolling like a seaman as he walked towards her.

"Good morning, Ms Sa. Have you eaten yet?" He was picking up some Chinese ways.

"Thank you. How about you? Let's go to the coffee shop," Cheng Cheng replied.

"You've got a message," said Sebastian, pointing to the blinking light on her pigeon hole. She walked over to the receptionist.

"There's a message for me, please, seven twelve," said Cheng Cheng, showing her room key.

The pretty girl smiled, turned, flicked off the light and gave her the envelope.

"Damn, it's from Johnston's attorneys. He won't be back in the Bahamas for two or three days. Arrogant so-and-so, I'll bet he'd be here if it was Tsui."

Sebastian didn't mind a few days in the Bahamas, and he said so.

"Never mind. A few days' holiday will do us good! Will I send a fax to your new secretary, what's-her-name?"

"Jane," she said sharply, then in a lighter tone, "Yes, OK, that's fine thanks. And can you check out the lawyer's office. Tsui said that it's about ten minutes' walk down Bay Street, in a small courtyard near Parliament Square. Let's eat first."

They sat in the coffee shop overlooking the bustling straw market and a MacDonald's, and had orange juice and fresh fruit.

"Well," Cheng Cheng said, "I think I'll get some magazines and sit around the pool this morning. What idle luxury!"

* * *

"Can I use this chair?" The tall, tanned girl looked down at Cheng Cheng. "There aren't many in the shade!"

"Sure," said Cheng Cheng, smiling. "Go ahead." She returned to her reading, looking at the fashion pictures. She heard the other girl settling down as she spoke again.

"Are you here with the banking convention?"

"No, just business," she said, glad of the company.

"Nice way to do business!" Cheng Cheng smiled, saying nothing.

"At the convention they work from eight thirty to two o'clock, and then it's all free time for the Bahamas, courtesy of Barings! Not bad!" The girl took a sip of the drink she'd brought with her. "What's your name?"

"Sa Cheng Cheng," and by way of explanation she felt was needed, "It's Chinese."

"I'm Ina Isaacson. My part of it is from Brazil!" That explained her lovely skin colour, thought Cheng Cheng. "I think I'll go in for a swim."

She got up, and with five languid paces came to the edge of the pool, diving in without a splash. She swam six lengths in the uncrowded pool before vaulting out, dripping, and slightly out of breath.

"That was very graceful," said Cheng Cheng.

"Oh! I was never out of the water for long when I was growing up! Besides, Ina means 'Dolphin Goddess', so I have to be good!" she said, laughing, crinkling up her nose. "Are you here alone?"

"No. I've got a security man travelling with me. A large, very fit Maori."

"Oh! I've seen him. Rather gorgeous!"

"Yes, he is. But strictly business. We're waiting for someone to join us. I think I'll send him golfing tomorrow morning."

* * *

Cheng Cheng and Sebastian were in the main restaurant, at the window, for their evening meal.

"Why don't you play some golf tomorrow? The hotel has some special deals with the Paradise Island golf course, and you can hire clubs."

"Sounds good! I could do with some exercise; the gym's not very good," he said, chewing his porterhouse steak. Cheng Cheng was missing her rice.

"And we can do some souvenir shopping in the afternoon. I've confirmed the meeting for ten a.m. tomorrow. Maybe we can leave on Thursday."

* * *

She came down in the pink hotel bathrobe, swinging a casual rattan handbag. She put her things down beside Cheng Cheng, smiled hullo, dropped the robe and went for a swim. Her bikini was even more micro than yesterday, a brilliant azure, like the sea lapping up onto the beach. Coming back and rubbing off with one of the towels, she turned to Cheng Cheng.

"Don't you swim?" she asked.

"No, I never learnt. Actually, not many Chinese do."

They smiled at each other.

"What are you doing this morning?" Ina questioned.

"Nothing really," Cheng Cheng replied, still smiling.

"It's going to be too hot to swim soon," she said.

"Let's cool down upstairs and drink some champagne. There's some in my mini-fridge, and glasses too."

"Good idea," said Ina, bending over and collecting up her things.

* * *

Cheng Cheng opened the bottle, filling the two cold champagne flutes, giving one to Ina and sitting down beside her at the coffee table. They sipped their drinks together.

"Champagne is all right at any time, isn't it?" said Cheng Cheng. She must have got her drinking open-mindedness from her Japanese genes; and her sexuality too, she thought. Ina grinned. She crossed her long legs and began swinging her manicured toes.

"They say that one of the pools is seawater and one fresh. I don't believe them. Anyway the chlorine's much too strong. I stink! Do you mind if I take a shower?"

"No, of course not," said Cheng Cheng, patting Ina's knee, her lips apart, smiling. "I'll join you!"

"Oh! Goody! Come on then!" said Ina, skipping barefoot down the hall.

* * *

Sebastian watched the elevator stop at the seventh floor before walking up the emergency staircase two steps at a time. In his bathroom he splashed water on his face, towelled away the sweat and water, then went back to his room. He switched on the receiver. He could hear the sound of running water and giggling. When they turned off the shower he would hear better.

No need to keep the tape. Tsui had told him it was an inclination of hers which might affect her strategy, and just to look out for her. The water stopped. He could hear clearly now.

* * *

They sat at the round conference table at the back of the small, trim office, walls of gentle pastels and earthenware vases full of flowers everywhere. Outside a mature bull vine lay on trestles, shading the patio, its large red flowers attracting a mass of brightly coloured butterflies.

The inventor, Big Johnston, or 'BJ', sat beside her, his weight creaking his Chippendale chair whenever he moved. Gregarious and a 'late night owl', playing backgammon with cognac till the small hours, he was also that unusual mix: an inventive mind and an excellent businessman, with property around the world. His two patent attorneys sat further round the table. Sebastian was waiting in reception, talking to the secretary.

"The trouble with the Hong Kong licence is Taiwan," Cheng Cheng was saying. "You're not able to patent in Taiwan now. That might jeopardize the exclusivity of the Hong Kong licence." The suave patent attorneys weren't about to admit their cock-up, not registering quickly enough in Taiwan.

"Why are you interested in Hong Kong? It's a tiny market," the inventor questioned her.

"It's our home base," Cheng Cheng said, without hesitation. "We plan to have the Transport Department start by putting them in every taxi. We want to help with our environment." At a profit, she thought. "Pollution from vehicles in Hong Kong is getting very bad."

There was a pause.

"What about China?" asked one of the attorneys.

"There's no market there. Won't be for many years. Not enough cars, and anyway their equivalent of the EPA won't be overly active. The Chinese government feels they should be allowed to develop first, like America and Britain, before looking to clean up their environment. Besides, most of their pollution is from solid fuel burning." She said nothing about the early planning going ahead for massive international joint ventures in car manufacturing.

"OK, let's do this. Let's half the licence fee for Hong Kong, and add two per cent to the royalty until the other half is paid. Draw up the agreement, Brian. Ms Sa, you'll have to send someone you can trust over to learn the know-how. We'll have the agreement ready to sign at nine tomorrow morning. In the meantime you go over to the lab with my secretary for the 'official tour', then all meet back at the house at seven for drinks and dinner. OK?"

But BJ didn't expect an answer, getting up and leaving the room, used to people doing as they were told. She had heard about the 'dinners' at the old governor's residency on the hill, overlooking all of Nassau; with its original and elegant furnishings, the swimming pool and the guests' cabin at one end. And the backgammon table in the drawing room worth more than half a million pounds. And the local staff.

* * *

The deal was signed and they were checking out. As the receptionist gave Cheng Cheng her receipt, she also gave her a large white A4 envelope with her name and room number written on it.

"This was handed in for you earlier," she said, smiling.

She opened it with the paper knife on the end of the hotel pen. Inside there was a typewritten ordinary envelope addressed to Tsui at the office and marked 'personal'. She threw away the big envelope and put the other in her Gucci briefcase. Who here knew that she worked for Tsui? The inventor and his attorney's office. And Ina.

* * *

They transferred to a Cathay flight as soon as they could. First class was to Cheng Cheng a luxury, and an unnecessary expense. But very nice. She had begun to teach Sebastian Wei-Ch'I on a magnetic nine-by-nine board. The challenging game of strategy and territory had been played for four thousand years. More subtle than mah-jong, chess, or backgammon, Mao Zedong required all his generals to play it. Known as 'Go' in Japan, it was studied through the centuries by the Japanese warrior class and Ninjas. Tsui excelled.

* * *

He sat in one of the Falcon leather chairs opposite his desk. Tsui was considering the Bahamian trip. He had sent Cheng Cheng down to the mailroom with the letter so that they could x-ray and open it. He had asked her to let no one read it. He was wondering who else he might know who was in or visiting Nassau, when Cheng Cheng knocked and came back in, looking smart in her well-cut black business suit. She was smiling.

"It's OK," she said, handing him the open envelope.

He took out the letter and read it.

"It's from Barings, London. They've heard rumours. Want to know if we, I, knew if China needed any US dollar finance for purchases overseas. Something about frictions between Taiwan and China. They're never shy about playing both sides of a situation! Wonder where they get their information? It's signed by a partner Ivan Isaacson. Mean anything to you?"

Clipper Lounge, Mandarin Hotel 1991

The Mandarin was simply one of the best hotels in the world, and only five minutes from the office. Tsui sat at ease in the bulky leather armchair at his usual table near the uncrowded entrance to the exclusive arcade, another home to him. The pianist played Gershwin through the drone of voices of the elite. He was waiting for Cheng Cheng and Antonia and afternoon tea. He had told the attentive but discreet waiter he would wait for the others to arrive. They had been shopping in Ocean Terminal on the Kowloon side, these days a bit less expensive than Hong Kong Island.

Whilst he waited he considered, planned, opening 'boxes' in his mind. The Comprador. For instance, why was he so against freemasonry? There were Chinese masons and lodges on the mainland. On the surface it all seemed fine. All men are equal. One god for a universal religion encompassing all religions. Tolerance, charity and truth. With six million members, averaging fifty each Lodge, they certainly should be a benign influence around the world. Though there were some oddities. He had crept his way out of Blue Lodge up the ladder of 'degrees', amused by their initiations, rituals and regalia, but learning more. He had been surprised to find out that 'brother' would perjure for 'brother', even in the highest echelons, in the case of treason and murder. Some records said freemasons had for centuries been in a secret cabal with the Jews, planning to seize by subterfuge the financial centres of the world. He had tried networking, building a 'Scots' society within a society, but, as the Comprador had said, it hadn't worked. Still, for him, the mainland lodges might be useful.

He saw Cheng Cheng and Antonia walking up the wide heavily carpeted staircase from the lobby, shopping bags banging against their legs. They had become good friends, which pleased him. They both kissed him on the cheek and settled down, almost engulfed by their armchairs. Cheng Cheng and Tsui ordered smoked salmon sandwiches and Chinese tea. Antonia had an éclair, and a slice of Sachertorte with black coffee. She was young and slim. He watched them laughing and joking and talking nonsense.

* * *

He had had his seven thirty meeting with the Comprador in a corner of the Chinnery Bar at the Mandarin. Later they said goodbye to Antonia and took the car back to the office. He wanted to call London. The building was deserted and silent as they passed the security guards at reception, who quickly stood up to acknowledge Tsui as they took the lift up to his office suite.

Cheng Cheng got him the number and he started to talk. She went to her office, knowing he'd be half an hour or so. London markets were still vital to Hong Kong and OSM, and the pound was moving.

He came to her office and she stood to meet him. They'd had little time for each other since he'd been back from China. He held her strongly in his arms. She stood on tiptoe and nibbled his ear, then whispered, "I set the noonday gun for eleven minutes!"

"Tell me all about Ina," he said, grinning.

THE LAKE OF THE OZARKS, AMERICA 1991

She sat in her car, smoking. It was still warm inside, as she had only been waiting five minutes, waiting for the minibus from Kansas City with the girls. The snow was falling gently on the Japanese garden, an attraction of The Lodge of Four Seasons resort. It was living up to its name. The arriving cars were crunching over the snow as they parked. Cars that had been parked overnight had four inches on their roofs.

She saw the minibus turn off the road and into the car park. Quickly she stubbed out her cigarette. As she got out of the car, she pulled up her collar against the driving snow. Opening the trunk, she took out her briefcase and overnight bag, and slammed it shut. Her miniskirt under her fur coat did little to keep her warm; her knee-length white leather boots helped. Quickly she joined the girls as they laughed and giggled their way into the warm foyer and to the crackling log fire. The driver shepherded them away from reception towards the ice rink.

There were only a few skaters, being midweek and no seminar in the hotel. The delegation from Taiwan stood in a small group, off to one side. They seemed nervous, but full of anticipation. They wore their name tags from Washington, and the girls were beginning to look for the man to which they had been allocated. Last year they had not done this. Heated arguments had ensued and the hotel had become concerned.

Each year, Li Kai Sing had brought his annual twelve-man delegation home through the Ozarks and the Four Seasons as an 'American bonus', which was much appreciated, valued, and vied for in his department.

The girl came up to him, looking him in the eye, knowing him.

"Hullo, Mr Li, how are you today? Shall we go for a coffee?"

She didn't wait for an answer, turning around as she spoke. She carried her own bags, knowing from experience he would not. Some of the Taiwanese were tentatively going on the ice, escorted by the girls. The others were talking about trying skiing, though they couldn't ski. The hotel 'skiing' was a golf driving range in the summer: one large slope with a single-pommel tow. The driving tees were enclosed to double as a 'ski haus' for hot chocolate and ski and boot hire.

The coffee lounge overlooked the Japanese garden, the falling snow gradually making everything into unrecognisable white mounds. The bamboo fountains were frozen in motion, an icicle hanging from their tips. They ordered coffee and jasmine tea.

"How's the trip been?" she asked, passing the time till the other members of the group were appropriately distracted, not expecting any meaningful conversation.

"Fine thanks. As to be expected. The snow is beautiful." Then after a pause, "I've never been here in summer."

"It's much busier. I don't think you would like it!"

He smiled, and looked again out of the window. How could she possibly know what he thought? What impertinence.

* * *

He had explained the situation to the hotel management, as he did each year, so there was no difficulty in taking her upstairs. They assumed that she was one of the escorts from Kansas, and that was fine by him. He opened his door and entered in front of her. She followed, closing and locking the door behind her. She threw her case in the bottom of the wardrobe.

Sitting on the bed, she opened her briefcase on her lap. He put on the radio as loud as he dared without disturbing anyone in the adjacent rooms and so that she would have no suspicions. He wouldn't strip search her – they were supposed to be on the same side. Before he sat down, he switched on his CW in his trouser pocket. His one looked like a lighter. He felt secure.

She came close to him, speaking in a whisper.

"Five F-fifteen Cs is a good order at fifteen million each. The boss thanks you. Same as last year, here's your American Express Gold card. You know the precautions. Use it unobtrusively, only in places that don't know you. You sign as 'Danny Leung' as before. The card is on a numbered account with Hypo Tyrol Bank in Innsbruck – more secure than Zurich. We'll pay each due date and the card cuts out when you reach your limit. OK?"

"OK," he said, taking out his gold pen, signing the card as Leung and putting it at the back of his business card holder.

"Oh! They want you to use the TECRO as little as possible. We won't be using AIT. We prefer to work direct with your department."

He didn't reply to the obvious. She snapped her briefcase shut and spun the locks for the opportunist thief.

Getting up and turning the radio lower, he asked, "Rum and coke, is it?"

"Yes, thanks."

He went over to the minibar and fixed her drink, then got a brandy for himself. Passing her drink to her, he said in a brusque tone, "We'd better go down and mingle."

"Yes, you're right," she agreed. "But do you mind if I have a quick shower first, please?" She felt she needed one after the drive from DC.

He did not answer, aggravated. She picked up her bag and headed for the bathroom. He heard the door lock and minutes later the shower start. Switching off the radio, he took his drink over to the window. The snow was still falling, heavier than before. He couldn't see the lake any more.

He began to think about the courier. Maybe she was learning too much. Certainly if she spoke out, his department would be compromised, and even the KMT would be severely embarrassed. He would be hung out to dry. He had checked out the Austrian banks. It was true their numbered bank accounts were more clandestine than the Swiss. They had even avoided the stigma of being found out dealing with the Nazis during the Holocaust, something which still plagued banks in Switzerland and Germany. Yet… his thoughts moved on to an endless puzzle that worried him: his country's odd relationship with America, and how he gained personally from it. America had no diplomatic relationship with Taiwan, yet they were their only military supplier. And the US was Taiwan's largest trading partner, though that was swinging towards the PRC, with Europe and Asia expanding. Yes, things were changing more quickly these days, even the KMT's dictatorial politics. He had to be careful. More open government was bad for him. Martial law had gone. The decree, issued as the delegation was about to leave Taipei, was a fair example of how long the conservatives had hung on. 'The period of national mobilisation for the suppression of the communist rebellion is over.' They always seemed in cloud cuckoo land to him, but he never spoke out.

* * *

He heard the door open. She came out dressed in a white roll-neck top that accentuated her rejuvenated breasts; jeans; and boots. She had dressed to fit in with the Kansas girls. Certainly he'd never seen her dress like that at the office.

"Let's go, shall we?" she said.

He followed her out of the room, not responding and not smiling, barging in front of her at the lift. They went in to the bar, where a junior member of the delegation was already warming up the karaoke with Bonnie Tyler's *Holding Out For a Hero*. Very good. Later on in the evening, when he was pushed, he would 'do' his 'anthem', 'Where do you go to my lovely, when you're alone in your bed?' It's always about control!

Hong Kong Sevens, Government Stadium 1991

"Who's going to win?" Iain was in the East Stand with Bruce and Sebastian. He and Bruce were back from school for the spring holidays, and Sebastian was enjoying the long weekend. Tsui gave all the Maoris who worked for him from South Auckland Security time off for the Hong Kong Sevens. They were standing together as a group, becoming slightly rowdy. Security was taken over by a local firm, which worried Sebastian each year.

"Even in the presence of Mr Sebastian, I'm going to pick Fiji!" replied Bruce, smiling at Sebastian.

"You might be right, but I've got a hundred dollars that says the Kiwis will be up for it!" challenged Sebastian.

"That's Hong Kong Dollars!" Bruce clarified.

They were watching the parade before the Finals. In fiesta spirit all the teams were on show, lead in most cases by their mascot. At the front a Chinese pipe band played. At the rear came the referees, each with a white walking stick.

The seven-a-side game had found an unlikely but enthusiastic home in the British colony. The seven-a-side game had started over a hundred years ago at Greenyards, the ground at the boys' school's town, Melrose. Bruce had been selected to play for the town whilst still at school. They were keen.

The three of them had pints of draught San Miguel in hand. The bars had been open at ten this morning and would stay open till ten at night.

"Rugby players know how to drink, that's for sure!" remarked Iain.

"Yeah, they do. But have you noticed how convivial the crowd? Hands across the nations and all that stuff. No fighting like those soccer hooligans. I wonder why that is?"

The question hung in the air unanswered. Sebastian was drinking slowly. He had taken out his light army-issue binoculars and was scanning the stands. He found Tsui with his brother Tsui Wai Kwok. They were talking with the taipan of Hong Kong Electric, probably about their upcoming fuel oil contract he'd heard them discuss. The taipans were more interested in the deals they made than the results of the various events they attended: racing, British pomp and circumstance; rugby, cocktail parties and receptions; yachting, yum cha and the elaborate Chinese dinner parties in private rooms, where they ate first and talked business afterwards at a separate conference table, the cognac bottles in front of them on a lazy Susan.

He heard the drone of the light plane. Turning, he trained his binoculars on the flight path. The plane was flying slowly along the line of the hills at right angles to the stadium. A streamer trailed out behind. He steadied his glasses, moving with the plane, and read the banner, still a long way off. 'Welcome to the Hong Kong Severns'. Spelt wrong, like the river. Unusual. He gave Iain the binoculars and took out his mobile phone, courtesy OSM. He went to the memory bank and punched a number.

"Peter, do you see the plane?" He spoke sharply.

"Yes, I've been watching," came back Sebastian's stand-in. The pilot was banking to the right, heading towards the ground.

"Get Tsui back into the grandstand. To the rear of the concourse."

"OK."

Sebastian turned back to Iain. "Are they moving?"

"Yes…" Iain paused. "They're moving quickly. Tsui looks upset!"

The pilot was flying straight between the grandstands over the empty pitch. It looked like a touch-and-go. As the engine roared in ascent, thousands of leaflets floated onto the pitch and into the stands. One lodged momentarily on Bruce's shoulder, then fell to the ground. He stooped to pick it up and read out loud.

"DEMOCRACY WITH VITO NO DEMOCRACY."

"What's all that about? Don't they mean 'not' democracy?" asked Bruce, always the editor.

"I don't know. But there'll be hell to pay. Patten won't be happy though, with his proposed attempts at democracy after a hundred and fifty years of autocratic colonial rule, and all that goes with it. Anyway, who cares?" replied Iain, turning back to the pitch.

"Your old man does. I'll go over and see him now," said Sebastian.

"Be quick though! Kick off's in ten minutes," Iain shouted after him as he pushed his way through the crowd.

"They have a point though, don't they, Iain? What about the UN Security Council? They all have a veto, don't they?"

"Mm," said Iain, non-committedly. "Probably done by the new Democratic Party," he said, almost to himself.

* * *

"I'm sorry, Tsui," Sebastian was saying, "I just wasn't sure. It was unusual."

Tsui had recovered his composure. "That's all right. You did what you thought was best. That's what you're paid for!"

"Yes indeed," rejoined Wai Kwok, "but aren't you on leave for the sevens? You shouldn't be interfering—"

"Excuse me," interrupted the temporary security man, coming to Sebastian's defence. "He saw a perceived risk and acted on it – nothing wrong with that."

Wai Kwok was still ruffled by being manhandled out of the stands.

"I'm sure Hong Kong Electric will think we're paranoid!" he said. "I think we've lost the contract."

"Never mind that," Tsui cut in. "You never know. Britain has enemies and this is a British colony and not as far away as the Falklands, for example, which is only an overseas territory, and tiny at that. And look what happened in nineteen forty-one. And Malaysia. And Korea. No, I'm happy with that 'interference'" and he turned and smiled at Sebastian and shook him by the hand. "Now let's go and watch the rugby."

* * *

Sebastian went back to join the boys and his men, knowing that he was not welcome as a guest in the corporate box.

"Everything all right?" asked Iain, well aware how tough his father could be in a very few words.

"Yes, fine thanks." He said nothing about his uncle, as the teams ran out. There had been no announcement about the plane. It would be in the news tonight, and in the papers tomorrow.

* * *

The match had been a display of wonderful open rugby with Fiji showing imagination and flair: flick passes behind the back at great pace, some long passes covering two-thirds of the field, devastating tackling, and pinpoint accuracy with the boot. In the end they were too fast, too fit and too imaginative for New Zealand, running out comfortable winners twenty-four to five: three converted tries and a penalty, to a try.

"Thanks," said Bruce as, unsmilingly, Sebastian asked Iain to give him the two-hundred-dollar stake, as they slowly made their way to the celebratory and holiday atmosphere of the crowded bars in the tented village.

* * *

Later Iain and Bruce were in the Fire-Fly night club in Wanchai, eating the pulutan – cooked beer snacks – provided by the Filipino management and drinking another cold San Miguel.

"I wonder if they can play Fats Waller?" Bruce asked, the beer beginning to work.

"Probably. The Filipino bands play talented music all around the world. Ask them. Fill in a slip."

"OK." And he did, then waved at one of the ravishing waitresses, who were mostly Manila girls. She smiled at Bruce and his blond hair and blue eyes. He had another advantage in the Far East, though he never knew why, just being a European and a Scot. She kept on smiling, and squatted down beside him to take his request. Bruce had no trouble with girls. She left, still smiling, giggling and wiggling.

"Are you going to stick with journalism when you leave Melrose?" asked Iain. He felt like talking. Must be the drinks and where they were. Exotic. A far cry from dormitory life, cold showers and beatings.

"Well, maybe. I'm rather attracted to PR though. You know people like me, trust me when they meet me. I don't know why," said Bruce. "Hey, look at that, Iain. Those girls want to join us!" Two slim microminied girls were nudging each other and laughing and miming "Cheers!" in their direction.

"No," said Iain, suddenly earnest. "Not in here. Nobody knows us. Tsui would crucify me."

The club was filling up with rowdy and happy people from the Sevens. The girls were soon picked up.

"Why don't you come and work for OSM when we finish school. The firm would train you. It's good here," mused Iain. "If you have money," he added, as an afterthought.

"Make me an offer," joked Bruce, not thinking he was serious. They often talked at school in front of the tiny coal fire of their two-man study about theology, ethics, life and what they could contribute. The Fire-Fly Club just didn't seem the place. The band was playing 'Air Supply'. To scattered applause the Filipina with the band began singing the stock single 'Two Less Lonely People in the World Tonight'. She sounded better than the original. They stopped talking, watching her. So far in their lives they had no time for nostalgia.

Shiga Heights, Japan 1992

The four of them had caught the direct flight from Hong Kong to Osaka and were now on the domestic one-hour from Osaka to Nagano City on their way to Shiga Heights for skiing. Tsui had a meeting. Even Cheng Cheng didn't know what about. She sat with Tsui. Behind them sat Tane, one of the Maori security, and Cheng Cheng's maid, Mary-Lou. Cheng Cheng had asked Tsui if she could come.

"She's never been to Japan. It would be exciting for her and amazing, right out of her environment. She'd learn a lot."

"OK! OK!" laughed Tsui. "Yes. Anyway, when I'm at this meeting – it's going to be an all-day affair – she can keep you company."

"What's it about?" asked Cheng Cheng tentatively.

"Never mind!" he laughed again, this time coldly and without feeling and, as an afterthought and as an all-encompassing explanation and closure: "But it's important." He had decided not to tell her about the China Deal. What she didn't know wouldn't hurt her.

The Japanese pilot interrupted them, like a travel guide, but obviously proud to show off his country to the *gaijin*.

"Those of you on the left of the aircraft will be able to see Lake Biwa, the largest in Japan. It is the third-oldest lake in the world, has fifty-eight exclusive species, and supplies drinking water to fifteen million people."

They looked at the immense lake below and the snow-covered Alps. Behind them they heard Mary-Lou squealing with excitement.

* * *

They were waiting for their luggage at the well-organised Nagano terminal.

"This is where we part company, Tane," Tsui was saying. "We'll meet you back here on Friday. They're going to take care of security from here."

"OK, Tsui," Tane said.

He turned to Cheng Cheng as she began speaking to him. "You're checked in at the Comfort Hotel – you should be all right there!"

Cheng Cheng was in a good mood. She handed him his hotel voucher. "Don't forget to visit the Zenkogi Buddhist temple – might be an antidote! The town grew up around the temple, which is one thousand four hundred years old—"

"Come on, Cheng Cheng! Leave the man alone," Tsui interrupted affectionately.

Mary-Lou was silent, anxiously looking out for the new suitcase Cheng Cheng had bought her, as the flight's luggage went around on the carousel.

* * *

Cheng Cheng and Mary-Lou pushed the trolleys through the doors, as Tsui went ahead to find the driver. With a wave Tane headed for the taxi rank, having already spotted their limo and their driver greeting Tsui. The tall, fit-looking Japanese looked the part with white woollen gloves and a chauffeur's cap.

"How did you know it was me?" asked Tsui.

"I was told." Was all he said with a brisk bow. Tsui said no more. As the only Chinese with two women in tow he'd be easy to pick out.

"We're going to Shiga Kogen Prince Hotel, right?" Tsui said curtly in good Japanese.

The man bowed again. "Yes, yes, Tsui," came the mechanical reply. He knows that as well, thought Tsui. Well briefed. The driver opened the curbside doors and the girls got in the back. Tsui sat in the front with the driver, who had left the empty baggage carts on the pavement behind them. As they drove, the snow began to fall.

"We've got about forty minutes to go," said Tsui, turning round and talking to Cheng Cheng and Mary-Lou. "Might as well have a nap."

"Isn't it beautiful? I've never seen snow before," said Mary-Lou in her youthful, breathless voice, putting her arm out of the window and catching the speeding snowflakes in her hand.

"Keep it closed please, Miss," the driver said, in passable English. From the tone of his voice she knew that the 'please' was superfluous.

* * *

Tsui and Cheng Cheng had their own ski gear. They'd hired everything for Mary-Lou, all in red, setting off well her round face and golden-coloured skin. The weather so far had been perfect – crisp and sunny – and the girls had been taking lessons every morning. The ski instructors seemed to be giving Mary-Lou extra attention, but she didn't appear to notice. She was learning very quickly, young and lissom, as good as Cheng Cheng already. Tsui had been able to put in a hard morning's skiing each day, pushing himself to the limit. In nineteen seventy-two, when he was twenty-seven, he had skied for Hong Kong as an individual at the Sapporo Olympics. He had raced in the slalom, coming in thirty-fifth. Not good, but at least he'd finished the course.

At lunchtime they met up at 'The Grenoble', a log restaurant on the slopes, where the cooking was European: a smorgasbord with borscht. Tsui sat by the fire with a brandy waiting for them. He saw Cheng Cheng wave as they came in. Their skis and poles were stuck in the snowdrift outside. They added their coats to the colourful pile on the rack by the door. Tsui got up to greet them, ponderous in his ski boots.

"How's it going?" asked Tsui, kissing Cheng Cheng on the cheek.

"Wonderful!" answered Cheng Cheng for them both, "and she's getting really good!"

"Well done!" he said, turning, smiling at Cheng Cheng's young maid. "After lunch we'll take you up your first chairlift, and then do some long gentle traverses down, each ending with a semi-Christie. That sound OK, Mary-Lou?"

"I'll try," she replied meekly.

"Let's eat. Oh! Cheng Cheng, while I think of it, my meetings tomorrow. You two'll be all right? In the afternoon, why not take the driver and go to the hot spas, for a change?"

"Good idea," said Cheng Cheng, happily.

* * *

Tsui, at eight thirty, was on the first lift to the summit. He had ordered a Japanese breakfast the night before. He had eaten bright and early and had left a drowsy Cheng

Cheng mumbling about being stiff and not being as young as she used to be, and looking extremely beautiful, sultry and inviting.

This morning the sun wasn't coming out. Leaden grey clouds hung close to the mountainside. More snow, thought Tsui. The slopes were empty. The early chairlifts rattled loudly as they went over the wheels at each pylon. A lone skier went racing down the piste. Looked like the build and height of the driver. He'd thought he'd seen him a few times on the slopes. Tsui slipped off the lift with ease, sliding down the ramp to the wooden cafe covered by a thick canopy of snow. He was ahead of schedule so he decided to go in, have a cup of hot chocolate and keep warm. He kicked off his skis and pulled open the door.

"Hot chocolate, please," he said in Japanese to the tanned young man behind the counter. "Thank you."

Paying, he carried it to the table by the window. He could hear the constant drone of the lift motor and the intermittent bouncing of the chairs as they went round the huge wheel taking them back down the run again.

* * *

He came out of the hut and put on his skis. With one push of his sticks he was at the edge of the track next to the rollers used for making the piste firm. The meeting place. There were more people skiing now, and the cloud was lifting. He could see the hotel and, beyond, more of the snow-covered Japanese Alps. It was impressive, but somehow in Japan there was a different atmosphere compared with, say, Switzerland. For instance, thought Tsui, this wasn't like going up the Gornergrat, skiing slowly down for a leisurely lunch on the sundeck at the old Riffelalp, surrounded by the European elite, before going on downhill to Zermatt, in the gloaming, and having a gluhwein at one of the chalets *après ski.*

Surely they wouldn't be late. He checked the time, two minutes to nine. There was little noise, just the chairlift and a few skiers calling out happily to each other. He heard nothing, till the one on his left spoke.

"Good morning. Mr Tsui, is it?"

They were dressed all in white: white skis and boots, white trousers and anoraks, white goggles. They were trim and wiry, looking superfit. He noticed, before he replied, that their clothes were flecked with red.

"Yes."

"Please, the sun glasses?" the man said, out of politeness taking off his own goggles. Tsui obliged, and they studied him, remembering the photos they'd been shown. Almost perfect English, thought Tsui. The other one spoke, this time with a faint American accent.

"The snow looks good today." His password.

"My grandmother thinks so," Tsui replied.

"Follow please," and they took off over the hill and down through the trees in the deep virgin snow. They did not hesitate or wait for him, assuming that he would easily keep up. They carried on in line of three, Tsui now in the middle, for about three miles, in a gentle descent. Abruptly the lead skier stopped on the edge of a small valley, pointing down with his ski stick for Tsui to observe, saying nothing. Tsui pulled up alongside him and looked down at the medieval mountain hamlet covered in snow.

The torii gates of the Shinto shrine, with its complementary buildings, stood apart up the valley, the sacred ground surrounded by a simple fence. Monks in red robes and villagers in working kimonos and getas were busily going about their work. On the far side of the valley a high waterfall was frozen into stupendous icicles, reaching more than halfway down to the valley floor. He looked up to the head of the falls and saw the straw rope strung across the river, marking a sacred site. The waterfall was one of their kami, one of their local gods.

Large lumps of snow fell from the trees beside them, disturbed by increasing wind. Without a word the two skiers set off down the slopes towards the village. Tsui followed.

* * *

They stopped before they reached the first torii gate and took off their skis, banging them together to get rid of most of the snow. They walked over to the bamboo fountain, which was rocking slowly back and forth, dispensing steaming water into the overflowing trough below. The bamboo made a resonant sound every time it emptied, echoing through the silence of winter. They took turns using a wooden ladle and pouring the warm spring water over their hands and into their mouths in an act of purification.

Following a swept path around the main shrine, they came the large residential building. Going through the tall front doors, they exchanged their ski boots for house slippers taken from the visitors' rack. The large room was covered with tatami. In spite of this, two adapted western style chairs had been put out next to the log fire, in deference to Tsui's culture and the possibility that he would be uncomfortable after hours of sitting cross-legged on the floor.

"Welcome, Tsui!" Takji Yoshida said warmly, bowing and, unusually, holding out his hand. Tsui shook his hand and bowed lower.

Takji was moderately westernised and spoke perfect English. A strong personality and a strong physique. One of those people who appeared to tell you everything and yet remained a mystery. Best have him as a friend. Tsui had known him at Cambridge, where they had been reading International Law.

He turned and walked back with Tsui towards the fire, waving his hand towards the armchairs. Tsui's ski partners had disappeared.

"Did you have a good run down, Tsui?" as they settled in front of the warm fire.

"Yes thanks. Invigorating!"

"Tea?" asked Takji, as a miko in her white kimono put a tray down on the table between them. Tsui knew better than to talk to her directly, but he was not surprised. These young ladies helped with duties around the shrine and at rituals. They could become priests, and, as with male priests, they could marry and have children. Shinto seemed so sensible.

"Thanks."

The miko served him Japanese green tea, which he loved. It always settled his stomach.

This, Tsui knew, was only the beginning. They would talk about all sorts of things for two to three hours before they even mentioned their business. In Japan the one-hour meeting didn't work.

"How long has it been?" Takji was saying.

"A long time!" he replied, looking at Takji, obviously fit, tall, pale olive skin and Japanese eyes. He must be about forty-two, thought Tsui, very young to be in charge of the Academy. How had he done it?

"Did you know, this area, with its hot spas and this Hachiman shrine, dedicated to the kami of war, was an escape, a place for R&R, for the samurai? When they moved out, the Ninjas bought it, about three hundred years ago from a local daimyo, who they had made broke by charging him the maximum fees possible for their services! Playing one daimyo off against the other. You know we went to the highest bidder, even in those days!"

Takji asked him many questions about the intervening years without, at any time, being blatantly intrusive. Tsui had learnt little from Takji that he didn't already know, though he had been interested to learn that Takji had been training as a Ninja even when he was at Cambridge. That explained his total lack of participation in student life. Tsui had tried to get him into the Student Union, whose politics Tsui enjoyed, without any success.

"Let's take a break, and get some fresh air," said Takji. "It's only a short stroll to the Offering Hall." They put on some clogs at front door. Takji crossed his arms as they walked, tucking his hands deep in the large sleeves of his winter kimono. It had started to snow and the wind was stronger. It would drift, thought Tsui. Leaning into the wind, Takji kept talking, turning his head to Tsui.

"The people," Takji said, nodding his head down the valley towards the village, "more or less live off the activities at the shrine, which is useful. We open the shrine in the summer months, which helps our cover. In the winter the road is closed. All the students act as Shinto monks. It works well and it is useful practice for them. Some of them believe in the tenets; most don't, but accept the traditions. It might be useful if I gave you a background sketch of the religion when we get back for lunch, though I expect you know already."

"No, that will be good," responded Tsui as they entered the Prayer Hall. Tsui copied Takji, standing slightly behind him. A bang on the drum to get the attention of the gods, three bows, prayer, two bows and two claps. Different from the Church of Scotland his mother had shown him.

When they got back to the meeting hall a large round table, covered with a white cloth, had been set up, with chairs for nine.

"We'll eat on our own first, if that's OK?" said Takji. Not a question, thought Tsui. Their lunch was already on the table: a black box of nigirizushi and a large steaming bowl of ginger congee.

* * *

Cheng Cheng and Mary-Lou had also got up early. As their rooms were in the East Building they had gone to the main restaurant for a buffet breakfast. The driver was coming at nine thirty.

"Let's first go on down to the wild monkey park, before the spa, instead of skiing. It's too wild out there," Cheng Cheng was saying. Mary-Lou could not answer; her mouth was too full. At buffets she piled her plate high. Cheng Cheng was always amazed that one so slight could eat so much. "They're wild mountain monkeys," Cheng Cheng continued, "so you have to be a bit careful; don't stare them down and let them start any contact. But they're so cute! Have you got your camera with you?"

"No, I don't…" she replied, her voice fading shyly away, feeling as if she should have one.

"Never mind, we'll have to get you one when we're back in Hong Kong. Whilst I think of it, I'd better tell you about the spa. The one we're going to has separate pools for men and women. Firstly, remember they are not like swimming pools, so no running about, no jumping or diving. And you won't need a swim suit. We shower all over – bring your shampoo – before we get in the hot spa bath. The water's very hot, so you have to get in slowly to acclimatize."

Mary-Lou was looking nervous, apprehensive.

"Don't worry. You'll be fine! It's fun! Oh! And they're sulphur baths, so there's a bit of a smell! Oh yes! I nearly forgot. Have you any tattoos anywhere?"

Mary-Lou now looked startled. "No, not at all."

"I didn't think so, but it's best to ask! The spas won't let you in if you have. They think you are yakuza, Japanese mafia! The only ones they let in are the tattoos of some Shinto kami, which pregnant mums have put on their bellies to ward off evil spirits. And that's not you, is it…?!"

* * *

The red-faced, hairy monkeys had their own hot spring pool, surrounded on three sides by high rock cliffs covered with fir trees running away into the wooded mountains, their natural habitat. In the winter, with snow on the ground, more monkeys came to the warm pool in troops. Hundreds of them altogether. Some of the late-born monkeys were still carried on their mother's backs. One of them was preening her baby whilst they sat in the steaming water.

Cheng Cheng went closer to them, her camera ready.

"Be careful, Cheng Cheng," called Mary-Lou, hanging back, thinking of the stories she had been told as far back as she could remember about the rabid wild dogs in her barrio in the Philippines.

Cheng Cheng took her photos and came back, smiling, to Mary-Lou. She took a photo of her with the snow-covered mountains as a backdrop. They carried on around the steaming pool in the crowd of tourists, walking arm in arm as many of the Japanese girls do. The driver had gone to the cafe to keep warm out of the wind.

* * *

In the changing rooms Mary-Lou had her towel wrapped firmly around her and was taking off her underclothes underneath, wriggling as she did, embarrassed.

"Come on, Mary-Lou, don't be shy. In Japan no one thinks anything of nudity! Sex in general, really. They don't have your inhibitions which you got from your church and the Americans!" Though when the inhibitions break down, look out, thought Cheng Cheng, smiling to herself.

They walked through to the baths into the heat. Some middle-aged Japanese ladies leant against the poolside, their feet floating in front of them, their breasts and large tummies. They smiled at the newcomers, and one of them waved. A row of showers, with soap and a wooden stool for each, ran along one wall.

"Let's wash, then," Cheng Cheng said to her maid, more like a command, as Mary-Lou was so obviously nervous. Cheng Cheng hung up her towel and walked naked, decisively towards the showers, Mary-Lou trotting behind her.

"Remember, have the shower really hot; it makes getting into the spa easier," said Cheng Cheng, more gently. She noticed that the young girl was resolutely facing the wall as she shampooed her hair. She looked delightful, thought Cheng Cheng, one of the few who looked perfect nude: so young and slender with a dark, tight bottom.

"Ready?" They walked over to the poolside and began slowly easing themselves into the water.

"It's too hot!" cried Mary-Lou.

"Don't worry; take it very slowly," answered Cheng Cheng. She noticed her firm, petite breasts with their dark nipples, and that, so far, she had only wisps of black pubic hair. Lovely.

Mary-Lou was beginning to relax, looking around, her wide eyes wandering.

"Oh! Cheng Cheng, you are bushy!"

"Yes," said Cheng Cheng, laughing, sliding easily into the steaming water. "Must be my Japanese ancestors!"

* * *

The snow had started again more heavily. Tsui and Takji were brushing it off their shoulders after a second walk as they came back into the hall. They stopped to change their shoes at the entrance.

The table had been cleared and a fresh red cloth had been put on. Water glasses and a pitcher had been left ready for them.

"Let's sit by the fire again," said Takji.

Tsui didn't answer, but walked towards the fire burning strongly around the new logs that had been thrown on. He was thinking about the second Ninja memo his people had given him, just before he left. It had told him that, leading off an ancient escape route, the Academy had developed an extensive state-of-the-art instruction facility, with the nine halls underground. It started with a general appraisal of the nine halls and it was suggested the trainee Ninjas develop the facet for which they show most talent. The first hall was mostly physical, going through to the ninth, which was mainly of the mind. He was wondering if he should ask Takji about it and decided not to. Probably, even if he did ask, he would not be shown them, or even have their presence acknowledged. And they would become suspicious, ask questions. He didn't need to inspect them, so long as the results were there.

"You probably know most or all I'm going to say, but it is interesting to consider how Shinto might affect a Ninja's performance, might affect me.

"Shinto means 'the way of the gods'. It is a divinity of objects and places. It is the archaic faith of Japan, at present living in harmony with Buddhism. Shinto does not have a creator, nor does it have sanctified writings. There is no proselytising, propagation or preaching. Interestingly, there is no totality of right or wrong. It is positive, joyful faith, in which humans are noble and bad comes from evil spirits. If, at any time, I had a need for gods, they would be Shinto gods: kami!

"Politically, because Shinto lacks formal structure, no hierarchy, nothing like a Bible or Koran, the faith leaves itself vulnerable to being hijacked for political misadventure, as has happened in the past. Continuing even today, ancient Shinto rights concerning a sacred empire are preformed at the palace in Tokyo, despite America saying the emperor has to be secular. But we have an interest in stability. We will always act accordingly."

Tsui was only half listening. Enough talk, he thought, let's get down to business. Takji was looking at him, waiting for a response.

"Yes, I am aware of what you are implying. For instance the fuss about your prime minister honouring your war dead.... But it won't involve us; all our operations are outside Japan."

Takji leant forward, suddenly alert.

"Wait, Tsui. Before you start, let me call the others."

"What others?" asked Tsui, feigning surprise.

"We have a council of elders, older and wiser than me!"

So you're not in charge after all, reflected Tsui.

"Look, there's a storm blowing up," continued Takji, walking over to the window and looking at the swirling snow. "Why not stay the night with us? I'll get a message to your people at the hotel."

"Thanks," said Tsui. Preordained, perhaps?

"Excuse me. I'll do it now," said Takji, bowing, as he left the room.

* * *

The door beside the fire opened and Takji walked in, followed by six older men in flowing red robes. Takji had changed into his contrasting white ceremonial costume. He looked formal and taller.

Tsui had to remind himself, as they filed in and around the table, that they were not Shinto monks but Ninja elders. Still, it was Takji who spoke.

"We are all here firstly because I know you and once knew you closely. Secondly, we're all here because we all know of the historical strength of OSM worldwide. We are told that the company started in eighteen hundred and fifty-one. Before then it was more or less a pirate operation."

Tsui cut in to divert Takji from pirate talk, though in the case of the Ninjas it might have been a plus. "Yes, that's right. We started five years before Happy Valley, the racecourse. So you see, we were even gambling before the Establishment!"

Takji didn't laugh, but smiled politely, drawing in his breath. This is getting serious, thought Tsui.

"Thirdly, you are here because our elders are interested in the little they have learnt of your proposal." And he nodded towards Tsui, indicating that he should speak. Tsui bowed.

"Your Ninjas will be asked to do nothing they haven't been trained for," started Tsui. "I am not able to discuss any details of my blueprint – you know all about surprise. I can say the martial plans are based on my experience in the British paratroopers and with the Taiwanese military, and on the current experiences and knowledge of two other serving officers and various other political personages. Also on information from one of our people in MI6. The operational plans are also based on the traditions and culture of the Ninjas. We will need twenty-nine and they will sign for ten years. If you want to proceed, and I too am happy, I will bring a copy of the agreement to our next meeting. At that time we can also discuss remuneration. It will be handsome." Brief and to the point. No mention of China.

Takji looked at the elders. As the table was round it was difficult to tell who was leader, if there was one. Usually he would be facing the main door. The old men were staring at Tsui. Takji spoke to him.

"Where will they be based? Hong Kong?" he asked.

"They will have no base." Tsui noticed the Ninja sitting opposite nodding, as if in agreement. Takji was surprised.

* * *

The fat, jovial Japanese man with the big, noisy group a few tables away, was coming towards them, smilingly happily. Cheng Cheng had noticed him around the hotel.

"I have a message for you," he said, holding out a folded paper. It was a bit crumpled and damp.

"Thank you," said Cheng Cheng, smiling and reaching out for it. The man did not stay. Cheng Cheng watched him return to his friends, and then unfolded the note.

Staying overnight. Tsui.

No double full stop, she thought. Hope he's OK. She passed the note to Mary-Lou. "Must be the storm on the mountain."

They poured the last of the sake in each other's cups. Mary-Lou had had three. It was the first time she had drunk the hot rice wine, and she liked it, though she could feel her cheeks burning.

"Let's go up and have showers, to get rid of the last of the spa. Then come through to Tsui's room, and we'll watch movies."

* * *

They were watching an uncensored Japanese love story with subtitles, provided by the hotel, sitting on the queen-sized double bed. Only the bedside lights were on, and the room was warm. Mary-Lou was combing Cheng Cheng's long black hair, making it crackle and shine in the subdued light. The movie was becoming sexy, and she giggled.

Cheng Cheng relaxed back in the down pillows, sighing.

"That's beautiful, Mary-Lou," she said softly. She let her yukata fall open, and uncrossed her strong legs.

"Comb my pubic hairs," she instructed. Mary-Lou stopped combing, looking at Cheng Cheng, laughing nervously. "Do it, or I'll slap your face," Cheng Cheng said sharply.

Mary-Lou acquiesced, still giggling, but quietly now, in anticipation.

* * *

"You will be aware," said Takji, "that our heritage is founded upon the work of Sun Tzu." Tsui nodded. "I have been asked to draw your attention to chapter thirteen, para nineteen, and I quote, 'If a secret piece of news is divulged by a spy before the time is ripe, he must be put to death, together with the person to whom the secret was told.' I am sorry to say this, but you, Tsui, are in this position now, 'if' etcetera. The more so we work together. The more knowledge we pass to you, the more we ennoble you, yet the greater your risks become, not only the risks to you but also the risks to those closest to you. Do you understand and agree?"

"Yes," replied Tsui, without hesitation. "I would expect no less. *Noblesse oblige* – with nobility comes responsibility."

The elder was nodding again as Takji continued.

"There is not much more to say. Your request is extremely unusual, and, as you lawyers say 'will have to be taken under advisement'. You must know a great deal about the Ninja Way to make such a request."

"Yes indeed," said Tsui. Perhaps he should respond. "The Ninja philosophy and methods are directly opposed to the samurai of old. They use secrecy and stealth, preferably in darkness, silently, unnoticed and unseen. They can accomplish in secret what great numbers of troops are not able to, and with the minimum of fuss. Unlike the Americans in Vietnam, for example. Wherever Ninjas can, they will use guile rather than violence, stealth rather than aggression, and secrecy over openness."

"All true," rejoined Takji, "and the modern Ninja is familiar with contemporary espionage technology. In addition, he will always plan his way out, as well as his way in. He is no 'suicide bomber'. This principle is not based on the moral high ground. His training is simply too extensive and too expensive."

Takji paused. The elders stood up, bowed and left the hall.

"Tsui," said Takji, getting up and stretching, "I have to go and talk with them. I think it went well. But I'm only the go-between! Dinner will be in about an hour or so. I'll have a miko show you to your room. You can wash and change. I think you'll find it comfortable. Not the Mandarin, but not like an ancient shrine either. Come down when you hear the next gong. I'll wait for you in the hall."

"Right," said Tsui, getting up and vigorously poking the fire, sending sparks flying up the chimney.

* * *

Tsui was at the high table, on the right-hand of Takji, in the dining hall with the students cheerfully talking and laughing as they ate; this was no solemn, silent order. Nearest their table were the senior students. At the far end of the hall sat the youngest, trying to look grown up. Their tables were surrounded with young miko helpers. Takji saw Tsui looking at the youngest students.

"They have one miko to two of them. I help with the young ones; it's fascinating. We teach them an almost unnatural awareness of all around them and we teach them balance and agility. They absorb the teaching like a sponge. They can race through the treetops like monkeys! Even at their young age we teach them disguise; they love it. Discipline is a wonderful thing. By the time they are twelve, at genbuku, we treat them as men." Tsui made no comment, so Takji continued. "We have two hundred students, from ages five to twenty-five. Most of their instructors are alumni." He used the American term, sounding international.

Tsui had noticed that the old men were not present. Takji sat at the centre of the high table. The other men and woman with him were youthful, in their early thirties.

Takji spoke again. "You see, we are training some Occidentals for work outside Asia. We also train some women." Their food came: katsudon and rice with pickled vegetables in blue-and-white bowls with chopsticks, and a bowl of miso soup. Green tea, no sake. "By the way, Tsui, if you want to talk business while we eat, that's all right by me. It's absolutely safe."

It may be for you, thought Tsui, reaching in his pocket and turning on his CW. He glanced at the Ninja beside him. He appeared uninterested in them, chatting earnestly to his neighbour.

"We will be running our operation in cells of five, sometimes in twos," Tsui tersely imparted.

"It seems to me, that dividing twenty-nine by five, you yourself will have an active role?" questioned Takji, smiling.

"It seems so," replied Tsui.

"You know, we'll have to give some basic training – about a week."

"Slow down, Takji! Before we take the next step, I want to set up a trial for a group of your people. I'll pay for the exercise." Again Tsui was brief and to the point.

"What do you have in mind?" asked Takji, leaning forward in his seat.

"The abduction of a taipan, Patrick Fitzgibbon, taken off Hong Kong Island, unharmed – within a month, which I shall nominate," said Tsui quietly and firmly, in his closing-deals voice.

Takji leant back in his chair, steepling his fingers. It wasn't necessary, he thought. But it would be good training and it would strengthen their relationship. It would help deliver the contract with Tsui, and he said he would pay.

"All right, Tsui," he replied, smilingly broadly and stretching out his arms expansively. "That's a good idea – get used to working together again. We'll have to discuss the detail before you go. Changing the subject, is it possible for us to procure some of those Chinese Whistles, like the one in your pocket?"

Showing no surprise and still not smiling, Tsui was non-committal. "Maybe. Maybe not. Probably. It will take time. I'll try."

* * *

Takji was walking his friend back to his quarters. There were more red-robed students about now.

"It's their free time now, before lights out," he explained. "Oh yes! I just remembered: one of the elders arranged for a masseur from the village to come up and give you a massage, as a sort of welcome. I hope you don't mind."

Tsui knew that he could not refuse. Anyway, it would be a good relaxation.

"No, that's fine. Please thank him very much."

"She should be here by now," said Takji, as they came to Tsui's door, which was open. She bowed deeply.

"I'll leave you in her capable hands," Takji said, smiling, as he left the room. The masseur had moved the futon nearer to the log fire. She helped Tsui take off his clothes and indicated that he should lie down. Under her strong hands he soon relaxed, warm and tingling, listening to the sounds of the fire. She moved slowly down his spine to his buttock, using fragrant oil. He couldn't identify the aroma, maybe sandalwood. She worked on his buttocks, moving her fingers from the centre out and firmly circling his hip bones. Relaxed as he was, he still felt himself become aroused. She had straddled his back with her knees so he was easily able to run his hand up her smooth inner thigh. When he reached the top his hand bumped into male genitals. With a bellow, he jerked himself up, grabbing for the towel. The masseur had already vanished.

There was a knock on the door.

"Can I come in?" called out Takji, laughter in his voice. Not waiting for a reply, he walked across to Tsui, who was now sitting on the edge of the bed. He was glad to see that he was grinning too. "I'm sorry, Tsui! We wanted to show you some of our skills. That was one of the Ninja instructors. Actually, one of the skiers who brought you in this morning."

"Damn! Damn! But that's good, amazing," admitted Tsui.

One of the young miko was hovering at the open door. Takji turned, and acknowledged her. Turning back to Tsui he said, "This miko will finish your massage for you. She will also be honoured to spend the night with you."

When the massage was finished, she simply stood up, facing the fire, and dropped her white robe around her ankles. Slowly she turned around, smiling happily at Tsui. She walked over to the futon mattress lying on the tatami and cuddled up under the huge eiderdown. Later, when the lights were out, the fire lit up her body.

* * *

In the morning, after they had discussed the exercise, Takji took him aside and told him, without being asked, that she was older than she looked at thirty-two. "She is a fully trained Ninja. She could have easily killed you several times last night!" Takji was laughing robustly. He had hardly changed since Cambridge. She too had vanished.

* * *

They were in the vast reception of the Shiga Hotel, waiting in the queue to check out. Cheng Cheng had their Visa card ready. It was gold, and had a limit of fifty thousand US dollars, paid off monthly by the accountants. It made her feel good. One of the hall porters came over to them.

"Good morning, Madam. Sir," he said with his habitual smile, talking to Tsui, and completely ignoring Mary-Lou, which annoyed Cheng Cheng, "I have a message for you."

"Thank you." If he had accepted Mary-Lou as part of their group, Cheng Cheng would have tried to tip him. Tsui made no comment, but agreed with Cheng Cheng. He was wondering what the message said. He had left strict instructions: no contact unless absolutely necessary.

Please phone ASAP. Kestrel. His brother.

"Give me some coins please," he demanded. "I need to use the phone." Cheng Cheng already had her purse out.

"That's all the yen I've got."

"That's fine, thanks. Won't be long."

He strode over to the bank of phones. No one was there, unlike in the evenings. Good, he thought. He dialled his brother's direct line, told him to call him back, and gave him the number.

"Hullo."

"Hullo." His brother seemed concerned. "It's about Vimana. She's a corporate spy."

"Who reported her?" Tsui asked.

"Sebastian. To me," replied Wai Kwok.

"Jesse! Hang on. Give me a minute," Tsui said. Pillow talk! It would just be gossip about the house.

"Does she know about 'it'?" Their parlance for the China Deal.

"No – I'm certain." His brother's reply was unequivocal. No need for anything extreme. There was no action yet.

"Right," Tsui said, briskly, in command. "Don't tell anyone, particularly Sebastian. Instant dismissal. You do it personally. Take all her keys. Stay with her as she gets all her things together and see her off the premises. Then tell security she's not allowed back for any reason. Better have the locks changed. I'll see the recruiters myself. We'll be back in early evening. Tell the Comprador I'll see him as usual."

He hung up and went back to Cheng Cheng and Mary-Lou. They were three from the front now.

"Anything important?" Cheng Cheng ventured.

"No, I'll tell you later." Tsui replied. He was looking at the eye-catching ski posters put up behind the counter. They were promoting Nagano for the Winter Olympics, still six years away. Maybe he could come back.

"Did you have a good time yesterday," Cheng Cheng was asking, as she paid their bill.

"Yes, I did. Very interesting. Some of it was hilarious! I'll tell you all about it on the plane." It was easy enough for lovers to talk in first class.

The Comprador's Place, Sai Kung 1993

They had left the car with the driver, parked near MacDonalds and were making their way through the surprisingly clean back lanes of Sai Kung, past the steaming laundry and out onto the main town square, where people were gathering after work, the older men airing their caged birds and some playing Go on concrete tables with concrete seats. The children, free from school but still in uniform, chased balls and whiz bees, dogs and each other, the teenagers shyly walking side by side, talking and laughing. They walked past the pancake man making huge thin crepes served with oily peanut butter from his push cart, the gas from his primus hissing as he cooked. He had a steady flow of customers.

"Now there's a good business to franchise!" said Tsui, with a smile.

"Yes, Tsui," replied Sebastian, "they're delicious. Have you tried one?"

"When we were growing up we practically bought the cart!"

They walked on towards the waterfront, knowing they shouldn't stop, striding out, like the blinkered foreigners rushing back and forth to their offices. At this time of day you were not allowed to take a vehicle down to the jetty, where small motorised sampans were plying full loads of customers to outer islands and distant promontories.

Sebastian cleared his throat. "I'm sorry about Vimana—" Neither of them had spoken of her since she was summarily dismissed last December. This was the first time Sebastian had been alone with Tsui since then.

"Don't mention her again," Tsui interjected abruptly. "If you have learnt the lesson from your critical error, so be it. Consider the matter closed."

Sebastian didn't speak.

* * *

They slowed down now as they reached the alley to the back door of the restaurant. The blue-tiled path had been hosed clean and the sealed, green district council skips stood in a neat row on the left-hand side. The Maori security guard leaning on the doorpost straightened up as they came towards him. Just inside two chefs and two of the Comprador's friendly triads were sitting at a square fold-up table on four tiny stools, playing mah-jong. The lull before the evening rush.

The Golden Carp restaurant was the best seafood restaurant in Hong Kong, some said anywhere. It had been open for more than forty years, back when Sai Kung had been a sleepy fishing village. Now it was patronised by rich tourists, who usually came by minibus from the big hotels, mostly for weekend lunch, when tables were put out on the promenade to cope with the crowd. Much more importantly and impressively, it was also patronised by the resident rich and influential Chinese. They came aboard executive junks which moored about a hundred yards offshore, before being ferried to the pier in sampans hired by competing restaurants and rowed by weathered old ladies standing upright in the stern with their single oar. They jostled around each new arrival, all the while shouting out the name and virtues of their restaurant. Or the businessmen came by road in air-conditioned Mercs.

The Comprador had bought the business through his company K. K. Chen in nineteen fifty-five. He had been lucky to keep all the staff, especially the chefs and the maitre d', Jasmine, whose devastating perfection and formality were excellent for business. They had all done well out of the transfer, each now holding some shares in the restaurant. Once the changeover had settled down, the Comprador had built a third storey on what was traditionally the owner's living accommodation. This old live-in flat had been combined with the new building to make a comfortable apartment, which the Comprador used as a second home well away from the frenetic commerce of Central; and near his cruiser, used for fishing and for some other meetings.

"Good afternoon, Tsui. Good afternoon, Sebastian," the guard said. "Mr Chen is expecting you," as he held the fly screen open for them. Tsui nodded, lowered his head and went in, glad to be out of the buffeting wind blowing off the sea.

"Thanks," said Sebastian, following. They were met by Jasmine in her golden cheongsam. She simply smiled, turned around and lead them back through the modern kitchen towards the manager's office. As they found their way through the equipment, all was quiet, except for one cook working with yum cha bamboo baskets at the steamer. The lights were dimmed. They could see the manager at his desk and hear the sound of his abacus rattling through some figures. The stone stairs to the Comprador's apartment lead out of the office, built across the back wall. The stairs looked ancient but were in fact part of the new building.

"Excuse us," said Tsui, getting a wave over the manager's shoulder for his trouble. Jasmine went ahead up the stairs, her hips moving rhythmically in front of him. Good for business.

They were standing on the upper landing outside the heavy, ornate steel door. Jasmine rang the bell and stood back. The door opened nearly at once. The young houseboy stood aside and bowed to Tsui whilst indicating that he should enter. He was much younger, about fifteen, than the houseboys at Laird House, who were middle aged or older. He had delicate features and thick black hair, neatly parted. He wore the usual uniform: black canvas slip-ons, black trousers and a crisp white tunic with a high collar. Maybe the uniform made him look younger. The Comprador's Achilles' heel, thought Tsui.

Tsui turned to Sebastian. "Wait in the restaurant, will you? See if you can get something to eat." He smiled at Jasmine and followed the houseboy in, as the other two went back downstairs.

* * *

The Comprador, elegant in a black, high-collared Chinese gown, was sitting with Tsui in wooden straight-backed armchairs with matching rosewood side tables for their yum cha, which the houseboy had brought before being sent out. They were alone by the window looking out on the esplanade, the ferries and the sampans. The sea beyond, dotted with islands, was still grey from the storm, the bigger waves white capped. As it was low tide, the passengers at the pier were going carefully down to the bottom of the wet steps: the girls in medium heels with shopping from the Shatin malls; the men with suits and briefcases; the amahs with the groceries; and polite children, with their schoolbags and the change for the fare clasped in their hands. Later, when they were underway, they would throw their coins on the deck for collection later by the crew.

As their turn came each jumped easily from the last exposed step onto the bobbing wet prow. The Comprador smiled as he saw Tsui looking out.

"You must have a view. But if it is only a view, it becomes tedious! You need activity in the foreground."

Tsui did not speak, but carried on watching the rush-hour throng. Away to the right, only a few hundred yards, was a different world: about fifty tanka junks moored together. 'Boat dwellers' to the British; 'vermin families' to the harsher Cantonese. He watched as the Tui Min Hoi sampan weaved its way through their anchorage, the passengers unwittingly having an insider's view of domesticity: dishes being washed for the evening meal, savage guard dogs barking, younger children scrubbing teeth in plastic buckets on their way to their bunks. The very youngest were restricted, tethered to their junk. In amongst this bustling confusion Tsui knew that the Comprador had some of his best spies and a sanctuary, should he ever need one.

Inside the apartment it was silent and serene, the noises and the wind cut off by thick double glazing. The Comprador spoke again.

"I know it's late for yum cha, Tsui, but it's always pleasant to have a snack."

* * *

As it was a cold spring day, he had decided on steamed dumplings – one kind with vegetables, the other with fresh crab meat – served in their bamboo baskets. They both had their own pot of oolong tea beside them to save the Comprador getting up and down.

Tsui looked around the familiar apartment. A minimum of rosewood furniture set out on some exotic Tibetan carpets now made in Nepal. Ming ornaments and vases standing on shelves and in alcoves, complemented by good lighting, and two hanging scrolls and a large landscape by Li T'ang as the centrepiece. None would be for sale in the tourist shops of Mody Road or Ocean Terminal.

By the entrance there was a small shrine to Buddha, fresh fruit in front of him. In the evening joss sticks would be lit and burnt there. Tsui wondered if Mrs Chen ever came here – there seemed no feminine touch. Absolutely no clutter.

The Comprador brought out his CW, which looked like a black Go piece, from an inside pocket and laid it on the table next to him. Unbeknown to Tsui he had not switched it on. He stroked his long thin beard, smiling, eyes twinkling with vigour.

"Shall we start?" he asked Tsui.

"Yes," came the reply, "but where shall we start?" Tsui deferred to the older man.

"I read the EIU report you sent over. Most interesting, that bit about the overseas Chinese. Thirty-five million of them, without counting Taiwan, with a turnover of five hundred billion. Compares well with the mainland at four hundred and ten billion. Quoted as 'the most dynamic capitalists in the world'. No challenges there. Commerce, they can manage."

"Locally the new governor is settling in. He is popular with the staff at Government House. He even has a nickname already, based on his love of dahn tarts. It is an affectionate Fei-Paang – Fat Patten. It seems he might rock a few boats with his waving the democracy flag. A bit cosmetic after one hundred and fifty years of colonial rule from London."

As he paused Tsui spoke. "But that autocratic rule has been good for Hong Kong."

"I agree," said the Comprador. "But not always for the Chinese. I still wouldn't feel comfortable living on The Peak. In balance, it has been good." He ate some yum cha followed by a sip of tea. He looked at Tsui and held his eye with his unwavering stare. "About the China Deal." He spoke slowly, deliberately. So it has begun, thought Tsui. "Your brother, Wai Kwok, should know no more details of the deal. It is for his own safety, and it will leave him free to run OSM. I will be the go-between. My family always has been for yours. Now is not the time to break with tradition." The Comprador paused, still watching the younger man, with his strong Eurasian features. For the first time, they were going into an arrangement for other than money. The risks seemed higher. "All we have is mutual trust," he said, almost to himself.

How did the Comprador do it? thought Tsui, reading his mind, knowing what he's thinking. They had talked like this once before on a visit to Tsui's father's permanent grave, placed secretly in a pine forest on company land near the bottom of the Kowloon Hills in the New Territories.

"Yes," agreed Tsui, "the same trust that has been so good to us all these years." He too paused, thinking of his father; no way would he have committed to this venture. Back to business. "My trip to Japan was most successful. They will have to gain local expertise in the terrain involved, but that's not a problem. They want Chinese Whistles – half a dozen. Check it out on your next trip."

The Comprador nodded and continued.

"I am going to the mainland once a month now. My contacts are growing in stature, both in Shanghai and the PLA. The right people are listening. About Taiwan. If you agree about Wai Kwok, I suggest you take on Taiwan."

"Yes, I will." Tsui knew that the Comprador was right, though he would miss his young brother's support. "I will bring Iain instead."

He heard the smothered intake of breath as the Comprador stood up and walked to the window.

"Are you sure? He is very young," the Comprador said, without turning round.

"He'll be older by the time we go. Besides, you know we favour youth in OSM! He'll be fine."

"You know how strong willed he is, like you and your grandmother! What will you do if he doesn't agree?"

"He will. Now what about our two 'experts' to complete the team? Have you talked to your nephew yet?" The Comprador's nephew was at UCLA in computers, some obscure field, and coming consistently top in his class. He was also a peace activist, like many of his peers.

"I'm beginning to make contact with him again."

"Don't talk to him too much before I've met him," Tsui rejoined.

"*D'accord. Bien sur.*"

"As to a PR/media. I have someone in mind."

The Comprador walked across to a red-and-gold-lacquered cabinet to pour them cognacs. Outside it was becoming dark. He drew the curtains and sat down, taking a toothpick from a small bowl, cleaning the gaps in his teeth behind his hand. The lights came on automatically, hidden lights above the landscape, mirror and Buddha, and two standard lights with Chinese shades beside their chairs. They talked details well into the evening. Finally some OSM business.

"Through the year," the Comprador was saying, "we have been changing our product and price range in OSM stores. We are no longer competing with Lane

Crawford. We are aiming at the Chinese middle class, the two-income family in Mei Foo Sun Chuen, for example. We see how we go this Christmas, which is growing and growing following the Japanese, and at Chinese New Year."

Later, when the houseboy was back, they went downstairs to eat.

CLIPPER LOUNGE, MANDARIN HOTEL 1993

Alexander had checked in to the Mandarin, as he always did when he was in Hong Kong. The welcome and the service were as perfect as ever, spoiling him for anywhere else, like the 'diner' in the Manhattan Hilton, where you ate breakfast at an alarming speed under the eagle eye of the old waitress. He had gone up to his room to clean up – a simple double room with a harbour view. Now he was with Tsui at his table on the mezzanine floor, directly across from the piano player, who was going through a medley from *Porgy and Bess* on the baby grand. Their green tea was on the coffee table between them as they settled in the expensive leather armchairs.

"Have a good trip up?" Said Tsui, watching his elder brother and wondering what he would think if he knew about the China Deal. "Hot enough for you? It's humid this summer."

"Yes and yes. I'm used to humidity these days, you know – a lifetime in the Philippines." There was an aggrieved undertone in his voice which Tsui hadn't heard for more than thirty years when his father had gone over Alexander to himself as heir apparent, the next taipan. He remembered the evening vividly. It was the same evening that the Comprador had knocked him out when he had become overly aggressive in karate. Once his parents knew that Tsui was medically all right, they had been delighted with the Comprador for teaching him a valuable lesson. Then after dinner, when the servants had been sent away, their father had given Alexander his ultimatum: stop his often spoken plans to marry his present girlfriend or leave the company. She was not a suitable wife for the next taipan. At twenty-four Alexander was furious, mad and stubborn. His 'fiancée' was a young maid in the household, one of the first Filipina maids to gamble on Hong Kong, and working illegally. Tsui remembered her well:

so breathtakingly beautiful and petite; deep-brown almond-shaped and sparkling eyes, golden-coloured skin and long shimmering hair. But she did not belong either to one of the rich Chinese families in the Philippines or to one of the long-established Spanish ones. In fact she was from a small provincial town in Leyte, where she had had only limited schooling, and she was Catholic.

Tsui was puzzled and felt sorry for his big brother, but understood his father. When he and Shelagh had wanted to marry she had at once been accepted: the 'daughter of a Scots shipping line'.

Alexander and his wife, as she soon became, were sent to the Philippines to manage the company's coconut plantation. Cerise had never returned to Hong Kong. The agreed story was that Alexander declined the responsibility and obligations of being a taipan, and that, despite the disappointment of his father, the honour would go to Tsui. It had worked out for them, both happy and married for twenty-eight years.

Now Tsui wanted a favour and his brother was upset about something. He needed more information.

"Have you had enough tea?" Tsui asked. "Let's go up to the house. It's easier to talk there."

Laird House, The Peak 1993

The two brothers stayed inside in the air-conditioning out of the heat. Alexander wandered round the tinted-glass conservatory, thinking of his childhood years. He had not been invited back into Laird House until his father's funeral; Cerise never had been. It used to infuriate him. These days it didn't seem to matter.

"Let's sit down and talk," said Tsui. "I've got the Comprador at seven thirty." The conservatory was at the back of the house, looking onto the cliff face of The Peak. It had been planted with a mass of tropical ferns and bamboo, covering most of the rocks, the retaining steel mesh and the concrete storm drains. Water ran down across it all like a gentle, misty waterfall. Inside there was a profusion of orchids – Shelagh's legacy. It was a peaceful spot.

"What's bothering you?" Tsui asked his elder brother directly.

Equally directly Alexander replied, "I had a letter from the board of directors in Manila."

The plantation was owned by a Philippine company; no foreigner could own Filipino land. Tsui kept control by appointing the directors. Alexander was only resident manager. "They are going to change the name, using the OSM logo. Bloody ridiculous. First the stud, now this."

"Don't bother yourself with that. You still get upset by little things!" Tsui teased. "What I've got to say could change all that. I propose that we transfer the farm to you and Cerise. The money side of it I'll sort out. The Manila Company will want 'fair market value'. Ownership is a different matter. It could be Cerise and the present company lawyer. We've got him in our pocket."

"Why are you suggesting this?" Alexander looked puzzled mingled with defensive aggression, standing up as he spoke. His height and strength were enhanced by his military style jacket as he stood looking down at Tsui, seeming the younger of the two. In the early days he had deeply resented his brother. But later he had begun grudgingly to admire him and how he ran the company. He admitted to himself that his own laid-back lifestyle with Cerise and Antonia suited him best.

"I could say I want to settle the score, even things up a bit now the families are growing closer. It's been a joy having Antonia living at the house for the past six months, and so on. But that would only be partly true. I have a challenge from the Comprador and Wai Kwok, which you can help me with. I want them to take over the day-to-day running of OSM." Tsui paused, wondering if he should tell his brother why and deciding not to, as he had already decided before their meeting. There was no need. "And I have to respect their judgement and decisions; it's the only way it will work."

"What will work?" interrupted Alexander, nobody's fool.

Tsui hesitated. "Well, that they run the show more.... Anyway," he said, breaking his brother's train of thought, "they want OSM to get rid of the stud; the usual stuff, returns too risky, too slow, not a core business."

"You won't do that; it's always been a passion of yours," declared Alexander, never one to hold back.

"Yes, I can and will. They need that reassurance." This time it was Tsui who stood up. He started pacing up and down between the plants, a sure sign that he was weighing decisions. "I want you to take over the stud. OSM can sell it to you for one US dollar. One of the benefits of going private again. We can do things we want to without being beholden to shareholders. All I ask is that I keep a half-share in Bellatrix. I don't want you to say 'No', but I know you might. It'll be a lot of travelling and work pressure."

And, as an afterthought, a light-hearted sweetener, Tsui added, "You could change the name back to Kawhia Stud."

Alexander walked over to the sideboard, where the Grant's and two Stuart crystal glasses had been laid out. He poured two decent-sized whiskies, no ice, and gave one to his brother, before walking over to look at the water trickling through the ferns. He didn't speak for a long while.

"You know I love the horses; working with them is mostly pleasure." He talked slowly and paused often, like most big men. "That's a very generous offer." He turned and faced his brother. "What's going on?" He sounded sympathetic.

"As I said, I want Wai Kwok and the Comprador to do the day-to-day hands-on management. I want to concentrate on our global strategies."

"There must be more to it than that?" Alexander said, pushing.

"No," Tsui replied abruptly, lying. "Well, what do you think?" he said, bringing their talk back to his proposal.

Alexander walked unhurriedly to his chair and sat down. Tsui did the same. They both took a long drink. Alexander swirled his whisky around in his glass, gazing at the amber liquid. Eventually he looked up, smiling kindly, and spoke openly to his brother.

"OK about the coconut farm; it should have been mine anyway. But thank you. As to the stud, that's not fair to you. I'll only do it if the stud is fifty-fifty with you personally."

Tsui returned Alexander's stare. They hadn't worked together for a long time. It would be good. He leant forward, hand outstretched, and shook his brother's hand. The taipan's handshake was his word.

"So be it!"

"Good," Alexander said, smiling even more. "Can we change back to Kawhia Stud?"

"Of course!" Tsui laughed at his brother. Stubborn as ever.

Alexander looked at his watch. "I have to go. I'm meeting Antonia at the Mandarin, then we're going to try that new Mexican restaurant in Wanchai."

"Have a good evening, Alexander. Take one of the cars."

"Thanks." With his long strides, he was soon at the door. Tsui called out to him, "Bring Cerise next time."

He turned, smiling boyishly, waving. Tsui was alone.

Niyogan, The Philippines 1993

Alexander enjoyed riding his Anglo-Arab around the coconut farm in the cool of dawn. She was a flea-bitten grey and strode out without encouragement, interested and ears pricked. He had brought her up from New Zealand from the Arab stud near Cambridge. She had some long and fancy name, but at Niyogan she was simply known as 'The Grey'. Today he was riding out to the north of the plantation to talk with his neighbour about this harvest's price of rice. Niyogan didn't plant rice, so he bought some in to supply his workers and their families. He liked to look after his people and on the first of each month gave them a bag of rice, two gallons of tuba and some virgin coconut oil for cooking. The girls used it for their skin and hair and the children's minor wounds. Cerise said he spoilt them, but he told her the plantation made them a decent living and they were not like the rest of OSM, 'in it for profit above all else'. But, with the price of copra falling, he was considering making virgin coconut oil commercially, like the foreigner and his Filipino wife on Mount Banahaw.

The tuba ration sparked parties with friends and neighbours. They got together in one of the nipa huts with guitars, singing local songs and drinking from a communal glass. They ate steamed bananas as they drank the tuba and used Pepsi as a mixer, only Pepsi. Coke didn't work for them. In their province of Leyte, Pepsi always outsold Coke; a fact of which they were proud. But the manager and Cerise complained about lost work hours on the second of each month. That was true, but so what? he thought.

The men were working around the house today, so the plantation was peaceful. He could feel the breeze on his face and hear it rustling in the leaves overhead. He could hear the twigs snapping under The Grey's hooves and the squeaking of the stirrup leathers on the saddle. Occasionally a bird cried out in alarm. He rode through the dry creek bed and jumped the fallen log on the other side. He hadn't expected it, but ownership made him feel good about the land. Yet he'd always felt at home at Niyogan, husbanding the property well for his family, for his workers and for future generations. Besides this magnanimity, he had tried to help the wider community, creating jobs by starting a small factory in their neighbouring town of Tolosa. It made old-tech cassette players which sold well in Africa, marketed for him by OSM. The factory now employed five hundred people and had a Japanese manager, which had caused friction at the start.

The Grey was on her toes now, tossing her head as they began coming down out of the plantation and her usual surroundings. He could hear the putt-putt of the small rice thresher drifting up to them from the valley below. He had often wondered at these transportable rice mills, introduced to the Philippines after World War II. They made polished white rice very popular and in the process lost most of the bran and nutrients from the rice. It didn't make sense to him.

Riding down the hill he could see through the palms the rice paddies stretched out on the flat valley floor, and some white herons fishing in the ponds. As they came out of the Niyogan lands a flock of tree-babblers flew out in front of them. The mare snorted.

"All right, girl," he said, patting her firmly on the neck, "they won't hurt us."

The owner of the rice farm waved at the man on the thresher. He cut the engine; they would have a break. Men, in the shade of the trees, were loading two fifty-kilogram sacks onto a small thin horse, no more than a pony. They had one sack roped on one side. One of the men was pushing on the sack so that the pony would not fall over, while another struggled to rope the second sack on the other side. Alexander rode up and got off, taking the reins over The Grey's head and giving her to the man who had come forward. He ran up the irons and loosened the girths so she would be comfortable and rested. Another man came over, carrying a fresh coconut, probably one of Niyogan's. With a sharp machete he skilfully cut off the top and handed the ready-made drink to Alexander.

"Buko juice, Sir?"

"Thank you." He took it and drank. "That's good!" He smiled at the man, stripped to the waist, weathered and tanned, muscular and short. Behind him his boss waved at Alexander, asking him to come over. He had moved across to the open hut at the edge of the field and was sitting in its shade. Alexander looked around at The Grey, saw that she was placidly nibbling at some grass, and strode over to join him on the bamboo seat.

"*Kumusta*?" the other man said, smiling and holding out his hand.

"*Mabuti*, Eddie; and how are you?" Alexander answered, shaking his hand and sitting down beside him. He propped up his coconut on the narrow cane table in front of them.

Eddie had been his neighbour for a long time, ever since his father had died and he had come to run the property. He had been an assistant manager with the Hong Kong Bank in Makati, but had decided to bring his family to, what he considered, a better life in the provinces. They had a good friendship.

"How's the family?" said Alexander.

"Good, thank you. Rowena has started university in Tacloban; the rest are still at high school or primary."

Eddie had eleven children. Alexander took another drink from his coconut. The morning was getting hotter. No point in hanging around, he thought.

"How's the harvest going?" he asked.

"Very well, actually. It's a good season," he replied in his American English. With careful management he was getting three crops a year.

"I checked out the wholesale price this morning." In fact, he had rang the office in Manila. "It's ten point seven eight pesos."

"That would be about right," he replied, looking out across the paddy field, shorn like a sheep, the stiff rice stubble left behind. "I'm charging six hundred pesos a sack in lots of ten."

Alexander did the calculation in his head. "That's OK. We'll take seventy sacks, please." In the early days he had paid cash; not any longer. They didn't talk for a while, watching a pair of eagles circling in the currents high in the sky. Eddie seemed to want to talk, but hesitated.

"What is it, Eddie?" Alexander prompted him.

"*Nag irum nun*. We had a drinking session at my place last night; the men from the mountain were down." He meant the NPA. "Their farmer friends were again complaining about your free rice, and how you steal the best workers! Now they don't like 'the Inchek's' tax return. They say you're far too honest and that's dangerous for them. Best be careful; this one could be more serious!"

HEATHROW AIRPORT, UK
1993

Iain and Bruce checked in with Cathay for Hong Kong at Heathrow. They missed some of the queues, travelling business class.

"I'm glad to be going back to Asia!" Iain said.

"I'll be glad to be checked through and away from this damned terminal to the welcoming arms, well, say smiles, of the Cathay flight crew!" rejoined Bruce. They handed over their passports and their tickets.

"An aisle seat, please," requested Iain.

For the past year, after finishing their final term at Melrose College, they and four friends had travelled on a Eurail pass through France, Switzerland and Austria, through all four magical seasons. Now, 'sabbatical' over, they had to start some sort of a career, thought Iain, but in what? Should he go directly into OSM?

They went through the metal detectors, with their carry-on bags, at last being disgorged into the milling crowd of duty free. As neither of them wanted to shop, they settled down with croissants and espresso in a quiet corner of the café, looking out on the tarmac and the green-and-white striped livery of their Cathay flight. They had twenty minutes before their first call.

"Are you ready for the new job," said Iain, biting into his warm English croissant, no butter or jam. They hadn't eaten since early breakfast.

Looking elegant and confident, picking up his coffee and crossing his long legs, Bruce replied with a laugh, a shrug of the shoulders. "I don't know! I talked my way into it, now I have to deliver." Bruce was going out to start the Hong Kong edition of *Trance* magazine. At first it was going to be four pages in the London edition. The magazine was owned by the father of the other wing-forward in the school rugby fifteen. "In the beginning I'm afraid it's going to be dealing with expats, till I can persuade more of your lot to go to the 'dos'!"

"Will you do much PR?" asked Iain inquisitively.

Bruce looked at him, wondering why the detailed interest. "I reckon it will be about one third PR, one third selling ad space, and one third writing copy," he replied.

"You'd better brush up on your sixth-form Mandarin and start on Cantonese!" continued Iain. "Where are you going to have the office?"

"Yes, you're right; a bit of Cantonese would be useful." Over the years Bruce had become accustomed to Iain's investigative conversations. Usually they meant well. "And I'm thinking of leasing in Tung Ying Building in Nathan Road. It's a good enough location, and a whole lot cheaper than Central. I like the layout: practical. And – before you ask! – I'll rent in Broadcast Drive: easy getting to work."

"I don't know what to do," Iain volunteered. Bruce was his closest friend and confidant. "I'm sure Tsui will want me to go to the States. I really don't want to. Canada would be very different: no gun culture. Vancouver is more than quarter Asian. But the business schools don't carry the same élan. Within OSM there's such a choice. Maybe I'll go onto the trading floor; that could be exciting!"

Bruce smiled and reached for his carry-on bag as their flight was called. He finished his coffee and picked up his *Economist*. He'd been saving this week's for the flight. He smiled again, this time to himself, as he recalled APH, his geography teacher, introducing them to the magazine: 'The best newspaper in the world.' He'd also played hooker for Wales, so they all believed him.

* * *

The Korean air hostess smiled as she put their gin and tonics on their tables – drinks before the evening meal.

"She's all right then, isn't she?" said Bruce.

"Yes," was Iain's monosyllabic response, as he watched her going back down the aisle pushing her trolley.

"Trust you to take the aisle seat!" joked Bruce.

Later, after eating and a bottle of Beaujolais – Iain was enjoying a brandy and Bruce a port – they had reached the giggly stage.

"You know," whispered Bruce, "I read in *The Age* odd spot once, that an ant can jump three hundred and fifty times his own height, like a man jumping over a vertical rugby pitch. And a pig has a minimum of thirty-five orgasms per encounter. Now there's some useless information for you!"

Iain chuckled, and turned to Bruce. "Let's get that tape out that we bought in France. Have you got it here? I'll get the hostie to play it over the intercom. Relaxing and so forth!"

"We shouldn't really."

The tape played soft classical music with bird songs intermingled. It also had hidden messages to encourage sexual activity. It was labelled 'Fashionable Techniques'. Substitute 'fashionable' with 'sexual' and you had the idea, they had said in the shop.

Iain got up, opened the overhead locker and handed Bruce his satchel. When the cabin had settled down and the lights had been dimmed he buzzed for a hostess.

"I hope I get the Korean."

"Course you will," said Bruce.

She came walking back towards them, swinging her hips. When she reached them, she smiled confidently and leant forward to find out what they wanted.

"Can I have another cognac, please," said Iain, "and could you play this tape? It's some quiet classical music. It will help my friend sleep; he still needs a lullaby!"

"Do you mind?" said Bruce, laughing as he spoke.

"I'll see; maybe," she said sweetly, taking the tape from Iain.

* * *

About two hours later, after the movie, they heard their French tape. It was very relaxing and seemed to give them a warm glow. There were several ringings of call buttons and passengers asking for extra blankets. The seat in front of them was pushed right back, and a few of the passengers walked up the aisle to talk to the hostesses in the galley. The Korean girl came to the young men. Gracefully she sat down on the arm of Iain's seat.

"Any more drinks, gentlemen?" she asked.

"No thanks, that's enough!" Iain answered for them both, all the time trying to think of something else to say to keep her there, her thigh pressed against his forearm.

"Do you live in Hong Kong?" Iain was surprised at himself – he wasn't usually so forward – but she didn't seem to mind.

"Yes," she said simply, then added, "in Kowloon Tong, with two others of us." She smiled. "I'd better get back; I'll be in trouble."

"What's your name?" Iain sounded a little desperate.

"Have you got something to write on?" He gave her his in-flight magazine. "It's Suk Soon," she said, writing. Iain smiled openly as she wrote down her Kowloon number underneath. Before handing back the magazine she glanced quickly towards the galley.

"Thanks. My name is Tsui; my friends call me Iain. I'll phone you."

As she stood up to go, a flicker of recognition went through her eyes. She knows who you are, thought Bruce.

"Yes, please," she said, smiling and patting him on the forearm. He watched her walking away. She turned and smiled at him again, before slipping out of sight behind the blue curtain.

"Well done," said Bruce enthusiastically.

"How old do you think she is?"

"About twenty-four."

* * *

They slept fitfully through the night, eventually being aroused by the false dawn of the cabin lights. Those passengers who were awake enough were being served fruit juice. Suk Soon gave them theirs and their tape from her pocket. She looked tired.

"Thank you, Suk Soon," Iain said quietly.

She smiled and went on to the next passenger. Later they had breakfast: cereal, mushroom omelette, black coffee and croissants. They didn't talk much, a little hungover from the night before. Bruce was finishing his *Economist*.

"Listen to this, it's pretty good, *The Economist*'s take on democracy.

"*Democracy is not just about elections. It requires political institutions and civil society, an independent judiciary and press, checks and balances, tolerance and debate.*

"Do you think Hong Kong qualifies? Singapore, for that matter?"

"No, I don't. But there again, I don't think some nation states should have democracy. Not yet, anyway."

Bruce had turned to listen to Iain. As he spoke, he noticed an athletic looking Maori from about six rows back get up and come towards them. When he reached their seats he leant forward and spoke softly but purposefully.

"Good morning, Mr Iain. I have a message from Sebastian. There will be a car waiting for you at Kai Tak. If you want to bring Mr Bruce with you, that's fine; he's been invited to stay at Laird House."

"Thank you, I understand," replied Iain wearily. Another irritating 'nanny' from Tsui. The 'I understand' bit he'd found useful for getting rid of them. Sure enough, he was returning to his seat.

The Maori was pleased with himself. He had heard that the boss's son could be difficult, flying off the handle for no apparent reason. He was wondering if he should put in his report the fact that his charge had been chatting up one of the hostesses.

ALNWICK ROAD, KOWLOON TONG
1993

Suk Soon and the rest of the crew came down the ramp at Kai Tak airport long before their passengers, though it was hard to tell which crew had brought in which passengers, there were so many early evening arrivals. The waiting crowd pressed against the rails of the walkway to the exit, lit intensely from the glaring advertising displays. In little booths down one side the car rental companies were hustling for business next to the Hong Kong Tourist Office, whose reps were handing out welcome packs which she knew included their useful street map and nothing much else, apart from advertising.

Drivers were waiting for their unknown passengers, whose names were written on signs they held, some being waved discreetly.

She walked on, following her flight crew through the noisy crowd, through the sliding doors to the warm night and to the long, well-disciplined taxi queue penned in by rows of tubular fencing. The taxi rank snaked forward, picking up passengers on twin roads either side of the traffic island. The line was long, but she knew from experience that it was fast moving, with the red Kowloon taxis arriving in an endless stream and stopping in groups of six, taking about twelve people and their bags with each stop.

Police waved their arms and blew whistles. Close overhead another jet screamed down for landing – one every three minutes.

"Kowloon Tong. Alnwick Road, please."

She had found that, with drivers, giving the suburb first helped; it must focus their mind on a general area, then in on the specific. She also knew that, unless one spoke Cantonese, the 'please' was a waste of time. True to form, the taxi driver took off with only a grunt as he slammed the meter flag over and the door closed. The small Buddha hanging from the driving mirror started swaying wildly. On the dashboard the sausage dog started bouncing up and down on his spring.

They raced along Boundary Road, turning right up Waterloo Road, the traffic lighter now in early evening. Just before the Baptist Hospital they turned left up the hill to Alnwick Road and her block of flats. She saw the old amah from her block exercising the family chow-chow and directing him, with much shouting and flapping of arms, to the dog toilet, a designated sandpit at the side of the road. She carried tissues to wipe him afterwards.

Suk Soon leant forward to give final directions to the taxi driver.

"Number twenty-two, straight on." She pointed forward. "Stop."

She paid him and took her little case on wheels and her shoulder bag out of the boot. She climbed the five flights of stairs, her bag banging against her hip. There were no lifts required, as the block was only five stories high, restricted because of the flight path to the airport. Good exercise, she always told herself. Opening the front door, she rang the bell as she went in. The flat was empty, so she went through the swing doors into the small, white-tiled kitchen to look at the rosters they kept on a board on the left-hand wall. First on the list was her Korean friend, her closest friend, Mi-na. She also flew with Cathay, and was in London till Friday. The third member of their renting group was Mary from Malaysia, and she was down in Sydney till Thursday. So she had the flat to herself for a few days. She went from room to room, pulling the curtains and putting on some lights. The two-bedroom flat was large by Hong Kong standards, but still very compact: a main bedroom with two single beds, and a single room, with the bathroom squeezed between. There was the kitchen and an airy living area. The floors were parquet, common in Hong Kong. She sometimes wondered where all the wood came from. Their Chinese landlord had put in modern furniture and some leather beanbags. And there was the roof garden, a real luxury in Hong Kong, which Suk Soon loved. Leaving her cases untouched, she went out onto the landing and unlocked the door to the stairs leading to the garden.

Coming out into the air, she flicked on the outside lights. The arbour, which gave shade and welcome respite from the summer sun, supported loads of green eating grapes. It covered half the roof garden. Scattered around the garden and along the parapets were all sizes of Chinese glazed pots containing kumquats laden with fruit; lemon shrubs; bonsai trees; and plants and shrubs she didn't know. The kumquats were given as gifts at Chinese New Year, the more fruit the luckier. By the door there was a 'money tree'. She would light a joss stick and put it in the pot on her way down; as they always did each evening they were home.

When they had moved in, the agent had pointed out three special clauses in their agreement. First, they had to water the plants as directed; second, the old man, the father of the owner, would have access to the garden each Monday to look after it; third, whenever typhoon signal five was raised, they would see to it that all the pots were taken down from the parapets. The old man had left a pith helmet and a light plastic raincoat for the job, hanging in the stairwell.

Suk Soon loved watering the plants at sunset. Tired as she was, she was happy to do it. She hardly heard the planes going in on their final approach to Kai Tak, turning right sharply as they came to the chequerboard, about half a mile away. It was true what people said: you got used to the noise. But they reminded her of Iain, son of OSM. She doubted she'd ever hear from him, once he was back amongst his family and his controllers. She wished she could talk with Mi-na.

* * *

He phoned late next morning. She recognised his young, confident voice at once.

"Hullo, Suk Soon. This is Iain. We met—"

"Yes,I remember."

"Are you all right, rested now?"

"Yes, thank you."

"I was wondering if you would like to have dinner at the Korean barbeque in Nathan Road. We could meet at the Holiday Inn coffee shop on the mezzanine floor and walk to the restaurant later, say on Tuesday or Wednesday?" he said, smiling into the phone. Always give them a choice, an 'either or'. That way they relaxed, feeling they weren't being pushed into an absolute decision. And smile – it came over the phone. A younger Comprador had taught him how to use the phone to his advantage, when they had been stuck in the Comprador's office by a typhoon when he was thirteen.

"Oh! Tuesday will be fine," she said, a little flustered.

"Seven or eight o'clock?"

"Seven, please." Did she sound too eager? "It gets so crowded and very noisy later on," she added.

"OK, I'll see you then." Now he sounded a bit nervous and bossy too.

"Bye." Suk Soon put down the phone. She wondered if he would be fun.

NATHAN ROAD, TSIM SHA TSUI 1993

They had met as planned in the warm and friendly atmosphere of the Austrian style coffee shop, upstairs from reception at the Holiday Inn Golden Mile. After a coffee, they walked up Nathan Road with the crowd and into the contrast of the Korean barbeque restaurant, all garish, blinking but welcoming neon. The restaurant was in the basement, a stark barn of a place with white-tiled floors and plain white formica tables. Each table could be connected to its own small gas cylinder on the floor. Overhead was an individual extractor fan which was lowered if you were having the barbeque, and which joined onto a labyrinth of ducting hanging from the ceiling. The bus boys wore rubber boots for swilling down. The restaurant won no prizes for elegant decor. But the quality of its Kobe beef was known throughout the Colony.

Suk Soon had been right; the restaurant was barely half full. Even so the noise of the Cantonese, coming here from work to relax and enjoy the food, was raucous. Suk Soon and Iain grinned at each other and started talking loudly.

"Will you have the barbeque?" Iain almost shouted.

"Yes please," she said, nodding her head vigorously, "and lots of Kim Chi, please." She nearly made the mistake of telling him to make sure he had some too. She had told him she was twenty-one, though she was really twenty-four. The newspaper article she had read had said he was coming up to twenty. She thought he looked and behaved a few years older.

"And Tsingtao beer; it goes well with the hot Kobe beef."

The waiter nodded and took away the menus. Another waiter arrived with a flurry of activity, slamming down the cooking hood and, with his other hand, dropping the barbeque in the middle of their table. Then he dived under the table to connect the gas with a hiss, lighting the barbeque on the way up, and setting it low. As he left them, three other waiters arrived with plates of meat and vegetables, bowls of sauces and Kim Chi, a steamed rice server, and two tall bottles of Tsingtao. Their waiter came back, switched the barbeque high, poured on some chicken stock and, with long chop sticks, doused some of the red beef in the runny chilli marinade, then adeptly threw it on the sizzling dome and left them to get on with it. They couldn't see each other for the dome so, as it was a table for four, Suk Soon quickly moved herself to Iain's side of the table.

"That's better," she said, smiling. "I can hear you now – and see you!" She busied herself with the cooking; spreading some of the vegetables in the trough around the base of the barbeque, feeling relaxed with him. She made sure he ate plenty of Kim Chi with his beef.

"Do you mind if I do the cooking? Some girls in Korea still like to be girls!" and she laughed softly.

"All right, that would be lovely… but what will I do?" questioned Iain, looking at her with a quizzical smile.

"Drink your beer, and tell me about yourself," she responded teasingly. On a personal level he was usually reticent, not knowing what to say.

"Oh, no! It's so boring."

"Come on," she cajoled. "Tell me about your schools." A bit of a gamble, but it seemed to be working, as he began to talk.

"All right then, if you're sure? First I went to the French international school here when I was four. Tsui, my father, told me when I was older that I went there because we did little business with France, and that might help! It did actually. I used to be driven with my amah back and forth by our present head of security. Then they sent me to Scotland, to Melrose College when I was thirteen."

"A bit young to be so far from home, wasn't it?" Suk Soon asked gently, filling his bowl with rice.

"I suppose so. To begin with I was pretty homesick and a bit scared. But I got used to it. That's where I met Bruce. He was on the flight with me yesterday."

"Yes I remember. The polite one! What was the school like?"

"It was terrific really. Set in acres of its own hilly and wooded grounds, even with its own golf course. It's the only school in Scotland that has golf and rugby as its major sports. And we had prefects and fags and all that stuff. It's an all-boys school. We used to climb the nearby Eildon Hills and visit the Roman camps. We were very devoted to Roman history!"

He looked at her and she looked back, a slight smile playing around her large and dark Asian eyes. She was so beautiful, so graceful even in these rowdy mundane surroundings, in control of herself, at ease. He felt fascinated by her, enthralled. A lady of the East.

"What about you?" he heard himself saying. Waiting for her reply, he went fishing for vegetables in the bubbling soup, using the little mesh scoops they had been given.

"Oh there's not much to tell. Two elder sisters and a younger brother. Spoilt! I went to school near home in Dobong and on to SNU, Seoul National University." He knew that SNU was one of the 'SKY' Universities, one of the three elite: Seoul, Korea and

Yonsei. "I took humanities. Then I flew with KAL, before I moved to Cathay."

"Why did you change to Cathay?" he asked.

"More international, a better clientele!" She grinned at him as she casually patted his knee, laughing. No longer hungry, they sat back and drank their beer as the last pieces of beef sputtered.

"Would you like a dessert, anything else to eat?" Iain asked.

"Oh no, not here, I don't think. Why don't we go back to my place? I think I've got a can of lychees and some ice cream!"

He was surprised. That would be even better. He had thought they would go on to 'Aquarius'. Who needs loud music! My god, this sounds all right!

"OK, that's lovely. But… there's something I meant to tell you earlier. Tsui's paranoid about the spate of kidnappings—"

"Not paranoid at all," she interrupted. "You read about it in the papers every day."

"Well anyway, there's always someone around; and this evening I intend to shake them off. Is that OK with you?"

"Are you serious?" She giggled her delicious giggle.

"Yes, I am actually. Our comprador is a partner in this restaurant. I've worked here washing dishes during some school holidays, so I can go through the kitchen. Bruce will be waiting out the back. What's your address?"

"Fortune Villa, Alnwick Road. Number twenty-two. Wait outside for me. It's a rabbit warren! I'll take you up to the flat. Oh, come on! Really, this is a bit CIA!"

"I'm sorry. I just get fed up."

"It's all right! It's fun!"

"Do you mind catching a taxi? Just give me five minutes."

"OK, James," she teased.

"Shut up!" he said, laughing, leaving the table.

* * *

He walked through the kitchen, waving to the staff he knew, taking care not to slip on the wet tiled floor. The refrigerated prep tables were loaded with cut-up vegetables and sliced meat ready to go out to the restaurant, and two chefs were cooking dishes which had been ordered a la carte. He saw the manager in his office, who acknowledged him and grinned lecherously. Iain pushed open the back door and went down the narrow, littered and stinking walkway leading to Lock Road. He saw Bruce and a taxi driver arguing about a parking spot, so he quickened his pace, calling out in Cantonese that they were just leaving and he didn't expect anyone to do that to their mother. They jumped in the car and slammed the doors.

"Where to?" asked Bruce, switching on the engine.

"Do you know your way out to Waterloo Road yet?" checked Iain.

"I should do. That's my way home now!" Bruce had just moved in to a furnished flat in Broadcast Drive.

"Of course."

"How's it going?" said Bruce, glancing at his friend.

"She's fantastic, really terrific. She's fun to be with."

"Come on, Iain, this is the one. Action stations!"

"Well, maybe. We're going back to her place for dessert."

"Say no more!"

They were working their way through traffic, north up Nathan Road.

"The car sounds good," said Iain, changing the subject. Bruce had bought the three-year-old silver Audi through the OSM dealership, a phone call from Tsui's secretary ensuring a good deal. His company budget had allowed for a half-decent car, a small office and some expat accommodation. They travelled on in silence for a few minutes.

"Do you think I should tell her?" asked Iain.

"Absolutely not. Don't even think about it!" came the reply.

FORTUNE VILLA, ALNWICK ROAD
1993

They arrived at Fortune Villa, and drove up the end to number twenty-two. There was no sign of Suk Soon.

"Let me off here, Bruce," said Iain; more an order than a request. "It's a lovely balmy evening."

"All right, Iain; it certainly is. Just relax!" Bruce swung the car around, dropped Iain off and headed out. Through the open car window he waved at Iain and shouted "Happy hunting!" just as a taxi's headlights swung in at the entrance. Bruce switched his lights off to let him pass. There was not much room and no response from the other driver. "And thank you, too," Bruce said to himself as he accelerated away.

* * *

He walked over to the taxi, opening the back door for Suk Soon and then paying off the driver.

"Perfect timing!" he said to her as she moved towards him, taking his hand.

He squeezed her hand, holding it firmly, smiling and looking into her eyes.

"You're so very beautiful!" he said.

"Thank you," said Suk Soon, staring back, holding his gaze. "Come on," she said, laughing lightly. "Let's go up."

They went into the communal hallway and up the mosaic-tiled stairs. His mind was racing as he followed her up to the fifth floor. He had little experience with women. Only with his cousin Antonia years ago at Niyogen, in one of the plantation's nipa huts during the monsoon rains. There they had been playing 'doctors', and he had ended with the brilliant words: "Somebody's got to know when to stop", and stop it had. Apart from a few passionate kisses and inadequate fumbles, one with the house matron in an empty dorm, that was it. The handicap of all-male boarding schools. He was watching Suk Soon's shapely legs go up the stairs in front of him when he noticed her simple black court shoes. They were very new; the soles were still whitish. Maybe she had bought them for this evening. She was opening the security door, then the metal front door, laughing and pulling him inside with her as she flicked on the lights. The apartment was humid and warm.

"There's some brandy in the corner cupboard over there; help yourself."

She put on some eighties music, some of Sade, then crossed the room to close the curtains. Iain nervously sipped his brandy.

"That's nice music," he said.

"Yes, I love it," she replied. "I'll just freshen up…"

* * *

When she came back from the small bathroom she was wearing a full-length silk Chinese gown. Her hair was down around her shoulders. Out of habit Iain stood up. She came closer, standing in front of him, smiling and looking up at him.

"Do you want the lychees now or later?" Suk Soon did not wait for his answer, but reached up and kissed him gently on the lips, pressing her young body firmly against him.

* * *

They lay together in her bed, holding each other closely, clothes scattered on the floor around them. He felt tranquil, calm and warm. She smelt so good. He wanted to talk.

"That was my first time," he said quietly.

She turned and looked at him. She nearly said "I thought it was", he had been so eager. Instead she simply said, "You were wonderful! So strong." She tickled him; he seemed too serious. This was meant to be fun.

He started to wrestle with her, laughing.

"Let's make it the second time, but this time I'll go on top: better control!" she said, giggling again and throwing her leg across his body.

* * *

He woke from a deep sleep to the sound of a bell ringing, on off, on off. Suk Soon was halfway across the room, going to the intercom, naked. She looked wonderful in the dim dawn light which was creeping into the room. He heard her talking but could not make out the conversation. She came back into the bedroom.

"It's for you." Her voice was deep and warm, though slightly annoyed. "It's for you," she said again, jumping back into bed.

"For me!?" He sounded surprised. "Who the hell…?" But he had a good idea.

"Yes, it's for you, if you're Mr Iain!"

He let his feet hang down onto the wooden floor, starting to look for his boxers, thought better of it and, becoming more awake, walked quickly into the living room.

"Who's that?" he barked into the microphone.

"Sebastian, Mr Iain."

"What are you… what do you want?"

"I needed to make sure you were there." Sebastian sounded tired and angry; no apology for disturbing him, them. "You know Tsui is in China. We have very strict and simple instructions. Please do not make things more difficult with some schoolboy pranks." Iain was getting aggravated when he heard Suk Soon come up behind him. She began to play with him. Sebastian was still talking. "You know how Tsui is, perhaps overly, concerned, particularly with the recent armed abductions by mainland gangs. I'll leave someone here…" and the intercom went dead.

"Don't worry, it's OK," the Korean was whispering, caressing him in the half-light, unrestrained, audacious. Iain began to forget the interruption, hanging up the phone and holding her head in his hands.

* * *

In the morning they ate the lychees up on the roof garden, sitting in the shade of the vine. She was wearing a red happy-coat and light-blue panties. She looked radiant.

15 Graham Street, Central 1994

Tsui walked up the steps in glorious morning sunshine, Hong Kong's Indian summer at its best. He wore an American baseball cap with his dark business suit. None of the people rushing up and down the walkway gave him a second look. Stalls of leather belts, silk ties and women's lingerie crowded in on either side. Some of the stall owners called out to him, not sure if he was a tourist or not. At Graham Street he turned left past the new yuppie fresh fruit juice bar on the corner with its stools and counters looking out onto the busy streets and its garish trani-display menu above the serving counter. Even at this early hour they were busy serving substitute breakfasts.

Tsui turned sharply into a narrow, darkened passageway and began climbing the steep and narrow stairs, the air pungent with rotting rubbish, the floors covered with the flotsam of squalor. Each landing's litter included cardboard boxes, some of them still occupied. He came to the third floor hallway, as grimy as the others. Stepping over some cartons, he used his key to open the deadlock on the heavy security door. The inner door was open.

Inside the small three-roomed office the dirty locked windows, covered with security grills and housing creaking air-cons, were opaque with grunge. Rubbish from the floors above hung on the outside. Giving some order, the rooms were set up like an old-fashioned call centre, with neat rows of cheap desks, each with its own phone and agents' directories. On the walls were colourful posters of travel destinations.

It had been Tsui's idea that it be set up as a dummy travel agency. When there was no one here the phones rang intermittently for the inquisitive neighbours, the resident janitor giving a human presence. Fifteen Graham Street was the first one of half a dozen planned safe houses, some on the outer islands, and Macau, to be used for debriefing and some rest and relaxation before resuming 'home life'.

The Comprador and the janitor were talking quietly in the middle of the main room. They stopped when Tsui entered. The Comprador looked incongruous but still dapper in casual western clothes: faded jeans and a Pierre Cardin polo shirt. The janitor, looking intentionally scruffy in an old unnamed boiler suit and without a cap to cover a balding head, bowed towards Tsui before leaving.

"Good morning, Tsui. Welcome back. I sent him down for a fruit juice while we're here."

"Good morning. Good. Where's the nephew?" The Comprador brought out his Chinese Whistle and switched it on where Tsui could see.

"I took the liberty of telling him to come in twenty minutes. Perhaps we can talk first," the Comprador continued, without waiting for comment. "First, before we start, there was news from Taiwan late last night. The KMT publicly concedes that The People's Republic of China controls the mainland; that's a joke! And at the same session they have made legal the National Security Council!"

"Thanks. We knew it was coming; it was only a case of timing. Both are OK with us, though the NSB can be a bit of a nuisance." Whilst he was talking he dusted off one of the desks and sat down. The Comprador remained standing, preferring to keep his clothes clean. Fastidious as ever.

"My nephew is both intrigued and interested. I have tested his loyalty. It is satisfactory." He stopped in front of Tsui.

"I would expect that, Comprador, from your family." Tsui paused. "But does he have the expertise? Does he know the technology?" He turned his piercing eyes on his comprador, who paused in turn, this time for a long time.

"Yes," he said softly but confidently. "He persists, almost insists, on being top of his class. And last night over some sake he told me, none too readily I might say, about some hacking he and a friend have been up to. For his part he got into the Pentagon and the CIA. He even created an agent. He thinks he might get paid soon!"

"Clever but risky, don't you think?"

"Yes, I agree. I told him to clear it all out and to destroy everything, including the main drive, of course. He said they do that as they go along.... He probably won't want to talk about the hacking, if that's all right with you?"

"OK," said Tsui, nodding his head in agreement, "but it sounds as if he's going to be a useful cyber spy. Incidentally, have you heard, the PLA are getting very active? The Pentagon is worried. A good cyber spy will do much more damage than ten physical ones. "

The Comprador made no comment. He felt that the taipan should know that he knew what was happening on the mainland.

"I've told him, if he takes this project on, there will be no connection whatsoever with K. K. Chen Ltd. He'll be on his own." The Comprador took a sip from his Evian, which he held in his hand, watching Tsui as he did so.

* * *

The nephew arrived precisely at the revised time. Maybe he'd been waiting downstairs. He was dressed like a Mormon going door to door, which was surprising. Tsui had been expecting a nineties hippy. Black shiny shoes and very short hair gave him a military bearing. He was tall like his uncle, and clean shaven. The left arm of his suit hung limp by his side; his arm was in plaster and a sling. He looked pale.

"Good morning, Tsui, Uncle," he said with a slight smile and accompanying bow.

"Good morning. Sorry we had to meet here; it's just more 'convenient', you understand?" The Comprador's nephew stopped smiling, his jaw set. He didn't speak, but nodded. "Let me come to the point," Tsui continued. "Your uncle tells me that you are being extremely successful in the US, both on and off the campus."

It was more a statement rather than a question. Nevertheless he replied, "Thank you."

"No! Don't thank me, thank yourself," replied Tsui. "It is well done. You will be having the scouts after you with share options and other enticing gifts. OSM wants to be amongst them, so don't rush in." Tsui began pacing around, stopping eventually in front of the whiteboard. The rattle of the cheap air-conditioning units interrupted his thoughts. Distracted, he picked up a marker and wrote a bold red 'seven' on the board. Uncle and nephew watched him steadily.

"Subject to your continued good results and demeanour, we will offer you a commission which will be in the low seven figures," Tsui said, turning to the 'seven' he had written. "It will be paid in cash – half at the execution of your contract and half on completion. Each contract will take less than three years. You will not work for OSM or your uncle; you will work directly for me. There may be a moral reason for you taking on the work, which will be clandestine. As is this meeting," Tsui added. He paused. There was no response.

"Would you be interested?" he asked.

"Would my uncle be involved?" asked the filial young man.

"Yes."

"Then yes, thank you, Tsui. I am interested and intrigued."

"A question, Nephew." The Comprador spoke quietly, with authority. "We will work in cells for security. What is the best, safest nomenclature?" Very simple and down to earth; no room for pure tech geeks.

"May I ask, how many cells?"

"Not more than ten," Tsui volunteered. Actually there would be five.

"The best way is to have no identification." He paused for emphasis. "If you do, don't use codenames, but a combination of numbers and letters; the letters lower and upper case; not less than six characters and not more than twelve. Some punctuation marks instead of letters, figures. Simplest is best; none is better." He spoke precisely and economically and with the confidence of youth. The answer was practical and correct.

* * *

Tsui came out into the morning sun, warming up as it reached down into the street. He was on his own as he headed downhill through a maze of crowded streets towards the harbour and the start of the elevated, covered walkway which would take him right into the reception floor of his office building. He still preferred the exercise of walking rather than using the downward-bound mega Central-Mid-levels escalator.

Before stepping onto the escalator to the walkway he stopped at the Chinese chemist shop hung with dried vegetation and cured animal parts, the shelves below loaded with tall jars, each labelled with the characters for their contents. In the back a Cantonese doctor was taking the pulse of a patient, with an assistant hovering around taking notes of the prescribed ingredients for the drink that would be made up, each part being weighed on the antique brass scales. Tsui paid ten dollars for his tonic drink, served in an old glass tumbler standing ready, with others, on a wooden tray by the door. The drink was black and bitter, a mixture of medicinal herbs with ginseng. When he was finished, Tsui was offered a boiled sweet to take the taste way. He declined, knowing from experience that the sweet was as bitter as the drink. He walked away and knew that by the time he reached his office he'd feel invigorated. Last night was not for sleeping. As he approached his office, he took off his baseball cap, pushing it into his jacket pocket.

Lobby Bar, Sheraton Hotel 1994

Sebastian was with his new Singaporean girlfriend in the lobby bar of the Sheraton at the bottom of Nathan Road. Coming in from the humidity, he was enjoying an ice-cold Steinlager. Tango had a gin and tonic. She was tall and graceful, precisely made up, and fun to be with when away from her peers. But, like most from her island state, she was a ferocious snob, which Sebastian enjoyed manipulating and exploiting, having no superiority complex himself. He had brought her to the ground floor piano bar so that they could 'bump into' Iain and Suk Soon, who he knew were meeting here at seven thirty. Iain, with his good manners, would ask Sebastian and his friend to join them for a drink. Normally Sebastian would not come here, the bar impersonal and too formal, though the piano player's music was relaxing. As the bar was almost part of the lobby, he sometimes felt as if he was a bellhop, sitting amongst the baggage of the Japanese tours. But he knew that Iain liked to come here to avoid 'the Peak people', whose gossip machine mainly operated at the Mandarin, the Hilton, the Hong Kong Club and the yacht club. His friends wouldn't be seen here.

Iain came striding confidently into the bar, wearing the OSM 'uniform': a dark blue suit, black shoes and tie; only his tie was bright orange. He had planned to be early so that Suk Soon and her flatmate would not have to wait in the bar on their own. Suk Soon had rang earlier to let him know that Mi-na, her Korean girlfriend, was back in town and would it be OK if she came too? He had agreed, happy to meet any of Suk Soon's friends. He had told Bruce, who had grinned broadly and simply said "Go for it, tiger!" But he didn't think it was like that… probably. He was looking round the bar just in case they had arrived, when he saw Sebastian with a girl, drinking at a corner table. Damn, he thought to himself, I didn't know that he drank here. Sebastian was smiling in recognition and raising his hand. Iain had no choice but to wend his way through the low tables and chairs to where they were sitting. Sebastian stood up, half turning to his companion.

"Good evening, Mr Iain. May I introduce my friend Tango?"

"How do you do," said Iain, holding out his hand, which met hers, held out languidly from the two-seater sofa. She smiled and said nothing. Iain had spent most of his holidays in Hong Kong and knew the mixture of diaspora well. He was pretty sure that Tango was a Singaporean Chinese, with her expensive clothes and very expensive jewellery, quietly stated, and her overly-assured presence, lounging back in the silk cushions as if her father owned the hotel, which he might.

"Won't you join us?" Sebastian was saying.

"I'm meeting some people—" he began.

"Never mind, they can join us too. Have a seat," interrupted Sebastian, with Maori authority in his voice, waving towards the empty seat next to Tango. Iain smiled as he sat down beside her. No matter, he thought, Sebastian was good company and they could leave after a couple of drinks. He turned, still smiling, to look at Tango. She was an attractive girl, self-assured. She looked Hokkien, as were more than half the Chinese in Singapore. He wouldn't try his Hokkien; and certainly his Mandarin, their lingua franca, was not yet good enough. He'd stick to English.

"I bet Tango is not your real given name, given by your family?" He asked, half teasingly.

"No," she replied, smiling back. "Actually, my family name is Tang."

"Not Tang Containers, out of Singapore?"

She hesitated, and then said, "Yes, that's right," looking down at her drink.

"We do lots of business with you!" Iain hadn't noticed her reluctance to talk about it. "We're with OSM."

She changed the subject from her family business by speaking about herself. "I'm with the *Straits Times*, attached to the Hong Kong office. More freedom!"

Yes, that's right, thought Iain, otherwise there's no way you'd be going out with a head of security, and a non-Chinese at that.

The waitress, in a discreet olive green long skirt and waistcoat, came with his San Miguel, the tall glass wrapped in a paper serviette to catch the condensation which was already forming. As Iain took a long draught, he saw the reflection of Suk Soon and her friend in the wall mirror behind Sebastian.

* * *

The Cathay girls had nearly finished their first screwdriver and Sebastian was mainly talking, more like questioning, Suk Soon, who was mildly put out and getting no support from the Singaporean, who spoke to no one. There was a slight tension in the air. To hell with the second drink, thought Iain, waving at their waitress for their bill.

"We live in Dobong now, one of the most northern suburbs. It's beautiful, with Mount Dobong and many public parks," Suk Soon was saying. Iain was signing for the drinks and leaving a tip as he picked up his card.

"We have to leave now, or we'll be late." They were going to the Korean restaurant again and they needed no booking, but it seemed the polite thing to say. He wouldn't mention where they were going. Why give Tango a chance to look down her Singaporean nose? She would probably not set her sights lower than The Pen's 'Gaddi's'.

"Please excuse us, Tango, Sebastian. See you tomorrow, Sebastian."

Head Office, Tsui Centre, Wanchai 1994

Travelling to the new head office was even easier, as the new office building sat on top of Wanchai MTR station. As the doors hissed open, Sebastian stepped out first and headed for the exclusive OSM escalator, which would deliver him to the main lobby, where his office was located.

The floor-to-ceiling window stretched right across the office, showing banks of monitors – the nerve centre of the building. The glass was bullet-proof and the heavy security door was always locked.

Sebastian opened the door with his card and his handprint. He nodded curtly to the morning shift and went into his spartan and efficient office. He went through his usual morning mail; nothing important except two coded messages for Tsui, who was back in again tomorrow. They could wait till then. His priority this morning was his one-page report for Tsui on Suk Soon. He switched on his computer and began his first draft. The phone rang. His secretary wanting his order for lunch. He thanked her, saying that he would be out, and then told her to take calls for an hour. He left his direct line active.

Ms Pak Suk Soon

DOB 15th July 1970

Educated at Seoul National University. BSc Humanities.
Hostess with KAL – eight months.
Hostess with CP – six months, long haul.

Early life household very poor. SNU later. Shares flat with other hosties, one a Korean, Mi-na. Close personal friend.

Mother, about ten years ago, was a high-class hostess (bar girl) working mainly from Westin Chosun Hotel, Seoul's top business hotel.... No, Tsui would know that, and he hated useless information. *Chosun Hotel. She still takes occasional customers, always (to her) foreigners and nearly always from a regular Japanese clientele.*

Father worked for US forces in stores. Became a procurer for servicemen. Married one of his girls, his present wife, who was pregnant with Ms Pak.

Now is believed to be in clandestine trade with the North. Therefore extremely dangerous and extremely volatile politically. One source suspects him of spying for the North.

In view of the China Deal.... No, that wouldn't do, he wasn't meant to know that much. *In view of OSM activity in the area....* No. *In view of Mr Iain's position with OSM....* No, leave out OSM. *In view of Mr Iain's position, it is recommended that the relationship be ended forthwith.*

He read through his work and printed out one copy. He deleted the file; in security their main drives were formatted bi-weekly. He took his report, and the two coded messages, and locked them in his wall safe; took his jacket off the back of his chair, and went to Delifrance for a coffee. Sorry, Iain, he thought.

WAI KWOK'S OFFICE, TSUI CENTRE, WANCHAI 1994

Tsui was waiting in his brother's fifth floor office, with leather-bound law books lining every wall. His secretary had told him he had been held up in court. She gave Tsui a cup of green tea and the *South China Morning Post*, and left him to his own thoughts.

He was here in Wai Kwok's office to sort out Iain and to tell him about the girl. They would do what was necessary, though unpleasant. The situation and the girl simply were not good enough.

Even though times had changed traditions, he still should have done what his grandfather had done for him. He smiled at the memory.

The *Swallow*, Hong Kong Waters 1959

Tsui and his grandfather were being driven down the steep and twisty road, flanked by hidden villas, on the other side of Hong Kong Island to the busy fishing village of Aberdeen. It was early evening of the first Friday after his fourteenth birthday. His grandfather was talking to him in an unusually gentle manner, but in a matter-of-fact tone.

"There will be a small crew to sail the junk, though it has an engine if you need it. And there are two servants from the house, and a cook to feed you and so on. The girl is nineteen, they say, though she looks younger to me. She's pretty. You'll be sailing around Lantau Island, through the harbour to the eastern New Territories to anchor off Sai Kung for a while. I'll send the driver over to pick you up on Sunday afternoon."

His grandfather had walked Tsui to the old fisherwoman with her small half-covered sampan tied up to the jetty, shook hands with him and left. Enthusiastically Tsui, in jeans, blue T-shirt and rope-soled pumps, climbed into the rocking private ferry. The old lady cast off and, standing up, began rowing with her single oar held over the stern. They came round the floating restaurant towards a spacious luxury junk, bobbing at her mooring. He saw the junk's name clearly as they rounded the stern: the *Swallow*, underneath the same in Chinese characters, then Hong Kong. The old woman expertly came alongside as he grabbed the handrail of the wooden steps, pulling him onto the first one clear of the water. Athletically he climbed on board, not needing the outstretched hands that reached down to him. It was nearly dark now as he stood on deck, looking around. All was shipshape and swabbed down.

"Good evening, Sir," said one of their senior houseboys, neat in Laird House uniform. "Will you follow me, please?" He turned and led the way to the main quarters below the poop deck. The door was open, diffused light from the cabin lanterns lighting their way. He ducked as he went into the cabin, the houseboy standing back to let him go first.

"Your usual Pimm's, Sir?"

"Yes, that would be nice," said Tsui, talking a bit louder to take any tremor out of his voice. The cabin had been divided in two by a heavy red curtain, which gave a warm feeling to the living part of the junk. He left his shoes by the door and walked across the polished deck to the low table, where he sat down cross-legged on one of the two dark red silk cushions. He felt the movement of the junk on the swell, usually relaxing.

The houseboy came in with his Pimm's Number One garnished with a sprig of mint and a slice of lemon. Without speaking he put the drink down in front of Tsui and left the cabin. Tsui heard subdued shouting in Cantonese as the engine started and they got underway. They would use power to get out of the congestion, and sail when they were clear of the harbour. The steady throb of the junk's powerful engine felt good to him, he being used to sailing and the sea.

"Will you eat now, Sir?" The houseboy was back again.

He hesitated, not sure of protocol.

"What about the girl?" he asked.

"She will join you when you eat," he replied, without humour.

"Then I'll eat now, thank you." As the houseboy left the room Tsui heard quiet footsteps from behind the curtain. It opened slowly, revealing a low candlelit bed as a young girl glided into the cabin. She was startlingly beautiful in a natural, diffident way. Her long black hair shone in the soft light as she walked gracefully with the movement of the junk to her cushion opposite him, wearing a silk cheongsam cut high to her hips. He could see that she wore nothing else. She smiled shyly at him.

* * *

It had been a never-forgotten experience. She had been told he was called Jack, and he that she was Sarah. She had experience, which she taught him with gentleness and understanding, and then with passion. She was lithe and supple and smelt of jasmine, fresh and lovable. Her skin had the golden bloom of youth. Of course he fell in love with her.

* * *

Inevitably, and in confusion, he was put in a sampan and delivered with one of the houseboys to his father's driver, who was waiting for him behind the Sai Kung piers and restaurants. The Comprador had been watching the transfer through binoculars from his new apartment.

Tsui never saw her again. She was sent back to her province in the mainland hinterland with enough money to look after her family and to help her village. The Comprador had negotiated. His father had ignored Tsui as he moped about the big house, except once at dinner one evening he tried a few jokes to lighten up the mood.

"What's the Hong Kong definition of a pervert?" And he answered himself. "A man who prefers sex to money!" And then, "What did God say to the Hong Kong Chinese who had asked him why he had put foreigners on earth? Well, some one has to buy retail!"

In the end they sent him away to his uncle in Taiwan until school started.

Wai Kwok's Office, Tsui Centre, Wanchai 1994

Suk Soon came down in the elevator in Swire House from the personnel office of Cathay Pacific. She was in a daze. They had told her that her contract had been terminated because her Hong Kong work permit had been cancelled. She had asked them why and they had said they didn't know why, just that the notice had been delivered by a uniformed immigration officer. They had given her a copy. It said she had to leave Hong Kong by Tuesday.

The lift doors opened and everyone rushed out, leaving her, bewildered, in the middle of the lift lobby. She thought of phoning Iain. As she turned to go, she was surprised to bump into Sebastian.

"Good afternoon, Ms Pak. How are you?" He paused, smiling. Suk Soon smiled back, vaguely in the back of her mind wondering how he knew her family name. She didn't speak.

"Mr Iain's uncle would like to see you. Do you mind? I've got a car."

Iain seemed to like and trust this Sebastian, she thought. She hesitated. This felt bad. Quietly she replied, "Yes, OK," and followed him outside. His broad shoulders stood out above the crowd. It was raining again.

* * *

"Come in, Miss Pak. Thank you for coming to see me," said Wai Kwok as his secretary ushered her in and he came round his desk, hand outstretched to shake hers. "Have a seat please."

He turned around and sat again at his desk, opening the thin file in front of him. Even from the other side of the desk she recognised the Cathay and Immigration letterheads. Two and two began to make four.

"I'm sorry about your bad news," Wai Kwok said deliberately, picking up his copy of the two letters. "Now for the good news. We hear that you have become a Legal Permanent Resident. You have been granted a Green Card for work in the US; and also a contract to join Continental's 'short haul' out of Houston." He pushed two envelopes towards her. "You will need to get your Social Security Number – your SSN – as soon as you get there."

He leaned back in his revolving chair, steepling his fingers and looking at her steadily. She did not pick up the envelopes. He reached into his inside jacket pocket and took out a fatter envelope.

"And ten thousand dollars US spending money. You have to leave by Tuesday midnight."

She picked up the three envelopes. There was no point in trying to fight the power and connections of the company: too much power, too many connections. She felt very sad, overwhelmed, but saw no point in being a martyr. Her family needed her remittances.

"Tsui expects you, once you are out of Hong Kong, to sever all relationship with my nephew, Iain Tsui. Good afternoon."

She did not speak as she turned to go. She was fighting back tears which she didn't want Wai Kwok to see.

THE PEAK WALK, VICTORIA PEAK 1994

The boys came out onto Lugard Road, more like an English country lane than a Hong Kong road, after walking up from Laird House. They broke into a fast jog at the start of the Peak Walk. Everything was shrouded in early morning mist, drips falling on them from the overhanging trees and shrubs. Soon they left the sealed road, which serviced the few old colonial homes tucked away in their luscious gardens, and were running on the wooden walkway which took them around the steepest cliffs, the walk following the contours around Victoria Peak.

The early morning fog often hid the spectacular view of the Hong Kong harbour, bustling with every type of shipping; her business district skyscrapers; and Kowloon; and Kai Tak airport; and, in the distance, the hills of the New Territories; and, on the other side, the view of the South China Sea, inward shipping mere dots on the horizon amongst the islands.

They ran in rhythmic step, their long strides covering the ground effortlessly, as they had run cross-country at school together. They didn't speak, keeping their even breathing deep and in time, as they had been taught. The fog began to lift, blown away by the strengthening wind, as they reached their halfway point: a green bench at the side of an open park at the crossover point from harbour view to open sea. They sat down, still breathing heavily, Bruce more than Iain. On the comparatively flat grassland in front of them groups of old Chinese men and women were systematically going through their traditional Tai Chi exercise regime: a continuous series of elegant, flowing movements, good for bodily and mental health. They wore loose-fitting uniforms – white tunics, black trousers – and plimsolls.

"How's Suk Soon? And Mi-na?"

"Funny you should ask: I wanted to talk with you," said Iain, getting his breath back. "Mi-na? Oh! Her flatmate. Actually, they're fine, terrific… but it's not that…. She's leaving Cathay to go to the States. Joining Continental out of Houston, for Christ's sake!"

Bruce was watching a sea eagle wheeling above them in the morning sun, not expecting anything more than some scintillating titbits about the liaison. He turned to his friend. Iain was obviously agitated and upset.

"Bugger, that's a bummer. What brought that on?" Bruce regretted asking as soon as he had.

"I don't know. She said she'd get a Green Card, which she always wanted. I don't know; it's all so sudden. She leaves on Tuesday. We're going to dance the night away on Monday at 'The Giraffe'. She seems cool, distant."

Distraught, he was talking much more than usual, thought Bruce. He wondered if Sebastian had told Tsui about Suk Soon; Tsui was back in town. Iain was talking again.

"So much for her name. It's supposed to mean 'pure and obedient'." He turned away, his voice failing him. Standing up, he began their run again. Bruce followed.

* * *

Suk Soon and Iain came into the Sheraton lobby out of the commotion and heat of Nathan Road.

"Phew! That's better!" he said, swinging his jacket over his shoulder as they walked to the lifts opposite reception. The external lift was empty so they had an express ride to the top-floor night club, with Hong Kong before them, as they stood silently, holding hands. There were a few people at the bar: mostly expats, and one tourist couple in the restaurant. Monday night and early, they were very quiet. Suited their mood, he thought.

They were seated next to the window, with a brilliant view of busy Victoria Harbour and the tall neon-clad buildings of Central, with The Peak a dramatic backdrop. The green-and-white Star ferries hurried back and forth, and the lonely junk of the tourist board went by, brown patched sails in the harbour. The sun was sinking fast, as advertising snapped on here and there.

Suk Soon was withdrawn, in a world of her own, across the table. Might as well be the Pacific Ocean, he thought. She looked so beautiful and so forlorn, in a simple black dress with a single string of pearls around her neck.

"What time's your flight?" he said.

"About two o'clock, but please, Iain, don't come out to Kai Tak. Let's say our goodbyes at Fortune Villa."

When the Filipino band came back, he danced with Suk Soon, holding her closely, her head on his shoulder, as the group played 'Feelings'.

* * *

He came back to his small office next to Sebastian's 'empire' after his hour with Tsui. His secretary walked in behind him.

"Coffee, Mr Iain?"

"Yes please, Margot; and hold my calls please." He'd have to phone Bruce. He reached for his business cards; he hadn't memorised or saved his new office number yet.

"Hullo. May I talk to Mr Bruce please? It's Iain Tsui." His office was all English speaking.

"Hullo, Iain. Good morning?"

"More 'news from the front'! You can use it if it's any good for your…"

"Rag?"

"Oh! Come on, Bruce, I didn't say that! Anyway, I've just had a meeting with Tsui. He wants me to go to LSE, London School of Economics."

"I know what LSE is."

"All right. All right. I'd be taking the three-year BSc, in International Relations. Tsui says it will be much more use than Harvard's MBA – you know that's only a two-year course."

"What do you think, Iain?"

"Well, I like Europe more, as you know, and flight time London to Houston's not too bad."

Bruce said nothing about Houston. He knew that Iain might kid himself but he really had no choice: whatever Tsui said was final, was law. He'd heard on the 'grapevine' that Suk Soon was only flying domestic for Continental. He didn't expect his friend would be seeing Suk Soon soon.

"Sounds like a good move. If you've got time, let's eat at Sabatini's this evening?" The change to 'Rome' might help his friend.

Queen's Pier, Central
1995

The Comprador's one-hundred-foot cruiser *Fusion* had come round to Central from Hebe Haven, where the Royal Hong Kong Yacht Club had their moorage for 'motor launches'. The Comprador had no use for the social club, but the marina facilities were good and only around a promontory from Sai Kung. She was lying off Queen's Pier next to Star Ferry terminal.

As soon as the crew saw the company car approaching, they swung her into the pier, and then backed her in like a Rolls Royce. There was a gentle bump as the stern hit fenders. Crewman held her steady with boathooks; no need to tie up to the bollards as the Comprador and Tsui were already striding towards them. Without hesitation the Comprador, and then Tsui, went down the landing steps, onto *Fusion*'s protruding stern deck, and up the short companionway to the main deck. Tsui said "Good morning" to the crewmen as they pushed off. Adjacent and above them, passengers from a docked Star Ferry purposely went down the wooden walkways to offices and hotels, shops and restaurants in Central, like so many shorn merinos at the sales.

As they got underway the powerful twin Man engines pulsed under their feet with controlled power. *Fusion* was making steady headway into the choppy waves. The

Comprador waved Tsui into a comfortable seat in the main lounge and sat down close by so they could talk in confidence. His houseboy was hovering in the background, wanting to give them tea.

The Comprador had bought the Falcon 100 a couple of years ago from a Dutchman for a song – considerably less than three million dollars. At the time the Comprador had happily misquoted Kipling when talking about the bankrupt expat he'd negotiated with: "Here lived a fool who tried to hustle the East!" *Fusion*, renamed by the Comprador, 'a blend of east and west', was a good-looking vessel, a hundred feet and white from bow to stern. She was handsomely appointed: all wood and leather, the best of Italian design. She had three spacious en suite cabins, a large living area, a compact galley, and crew quarters. The master cabin had a spa bath.

They were heading round the north end of Lantau Island to personally check the final phase of their contract with the new airport authority for site preparation. Then they would cruise around Lantau and head due east past Cheung Chau, Lamma Island and Stanley Point, before heading north back to Sai Kung. Lunch would be served on board; they would have plenty of time to appraise the China Deal. He let his thoughts wander to Cheng Cheng. It had been a hard week; he'd hardly seen her. He hoped she would come out with the car to meet him.

* * *

"Did you hear about Barings?" Tsui asked the Comprador, as he glanced out of the window at the noise of a Macau hydrofoil going by in a plume of spray. The main cabin had long windows on either side and forward, not portholes.

"Yes. It looks as if the bank will go under," said the Comprador, taking his lid off his porcelain cup and sucking in a little of his tea.

"What is edifying," continued Tsui, "is the speed with which it happened, inside a week from one rogue trader, losses of over one billion US dollars. Lousy senior management! Tsui finance is enhancing their Chinese walls and reviewing its derivatives—"

"They'll have to be stronger than Mandarin umbrellas!" butted in the older man. "However, I read that his false, exceptionally high arbitrage profits got everyone their bonuses! No wonder no one blew the whistle! A lesson indeed!" The Comprador chuckled to himself.

They were approaching Chek Lap Kok as the Comprador went to his cabin to change out of his office suit and Tsui went out onto the stern deck. He saw the temporary jetty they were heading into and, beyond, the busy site of the new airport; dump trucks and heavy machinery creating a continuously rising dust cloud. They had flattened Chek

Lap Kok and Lam Chau islands to make about twenty-five per cent of the location, the rest being reclaimed from the sea. The site was about the size of Kowloon Peninsula. The new airport project was, at the moment, the biggest engineering project in the world. The earth moving and dredging operation would be the fastest ever and well within the time frame.

The Comprador joined him on deck, looking very trim and youthful in a dark grey, almost black, tracksuit, and grey Prada sneakers. Tsui put on his baseball cap.

"Hullo, Comprador. It's looking great. How's Harald doing?" He was their German overseer.

"Outstanding. He's a good man, you know that. The site engineer did some performance calculations. The consortium is moving roughly ten tonnes per second."

The site engineer's Land Rover met them at the jetty, then sped them away to the cluster of prefab offices.

* * *

They had rounded the tip of Lantau Island and were now heading east, back in territorial waters: they'd have to be alert crossing the busy Lama channels. In an hour or so they would be cruising by what he had called since he was a kid 'the backside' of Hong Kong Island.

Tsui pulled off his tie, opened his collar and leant back, relaxed, in his soft buckskin armchair. The cabin was always kept at a comfortable temperature. One of the young chefs from the Golden Carp had made them a simple but satisfying lunch: Mongolian lamb hotpot with plain rice, and sweet and sour cabbage soup. Spring had not arrived this February; on deck it was still cold.

The Comprador was talking to his houseboy in Shanghainese. All his staff, like himself, were from Shanghai. The Comprador thought Tsui had only very basic knowledge of their mother tongue. In fact he had brushed up on his Shanghainese and Mandarin during his time in Taiwan. The Comprador was talking in clipped tones, telling the young man to keep out of the galley once lunch was finished and to go out on deck. He ordered them fresh tea.

The master of *Fusion* dropped back to about ten knots as they hit some rough water. He had been instructed to give them an easy ride.

"I read somewhere," Tsui was saying quietly against the throbbing of the powerful engines, "a report, from one of the ubiquitous Senate committees, that 'elitist covert operations pursue foreign policy objectives without public or democratic support and therefore act against US democracy'.What about the veto at the United Nation's Security Council?"

The Comprador looked across at the taipan. To those who were not part of his inner circle Ysui was unapproachable, intimidating. With piercing blue eyes and black hair, a thickset jaw and olive complexion he was often taken for Italian, if not Mafioso, except for his slightly slanting eyes. He was a man of unlimited ambition. The Comprador had also found him a man of the highest principles, a 'tilter at windmills'; but at the same time – an unusual combination – he was eminently practical. To reach his objectives he had a deadly streak, like the king cobra, the snake that spits its venom.

"Taipan, with respect, you sound like a student discussing political science!" The Comprador smiled, keeping his tone light, not wanting to anger the younger man yet knowing that one of Tsui's strategies was that if two executives always agreed, one was superfluous. "What is necessary is to know what covert black operations they are up to, what POTUS is hearing from the Foreign Intelligence Advisory Board. We need to know what they are doing, or undoing, before they do it. We don't want them running amok in the middle of one of our missions, our operations."

Tsui was staring intently at him. As the Comprador paused Tsui interrupted. "Agreed, but I think the PFIAB is the wrong organ of the body politic. We need to know what's happening in SOCOM, Special Operations Command. We've got plenty of time: the provisional target day is still ten years away."

"Maybe so, but time goes by. We have a lot to do… though time is also our ally. But SOCOM is not enough. We need information from inside MI6, to include SAS. Furthermore…" – and here the Comprador looked around to see that his houseboy was still on deck, and checked again to make sure his CW was active – "…we need to infiltrate MOSSAD. They could cross our operations."

"You're right, of course. They have a long reach. Damn! Their language makes it very difficult—"

The Comprador interrupted. "You see, Taipan, we are too dependent on the Vikings." Their codename for their Ninjas.

"No, Comprador. I know they haven't signed up yet. But they are committed. I now know that without our finance they would revert back to their ancient character. And, as you already know, Comprador, about ten per cent of their intake is Occidental these days. There's still time to train someone up. Besides, we are not planning to change or stop their operations, simply to know what they are doing." But he could see his comprador was not convinced. He changed the subject.

"The US psyops videos for 'putting over US views' are now being contracted out to American private advertising firms; but they're not for viewing at home! Different from the British Council. Never mind, I've got the research department listening in. And they're still doing their report on the Black Dragon Society. You know they were the grandfather of the yakuza? In nearly fifty years of operation throughout Asia they never lost an operative."

The Comprador did not respond, going on to the next item on the agenda, which they kept in their heads. "The 'bearer bond' state of affairs is as we suspected. A TCI-registered company is empowered to issue bearer bonds; and the same applies to a branch office opened in Hong Kong. In passing, it is interesting to note that our local Inland Revenue department treats such an entity favourably. So we need to start that company – have you a name in mind?"

"No, just take a new shelf company. For directors and shareholders use Cheng Cheng and one of the locals, like before."

"Taipan, I must strongly object to our using—"

Tsui interrupted abruptly and spoke sharply. "You object to my using Ms Cheng Cheng. I know. Get used to it! And we'll open the account with US two million from Austria." Whilst he was talking he saw the sharp look of disapproval from his partner.

The Comprador spoke, anger still in his voice. "Let's have a break; some English sandwiches, perhaps?" Without waiting for Tsui to reply, he clapped his hands sharply above his head.

* * *

The sandwiches were served: brown bread, and smoked salmon from Scotland garnished with French capers served with cold Seaview Brut from South Australia. They didn't talk for a while, pretending to enjoy their tea. As Tsui looked out to port he could see the different aspect of the southern side of Hong Kong Island going slowly by. Far astern, a heavily laden container ship was making its way to the terminal.

Tsui glanced at the Comprador, who was still looking young and vital, dressed again in his trademark black. They had known all their lives that their generation had been destined to work together, predetermined by generations of family history. At times their working relationship had been fractious, but as they matured it became more fruitful.

"The London Philharmonic was through last week on its way to Tokyo for a tour of Japan," Tsui said, breaking the silence. "You remember my cousin plays lead flautist?" They talked as they ate and drank, two mixed cultures – the Comprador's Chinese with French, and Tsui's Scots mixed in with ancient and modern China. They talked about the new Mayor of Shanghai, Bellatrix's new foal in New Zealand, the Grant's takeover and the Comprador's computer nephew. The Comprador himself had no sons, so he had to choose one of his nephews to take over K. K. Chen. Tsui was lucky to have Iain.

When the Comprador's houseboy had cleared the table and had again taken up his position on deck, Tsui started to talk once more about the China Deal.

"As you suggested, I have put the same team as researched the Vikings to look into the operation of the French resistance in nineteen forty to forty-four, and also XU, the intelligence organisation in German-occupied Norway. We will learn from the report. Also they'll have a look at the IRA and the Lebanese mafia."

"Good," said the Comprador, reaching for his briefcase on the seat beside him. "Why do they think they're doing the work?"

"For security, checking terrorist groups and their 'minders'," replied Tsui briskly, as though the question didn't need asking. The Comprador looked at him, raising one eyebrow in his cultivated mannerism. Without speaking, he opened his briefcase and took out a single A4 sheet and passed it to Tsui, who, intrigued, began to read.

> *WE DETERMINE to save succeeding generations from the scourge of war, which twice in our lifetime has brought untold sorrow to mankind; and to reaffirm faith in fundamental human rights, in the dignity and worth of the person, in the equal rights of men and women of nations large and small, and to establish conditions under which justice and respect for the obligations arising from treaties and other sources of international law can be maintained, and to promote social progress and better standards of life in larger freedom...*

Tsui paused for a long time, staring at the document then, looking up, transferred his stare to his trusted comprador. The sounds of *Fusion* permeated the cabin. Eventually he spoke.

"Nearly fifty years on, and what do we see? Who are these phantom members of the world's greatest, most obstructive and expensive talking shop? If I ran the UN, I'd feel an absolute and ineffective fool! I would turn down any offer of leadership. Who can wait for them?" With passion and disgust Tsui screwed up the paper and threw it on the floor.

The Comprador silently stooped to pick it up.

* * *

They had gone out on deck as they headed into Sai Kung bay, wrapped in parkas against the chill wind. They would come into the new Hong Kong Jockey Club pier, next to the swimming pool. It had been built for their new golf course on Kau Sai Chau. It was a public course, two eighteen-holes by Gary Player, and another example of the Jockey Club's 'good works'. The light was fading fast, unlike the gloamings in Scotland, and the crew had on the running lights. The same was true of the grey WJB that had been following them all day. It had a top speed of forty knots, and was as fast as any boat in

Hong Kong waters, police or smuggler. Sebastian would be on board.

As *Fusion*'s engines slowed tsui saw a company car, with Cheng Cheng standing aside watching them through glasses. He smiled and slowly waved at her. She took one hand off the binoculars and waved back. He was reminded of Winston Churchill's use of John Milton: 'They also serve who only stand and wait'.

In the dark he saw the upright figure of the Comprador holding the rail and looking dead ahead. He felt the power and magnetism of the elegant and remote Chinese in meditation. Drawn to his philosophical mood Tsui moved closer to him, beginning to speak. "Well, Comprador, when all is said and done, the only reason for living is to improve the lot of future generations."

For a long time, as *Fusion* drew closer and closer to the pier, the Comprador remained silent, not moving. Then, turning to Tsui, he spoke quietly, but very clearly and with a soft intensity.

"Taipan, let me quote again our Confucius to you. 'By three methods may we learn wisdom: first by reflection, which is the noblest; second, by imitation, which is the easiest; and third by experience, which is the bitterest.' He does not imply that easiest is inferior…. And another one which we may come to understand as an absolute, and which we may come to embrace, 'To know what is right and not to do it is the worst cowardice.' The axis of power is swinging to China and Taiwan."

* * *

They passed the signs to Clear Water Bay on their way back to Hong Kong, the Mid-levels and Macdonnell Road. Cheng Cheng snuggled up to Tsui and held his thigh.

"How was your day?"

"Looking good," he replied, relaxing back in the Mercedes.

She knew that he had spent all day with the Comprador, an unusual happening, but she also knew not to be inquisitive. She merely smiled, snuggled up to him again and, in a while, talked of something else.

"Do you remember Ina Isaacson in the Bahamas?" she asked.

"Yes," said Tsui, turning towards her with a boyish grin. "Yes, I do."

"Well, her husband was a partner at Barings. They lost everything, even though it wasn't his department. They had to sell the house in Surrey. He lost his job. He's coming out for interviews."

"Yes, I know. Our finance department is one of the people on his list."

OSM's Finance department was as big as most private banks.

"Oh! You know everything!" That's the taipan's job, he thought. "Would it be all right if I showed Ina around? She hasn't been here before."

"Yes, of course," responded Tsui, without reservation. "Do you want a car?"

"No thanks, we'll use the MTR; we're not ancient! And it's quicker."

OSM had known about Isaacson's trip out for a few weeks. They were going to make him an attractive offer. Tsui needed to know what he and his contacts had been up to in the Far East.

"Just find out whatever you can about their visit," he added distantly. He felt in his pocket for his CW and pressed it to switch it on. "Actually I want you to go back to the Bahamas next month. I think we're going to cancel the contract. We'll sort it all out in the next few days."

* * *

Ina and Cheng Cheng had started early in Central. They had done The Landmark, Princes Building and Alexander House and had dropped in at the gracefully ageing Pedder Building to eat at the popular and in-fashion Kigasawa Japanese, where they were having noodles and green tea. Cheng Cheng had phoned Mary-Lou to take away their morning shopping: Ina's back to the Ritz-Carlton and hers back home. Mary-Lou was leaving, loaded down with bags.

"How nice to have a proper maid," Ina was saying. "We have to make do with au pairs and most of them don't like doing too many chores. Too much an equal really. How did you find Mary-Lou? She seems so nice and polite. And young and beautiful!"

"She came from Tsui's brother's coconut farm in the Philippines." Cheng Cheng hated to use the word 'plantation'.

"Oh! A provincial…" Ina seemed more of a snob than she remembered.

"How's your trip going?" Cheng Cheng asked.

Ina looked across the table at her, smiling, as radiant as ever, and beguiling. She reached out to pat Cheng Cheng's hand, and then sighed as she replied, "Not well, actually." Ina looked down at the table. "No one wants to know about ex-Baring boys! How times change and so quickly too! He's been turned down everywhere he goes. He's only got ANZ Private and your OSM Merchant, and then he's down to cold calling, poor soul."

Cheng Cheng would tell Tsui. But he probably knew already.

"But what about all his China contacts?"

Ina had been boasting in the Bahamas of her husband's contacts, about playing tennis with the Mayor of Shanghai and giving him a dozen Slazenger rackets, unavailable on the mainland. And how the Mayor's star was in the ascent, and he was about to make a big move to Beijing.

"They don't want to know. I don't understand it."

"It's probably all a game," said Cheng Cheng, refilling her friend's tea. "There'll be messages at the hotel when you get back!" But she knew there wouldn't be; Hong Kong could be a cruel and cunning place.

"Let's get going," said Cheng Cheng, waving her card discreetly at the waiter. "We'll take the MTR along to Admiralty. There's an exit at Admiralty that will take us right into Pacific Place. We'll avoid going out in the wind and rain." She put her card on the waiter's tray, turning to him, smiling, as she did so. Then to Ina, "Did you know they've put up the first typhoon warning this morning? It's only a standby signal really, nothing to worry about. This one's called Sybil – why do the always give them girl's names! It's expected to miss Hong Kong and make landfall west of Macau."

* * *

In the tranquil Pacific Place they had covered all the shops they wanted too, tired but satisfied. They were in their last one, the very exclusive and expensive 'Sheer Elegance', their slogan simply 'Lingerie for the Rich and Famous' – a Hollywood steal, but it got the message across. Cheng Cheng and Ina were giggling at some skimpy silk bikinis in vibrant colours and priced, like everything else, in US dollars.

"Ninety-nine dollars: a lot of money for something designed to cover very little!" joked Cheng Cheng, her arms full of stuff she had picked out for herself and Mary-Lou. They went over to the 'customer service' desk, taking the ornate chairs offered them. Nothing so infra dig as 'cashier' at Sheer Elegance.

The young manager came over to them. "Have you heard, Madam? Number eight signal just went up. Sybil turned. We'll be closing shortly." When number eight was hoisted everyone left work, most going home, and schools would close. Star Ferry would stop running. They collected up their second lot of shopping bags and headed for the exit.

Stopping at the main entrance, they looked outside at the rain lashing down and the palm trees bending over. The doormen had given up using umbrellas and were rushing customers into open taxi doors, their chin straps firmly in place. Cheng Cheng grabbed Ina by the arm to get her attention. She had to shout against the gusts of wind howling through the automatic doors as they opened and closed.

"They won't take short trips like to the Ritz any more: we'd better share with anyone going up to the Mid-levels, to my place. Otherwise we'll be stranded!" She didn't want to have to trouble Tsui.

"OK. It looks pretty wild."

As they ran for the first taxi the rain soaked them and the wind took their breath away. They had to turn their heads sideways and use their hands as a windbreak to breathe at all. Ina copied Cheng Cheng, and the taxi door slammed behind them: no one else for Mid-levels.

* * *

The driver went down into the underground car park, out of the wind, rain and flying debris. They had circled fallen trees and driven through floods from overflowing storm drains. On some corners the taxi had shuddered and weaved about as it turned into the full force of the gale. All the time the driver had been swearing vigorously in Cantonese. It meant nothing to Ina, and Cheng Cheng chose to ignore it. They began to collect their things and started to giggle. Cheng Cheng paid the taxi driver double, the custom during typhoons. Right away he started reversing rapidly out into the storm, no thanks, simply a grunt. The girls started to walk across to the lift, still giggling.

"Mary-Lou will be glad to see us," said Cheng Cheng as the lift doors closed, trying to compose herself now she was somewhere she might be recognised. "I think they have even more typhoons in her province in the Philippines than we do here. She gets scared and spends the time sweeping and sweeping the living room floor!"

As they came into the flat Mary-Lou looked up, smiling, pausing, soft Filipino broom in hand. She was in Cheng Cheng's flat because it was leeward of the typhoon and she would get some company. She had taped up all the windows as she had been instructed, and closed everything tightly.

"Hullo! Mary-Lou. We've got to get out of these wet clothes. Can you find Ina a yukata, please?"

Cheng Cheng took Ina through to her bedroom and, giving her a bath towel, showed her the en suite. They put their shopping on the silk bedspread of the queen-sized bed. Cheng Cheng heard her mobile phone ringing in her handbag in the hall.

"Will you get that, Mary-Lou?" Her maid came running, the phone in her hand still ringing. It must be Tsui.

"Hullo?"

"Are you all right?" Tsui's strong, confident voice coming clearly over the phone.

"Yes, thanks. We're at the flat."

"I heard. Stay there till it's over. It's going to be a wild one. Several ships have broken their moorings already. How's Ina?"

"She's fine." How does he always know? Then she added somewhat lamely, "She's with us now."

"Fine. The landlines are down now. I'll try and get a message to her husband at his hotel. Forecast is that it will blow through overnight. If it does, I'll send the car down for you so we can have brunch at the house. Remember I want you to do another trip to the West Indies."

"Where are you?" Not a good question, she thought, so she added, "Are you OK?"

"Aberdeen and yes."

Dial tone buzzed in her ear. She smiled at Ina, who was rubbing her hair with the towel Mary-Lou had given her.

"He'll try and get a message to your husband. The phones are down. It's not safe to go anywhere now."

Mary-Lou brought in some tea for them: English tea, white and sweet. For the storm I suppose, thought Cheng Cheng.

"Make some for yourself, Mary-Lou. And come back in. Let's try on some of our shopping! I bought you some fun things…"

Mary-Lou blushed, smiling bashfully as she left the bedroom.

Taipei, Taiwan
1995

Tsui had left the company apartment in the cool of early evening and was travelling along Jenai Road. Soon the taxi would turn right into Shinsheng Road North and the rush-hour traffic. He was due in the lobby of the Taipei Grand Hotel. Kite had become active again.

Since he had become a sleeper in nineteen eighty-nine, Taiwan had become less of a 'military garrison' though it still felt like a nation on 'alert', with army personnel and their vehicles a fairly constant presence. For the country's political leaders the PLA was never far away. In reality less than two hundred kilometres.

Kite had arranged a shopping hostess for him to bring to their meeting at the Jardin de Paris 'short-time' near Snake Alley. As the taxi pulled up at the Grand, looking like an Emperor's palace on the hill, Tsui told the taxi driver to wait if he wanted to double his fare. He ran up the steps and through the massive doors, held open by bowing doormen, into the great lobby busy with guests and checking in and out. He hardly noticed the luxury: the huge vermilion-painted pillars, the regal archways showing off the high atrium with its tiled and vaulted roof. He was looking for his girl, who would be wearing a salmon-coloured tailored dress and carrying a Mitsukoshi bag. He saw her at once, standing by one of the pillars, tall, conservative and blending in to her surroundings.

He strode through the crowd towards her.

"Good evening. Are you Jade?" Tsui spoke in curt Mandarin.

"Yes, good evening, how are you?" She replied in flawless English. That will do, thought Tsui.

"Shall we go? The taxi is waiting." He took her arm peremptorily and walked with her through the throng.

In the taxi she tried to make small talk, irritating Tsui. Then she said, having run out of idle chat and things to talk about without response, "John tells me you're from Hong Kong."

Tsui sat up and turned to look at her. That's strange. Kite would never give her any information. Tsui grunted in reply and settled down again in the taxi's well-worn seat, now being more watchful. He would tell Kite.

* * *

Tsui picked up their room key at reception and took the lift, small but clean, to their floor. Their room was like the lift, small but clean, with a heavy smell of lavender deodorant in the air. As they stood looking at each other, they heard next door the sounds of bumping and squealing, louder than the piped music. Tsui spoke first.

"I have to go down to Snake Street for some medicine. I'll be about twenty minutes. Have a shower if you like," and he left her a little confused.

Out on the landing he recalled the third floor room number Kite had given him. One floor up. He'd use the stairs. He passed a young man going down, turning his head to the wall, not wanting to be recognised. Coming to twenty-nine, he knocked twice lightly. The door opened a little.

"Who's there?"

"Osprey." Still using them, in spite of the nephew. It sounded quaint. Maybe they should change.

"Come in," said the voice. It was Kite.

The lights were dimmed and the room was full of smoke. Kite was smoking again.

"What's all the fuss," said Tsui, coming straight to the point and sitting down at the modest dressing table. His CW was already on. Kite, sitting on the edge of the bed, was also direct.

"It's about Flycatcher," – codename for the Minister of National Defence. "Our other man thinks he's taking half our contribution and sending it off to Switzerland."

Perhaps that would explain the hiccups with Sinbad Fuel Systems and the cooling of relationships with the Merlin's China contacts, Tsui thought to himself.

"How sure is he?" asked Tsui.

"About ninety per cent," replied Kite, laconically.

"OK, I'll deal with it. Good work, Kite," said Tsui, getting up. "Oh! By the way, that Jade girl knew I came from Hong Kong. Did you tell her?"

"No," Kite spoke emphatically, then paused, thinking. "She must be a government 'nanny'." He wondered what had happened to his girl; or was she the same one? "I've got two people outside. I'll have them check your room. We must go now. Goodbye, Osprey."

Tsui nodded, already going for the door.

* * *

When Kite's two men checked Tsui's room, the door was open and the room empty. No girl.

Quemoy, Taiwan 1995

They had left the OSM jet parked at CKS international. Tsui had offered it; Li Kai Sing politely refusing, saying it would look better to take the Air Force shuttle. Tsui noticed that the Minister had put on weight, about two stone, in contrast to his staff travelling with him: two slim and dapper army captains and a diminutive but pretty secretary.

The company was a discreet contributor to KMT campaign funds, so Tsui was asked over for some 'occasions'. This time he was going to Quemoy to review the troops with Li. He had never been to the island fortress, which had been Chiang Kai Shek's strategic buffer against the communists. It was only two kilometres from Fukian province on the mainland. Tsui thought back to when it started, when he was still at school. Some people in Hong Kong, particularly those who had lived through the Japanese occupation, were anxious. They called it 'The Second Taiwan Straits Crisis' and it had caused a commotion with the superpowers and the loss of over a thousand ROC lives. The shelling went on for nearly two months until, with pressure from the US and the Soviets, the combatants had come to a quasi-agreement. Each side shelled on alternate days, Sunday being a rest day, the rounds charged only with propaganda leaflets. They had continued to do so for nearly twenty years. Nothing achieved but the status quo. Madness. Now nineteen ninety-seven was coming to Hong Kong and Taiwan was watching closely. Quemoy meant Golden Gate. The rank-and-file PLA really thought it was.

Tsui was looking out of the window at the approaching island, only forty-five minutes out from Taipei. He could now see the 'Fury F-fourteens' from the Korean War scattered around the runway as inept decoys.

Excessively deferentially, one of the captains came across to clear his tray. The flight sergeant called out for seat belts to be fastened. Tsui saw the runway flying past underneath them. They touched down with the usual military bumps. Nothing too alarming, Wai Kwok, thought Tsui. The secretary smiled at him.

* * *

The staff car was waiting for them, with ensigns flying and a two-dispatch-rider escort. As they left the airport Tsui saw through the pine trees the military barracks, and fighter planes in hangers. Though Quemoy had been open to the public for three years, it retained a garrison of ten thousand and a definite military presence. They were the last flight in at two thirty. That would allow the runway to be used for the troops to train for the march past tomorrow afternoon for the Double Ten Parade. Li had excused himself from duties in Taipei to inspect this frontline outpost, and to have time with Tsui.

The car took them along a wooded avenue at the head of a beach facing China, the defence against landing craft and tanks, great steel girders row upon row, pointing out to sea. In Tsui's research department briefing he had read that the girders had become festooned with oysters, which the women of the village harvested, risking old mines. It had created significant income for the island.

Their hotel, the Kinmen, was simple and adequate. Tsui's double room had air-con. It looked out onto the street with some restaurants opposite. In the morning it would become a lively open market. On the tiled rooftops opposite he could see brilliant red peppers drying in the sun. Showered and changed and deciding to keep his shoulder bag with him, he caught the lift down to the bar. Li was there already with the two officers, and a locally distilled Kaoliang in his hand. He looked pleased with himself. Drinking too much, thought Tsui. The Minister was already filling up a shot glass for him.

"Good evening, Tsui."

"Good evening, Minister. Thank you." As he sat down, Tsui ordered fried oysters for all of them from the tray of a passing waitress.

"Is your room all right, Sir?" said one of the junior officers.

"Yes, fine thanks." He took a sip of his drink and followed it with an oyster. With a nod from Li the aides-de-camp got up quickly, muttering their apologies, and left. The bar was filling with a mix of visiting Taiwanese and foreigners: Japanese, some Europeans and locals. The noise level was increasing and the karaoke went on as Li leant forward. "Have you got something for me?"

"Yes, but not here, surely."

"It's all right. No one is taking any notice of us. You're not going to carry that case around with you all the time, are you?"

"Maybe later." Tsui was annoyed. It had been difficult enough getting to his hidden safe on the OSM jet after the immigration officers had left. He didn't want any stupidity at the moment. Putting his hand in his pocket, he continued conversationally, or so it looked. "I am concerned with the slow progress of Sinbad Fuel Systems. It seems to be grinding to a stop because of the bureaucrats, and your patent laws aren't helping." Would the Minister believe him? He might guess the real reason: that the PLA would do a lot better with it and it would score OSM points in China, and that the Minister was not trusted any more. Li looked unconcerned.

"I'll try and speed things up, I don't know."

"Don't worry. Our board…" – that was Tsui – "…have decided to take it to China."

Li sat up, and folded his arms across his large belly. He did not reply. Otherwise he still seemed unperturbed. He refilled their glasses and, smiling at Tsui, his piggy eyes twinkling, threw his shot back.

The bar was packed now, because of the holiday. Most of the customers were trying Kaoliang and rowdily enjoying themselves. Tsui looked around and decided that no one was watching them in this crowd. He quietly reached for his shoulder bag on the bench seat beside Li, took out the large brown envelope and laid it on Li's lap. His podgy hands held it firmly. The Defence Minister knew he wouldn't be searched.

The Lobby, Hong Kong Hotel 1996

The Comprador looked nondescript without his beard and wearing a shabby grey suit with a dull green tie and tinted glasses. The group he was part of were milling around the hall porter's desk, waiting for their guide, shepherded gently by an assistant manager. OSM travel organised these tours into mainland China to visit 'ancient cultural sites'. In fact they were sex tours taking the 'clients' to exotic surroundings and lithe, nubile young girls unavailable elsewhere. They used the tours as cover for getting in and out of China.

The tour guide arrived and, waving a blue-and-gold OSM flag, led the small group out of the hotel through the sliding doors into the heat. They waddled across the forecourt to the new white Mercedes minibus, engine running, air-conditioning on. They climbed into the bus in crocodile, watched by two well-built security guards who were travelling with them.

* * *

The drive had been uneventful. They had queued up at the border for about half an hour, the heavy traffic mainly working trucks, the local powerhouse of trade. The Japanese man next to the Comprador earnestly wanted to practise his English. The Comprador had eventually frozen him out by pretending to sleep.

They were coming to the centre of Canton, now Guangzhou, the Flower City. The driver slowed down as more bicycles clogged the streets until he swung off and into the White Swan Hotel, opposite Shaman Island and the old colonial buildings. They would stay here for a couple of days' obligatory sightseeing before heading out of the city.

* * *

They seemed to have lost their minders. Their agent had paid them off. The minibus turned into the bustling ferry terminal as the streetlights came on in early evening, pulling up alongside a shipshape, covered and motorised sampan. The party went timidly down the gangplank, looking nervously around. The Comprador too was alert, anxious to get on board and away.

The helmsman guided the boat expertly through the shouts and teeming seaborne traffic heading towards the western side of the Pearl River Delta and the labyrinth of tributaries that fed into the estuary. As they cleared the crowds the sampan engines found their rhythm, and darkness grew in upon them. The young girl deck hand, all in back and in tune with the movement of the boat, had served them rice cakes and rice wine. The Japanese began to laugh and joke and sing, their voices rolling across the darkened water, till the girl came back from the makeshift galley in the stern, admonishing them with vigorous hand signals and asking them to be quiet. The Chinese amongst them kept to themselves, apart. Most of them were smoking, the tips of their cigarettes glowing like fireflies. They were a risk, but one they had found they were unable to prevent, only to discourage.

They were away from the wharfs and godowns now, the industrial city and its waterways left behind, the open countryside on either side made apparent to them by a lack of lights, and the tall reeds growing on the riverside. Without warning the glow of a small village came up on the port side. The helmsman cut back the engines and the sampan crept towards the wooden jetty as the girl threw over the tyre fenders.

The group climbed out, with grunts and heaves; the young, as the middle aged, stiff from their trip from Canton. They ambled up the walkway in the balmy evening, the Japanese talking and snickering amongst themselves, towards the deep yellow lanterns glowing warmly and bathing the old farmhouse in subdued light, like moonbeams. The manager came out to meet them, waving his hands affably and walking across the pleasant Zen garden, which had been made out of the ancient working courtyard. Most of his customers were from Japan.

They went up the broad wooden stairs into the house, which was much the same as it had been for generations, hidden away in the countryside, escaping the ravages of the Forty-nine Revolution, the Cultural Revolution and finally the meddling Department of Tourism's arty renovations. Here the heavy beams were showing, the ceilings and walls rough cast. The carved lattice work of the window shutters let in the breeze and daytime light. Intricate carving was on every surface. The furniture was sparse. Confucian scrolls hung on the walls. Healthy-looking plants on ornate wooden stands took up every corner, and drying herbs and peppers hung from the wooden arch leading into the garden.

From there the present took over. Above the glitzy bar a huge prototype plasma display screen showed a young, gracious, and nude Indian couple enacting scenes from the Kama Sutra: sultry Indian foreplay and sex acts.

At the other end of the outsized room, surrounded by the large already-laid dining table, there was a small raised stage. As they came away from the bar with their drinks and settled down at the table, two girls danced in traditional costumes to traditional village music. The Comprador held back, leaning against the bar, cognac in hand. The barman had sold a few Grant's. He was idly watching the Indians. It would be a few more hours before he was picked up.

The manager came over, covered tea mug in hand.

"Good evening, Comprador," he said, bowing. "Have you eaten?" The Comprador nodded vaguely, so he continued. "Did you know?"

He probably did. He was an information gatherer. That was the cornerstone of his companies.

"Did you know that Jardine Flemming dropped a further ten points in late trading? Where do you think the stock market is going? The biggest casino in the East!"

The manager always tried to impress the Comprador with his knowledge of business even from this backwater. The Comprador, sitting up very straight on his bar stool, stroked where his beard should be, in pretended contemplation before speaking. Odd without the beard, he thought.

"Flemming's are big – twenty-two billion US under management. They'll take a battering, and the exchange will dip for a while. But more importantly for us, OSM Merchant is unchanged, solid as a rock." He stood up to stretch, standing taller than the manager, his muscles supple from Tai Chi. He changed the subject to gain a local insight. "I hear the snakeheads are busy again?"

"Yes…" said the manager, hesitating. "They're cutting into our cheap labour—" He was interrupted by cheering and clapping from the tables around the stage. One of the Japanese had jumped up on the stage and was dancing suggestively with the girls.

"They're getting restless. I'll have to sort them out. Can I arrange someone for you, Comprador – there's still time."

"No thanks," replied the Comprador, curtly. Then as an afterthought, "But I would like some of your Szechuan snake."

The manager smiled, bowed and left him. The Comprador picked up his drink and strolled unnoticed into the garden, knowing his food would follow him. He wanted to take a look at the two houses either side, which, a short time ago, they had taken over to avoid complaining neighbours.

Foreign Correspondents' Club, Central 1996

Bruce was crossing the top end of Ice House Street on his way to the Foreign Correspondents' Club in the old colonial ice house, where he was meeting Katla for a Friday evening drink to start the weekend. He had decided to walk to clear his head after a meeting at OSM.

He had met Katla soon after he arrived in Hong Kong, at a formal luncheon at the club where Anson Chan, the private school girl who had risen to high position in the Civil Service, had been talking obliquely about the handover and democracy. Katla was a club member in her own right, being the correspondent for BT – *Bergens Tidende* – Bergen's highest-circulation daily. After the lunch they had moved to the bar, enjoying each other's company. Two hours later they had taken a taxi back to her place in Mid-levels. Tearing off their clothes and landing on the bed, she had thrown her legs around him. That first time she had come quicker than him, crying. Later she had said, as she pulled him down again, that it had been more than a year. Locals and expats seemed to be scared off by her Scandinavian beauty: startling blue eyes, blond hair and long legs. She was a little taller than him. Bruce smiled at the memory as he pushed his way in at the central door and signed in.

As he walked up to the bar he noticed her coming back out of the cloakroom, punctual as ever. From Hong Kong she covered all of Asia. Coming towards him, smiling and looking radiant, she waved at him in recognition. Coming close to him, she squeezed his arm.

"Hullo, sailor!" she said, as he kissed her softly on the cheek.

"Gin and tonic?"

"Thanks."

* * *

They took their drinks to the fringe of the crowd, the main bar always busy on a Friday, and found a table in relative calm. He raised his glass.

"Of all the gin joints," he said.

"Of all the gin joints," she replied, smiling, relaxed and confident. Her English was near to perfect, her voice deep and husky, her Norwegian accent seductive. For Bruce she was giving up smoking. He'd brought some nuts and olives over to their table to help.

"How did you get on with Iain?" Always to the point.

"Good, a bit heavy really. He was doing his OSM bit. They've offered me a job!"

"Is that good?" Katla asked on impulse.

"I don't know! It's in PR, which is good; and obviously it would be more secure, with better prospects etc. etc. Might be a better stepping-stone to starting my own business if I wanted to one day. But I don't know. They seemed deadly serious. Even his old man dropped in for five minutes."

"Tsui?" she asked.

"Yeah. He's very nice really. But I don't know. They seem pretty demanding."

"Like what?"

"Well, you know I'm thinking of going to live in Sai Kung, especially now that the Gary Player courses are open on Kau Sai Chau."

They all enjoyed their golf, and Katla was good, playing off three. All that lithesome height.

"I told Iain about the idea last time we played at Deep Water Bay. And he said that if I worked PR for OSM I'd have to live on the Island. Even said there's an apartment coming up in the same building as Tsui's secretary, what's her name?"

"Come on, Bruce! You've got to do better than that! It's Sa Cheng Cheng."

"Yes, that's right."

"What about salary?" Again straight and to the point!

"Well, Iain knows what I get." And so do you, he thought. "He says they'd pay one third more."

"What do you think? That's good," she continued, answering her own question. "And all the benefits of working here. And if they give you overseas assignments, that's tax free!" She seemed excited. "What are you going to do?" It seemed as if she had made up his mind already.

"I'm going to think about it. I asked for a week, and Iain gave me the weekend – he's away now in Manila, for a bit of R & R! One other thing, it's confidential, though…" – he looked around to see if anyone was listening to them, then leant towards Katla – "…they're going to buy a radio station, and they want me to be involved."

"That'll go well in the business page of BT back home," she teased.

He landed a gentle but well-aimed kick under the table. She grabbed his foot and pressed it between her thighs.

"Hullo! Hullo! What do we have here?" Tony Parker's large body loomed over their table. Bruce rapidly retracted and slipped on his Hush Puppy. The bar had filled up now, bursting at the seams, the Chinese barmen working flat out.

"Hi! Tony. Top of the whatever it is…"

"Good evening will do." Tony was a formidable character, a staffer for the *London Telegraph*, and an ex-president of the club. He still acted as if he had the authority. He was about forty-eight but carried it well. He had wanted Katla since they had been coming to the club; the second main preoccupation of Hong Kong, after money – older men with younger women. The source of much shopping. Katla told him to take no notice – he wasn't her type. That didn't stop Tony.

"It's getting too crowded here," Tony was saying. "A bunch of us are going to Soho – want to come?"

Katla smiled at him and turned to Bruce. "Why not?"

"Sure," he said, "why not?" At twenty-four she was two years older than Bruce, and much more worldly-wise. Going straight from high school into the paper, she already had seven years' experience, and had travelled the world in the last three. Her father was a director, which had made her life easier.

She felt she could handle most situations. Bruce wasn't so sure. Anyway, they'd go. Soho was the present hot spot for night life on the Island. They'd have fun and probably wind up down at the all-night open-air restaurant, his favourite.

Head Office, Tsui Centre, Wanchai 1996

Cheng Cheng was happy. All was well with her world. Jane was fitting in and there were no major 'panics', 'challenges' in Tsui-speak. Ina had gone back to London on Thursday, no job offers yet. Yesterday Tsui had given her a superb evening at his suite at the Grand Hyatt, perfect room service in every way. She sometimes wondered where he learnt it all. Even the weather outside her office window was beautiful, a real Hong Kong Indian summer.

She went through to the outer office.

"Jane. Are all the divisional reports in for October?"

"Yes," she said looking up from her computer, "all except Australia and Oceania. They shouldn't be allowed their head office in the Cook Islands!"

"Late again. We'd better—"

"I've already sent them a hurry-up fax," Jane interrupted, smiling and waving the pro forma page at Cheng Cheng.

"I'll be out of —" She never finished her sentence. An explosion shook the new partition walls.

"What's that?" called out Jane, looking frightened, and half under her desk.

The large frame of Tane appeared in the doorway.

"It was in the flowers," he said to no one in particular, shocked but in control.

"Was anyone hurt?" Resolute calm in her voice.

"No," replied Tane, now looking at Cheng Cheng. "No one's hurt. Just a loud bang."

Tsui came bursting out of the conference room.

"Report?" he barked at the security man, still moving towards Cheng Cheng. He noticed Tane's gun still holstered. The Kiwi had recovered his composure.

"Whatever it was, was in the flowers. I noticed the courier heading towards Ms Cheng Cheng's door. So I tackled him into the bed of rubber plants." He knew that all packages were meant to be left at reception, checked and taken around the building by OSM staff.

"Where's the courier now?"

Tane swung around to look where he had left him, sprawled in the plant bed. He'd gone.

"I don't know, Sir… Tsui."

"Cheng Cheng, phone reception. See if they can hold him there. Jane, get a hold of maintenance and have them clear this up. Follow me." Tane followed him in to Cheng Cheng's office. "Have a seat, Tane. Quick thinking. We won't get the police in. Anything else you can think of?"

"No, Tsui. It was all a bit…"

"Make your report to Sebastian. You might remember something." He called to Jane, "Get Tane some tea, please…. Tane, ring downstairs for someone to come up and relieve you. We'll give you a bonus. Twenty thousand dollars," adding on his way to his office, "Hong Kong Dollars, that is!"

* * *

Tsui was a bit shaken and extremely angry. He reached for the button on his intercom.

"Cheng Cheng, in here," he snapped. She came in at once, calm as ever. Tsui was pacing already, looking at his new harbour view as he did.

"Who the hell was that!? Of course we've got loads of enemies! Maybe trying to get at me through you. Better beef up security. Have Sebastian find out and fire the person or people who let the courier through reception." Cheng Cheng was taking notes, still standing, as he walked and spoke. "Maybe it was anti-Japanese. They will keep visiting Yasukuni, and there's that article in Bruce's rag about me: no, if they did it, it would have been more lethal. I know, how about Vimana's Indian backers?"

There was a timid knock at the door.

"Enter!" He shouted. Jane came in, obviously nervous.

"The cleaner found this when he was…" she said to Cheng Cheng, handing her a stained and crumpled card and leaving immediately.

"A card with the flowers – It's from Asiaway."

"What! Oh! Stupid bastard…. Sa, get me Ian Ross on the phone."

"Tsui, it's the middle of the night there," Cheng Cheng responded.

"Good." He looked at her dismissively.

* * *

"Ian Ross." The voice sounded sleepy.

"Your little joke was not appreciated," his voice fierce with repressed anger.

"Oh, come on, Tsui. It's our fifth—"

"I want someone over here to explain this nonsense within forty-eight hours." He hung up.

* * *

He had sent Susan Tang. Smart. They were in Tsui's office. He was more composed now but just as angry. More dangerous.

"Have a seat," Tsui said briskly in Shanghainese. "I've no intention of having any partners who are idiots, fools."

Susan had had the flight out to prepare herself. She expected him to be aggressive. "First, apologies from Ian. A university prank."

"Some university, some prank," Tsui retorted, borrowing from Churchill. "Does he know our security carries firearms? Someone could have been hurt. Or blinded. Did you know about it?"

"No, not till after the event." Unlikely, thought Tsui. "Just the sort of barbarian hare-brained stunt Ian gets up to. You know it's our fifth anniversary of the first one, George Street, Croydon," she continued, "and the fifteenth restaurant opened on the fifth, on target. So he's on a high, and with the rollout of the first national franchises as well. And you know November the fifth is Guy Fawkes Day; he wanted to get back at you for your 'one-hour-meeting gun'!"

"And I suppose you know what happened to Guy Fawkes?"

Not waiting for a reply, he got up and started to pace. That's better, thought Susan. Cheng Cheng came in with green tea, not looking at either of them, her demure face on.

Tsui kept walking back and forth, thinking, not speaking for several minutes. You could say an error of judgement. How could he use it to his advantage? Asiaway was doing well, on target for one hundred and fifty outlets after ten years. They could use the Comprador's idea. When Asiaway was in all its global territories they could use the networks for marijuana distribution. Tsui smiled to himself. They could package in Chinese cabbage takeaway cartons. The firm back in the old trade. Besides, marijuana wasn't a drug really, except to the paranoid. And it would make a wonderful diversion for the CIA.

Susan was getting restless. "We are very keen—"

Tsui held up his hand. "Let us learn from this error of judgement and carry on. But you owe me a favour later, much later. Agreed?"

"Oh! Thank goodness," cried Susan, beaming with relief. "Yes, of course, agreed," then adding, "If there's anything I can personally do at any time, just let me know."

Tsui nodded peremptorily.

"Let's have a peacekeeping dinner before you go back. Where are you staying?"

"At the Grand Hyatt."

"Good. I'll meet you at the champagne bar. Eight thirty."

* * *

Tsui was dropped off at the Harbour Road entrance.

"I'll call you when I need you."

"Yes, Tsui," replied his driver.

He strode out across the forecourt and into the art deco lobby. Eight thirty by the clock behind reception. He felt fit and well. Since starting the Ninja exercises he'd lost three kilos and had toned up visibly. He knew he was economically powerful; now he looked and felt physically powerful too. Women found the combination hard to resist. He didn't think he was conceited. It was just a fact.

He heard the jazz trio as he came into the bar. Susan had a table away from the music and the entrance. Clever girl.

"I'm sorry," said Tsui, "I didn't mean to leave you on your own, waiting."

"No, that's fine. It's only eight thirty, and they looked after me. I got a bottle of Veuve Clicquot Yellow Label. I hope that's all right." The champagne stood on ice beside her. The waiter was filling Tsui's glass.

"Thank you. And some black caviar."

Susan was looking very Chinese this evening. Different make-up. Not the kid of a few years before, but now a beautiful woman. She wore a deep red Versace, setting off her shining black hair. Around her slim neck hung a simple but heavy gold necklace, a favourite with the Chinese. As she sat back in her chair, crossing her legs, Tsui noticed her black high-heeled shoes held on with delicate straps, highlighting her slim ankles and long legs. Captivating.

They listened to the jazz, not too loud to spoil their conversation. They talked mainly about Asiaway; common ground. As the champagne was ending Tsui leant closer.

"Where do you want to eat? Do you want to have room service or do you want to go to the Chinese restaurant?"

"You choose." Her voice soft and low. Then, rationalising, she said to herself, It's only business, money. And she remembered with a smile that she was in Hong Kong.

He took the card key to his suite out of his wallet and slid it across the table to her, smiling.

"It's on the twenty-fifth floor. Pick up your own room key at reception and then just ride on up. I'll have your calls held," Tsui said, waving for the chit. "I'll join you in ten minutes."

Convention Centre, Wanchai 1997

Sebastian and Tane had insisted on walking him to the handover ceremony. They were weaving through the crowds on the overhead covered walkway that connected the Grand Hyatt with the Convention Centre; better to walk than take the car into the chaos and pouring rain. They passed the enterprising young man selling cans of 'the last free air in Hong Kong'. Tsui smiled and nearly stopped to buy one. With that kind of attitude, change of ruler would make little difference to the soon to be ex-British colony.

As they went along Tsui was thinking. It had been a good day. They had finalised the purchase of *Trance* for all of Asia, mainly to have more leverage with Bruce. He had at last persuaded the Comprador to agree to expand their magazine publishing on the mainland, particularly in soccer, which was booming, and on the Hong Kong races, which was huge and beginning to interest the rest of China. Not many people knew how big the racing was. There was more money put on one race at Happy Valley than on a whole week's racing throughout the UK.

His thoughts turned to the handover and all the pomp and circumstance, which England did with such aplomb. The Prince of Wales was to be there, not the draw card without Diana, and Fei-Paang would no doubt look statesmanlike, despite himself. The Chinese premier and president, and the British prime minister and foreign secretary were in town. There was to be a banquet for four thousand and Simon had won the contract. He expected to make eight US a head, about a quarter of a million Hong Kong. Tsui was glad to hear that the Lizard was at the high table, his influence still strong.

After the fireworks, the speeches and the lowering and raising of flags, the Prince and the ex-governor would leave dramatically on the royal yacht. At midnight Chinese troops would cross the border and Hong Kong would hold its breath. Except for those who knew.

Hakone-en, Japan 1997

The sleek black Crown, with its white cotton seat covers, was cruising quietly along the mountain road. The pine forests flashed by the windows, all shades of greens – no snow yet in late summer. Tsui turned from looking out the window, to glance at the two young women snoozing beside him. In Tokyo he had asked for the escorts to come with him for the weekend so that he would fit in better with the other local tourists and foreigners. He gently nudged the girl next to him, the one called Yohko, the one who spoke English. Tsui had decided not to use his Japanese this weekend…

"Hi!" she said dutifully.

"I just want to let you know before we arrive, there is no sex this weekend – unless you two want to!"

Her big almond-shaped eyes widened and she began to chuckle, holding her hand in front of her mouth and looking away from him. Her friend moved restlessly beside her.

"What's he say?"

"Typical!" Yohko retorted, but still suppressing her laughter. "It's always the nice ones don't want it!"

The driver half turned, sliding back his plastic partition.

"Tell the *gaijin* we'll be there in ten minutes."

* * *

They had been travelling for some time along the shoreline of Ashino-ko, Lake Ashi, one of the beautiful mountain lakes in Hakone National Park, and less than one hundred kilometres from Tokyo, but centuries apart.

They were skirting the south of the lake, the driver slowing at the old Hakone checkpoint which, as a young man, Tsui had gone to see during a day trip to Hakone from the seaside resort of Atami, over the mountains. He remembered the history: built in six hundred and something by the Tokugawa Shogunate, Hakone was checkpoint eleven of fifty-three controlling the ancient Tokaido road. He remembered being told that the cedar-lined Tokaido ran for nearly five hundred kilometres from the Shogun in Edo to the Emperor in Kyoto. Japan's ancient heritage all around them. He looked across at the girls. They were busy with their make-up for the arrival at the hotel. He wouldn't bother them.

* * *

The girls hung back, feigning shyness, as they checked in. He felt sure it wouldn't last once the room door closed. They took the lift up to the fourth floor, the driver staying on, for his room at the back and higher up. It was during Tsui's last Ninja briefing that he had been instructed never to sleep higher than the fourth floor, the highest you could jump from with an expectancy of survival. The bell-boy put their bags on the luggage rack, leaving without asking for a tip.

They were in the main building of the Prince Hotel, about a four-star resort hotel. The girls were more than happy, busying themselves with unpacking and taking their toiletries into the bathroom. He walked over to the window. They had a room overlooking the lake. The mist was low down the mountains this evening. He turned and called out to Yohko through the open bathroom door.

"I have a friend coming tomorrow. Eleven o'clock. Otherwise we're tourists. You'll take the round trip ferry ride at ten thirty." Tsui leant into the bathroom and held up his fingers so there would be no mistake. "Ten thirty tomorrow morning. You might even see Mount Fuji. OK?"

"That's OK by us," she replied. She took off her top and began to undo her brief skirt. "We going to take a shower, OK with you?" She smiled broadly at him, her eyes dancing.

"Fine. Come down to the karaoke bar afterwards." He had to act like a tourist too.

* * *

Tsui was up early and walking briskly to the jetty at Hakone-en. In late summer the air was crisp and the sky clear, if you were lucky with the drifting fogs. Even at this early hour there were others also hoping for a clear view.

The broad planks of the pier resonated under his feet as he passed an old man fishing. An *Ohayo Gozaimasu* got no response: too many tourists, too many 'good mornings'. The black bass were more important. Tsui intentionally kept looking down until he reached the end of the pier. He turned to his right, looked up and there he was: Fuji San, the highest mountain in Japan, a sacred place, his near-perfect snow-capped cone thrusting up into a clear blue sky, and reflecting in the still water of Ashino-ko. Tsui didn't move, enthralled by the spectacular power and natural splendour.

His reverie was broken by a group talking and laughing and taking photos. As he started back for the hotel he saw the striking orange-and-red torii gate out in the water, not far from the terminal. He paused briefly, as if accepting this as a mystical place.

He wondered if it would still be clear when the girls went out on the ferry.

* * *

He left the door closed but unlocked so his visitor would not have to wait in the corridor. His room was near the fire exit. He had hung up the 'Do Not Disturb' sign. Five to eleven.

At eleven the door was opened and closed quickly, then locked all in one motion as Takji Yoshida moved into the room. He didn't stop but nodded at Tsui as he went over to the window. In one sweep he closed the curtains. Turning to Tsui sitting in one of the armchairs, Takji spoke for the first time.

"If anyone notices from outside, they'll think we're timid young lovers!" he said smiling. "Good morning, Tsui." He looked very different. Gone were the flowing Shinto robes. He wore a nondescript grey salary-man suit with a drab tie. His shoes were scruffy, down at the heel, and unclean. He carried a tacky grey plastic briefcase. He looked like someone no one would notice in Japan.

"Hullo, Takji. How are you?" Tsui noticed that he behaved differently too – not the relaxed host but sharp, alert, taut as a new wired fence. Takji glanced at the coffee table, saw the single Go piece and looked back at Tsui, who nodded in confirmation. As he did so, Tsui reached under the coffee table and brought out a black velvet bag, passing it to his friend. Takji cautiously looked inside. The bag was full of Go pieces.

"The heavier ones are the real pieces." He didn't need to tell him how difficult it had been to acquire them. Takji bowed deeply. He put them in his briefcase and brought out the three-page agreement.

"I think everything is as it should be now. If you concur, that only leaves the payments."

"Takji, tell me. How much goes to the shrine?"

"That is the decision of each Ninja, but it has to be not less than twenty-five per cent." Clear and concise, thought Tsui.

"Right. The Comprador and I," always better negotiating with the appearance of two decision makers, "have come up with this, all in US dollars. Two hundred thousand during training, two million in quarterly increments during service, and three million at the end of ten year's service. Each Ninja can nominate an inheritor." One hundred and fifty-six million in total, he had told the Comprador – about a medium-sized takeover.

Takji took out his abacus. For a while the only noise in the room was the clacking of the beads under his nimble fingers. Quicker than Tsui's Casio.

"That is simple and clear. We are able to agree." He seemed eager to leave as soon as possible.

"I have only one other question, Takji. Are you embedded in Naicho?" Naicho was Japan's central intelligence, euphemistically called 'Cabinet Research Office'.

"Yes, but don't forget it's not as simple as most. In Japan many other small agencies still exist. I must go now. As is our habit, when we have digested the agreement, we will destroy it, any copies and computer files. We will do this by the end of this day. Can you?"

Tsui had half expected this but was still surprised. "Yes, right. I will do."

They were both standing now. They bowed equally.

"*Sayonara*, my friend," Tsui said. As the door closed Tsui went to open the curtains to let the light in. Takji was staying with friends in the town in an okiya, a small Japanese inn.

Tsui looked out at the lake again. The mist was rolling down the pine-clad mountains and hugging the shoreline. No Mount Fuji for the girls. He had told them to meet him at the hotel onsen when they got back. He'd better go down now. Later they would eat at the barbeque, a delicious and delicate experience, nothing like in the West. After lunch they'd go up the ropeway. He went through to the bathroom and put on the house yukata and slippers, then tucked the agreement in the sleeve. He hoped the hotel had a shredder which he could access. Later he would throw the shredded material on the embers of the barbeque.

Coloane, Macau
1998

The four of them had come down on the hydrofoil, all sea spray, noise and seasickness. Tsui had decided against flying the OSM jet into the new Taipa airport. Too conspicuous. Besides, Alexander was borrowing it to take Bellatrix up for the international meeting in Hong Kong next weekend.

They were met by the OSM car, an old grey Volvo which wound through the Portuguese-named streets to the small office suite in an old yellow-and-white colonial building overlooking one of the squares. They were ushered in to the compact, well-appointed conference room. A young Eurasian girl in OSM uniform gave them tea, coffee and biscuits on a bamboo tray. Cheng Cheng instinctively got up to serve.

After the obligatory fifteen minutes' 'talk' with the manager they walked after their luggage, which the driver had taken on ahead to reception at the Lisboa. After the group had checked in Tsui spoke to Sebastian and Tane.

"We'll be OK now. See you back here this evening about eight thirty. We'll go out for some Portuguese curry; don't worry, Tane, it's mild enough!"

"Are you sure you'll be OK?" said Sebastian. "Where can I contact you?"

"Don't be concerned," Tsui replied briskly, spinning on his heel as he grabbed Cheng Cheng by the arm on the way to the lift lobby. Once in the room Cheng Cheng unpacked while Tsui read his messages. Another day, another hotel. Tsui checked his Omega. Ten thirty already.

"We'd better get moving…"

"Is everything all right?"

"Yes. Why?"

"You seem so… preoccupied," she said, moving closer to him.

"Sorry. It's going to be a tricky meeting. And we have to be a bit devious. Come on."

Tsui walked ahead of her out of the door, towards the fire exit. He went down three flights and then cut back to the lifts. They rode down directly to the ground-floor casino. Inside, he took her by the arm. They wound their way through the morning crowd, mostly Chinese, to the private rooms, where the floor manager met them.

"Follow me, please."

He took them through the guarded staff exit, through the changing rooms and down a ramp to the heavily locked and barred staff exit. Once out on the street the manager left them to take the waiting taxi.

"Coloane," said Tsui. The driver smiled and nodded towards Cheng Cheng. Different from Hong Kong. They took off round the roundabout heading south on the Macau–Taipa Bridge. Traffic was good and in fifteen minutes they were coming off the Coloane causeway onto the old island proper, the countryside of Macau.

Tsui leant forward and talked quietly to the driver. "Ristorante Fernando, please."

"Yes, Sir. Very good restaurant!"

The taxi slowed down as the road wound through woods and hills. They passed the country club and the massive Westin hotel, looking like part of a displaced pyramid. In places they went through ancient, well-kept villages with tree-lined, shady streets. Pleasant red-roofed villas had been built on the slopes behind.

The driver turned sharp left into the dead end which led to Hac Sa Beach and the restaurant. Tsui knew the other way out. The black sand beach was not busy at end of season, but the famous restaurant would be, even at noon. Better cover than an empty one.

He smiled at Cheng Cheng's quizzical expression as they walked towards what appeared to be a hut, overgrown with a huge vine hat. Once inside the tiny fascia expanded into a large rustic restaurant with flagstone floor and brickwork walls. Ceiling fans went slowly round, moving the sea air. There was an open-air bar.

* * *

The waiter cheerfully waved them over to a small, just-vacated corner table. As they sat down, Tsui declined the menu held out to him, knowing what they wanted.

"Thank you. We'll have the Macanese baked cod and we'll have Chinese tea please." No Portuguese lager today. He needed a clear head.

When the tea arrived with some fresh baked bread to 'keep them going', Tsui reached across the table, smiling at Cheng Cheng and filling her cup. She was looking radiant in autumn colours from Sussan.

"You look beautiful today."

"Thank you," she said, smiling back. As he poured her tea she curled up her first and second fingers of her right hand and tapped the table top, an old way of bowing to the Emperor when he was travelling in disguise. Tsui laughed.

"You may well kowtow. You know very well that he who pours the tea pays the bill!"

* * *

The cod had been delicious and there had been plenty of it. They were sipping more tea from the replenished pot. Tsui looked at his watch.

"I'll have to go through soon..." Cheng Cheng said nothing but kept looking at him. "...You go first, I'll hold back and pay. When you get outside, go along the beach and get a coke."

"No," she said, smiling. "I'll try and get an OSM can of coconut juice!" The drinks division had just launched it. Alexander had been coerced into helping, much to his annoyance.

"OK, good luck. Anyway, the Macau car will pick you up back at the road at three."

She got up gracefully and walked to the restaurant door, looking forlorn and lonely. She didn't look back. He questioned his decision. It wasn't worth not telling her.

* * *

Tsui paid, tipped and thanked the waiter. After a few minutes he got up and went to the back of the restaurant and down the narrow corridor which led to the private rooms. Without hesitation he went in through the first door on the left.

The small room was thick with smoke. The occupants had just left the dining table, which was being cleared by their waiter, and were settling down at a round conference table complete with notepads, sharpened pencils, jugs of water, tumblers, and the required two bottles of cognac.

There were three men facing him. In the place of honour, the chair in the corner diagonally across from the door, Tsui was astounded to see the Comprador, who very discreetly nodded in his direction as Tsui caught his eye. He shouldn't have been so surprised: originally these men were his *guanxi*. The other two men were dapper even in their dark, ill-fitting suits, off the peg at some mainland department store. Yet underneath they looked fighting fit. The younger one was busy pouring four cognacs.

"Good afternoon, Tsui," said the elder. There were no introductions, no handshakes. In front of each one was a Go piece. Tsui took out his, switched it on and laid it down in front of him. Like adolescent schoolboys, he thought. Drinks dispensed, the young man collected up the notepads and pens. No records or recording. The older man from the PLA began to speak in Mandarin.

"Next year these meetings will be much easier and we'll be able to wear our uniforms, the fancy new ones! Macau, like Hong Kong, will be ours." He smiled a toothy smile at Tsui.

* * *

They were lying still, relaxing after their lovemaking, in their king-size bed with the room lights dimmed. Tsui had been holding Cheng Cheng for a long time as she dozed. He would tell her part of the plan without details. Gently he shook her awake.

"Sa, wake up."

"Yes, Tsui," she replied sleepily and sweetly, as she wriggled upright against her pillows.

"This China Deal. You should know about it..." Cheng Cheng turned in his arms, kissing him on the neck, entwining her legs with his, smiling and saying nothing. "... We are planning to improve some national governance, starting with Asia. Do you remember Nikita Khrushchev: 'Politicians are the same all over. They promise to build a bridge where there is no river.'? The incompetent, corrupt and greedy can't be allowed loose any longer."

HEAD OFFICE, TSUI CENTRE, WANCHAI 1998

"Did you know that the US secret services collaborate with the PRC?" Tsui was talking to the Comprador across the conference table in his office suite, which had been put together exactly as his old office in Central, though the carpets still smelt new.

The Comprador was reading his notes and nodding at the same time. "Two years ago they opened an office here. I hope they don't get in the way; they seem to specialize in disaster by 'friendly fire'."

The Comprador was in a suit, like Tsui. They were both 'back in the office' this week. They sat at either end of the massive conference table, Tsui at the head, though often it didn't seem so. They were expecting Iain. This morning they were reviewing the China Deal.

"So we are agreed, each cell will be from one to five people?" Tsui asked.

The Comprador did not reply directly. "What of the make-up of the Alpha cell? How many and who? I would not like, and consider it unwise, for my nephew to be in the Alpha cell."

"Why?" Tsui asked. He approved but wanted to know what the Comprador was thinking. Unlike Macau. He had asked the Comprador about that. He had simply said that Tsui's surprise would serve to strengthen his *guanxi*.

"I don't think he's capable, mature enough, to be part of the final decisions." The Comprador stroked his half-grown beard as he spoke, staring with piercing eyes at Tsui, again making the point about Iain's youth. What would he think of his latest decision?

"That's agreed then, though for a different reason. I think his focus would be too narrow, too confined to and relying too much on computing." Tsui paused, drawing breath for the fight ahead; he didn't hold back. "I'm bringing Cheng Cheng into the cell. I need her as the link to the computers and for admin, both with—"

"No! Tsui, I can't agree!" The Comprador's reaction was immediate, explosive and predictable. "This is no enterprise for a woman!" He was standing now, fists clenched, leaning on the table. "I would rather not participate than allow—"

"There is no way back now, Comprador." Tsui stood up himself and walked slowly round the table to the older man, confronting him face to face. It had to be said. "It's not that she's a woman; you have many in your top echelons. It's because she is not pure Chinese, a Jap mixed-blood!" Tsui used the offensive abbreviation through clenched teeth. His voice was quiet and threatening.

Within OSM any hint of racial prejudice earned instant dismissal or worse. Such a challenge in this room was unthinkable. They were reaching a position from where there was no retreat. They stood toe to toe. Eventually the Comprador stood back, still quivering with pent-up rage.

"I must leave. I need to…" The Comprador strode imperially to the door. When we was halfway there Iain came in. He gave way and held the door open for his tutor.

"Good morning, Comprador," he said, with a slight bow.

The Comprador did not speak or hesitate in his stride. He charged through the doorway as if Iain was not there.

"Good morning, Tsui," said Iain, moving towards his chair. "What's up with the Comprador?" He sat down, pulling the A4 pad and pencil towards him and taking a sip of water. His father did not reply at once, continuing to write in his personal diary. The only sound was the ticking of his mother's antique grandmother clock. Otherwise silence.

It was obvious they were father and son, though Tsui looked more Asian with a darker complexion and sloping eyes. He was also heavier built, like a prize fighter. Both wore a dark suit and tie, the younger man's tie bright red, standing out against a sky blue Sea Island cotton shirt.

"Sometimes we don't agree." Tsui said no more and Iain knew better than to continue. The minutes ticked by.

"I'll tell Cheng Cheng to cancel the meeting. We'll reschedule at the Riverside during the races at Shatin: Bellatrix is running." Tsui was looking directly at his son. Yes, he was young, but he had always trusted youth. But was he an idealist like himself? Would he place ideals before, and a long way before, practical, mundane considerations like making money, and women? He'd better find out.

"The China Deal is about improving national governance, first in Asia. It's a not-for-profit enterprise." Iain looked at his father steadily, appraising the older man. "The US Americans, and to a lesser degree the United Nations, continue to rant about democracy as a panacea for mankind. In fact it does not matter if it is Lee Kuan Yew's authoritarian Singapore, the colonial power in Hong Hong, the democratic mess which is India or the suspect lobbying democracy of the US. As long as governance is for the good of the people, that's good enough."

REGAL RIVERSIDE HOTEL, SHATIN
1998

They used The Riverside for small management meetings in the resort atmosphere away from the office. It was a nondescript hotel, where they came and went unnoticed. There were five entrances. Even so, they arrived at staggered intervals. Today the hotel was busy even in mid-afternoon. This was where junior executives brought their girls and mistresses, often before the end of the race card. They giggled in the elevators, at the minibars and when room service came, as they did.

In the OSM suite the bed had been replaced by a round table which could seat ten. It had been arranged for five. As Cheng Cheng came in, Tsui turned away from the tinted window, where he had been looking out at the slow-moving Shing Mun River, which had been channelled through the reclaimed estuary. In the hills beyond he could see the pagoda of the Ten Thousand Buddha Monastery jutting out of the trees.

"Right. Good afternoon, everyone. Let's get started."

They moved to their seats, not speaking. Only water and glasses were in front of them: no brandy, no yum cha, no writing materials.

"First, no notes, please. And obviously, no recording," though the CW was already on in his pocket. It had taken all his powers of persuasion and a personal visit to the K. K. Chen office on Kowloonside to persuade the Comprador of the use and worthiness of Cheng Cheng. They sat now, quietly ignoring each other. Tsui had their attention. As always, he would keep it short.

"What you are about to hear represents my philanthropy for all humanity." He paused deliberately, slowly looking around the group. "Improved National Governance. With apologies to the Dutch, to be known as ING. This is unlike some of my peers, who want to spend their money on saving lives, of which there are already too many. I have no time for this fashionable philanthropy: saving lives to put them back in misery.

"Without going into lengthy philosophical and erudite arguments, the yardstick, the benchmark, is simple and ancient: governance for the good of the people. Simple. Any man or woman can be the judge of that." In turn he looked steadily at each of the other three, going slowly round the table again. "But here's the rub… As you may have guessed in the months and in some cases years we've been talking about the China Deal, and as has been recorded in the history of our time and before, the only way to achieve this better governance in most cases is by force, direct and or indirect."

He stopped talking, looking at each of them in turn. Iain was moving in his chair, changing his position; Cheng Cheng was staring back at him, studying his expression; the Comprador was unobtrusively watching Iain. Tsui started talking again, moving smoothly into some of the detail.

"When we start we will send a warning letter totally anonymously from Geneva to all heads of state. There are less than three hundred so that won't be difficult. There will be no second warning for those nation states we strike: we need Lao Tze's 'golden principle of surprise'. We will have our own mercenaries, under my absolute command." Tsui and the Comprador had agreed that the Ninjas would not be mentioned.

"There will be five people in the Alpha cell. Memorise, please." There was no whiteboard. "The Comprador is one and his cells will be responsible for the PLA and China. His codename is Merlin. In connection with the China Deal we will start using these codenames immediately, probably for a short time. The still-missing link will handle PR and press releases, true and false. They will be assigned the codename Harrier. Cheng Cheng will be in charge of computers, continuity and admin: code Falcon. Iain will cover commercial and inter-government liaison. His codename is apt: Eagle. I am Osprey and my field is strategy. Over the next years I will personally work with each of you to fill in the gaps, cover the detail necessary for success. Any questions we will deal with then, not now."

He paused for a drink of water and for observation over the rim of his glass. He had their undivided attention.

"Finally," said Tsui, clearing his throat, "as I've already told you, the operation, once started, will run for an initial ten years. You will be committed to the first ten years, but you will be paid for each mission. Each mission will earn five million US dollars, which will be paid to you in Panamanian bearer shares."

Cheng Cheng and Iain looked surprised, shocked. She held up her hand as if to speak, then changed her mind. Iain looked at his father, then at the Comprador, eyes wide, leaning forward. It was a significant amount but Tsui wanted their total commitment. Money was the great motivator. Besides, you had to look at it in context. Take IPOA, the trade association of private military companies. Its rumoured turnover was one hundred Billion US dollars, and scant success to show for it. The Comprador and he had discussed their proposed amount at length. Finally they had agreed that it was justified by the risk, the personal risk to each of them.

"Later, I will take targets under advisement with the Alpha cell, but the final decision will be mine."

STAR FERRY HARBOUR CROSSING 1998

Iain sometimes took a Star Ferry: the snub-nosed, twin-bowed, green-and-white ferries which plied constantly between Central and Tsim Sha Tsui. She and her sister ferries worked as a team, with near military precision. More were commissioned during rush hour. With all the harbour tunnels people thought the ferries would die. They hadn't; passenger numbers were still high and more than half of them were tourists.

Iain found an empty row of seats, swung the wooden back over so that he would be facing forward, then walked sideways, like a crab, to the outside seat next to the rail. Looking back he saw Tane striding up the ramp before it was raised by the weathered and uniformed deck hand. Tane carried a large brown legal envelope with its string closure – the Hong Kong 'briefcase'. He needed to fit in. Iain did not acknowledge him but turned away to the grey water of the harbour.

The leisurely crossing took a little over five minutes, the passage shortening through the years as more of the harbour was reclaimed. Even so, he found it strangely relaxing. He and his amah had been using the ferry since before he was a schoolboy. As he watched ferry give way to ferry in the busy harbour his thoughts moved back to today. He had been with Tsui for an hour this morning in Tsui's inner office, continuing Iain's briefing. At the end of the meeting Tsui told him that he was considering Bruce for the PR slot in the Alpha cell. Tsui said he'd spent a lot of time with him since OSM had bought out his magazine. He wanted Iain 'to sound him out'. He hadn't asked Iain for his opinion, simply told him. So he was on his way to 'tiffin', which no doubt would lead on to drinks somewhere. Tsui was well informed: he knew that Bruce and Iain were 'blood brothers' from Melrose College.

His thoughts were disturbed by the gentle bump of the ferry on the Kowloonside pier. Most of the passengers were crowding round the raised exit ramp, waiting impatiently for it to drop, like so many cattle at the slaughterhouse. He picked up his briefcase and stood up. In the distance he saw Tane talking earnestly to a tall, slender girl. She looked Indian. So Tane wasn't following him as he'd assumed. Before they got lost in the crowd he recognised her. Vimana. He'd have to tell Sebastian.

Iain let the surging crowd take him up the pier and out onto the concourse surrounded by newspaper stands and snack bars. The big roundabout took the buses and taxis back out to Tsim Sha Tsui. This was the end of the line. He joined the long queue at the taxi rank. He would not have to wait long: taxis were leaving every few seconds, in batches of three. Soon his turn came. He almost fell in and slammed the taxi door closed as the driver took off.

"Tung Ying Taiho." Bruce's office building in Nathan Road. They accelerated away from the curb, pushing him hard against the door. He hoped it wouldn't open. As they swung out into Salisbury Road his mobile rang.

"Hi, Bruce."

"Hullo, Iain. There's been a change of plan, if you don't mind? Where are you?"

"In a taxi, turning into Nathan Road. What is it?"

"I'll meet you in the lobby of Happiness Hotel in fifteen minutes. You know, up Nathan Road just before Jordan?" He knew where it was but said nothing.

"What's up?" Iain didn't like spontaneous changes.

"I got a call from their PR man. You know, the Australian guy. I'll tell you when I see you…" and he hung up. Damn.

Iain leant forward and tapped the driver on the shoulder. "Not Tung Ying Taiho, go Happiness Hotel," he shouted. The driver grunted. Lucky for Iain it was on the driver's way to his depot for the four o'clock changeover.

Happiness Hotel, Nathan Road 1998

The traffic had been light mid-afternoon, and he had arrived at the hotel in less than Bruce's fifteen minutes. He went up the steps past the two rampant stone lions, just like the Hong Kong Bank. The hotel used to have a wild reputation when it was used by Americans on R&R from Vietnam. Since then it had been taken over by a Chinese group focusing on a local clientele, and had dragged itself up to three-star standard. He read their copy of the *China Post*, waiting for Bruce.

"Sorry I'm late." Bruce always seemed to be in a hurry. He slumped down in the other chair. "Still hot outside. Bret will be here in a minute…. Don't ask any more; it's a surprise."

* * *

The three of them took the lift to the top floor and walked along the landing. Bret nodded at the old houseboy for that floor, who smiled knowingly as he bowed. Bret stopped at one of the room doors, opening it with his master key. They moved into the well-lit windowless foreshortened room, Bruce closing the door quietly behind him. Inside there was only a red settee and a table against one wall, on which stood two rows of brandy balloons and bottles of cognac.

"Anyone for a drink?" asked Bret. Neither of them spoke. The ceiling fan was turning, with little effect. "OK. The room we are going into will be dark, so I'll be switching the lights off in here before we go through. There will be no talking or uncontrolled sniggering, as the Chinese tend to do. OK? Right let's go!" and he walked over to the second door and the light switches, which he flicked off. He paused to give their eyes time to adjust, and then lead them through to the other, even smaller room.

At once through the picture window, a two-way mirror, they could see the well-lit bedroom next door. A young Asian girl, Thai or Filipina, about sixteen or eighteen, thought Iain, was teasing a dark-haired, heavy-set, mid-aged European by playing tag around the room, laughing as she evaded his grasp. Adeptly she sidestepped the man and playfully pushed him back onto the bed. Almost as soon as his back hit the bed she began a graceful striptease, starting with her tight Jimmy Hendrix T-shirt, revealing her small breasts and erect dark nipples. Next she undid her zip and began wriggling out of her hugging designer jeans, dropping them to the floor over her white ankle socks. She stood at the end of the bed, legs apart, in a fawn microbikini. The colour matched her skin. Slowly she began playing with herself and smiling at him as he tore off his clothes.

Iain pushed past the other two, embarrassed. He thought naively that this was their private time, no need for voyeurs. He hoped they didn't know the 'fingernail test'. Ironically, when he was watching, he'd all the time been reminded of the birdwatching hide on the banks of the Tweed near Melrose.

Back in the anteroom Iain helped himself to a cognac and waited for the others. Shortly his lights went out as they came back. When the door closed behind them, Bret put the lights on again and poured two cognacs. He turned to Iain.

"It's OK, you know. The girl's one of ours. She knows what's going on."

Iain didn't speak. He imagined the manager and Bret had a profitable sideline going… He turned to Bruce. "Cheers!"

Laird House, The Peak
1999

Tsui was waiting for the Comprador, whisky in hand, leaning on the stone balustrade. He wore no jacket in the still warm autumn evening. Deep in his own thoughts, he gazed down at the harbour, ferries busy with the end-of-day trade. Gone now were the lights of flights landing at Kai Tak. Chep Lap Kok had opened in July, the landing approach hidden behind Lantau Island. The new airport was having serious 'teething problems', but they were not his problems. They had helped with the reclamation and had already taken their share of the twenty billion US dollar costs.

He heard two people walking quietly towards him across the flagstone patio, not talking. He was amazed how his training was sharpening his senses. Turning slowly, he caught sight of the Comprador and a houseboy coming towards him out of the shadows.

"Good evening, Taipan," said the Comprador quietly. The houseboy bowed and left them as Tsui moved lightly to the drinks table.

"Cognac?"

"Thank you, Taipan."

"Slainte-mhath!"

"Wen Lie!"

Tsui's principal adviser wore an open-neck white silk shirt with black trousers and shining black shoes. Tonight he wore a heavy gold chain with an encased Buddha around his neck. He seemed relaxed, in harmony with his environment. There would be no confrontation tonight.

"Did you read Patten's book yet?" said Tsui, conversationally. "He got it published in spite of Murdoch's kowtowing," he continued, not waiting for an answer in case it caused the Comprador any loss of face if he hadn't read the book. "It's certainly academic, even turgid, but argued well. He's a bit more than a dahn tart! He even quotes Amartya Sen's argument that 'In the terrible history of famine round the world, no substantial famine has ever occurred in a democracy'. That's maybe partly true. But that's not the only way, as we know. Why be a blinkered democrat? Government for the people doesn't have to be, shouldn't be in some cases, a democracy."

Tsui picked up his cutglass whisky tumbler, redolent with Grant's. He took a slow drink whilst watching the Comprador and waiting for him to speak.

"Indeed," came the reply, followed by another long pause. "I have now come directly from a meeting at my office with Cheng Cheng. She asked to see me."

In turn he studied the taipan. Tsui hid his surprise and feeling of duplicity, smiling silently. The only sign he gave was a slight widening of his eyes, imperceptible in the soft light. The Comprador spoke again, quietly but clearly, coming incisively to the point as usual.

"She wants you to stay based in Hong Kong as the figurehead of OSM, not go to China. She cites, whilst easily admitting her personal preference, two reasons. One, that you…" – and here he paused, turning around to make sure the houseboy had gone – "… that you would be able to better control the China Deal from here, and two, equally important, your cover would be much better." He paused again, stretching his fingers and leaning back, emphasising his authority yet belying it with his words.

"Taipan," with the slightest bow of his head, "of course it is your decision. We are hardly a democracy ourselves, are we?!"

Was that a criticism or a joke?

Tsui replied brusquely, "I will let the Alpha group know."

The two men did not speak, both immersed in their own thoughts and strategies.

Tsui considered why Sa had 'gone behind his back', or had she? He had lost considerable face, but what was that? If she had asked him directly he would certainly have said no. Now he would consider it.

The Comprador was deliberating how best to protect Tsui's own woman from the younger man's impetuosity, given his apparent position of power. The only way the OSM Comprador could show his actual and moral superiority would be to —

Tsui interrupted his thoughts. "The airport is finished," Tsui said. "Have we paid off all our government agents?" 'Government agents' was their euphemism for government officials on their payroll, bribe takers.

"Yes," was the Comprador's monosyllabic reply. Gradually they moved away from Sa Cheng Cheng.

"Have we put in the tender for the radio licence? We don't want Metro Radio taking all the kudos with their documentaries *Knowledge Changes Fate* and the like!"

"It's all taken care of, Taipan. We applied through K. K. Chen, not OSM as you suggested, though I'm not sure about letting a 'pirate' use our frequency to disseminate our CD News. Too close to the home, perhaps?"

"I agree. We'll find another angle," Tsui replied, relaxing as they talked. "And Bruce is running the station. We'll have to confirm the name."

"Bruce likes 'Rebel Radio'. I doubt they'll accept that," the Comprador said, almost to himself.

* * *

The master bedroom at Laird House was huge, easily accommodating the two king-sized beds and the breakfast nook which looked out onto a veranda, with a view of the green vegetation of The Peak. The large windows were covered with heavy cream curtains hung from poles and wooden rings. The ceilings were high, mainly for coolness, and a large fan circled above them, slowly moving the air. Sa and Tsui's clothes were scattered over the white carpet, left as they had fallen.

They had slept naked, as they were after their last orgasm, dead to the world. Tsui woke first and slowly turned over, nibbling her ear.

"Are you awake, Cheng Cheng?"

"I am now!" she said, giggling and smiling. Sunday morning, and this Sunday morning they had some hours together, she thought. She stretched like a cat, and reached out for Tsui. He pulled her arms down and held on to them firmly.

"Listen, sleepy head. You did the right thing, going to see the Comprador. Well done, little one! And well done is better than well said. You're right. On reflection, I have decided to stay based in Hong Kong. You're the first to know."

She reached up and kissed him without talking. He let her arms go and rotated her nipples in the way she liked. Softly groaning, she rolled her slim body on top of his.

TAI MO SHAN, NEW TERRITORIES 1999

The two men had stopped for a rest halfway up the five hundred steps leading to Man Fat Monastery. Alexander took the roast suckling pig off his shoulder and rested it on the counter of an empty fortune-teller's stall. The souvenir sellers and fortune-tellers wouldn't be around for several hours.

Both men were fit, hardly out of breath after the long climb. They both wore comfortable sneakers and loose-fitting tracksuits. Tsui carried their water bottles. Turning round, they looked down the worn stone steps they had climbed. Eventually the steps disappeared out of sight round a bend before they could see their starting point.

Unmoving and silent in the early morning tranquillity, they watched the sunrise through the dripping pine trees. They were able to catch a glimpse of the racecourse and, closer, the Shatin KCR station. Seeing the track and stands reminded Alexander of the racing this weekend.

"Bellatrix has settled in well at Happy Valley this time," he said. "Every horse now has air-conditioning and access to swimming pools ahead of much of the human population." Alexander didn't expect a response from his brother to such a socialist remark. "Micky O'Brien is calmer these days. Beginning to wake up to the fact that his career won't just go on for ever. I think this time we've got a real chance in The Cup…"

Tsui seemed preoccupied with today. Each year they went to the temple and on to their ancestral grave on the anniversary of their father's death to avoid the crowds of the Quing Ming festival, though Cheng Cheng went to the festival on their behalf with a maid and one of the Maoris from security. Today he had asked her to stay home with Cerise and Antonia, as he wanted some time alone to consult the ancestors.

They set off again, this time Tsui carrying the pig, climbing the steps rhythmically, side by side. Tsui was in reflective mood, enjoying the chance to talk with his elder brother.

"Big change is coming, big brother. It will touch everyone. Even you, tucked away in Niyogan, and the stud in South Island. Everyone, everywhere. China is coming — "

"I know, I know," butted in Alexander, "but remember Grandfather's favourite maxim: 'The only constant is change.'"

"Yes, but this is big change. If China manages social order with sound economics, America will no longer be leading the world, much to the relief of many Americans and most other nationals. The way they're going it will be like the fall of the Roman Empire! Their Temple of Democracy, their insistence that democracy is the only way, at least on the outside, will bring their downfall."

Tsui decided again, after arguing with himself for days, not to tell his brother about the China Deal. He continued with his diversion, knowing his brother sensed something was happening at OSM. "For example, Japan has more economic ties with China and, by some measures, is already China's biggest trading partner, ahead of the US. China supplying cheap manufactured goods, whilst Japan supplies the heavy machinery to make the factories hum."

Alexander grunted in reply. That wasn't what his brother wanted to talk about.

They were reaching the top of the steps, the graceful red-and gold-pagoda towering above them. Inside the smell of incense from joss sticks and from bell-shaped coils suspended from the ceiling permeated everywhere, clouds of smoke hanging in the still air. They had been coming to the Man Fat Monastery ever since it had been founded and they had been able to climb what their amah called the 'stairway to heaven'. Their family had donated one of the more than twelve thousand handcrafted Buddhas housed row upon row inside the monastery's buildings and gardens. It had taken the Shanghainese artisans ten years to complete, giving each Buddha an individual expression. Their one had a very cheeky grin which had always made them laugh. After their Buddha he remembered the monkeys.

Grown up now, they laid their suckling pig, one of their grandfather's preferences, on the offering table, bowed three times and prayed. Alexander moved away to burn the paper money, note by note.

Once they had lit joss sticks for their ancestors, a saffron-robed monk came to them and led them to the dining hall for vegetarian breakfast. Might this be a possible sanctuary? thought Tsui. On the way out Alexander left their donation envelope at the door.

* * *

When they came out on the top steps Tsui stopped and called his driver on his Nokia.

"Twenty minutes, please."

The way down was easier and quicker. The cool early morning air was good. They started jogging down the steps, in time together, remembering their youth. At the halfway mark they broke into a walk, as if by agreement. When he had caught his breath Tsui spoke, brisker now, back to business.

"Alexander," he said, turning to his brother as they strode down the steps, "there has been a challenge to your ownership of Niyogan. From the number crunchers. It was really Wai Kwok's fault, not doing 'his thing' correctly for once. We fixed it. It's a hundred per cent now. He'll send you down the paperwork. I wanted to let you know myself."

"Are you quite sure? I've got used to the ownership thing! How about the factory? It's going well," Alexander replied, his calmness surprising himself. Must be the exercise.

"Yes," said Tsui, looking straight ahead.

Alexander changed the subject again, feeling tension in his brother's monosyllabic reply. "We've just finished a large nipa hut over the hill from the house. We use it for beer and guitar parties. Some nights Cerise and I sleep up there."

* * *

As they came out of the trees the car was waiting for them at the roadside. They left Shatin, taking the side roads towards the foothills of Tai Mo Shan, Foggy Mountain, where they leased large tracts of land from the government for forestry, amongst which their ancestral grave was hidden. On a bend they swung off the sealed road onto a ride used for forest work and fire control. The driver slowed even more as the surface became rougher and they were thrown about. After quarter of an hour the track petered out and stopped in a little lay-by made for parking and turning. The grave was a further half an hour on foot. As they got out the driver gave Tsui a 'Park 'n Shop' plastic bag which Cheng Cheng had prepared. Tsui checked inside: fresh shiny oranges and red apples, some bland dim sum and a bottle of Chinese wine.

"Two hours or so. All right?"

"Yes, Tsui." He was a good driver, supplied by South Auckland Security. SAS. As usual he smiled to himself at the thought. Good for the Kiwis.

Alexander and Tsui set off, Tsui carrying the offerings for their ancestors. Neither had a need to speak as they walked through the man-made forest, row upon row of regimented pines stretching out on either side. All they could hear was the steady tread of their feet and the occasional call of a startled bird. A soft, misty drizzle began to fall.

It reminded Tsui of the start of a grouse shoot in Scotland. Shelagh had been with him.

After a vigorous walk the brothers came to the permanent grave, unpretentious, in an attractive clearing placed on a gentle, south-facing slope. Feng Shui experts had confirmed that the C'hi flowing down the slope and over the tombs was exceptionally strong, the trees only weakening it a little. The ancestors were happy. The simple marble foot stones carried the names and dates chiselled out boldly in Chinese characters. The family used no photos.

Tsui followed a number of religions. To his western friends Tsui said it was 'for insurance'. At school he had been a Presbyterian. In Hong Kong he followed ancient tradition, and Chinese Ancestor Worship was part of that tradition, as was Buddhism, Taoism and Confucianism. He knew, to his advantage, that Ancestor Worship preserved family loyalty and lineage. It maintained filial piety, respect and honour. Ancestors were informed of any major decision, and their wisdom and guidance was sought by the head of the family, now, by mutual consent, Tsui. Ancestor Worship was the one he believed in and respected. He hoped he had done enough to appease his grandfather with his offering of roast pig. He was going to ask a favour.

The brothers approached the tomb and stood side by side at the foot. Clenching their right hands, they covered them with their left and bowed respectfully. Alexander crossed over to the shed in the trees and returned with a digging fork and broom. They cleaned the grave and its surroundings. Finally Tsui poured some of the wine on the ground and laid out the foods and rearranged the bowls, chopsticks and small pottery cups. They bowed again, stood motionless for a few minutes, and bowed again. Slowly they walked over to the wooden bench at the edge of the clearing.

They sat, looking at the grave. Eventually Tsui unzipped his jacket pocket and took out a silk pouch. He handed it to Alexander, who looked back at him quizzically. He felt inside and pulled out a chop. Looking more closely he recognised Tsui's chop, his Chinese signature for all his affairs. Before he could say anything Tsui held up his hand and spoke in his brisk business tone.

"I cheated and had a copy made. If anything happens to me you will be able to expedite matters."

Alexander put the chop back. He asked no questions: there would be no point. But he could perhaps give some advice.

"Remember another maxim Grandfather loved to use: 'Rule a great empire as you would cook a small fish.'"

Tsui smiled, saying 'Yes' almost to himself. Then back to the present. "Do you mind, Alexander, going back now? I want some time on my own."

Alexander did not reply. He stood up, zipping the pouch in his pocket, bowed to his ancestors and left the clearing. He understood his brother's compulsion.

Tsui walked over to the graves and bowed again. The rain had stopped. He looked around. Nothing. He began to talk to the ancestors in a murmur that could hardly be heard.

"We have reconciliation with Alexander. With respect, I think it's about time. I hope that makes you happy. You know about the China Deal, how important it is to me and, I believe, to humanity. Please, and with respect, I need your continued help. And can you do me another favour please? Will you please help Bellatrix win on Saturday? It may be our last chance…"

He bowed again and picked up an apple and an orange. He took them over to the bench so that he could eat with his ancestors. He put the orange peel in his pocket and threw the apple core into the trees for the birds. He bowed one last time and followed his brother out of the clearing and down the track. He decided to jog for the fun of it, pleased to have done his filial duty. As he came round the last bend he saw Sebastian's car leaving. So, in spite of his instructions, they'd been there again this year. Attribute the Comprador.

CHUNGKING MANSIONS, TSIM SHA TSUI 1999

Iain and Sebastian got out of their taxi at the same time as some flustered Saudi Arabian contract workers, heading home loaded down with excess baggage, pushed their way in. They stood and watched as the last case was pushed in on somebody's lap. The taxi pulled out, indicating but regardless of traffic. It would be heading for Chep Lap Kok, forty-five minutes away.

They stood for a moment in the teeming crowd, mainly Chinese, wandering and weaving their way up and down Nathan Road, apparently aimlessly but in a hurry, either lost in their own dream-world or shouting into their mobile phones. Iain and Sebastian smiled at each other and pushed their way up the few steps at the entrance to Chunking Mansions as they were offered cheap brand-name watches, young sisters and software by English-speaking traders. The entrance led to the pungent smell of unwashed bodies and too many curries and to the packed hallway for the five tower blocks of flats used as boarding houses, restaurants and businesses which made up the multinational, hectic and semi-legal world of Chungking. The police rarely visited above the ground floor.

Beyond the lobby were dimly lit arcades, hardly air-conditioned, dust covered ceiling fans slowly moving. The compact shops, brighter inside, sold silks from colourful bolts; the latest toys, box upon box; luggage; and calculators of every make. A stall, squashed against a free wall, sold groceries, girlie magazines, fruit and beer. On the other side there were three small restaurants: Bangladeshi vegetarian, Indian and Pakistani. The customers in Chungking were mainly from the subcontinent, Africa and some of the poorer south-east Asian countries. Not many Chinese inside, unless they financed one of the businesses. And very few *guilos*.

They had decided to have a curry first, as the travel agent they were going to on the seventh floor would still be closed for lunch. Sebastian pulled open the glass door. Once the owners saw the 'foreign devil' coming in behind they hurriedly started to wipe the best formica table and stools, at the same time flapping away their tardy Asian customers. The chef peered out of the boxlike kitchen, chopper in hand. Iain hated all the fuss: unnecessary and unfair. A pretty girl appeared, ushering them from the door to the table about five yards away, banging down two glasses of obligatory hot tea and two plastic menus in English, which she had tried to wipe clean. All the while, unlike Chinese waiters, she had kept smiling and chattering away in her own Malayalam. Despite shabby and messy appearances, the restaurant had the reputation of serving clean food and outstanding curries.

Sebastian sat with his back to the corner and facing the door. The regulars started talking again in their own languages, glancing at them surreptitiously. Even though the SAR police claimed Hong Kong the safest city in the world, Iain was still glad of company in situations like this. He put his brown envelope on the inside end of the table near the wall. Sebastian leant forward, smiling, relaxed, speaking quietly.

"Don't forget this is the Ketchup Gang's territory!"

Iain nodded and grinned. Casually he rested his elbow on the table on top of the envelope.

There were many gentle scams in Hong Kong and the Ketchup Gang was one. They operated in pairs, usually Indian or Pakistani. The first made a large ketchup stain on the unsuspecting victim's clothing. He was then courteous enough to point the stain out to the mark and would earnestly try to clean it off, all the time loudly apologising. He might even offer tissues. In the resulting confusion the second operator would make off with the victim's suitcases or briefcase. Even bum bags were not safe from an open razor slash.

Sebastian ordered the 'special', always a good idea in local restaurants. Lamb curry with rice and popadam. Outstanding.

* * *

They moved across to the lift well and joined the crammed, multinational and sweating queue. There were about fifty people waiting, with all their luggage: cases, cardboard boxes, various shopping and plastic holdalls, filled to bursting. The old lift took ten people, not allowing for luggage. It had a warning buzzer and would not go when overloaded. Each time this entailed heated discussions, usually in frantic sign language, about who should get off. At last it was their turn. They walked on to the juddering lift floor. They were squashed against the back wall so Sebastian held up seven fingers. Number seven was punched. Now nearly all the floor indicators were on, but the alarm continued and the lift didn't move. A short fat Englishman from Manchester tried to make a joke.

"All together now… breathe in!"

Eventually a large Nigerian lady in flowing robes was pushed off, with her bags, protesting, and the lift began its slow ascent.

As they came gradually to each floor Iain thought about the time when Bruce and he had checked in a cheapskate school-friend at Chungking Mansions as a joke. He had not flinched when the Chinese owner of the Double Luck Guesthouse had shown him his six foot by six foot room with no window, except for a slit above the door, and a wooden bed. The laugh had been on them when he had got to know the Philippina maid who cleaned the hostel, and she had moved him into a larger en suite single room with a window and one of the telephones, all for ten US dollars a day. The maid wasn't included.

The lift reached the seventh floor. They struggled out, some of the passengers for higher floors having to come out too, holding the doors open desperately in case the lift went on without them.

Travel-Wise was open again and already busy with customers talking loudly at agents strung along a simple counter full of computers, which ran the length of the room. Travel-Wise was a general travel agent specializing in Taiwan, as the posters on the walls indicated. Iain, with Sebastian towering beside him, went up to the counter. He had to interrupt one of the girls to get attention.

"Mabel Kwan, please," he shouted.

The girl did not speak to him, but turned and shouted in Cantonese at an old lady sitting on a bamboo stool in a uniform of sorts: a high-collared white cotton amah's smock, black trousers and slippers. She grunted, stood up and waddled out of sight around the back. Could be she owned the business, thought Iain.

They kept their position at the counter with a struggle. In a few minutes Mabel Kwan came out of the back office: a typical Chinese business manager, efficient, smart and decisive in designer jeans and an Elton John T-shirt; he'd recently been booked at the Island Shangri-la. She came walking towards them, throwing back her black shoulder-length hair and holding out her hand.

"You must be Iain?" she said shaking both their hands, whilst alternately looking each of them in the eye. No time for formal introductions. "Ms Sa says you will have an envelope for me."

Iain was taken aback by her aggressive but friendly demeanour.

"Yes, Ms Kwan."

"Mabel will do!" she chided, taking the envelope and handing them two business cards in return. No tea, coffee table books or chitchat. "Thanks."

With a smile and a nod she left them. They both watched her go, checking out her active figure. Nothing left to do, they turned to go, grinning at each other. As they came out on the landing the fire alarms started.

"Probably another false alarm," said Sebastian. "Better use the stairs. This place is a real fire trap with all the rubbish thrown out of the central windows and piling up. Go up like an Aussie bushfire! Though it's a bit better now."

They seemed to be the only ones taking any notice of the alarm as they jogged down. So this is what Tsui meant by a bit of hands-on experience. They had reached the third floor. Iain came to an abrupt halt, face to face with a wall. The fire escape stopped.

"This way," said Sebastian. "We have to take a detour through the Shanghainese restaurant."

"Lucky there's no smoke."

To the surprise of some late customers a mixed group walked between the tables and on to the escalator out onto Nathan Road. Tane came out last.

Two red fire engines were double-parked amongst the traffic, their crew running around looking for the fire. Iain looked up at the building. No smoke yet.

Pearl River Delta, China 1999

The Comprador sat upright on one of the bench seats forward, looking straight ahead. The future taipan leant forward, listening to the quiet voice of the agent, which was sometimes drowned out by the windblown sound of the engines and the slapping of the water on the sampan's bows. Iain knew he had a lot to learn from this man. But so far the Comprador had talked in terse pleasantries. They were taking another load of Japanese tourists upriver to the old farmhouse. It was Iain's first time.

"I hear that Bellatrix won the Hong Kong Cup," The Comprador said, looking across at his young companion in his old school tracksuit and the dirty old runners he used on The Peak. Casual enough. Iain nursed his green tea against the gentle swell. The Comprador had politely declined anything from the sampan's galley.

"She won easily. Favourite too," replied Iain. Like his father, thought the Comprador: economic with words.

"Pity she was not a stallion. They could have made some real money then. Did you know they have taken the stud out of OSM? Tsui and your Uncle Alexander are running it now. A good thing too."

"No, I hadn't." His father nearly always kept him on a 'need to know' basis, which was exasperating. "I agree with you, it's a good idea. The old man…" – Iain noticed the tilt of the Comprador's head, querying, disapproving – "…I mean Tsui, needs an outside interest apart from — " This time the Comprador held up his hand up imperially. Iain stopped talking in mid-sentence.

They sat in silence, looking out at the darkness. Iain was wondering how he could get to know this austere, efficient, but ruthless and sometimes devious man, when the Comprador spoke to him again, turning round and leaning towards him so that their faces were close together.

"Iain," he said, surprisingly gently, "there are some things you need to know. For instance, did you know that we're in the arms trade?"

Iain hesitated. "No."

"Well we are, in a limited sort of way." What did that mean? thought Iain, and was it legal? "A good example is one of the very latest American man-portable surface-to-air missiles. We took a crate on board one of our coastal tankers at Kaohsiung. She brought it in to Canton and we're towing it, waterproofed and submerged, upriver." The Comprador paused, looking round, making sure nobody could overhear; his CW would take care of anything else. "To my, our, contact with the Forty-second Group Army."

Iain looked startled. He also took a quick glance over his shoulder.

"You might have told me." he said with controlled anger.

The Comprador looked irritated. He muttered to himself in French, then spoke calmly but sharply, "You did not need to know!"

Iain stared back at this key man. "Why do I need to know now?"

"Tsui wants you to know more about operations," was the short reply. The Comprador's attention had been taken by yet another boat approaching on its way downriver. It was slowing, its lights beginning to bob up and down. Suddenly its spotlight came on, slowly strafing the sampan from bow to stern. The local police launch. Using a megaphone, a voice carried across the dark water, telling them to heave to. Rapidly the launch came around their bow and alongside. The old man left the helm to the young girl. Dressed in black, she was hard to pick out in the dim lights of the galley. The Comprador leant even closer.

"Don't get up, and keep your eyes down. It's only routine."

The old man was talking to the commander. They were speaking Hakka. Iain understood only a few words, as he studied the grain of the deck. Out of the corner of his eye he was surprised to see two of the tourists stand up and move swiftly to the galley. They stood still in the shadows, next to the girl.

The commander was leaving with the 'access fee', calling cheerfully to the old boatman. The police crew pushed off with their boathooks and the launch swung wide of them, continuing downriver. The searchlight went out and they could feel through the deck the increasing rhythm of their engines pushing them forward. Iain heard the Comprador sigh quietly in relief.

"It was routine. They didn't know about the crate," the Comprador said softly. "You see those two passengers get up?"

He had decided to tell Iain more than his father had instructed. If you were going to trust the young they had to be allowed to be a real part of the team.

"Yes. What were they doing?" demanded Iain. The Comprador studied the young Eurasian before replying. A little anger in his eyes.

"They were for 'just in case'. And I wanted to see them work close at hand. They're part of our shock troops, our 'Vikings'. They're Ninjas."

"What?!"

"Can you pick them out of the crowd now?"

Iain looked slowly through the group.

"No, damn it, I can't."

* * *

"Well, that's one thing you won't find in 'made-in-China.com'!" joked Iain.

The Comprador held up his hand. Cease and desist, thought Iain. He was finding it difficult to concentrate on their conversation. The Indian couple and their soundtrack from behind the bar took most of his attention. The Comprador, somewhat exasperated, picked up his drink and indicated that Iain do likewise.

"Come."

The Comprador led the way out to the peace of the Zen garden. The stones had been watered, cooling the whole courtyard. A waiter followed them and put two cushions on the damp benches. The tourists were eating, watching the dancing. They were distracted enough.

"Taiwan is very important to our China Deal." The Comprador talked earnestly, wanting to pass on as much information as possible before he had to move on. The decision had been made to keep Iain fully appraised. "You know that China has more than seven hundred missiles aimed at Taiwan. But how many are actually primed? How many decoys? Is America Taiwan's only arms supplier? Our main contact is the Minister of National Defence, but he is becoming a liability. Because of him we are moving Sinbad Fuel to the PLA. Even if the army is the only user, volumes will be great and they will make good profits, which will help us." He paused and looked at the younger man. He looked weary. "That's enough 'briefing' for one day." As he spoke the manager came in and whispered in the Comprador's ear. He stood up, placing his hand on Iain's shoulder, an unusually familiar gesture.

"Don't get up. The package is ready. I have to go. Eat, drink and be merry. The manager will look after you." The Comprador smiled briefly, turned around, and walked out into the night.

* * *

The manager lead Iain back inside to an empty seat at the main dinner table.

"I'll bring you the courses they've already had, Sir."

"Thanks." Iain was too tired to be bothered with his usual reproach about the 'Sir'. The two Japanese either side of him half got up and half bowed, not easy to do after much sake. He felt like drinking too, picking up and finishing his double gin and tonic. The waiter beside him whisked away his glass and moments later returned with a new drink and his ika maru-yaki: grilled squid with teriyaki sauce. The squid was delicious; he hadn't realised how hungry he was. He looked round, casually trying to pick out the Ninjas. Real Ninjas? It can't be, he thought. The girls were still dancing, with less and less clothes. They took turns. The loud music had been changed to karaoke and the boisterous customers were raucously singing. One of the girls was not dancing, sitting gracefully at the back. She's the pick of the bunch, thought Iain. She looked calm and elegant in a light-brown batik sarong and blouse. Iain had been told they were not country girls, though they pretended to be. They were brought in from Guangzhou to avoid any local trouble.

Once the meal was finished the tourists began to dance as well, but with none of the graceful rhythm in their movements. Iain stood up, politely but firmly declining an invitation to dance, and walked, a little unsteadily, to the bar. The girl in the sarong had gone. The manager met him at the bar.

"A nightcap, Sir?"

The video at the back of the bar was off so he watched the young girls, sinuous and sensuous, hips rotating. There hadn't been many since Suk Soon. The manager was back again.

"May I show you your room, Mr Iain?"

That's better.

* * *

The girl in the sarong was waiting for him, sitting on the bed, hands in lap. As he came in she stood up and walked towards him with feline poise, smiling and barefooted. He didn't move away as she kissed him on the cheek. Stepping back from him, she dropped her batik to the floor. Iain looked down. She had dense and shining black pubic hair. Not Chinese, he thought. Her legs were slender and light brown. With expert fingers she began to undress him. She pulled her blouse over her head, showing him her tiny breasts and long dark nipples: they stood erect as he stroked her.

"Come," she said, taking his hand and turning towards the bed. She lay on top of him, taking him easily. He saw her in the ceiling mirror, her young body clinging to his. As he watched, her tight buttocks began to move round and round. Long before he meant to he exploded with a cry.

"Suk Soon!"

With limited English and no Korean, the girl thought she understood.

Tram Terminus, The Peak 1999

Takji Yoshida was tense, as he wanted to be. He was mingling with the dozen other Ninjas, five of them girls, who were being Japanese tourists taking photos of the tram's arrival and of themselves. It was a birthday outing and some of the men appeared a little drunk. Some were fooling around wearing Bill Clinton masks and blue T-shirts emblazoned in red with the single word 'Acquit!'

Takji walked a little apart, as 'group leader', sitting on a bench where he could watch the car park and the passengers coming off the tram, just in case. The late autumn sun warmed the back of his old grey *saranman*'s suit.

Tsui had given him this month of September for their trial. They had been watching Fitzgibbon since June. Now their well-rehearsed plan was in motion. Two Occidental Ninjas had hired a Honda Accord and had checked into the Ritz-Carlton, with its imitated old-world charm and five-star luxury. They were posing as stockbrokers from the Manila Exchange trying to get their products into mainland China by way of Hong Kong.

They knew that the 'target' dismissed his driver-cum-bodyguard when he was at the big hotels. They had learnt that he was the penultimate speaker at a stock exchange seminar held in the Ritz-Carlton ballroom. The two 'businessmen' had signed in for the seminar. They would put a diuretic in the speaker's water before the target took his turn to speak. That would ensure a visit to the washroom, not an unusual occurrence with his drinking reputation.

* * *

The door opened and Fitzgibbon came hurrying in. The Ninjas were already there, standing at the stalls, the outside two of three. The target came between them whilst they shook themselves off and zippered up. One of them turned and smiled at the taipan as they both stepped back. In the same movement they swung their syringes, aiming for the thighs, adroitly injecting the rapid-action muscle relaxant. Fitzgibbon swung around, spraying everywhere, instinctively turning back to his stall. The Ninjas held his arms in a steely grip.

"Fuck off. What the—"

"Relax," snapped one of the Ninjas, with dry humour. "Zip up; we're going for a picnic!"

"Behave," said the other, more menacingly, "and you'll live till tomorrow."

They swung him round and headed for the door as he began to stagger. They turned right for the lifts and hit the down button. As they waited Fitzgibbon began to sway and mumble. The lift doors opened and two Chinese seminar participants, complete with name tags, stepped out. The first Ninja began to laugh and spoke directly to the men in European English.

"Another wet lunch for him!"

The Asians didn't smile but nodded understandingly. They would be reluctant to 'help the authorities', he thought. Too much attention.

The threesome stepped into the lift. When the doors began closing one of them pressed 'B' and kept it pressed. They went straight down to the basement car park.

* * *

Takji saw the Accord approaching the car park, with a driver in the front and two passengers in the rear seats. Not unusual for Hong Kong. He turned to the group, still milling around the souvenir shop.

"Time to go!" He called out to his 'group' in Japanese, acting as their 'guide'.

Right away they changed direction, wandering back towards the car park where the Accord was now parking near their minibus.

As they got out of the car they were greeted by the 'partygoers'. One of the passengers was wearing a Clinton mask and T-shirt. He appeared drunk like others in the group. Some of them started getting in the bus, taking the new 'guest' with them. One of the girls was carrying his jacket.

The two Occidentals got back into the car and calmly drove out of the car park, heading down Peak Road. One of them looked at his watch.

"The final speaker's still got ten minutes to go, allowing for the target's missed talk. We'll be on the expressway before he's even missed."

They had taken the car for a full week so it would not be reported for at least five days. They would leave it in the car park next to the passenger terminal. Their cases were in the boot.

"We'll be at the airport exactly on time. Very good."

Soon they were on the Airport Expressway. They were going back to Osaka, one via Beijing and the other via Seoul. On different passports with current Hong Kong entry stamps.

* * *

The minibus went over Wan Chai Gap through Repulse Bay and around to Stanley Point and on out to the public pier at St Stephen's beach. Takji had been reading a local war history of Hong Kong. He knew St Stephen's College had been used by the Japanese as an internment camp, and of the atrocities there and elsewhere on the Peninsula. It all looked peaceful enough today, he thought, as he looked steadily out of the window, streets and market, busy on a Saturday in the sun, locals and tourists enjoying their weekend. Nothing untoward. The more the merrier.

The minibus stopped at the end of the pier to the raucous sound of a Japanese drinking song: the target wasn't hearing. He had been encouraged to take three sleeping pills on the way.

The hired launch was waiting for them, engines running. Five of the Ninjas walked down with a very drowsy Fitzgibbon, helping him on board. Immediately the Ninja at the helm pushed off and they slowly headed out of the bay towards Po Toi. The rest of the party wandered off towards Stanley Market for more 'sightseeing' and 'shopping'.

* * *

The rocky island of Po Toi was about three kilometres south-east of Stanley Fort, and was nowadays virtually uninhabited. It was mainly visited by ferry loads of people using the well-marked country trails as an escape from urban Hong Kong.

Today there was hardly any wind, the sea calm and the crossing comfortable. The Ninjas laughed and talked loudly, as if enjoying their holiday. Fitzgibbon had drifted off to sleep again, relaxed more by the steady movements of the boat and by having his head nestled comfortably in one of the girl's lap.

* * *

One of the Ninjas had come over on the first ferry last Sunday morning. He had mixed in with the crowd, wearing a dull green tracksuit, sneakers, sunglasses and a worn-out baseball cap, and had a Nikon camera slung over his shoulder. He had tagged along with a cluster of day trippers, who had a loudmouthed guide. He showed them the ruins of Mo's House, the haunted house below Coffin Rock: a local landmark. The guide said the house had been abandoned after an attempted kidnapping by pirates of Merchant Mo and his family. He added, whilst walking away, that during the war

Japanese soldiers had been stationed there. Some in the crowd glanced surreptitiously at their fellow tourist. Good, he thought, climbing back with the others onto the main track, this would be an auspicious place for their purpose.

* * *

As the launch came in, bumping the pier with her old tyre fenders, they shook Fitzgibbon half awake. The last of the ferries had gone back to Stanley with the tourists. Left were a scattering of junk parties, some launches like theirs and one or two permanent residents pottering about with their boats. They started laughing and shouting again as one of the Ninjas lifted Fitzgibbon onto the jetty and began to carry him, upright, to Mo's place, all the time making out that he was drunk. Only the Ninja's extreme fitness and strength made it possible. The helmsman wandered up two minutes later.

Hidden by the ruins, they took Fitzgibbon's mask and T-shirt off. The girl tipped out on the grass, from a plastic bag she had been carrying, his jacket and a blanket. She rolled up the jacket to make a pillow. Next she threw the blanket over him and moved him into the recovery position. The 'leader' had already put handcuffs on his ankles and wrists, his arms held behind his back. He wiped off the cuffs and the keys, throwing the keys on the grass, where they would easily be found. The target was secure and asleep.

On the way to the launch, in the fading light, another of the Ninjas wore a Clinton mask and T-shirt. He pretended to be exceedingly drunk.

* * *

The main part of the unit was returning to the minibus from the market when the launch gently docked in the failing light. The Ninjas leapt agilely out, leaving the helmsman to take the boat back to the hire yard further down the beach. Within minutes the bus got underway. Round the corner they stopped to pick up the Ninja returning from the boatyard.

One of the girls went round the bus with a black plastic bag she had folded up in her pocket, collecting all the masks and T-shirts. They turned in at Repulse Bay shopping mall, driving round the back near to the rubbish skips. It was dark now. The girl with the black bag, firmly tied, jumped down and moved with stealth from shadow to shadow, almost invisible. Gently she lobbed their disguises into the rubbish.

They took the Aberdeen Tunnel on their way to the airport and left the minibus in the car park with the Accord. Going into the terminal at different entrances, they split up into ones and twos, taking different destinations out of Hong Kong. Before he boarded his flight Takji phoned Tsui on a mobile, using an untraceable SIM number.

Soon after Tsui rang Maynard, telling him to have Fitzgibbon picked up on Po Toi at Mo's House.

LAIRD HOUSE, THE PEAK
2000

The elite of Hong Kong's business world came to Laird House each year to see in the New Year. If you weren't invited, you hadn't made it yet. No government 'bigwigs' received invitations, so it tended to be an informal affair. The format was more or less the same each year: a Filipino band playing beside a small dance floor put down in a corner of the drawing room; cocktails on arrival, served from a bar set up in the dining room; an extravagant buffet in the same room, catered by the Mandarin; at midnight, a wander out onto the great patio, weather permitting, for a grandstand view of the fireworks set off from barrages strung out in the middle of Victoria Harbour; and finally, a 'surprise' floor show for those who wanted. Since Tsui became taipan, on the advice of Lao-Tse enemies and friends alike were invited.

Tsui, in well-cut dinner jacket and black tie, mingled, with Cheng Cheng beside him. She looked ravishing in simple black by Prada, complemented by a diamond-studded necklace sparkling against her dark skin. She wanted to look good for Ina, and, of course, for Tsui. Dutifully they listened to the latest gossip: personal and business. They came to a group crowded around Fitzgibbon, who was regaling them with the story of his kidnapping. Earlier in the evening Tsui had been annoyed when Fitzgibbon arrived partnered by Vimana, though Cheng Cheng had quickly calmed him down. Vimana clung to Fitzgibbon's arm now, looking elegant though nervous, in a colourful, sparkling Indian formal gown and sequin-encrusted shoes. A little too much.

"I don't know. It all happened very quickly. They were very efficient. There were lots of them…" Fitzgibbon paused. "…Lots of slit-eyes, I think."

Out of the corner of his eye Tsui saw Takji standing at the edge of the listeners, smiling whimsically. Dressed in a modest and ordinary dinner jacket, Takji melted easily away in the crowd.

Bonito Island, The Philippines 2000

This was the only time he had defied his father over a major issue. In some ways it felt good, though he was nervous about the fallout.

Iain and Bruce had excused themselves from the Laird House party on the grounds that everyone was too old and that they needed some R&R in Manila at the younger Soriano's annual bash. Cheng Cheng had backed them up. On the second day in Manila Iain had slipped away. Tane had become anxious, asking Bruce where he had gone. Sticking to their plan, Bruce told him that Iain had probably gone up to Baguio with some friends to get away from the heat. In fact Iain had rented a Hertz car.

As the Philippines drove on the right, he cautiously headed south to the port of Batangas. From there he had hired a local banca: a dug out canoe with outriggers and a roof of bamboo, mainly for the sun. It had taken the outboard engines about forty minutes to reach Bonito, the last ten outside the bay in open water where the portside pontoon had lifted three feet out of the water, and he'd been glad he was a strong swimmer.

The following day Bruce had met her at the airport and had hired a limo to take her to Batangas. He had put her on the Island launch, which Iain had persuaded the manager to send across.

Bonito was an exquisite pacific island complete with swaying palms and a small beach. There was a central densely-covered hill and a shell-covered path around the perimeter, which was a gentle half-hour stroll, and there was the famous diving.

The private resort could accommodate fifteen guests. But at this time, with so many people with their families and it being midweek, they had the place to themselves.

They had spent the first thirty-six hours in their room, blaming jetlag. Food had been delivered to their door every three to four hours and, after a discreet knock and a call of "Ma'am. Ma'am. Please eat now", it had been left, covered, on the veranda, later to be grabbed by them in various states of undress.

This was the first time in six years that they had been together on holiday independently. In the dawn light he looked down at Suk Soon sleeping, relaxed, a faint smile touching the corner of her lips, naked after early-morning loving. He adored her for the way she gave herself to him in complete surrender. As he gazed down at her, replete, he decided to live with her and to hell with the consequences.

THE COMPRADOR'S PLACE, SAI KUNG 2000

He walked carefully through the frenetic Sunday-lunch kitchen, keenly aware of the slippery floor and that everyone else had right of way. Amongst the noise the call-order waiters shouted out their orders in singsong Cantonese. Junior chefs kept chopping the ingredients, using gleaming cleavers and large log chopping boards. The chefs stood in front of the immense heat thrown off by the eight-burner wok cooker, turning quickly now and then to the stainless bench behind them for the bowls of prepared items they needed for the dish they were working on. Their condiments were in front of them in heavy pottery containers on a shelf high above the flames, and their ladles hung on the rim of the exhaust hood. As they tossed the food in their woks they added a satisfying rhythm to the bustling sounds. With skill, one of the chefs turned and tipped his finished order out of his wok onto a warm, oval Golden Carp serving platter. More happy customers, thought the Comprador's nephew. More money in the bank.

He knocked deferentially on the manager's paned door and went in. The manager was out talking to the customers and keeping an eye on everything: the bar, the outside tables, Jasmine, the kitchen, the large glass tanks where men in rubber boots and aprons were catching the customers chosen live fish, all with a slight smile as he personally identified his customers by name. In his place the accountant was analysing last night's figures. He looked up into the large mirror in front of him, nodded, and went back to work. The nephew went through the door opposite and began climbing the stone stairs to the Comprador's apartment.

The Comprador himself opened the door. Sunday was his houseboy's day off. Unusually he was wearing a royal blue silk Mandarin gown with a high collar and long sleeves, making him seem taller, more austere and younger.

"Come in, Nephew." The Comprador spoke formally. "Over there," waving his hand towards the two chairs by the window, with a steaming blue pottery Chinese teapot and cups on a carved side table by the younger man's chair. The nephew would be doing the serving.

The nephew walked over and sat down where he had been told. He felt nervous and apprehensive. He had been told by his uncle to dress casually to fit in with the weekend crowd. Now he felt decidedly underdressed. The Comprador indicated that he should pour his host's tea then help himself.

"What do you think?" said the older man quietly, and yet abruptly and directly, a mannerism to which his nephew was becoming accustomed. More like an American executive than a Chinese patriarch.

He paused for a moment. No need to rush in. He took a long sip of tea. What madness was this? Did he need this? With his degrees complete and his paper translated and published in Technion IIT, job offers were pouring in and they weren't miserly. Ironically, he'd had one from the CIA.

"Morally it is a sound idea. Practically it's…" – careful now, choose the right word – "…it's interesting."

The Comprador was stroking his chin, pensive, adding to his final decision. "There are things you need to know, though you should not." After all, his nephew was the 'heir apparent' to K. K. Chen and, despite what Tsui said, the China Deal would touch their companies. "The China Deal will be divided into cells: an Alpha cell, Beta cells and Gamma cells. You will be in a Beta cell and I am your upline contact. Normally that is all you would know. But – because of your unique position I have created for you with the family – I have decided to tell you more."

The Comprador was becoming animated by the deal and by the trust he was investing in his protégé.

"The others in the Alpha cell – you already know about Tsui and me – are Iain, Bruce and Sa Cheng Cheng." His nephew showed no concern, being much better at dealing with female executives, even female taipans, than the Comprador. And he doubted if he knew Sa's background. "If anything should happen to me, your contact will be Bruce. One final thing…" The Comprador paused, continuing to gaze out of the window towards the horizon. Eventually he turned and held the young man in his piercing, withering stare. "…Finally, I have a copy of Tsui's jade chop, the seal of the House of One Sun Moon, OSM." Watching closely, he saw the shock in the younger man's eyes. Now his nephew was looking down at his well-worn sneakers, head turned away in disbelief. That defiles a sacred trust. He decided to ignore the information with a distraction.

"Uncle," he began to respond. He should be with his friends, enjoying the mountain bike trail on Lantau and riding along the rocky shoreline of Silver Mine Bay. "Uncle. You always tell me not to worry about the money, that sufficient will always be provided. But this decision is life—"

The Comprador held up his hand autocratically. "You will have a Gamma cell. Your people will be paid US dollars one hundred thousand per assignment. You will be paid, per mission nominated by Tsui, one million US dollars." Again, the flash of surprise. Lucky he's not negotiating with the Chinese, thought the Comprador. "The security of your people will be your responsibility. No unnecessary mistakes, please. Bring in only people you can trust. Be wise! Computers are your discipline. In that sphere you are outstanding. But remember Einstein: 'The difference between stupidity and genius is that genius has its limits.' Your first assignment will be to break into…" – he disliked the word 'hack' – "…the military intelligence network in Myanmar, particularly as it effects the office of the commander-in-chief. You can do this assignment yourself, as if you were in a Gamma cell." The Comprador paused, then continued incisively, "Follow the edict of Sun Tzu: 'To know your enemy, you must become your enemy.' That is all for today. You may go."

Regent International Hotel, Chek Lap Kok 2001

Despite the competition and the challenges, Suk Soon had worked her way back onto 'long haul' with Continental. Calling in a few favours, she had made it onto the inaugural non-stop flight from Newark to Hong Kong, over the North Pole and sixteen hours in the air. The first officer had teased her, saying they had taken on extra barrels of fuel in the hold just in case. She knew they would be heavy at take-off, but she didn't let herself worry. That was not her concern. At least the Continental layout gave them a rest station above the cabin.

Yesterday she had phoned Bruce, who had become a good friend, to ask him to make sure that Iain was in town for her long stopover, if possible. She wanted to give him an unexpected gift without too much surprise. She was looking forward to being in Hong Kong again after seven years. It was her favourite city. She missed it, she missed Iain and she missed Fortune Villa. There had been other men and other girls, but her fantasies always seemed to come back to Iain. They were on final approach now, everyone back in their jump seats and strapped in.

The landing was perfect, gliding onto the tarmac, and the passengers soon disembarked. The cluster of cabin crew, in Continental's smart beige, blue and gold uniforms, mostly pulling small foldup trolleys with their overnight bags, followed the flight crew down the gangways and into the immigration hall. They headed to the left and their own special gate, and were through immigration and customs and out of the concourse before their passengers had collected their bags. The captain and the purser went off to talk to the local press.

Continental, like lots of airlines, had decided to use the Regal Airport Hotel for their crews. It was only a few minutes from the terminal in an air-conditioned link-bridge. The small wheels on their bags and trolleys purred in unison as they walked, joined by the crisp clacking of their heels. There was little talk, most of them looking forward to a shower and rest. It was early morning in Hong Kong and they had the walkway to themselves. They entered the hotel and crossed the shining marble floor to reception, the trolleys silent now, the heels still clacking. Some guests turned to look. The well-lit lobby, decorated in whites and blacks, was vast, serving as it did over a thousand rooms. In the far corner, on a low mezzanine, they had put a coffee shop. All rather clinical.

"Good morning. Welcome to Hong Kong and The Regent," said the smiling receptionist. Another receptionist came to help her. She was carrying an envelope.

"Excuse me. Is there a Miss Pak amongst you?"

"Yes, that's me," said Suk Soon, holding up her hand discreetly.

"This is for you," smiling as she handed her the envelope. Suk Soon looked at it. Hotel stationery. She recognised Iain's private school handwriting.

Suk Soon. I'm at the coffee shop in the lobby. Iain.

Always precise; no room for error. She smiled to herself as she turned away.

* * *

They had jumped in the shower together. He had been glad he'd kept lifting weights in the gym at Laird House. He looked hard and trim. Suk Soon looked as fantastic as ever. Edible.

* * *

She had been sleeping as he watched her, whilst he drank the champagne out of the fridge. She woke up lazily and they talked.

"I had them upgrade you to this Cabana room at no extra cost. They want OSM to use their conference facilities! It's a bit bigger and the breakfast veranda gives the impression of more space. Less like a mailbox."

"Thank you, Iain," and she leant across the bed and squeezed his arm, digging her nails in.

"Ow! You vicious…" and they wrestled until he had her pinned down. Later they talked again.

"How is your family?" He wanted to talk about Tsui.

"Very good, thank you. My mother keeps telling me to thank you for the TV." He'd had the Seoul office pick up the latest prototype wall-mounted plasma model from Sony. "You shouldn't have. And my eldest sister is pregnant again. How are your father and his wife?"

He let that go.

"They're good, thanks – though I am disturbed about this incredible deal he's got going. And he's involving others. Even Bruce, I think. I thought I was in business to make money."

Suk Soon sat up straighter in the pillows. What could that mean? she wondered.

"And I'm going to talk to him this weekend – it's Cheng Cheng's birthday – about you and me."

Suk Soon looked alarmed.

"Don't look so worried! He's not that bad! Let's get dressed and go down and have some yakitori and sake at 'Izakaya'. It's the latest 'smart place'!"

PLA Garrison, Zhuhai, China 2001

The spotless Brilliance ZhongHua picked up the Comprador outside the hotel. Besides the army driver, a captain in dress uniform sat rigidly in the back seat. The driver jumped out, opening the rear door and saluting smartly as the Comprador stooped to get in.

Macau in spring was invigorating. The early morning sun lit up the yellow ochre-and-white Portuguese colonial buildings as they wound their way through the narrow crowded streets on their way to the border control, still maintained, between the old European enclave and Guangdong. As they approached the queue of mainly trucks and buses waiting to leave the SAR, the driver slowed. They came to a plaza which let on to the border gates, veering off to the left towards a vacant and closed gate. As they approached, a border guard ran out and raised the barricade. He waved them through whilst trying to salute. The captain ignored him.

They came out into China proper, with farmers and their water buffaloes and their women planting in the rice paddies. Gradually light industry and speculative housing encroached on their land. The army sometimes had to intervene.

Most of the forces deployed in Macau were stationed at the barracks in Zhuhai, fifteen minutes up the coast. They drove along smooth concrete roads in air-conditioned comfort. To pass the time the Comprador decided to have some fun with the silent captain.

"Major," he said, speaking Mandarin and behaving like an ignorant civilian, "Why are residents of Macau SAR prohibited from joining the PLA?"

The captain looked a little startled as he squinted at the Comprador. Eventually he replied.

"It is a matter of ideology."

* * *

The Comprador had been to the Zhuhai barracks many times before and knew that they would be able to see the guardhouse as soon as they came round the next corner. He reached into his jacket pocket and slowly took out a sky blue beret. He adjusted it on his head, looking in the driver's mirror. There was no insignia but the beret complemented his grey suit and raw silk sky blue tie. A little subterfuge never hurt. From a distance he was often confused with UN personnel. So much the better. Anyway, they were planning to do the UN's work for them.

Recognising the ZhongHua and knowing it was due back about now, the guards double-marched to raise the barrier pole. Once it had passed the point of balance on its way to vertical they let go and presented arms. The Comprador touched his beret in salute, feeling as if he were in uniform. The captain acknowledged them this time, his own people. They looked well turned out and disciplined as they held their salute. Among the elite of the PLA.

The driver stopped outside the mess hall. Before going in the captain took the Comprador on the quick, almost mandatory visitors' tour; he was particularly proud of the new Historic Photo Room. Returning to the mess hall the captain collected their tea and led the way to their usual austere meeting room. They sat without talking, watching the steam rise from their cups. It seemed colder than Macau. Across the parade ground the Comprador heard the beat of the regimental band's traditional drum music. In command of this outpost, close to western influence, was a major-general. But the Comprador had come to meet with a visiting general from the headquarters of the Guangzhou Military Region, one of the Comprador's best contacts.

General Wang came bursting into the room like a fighting cock; fit, energetic and small. He was more like a Shanghai businessman than a senior-ranking field officer. He was extremely self-confident, born of his commercial success and wealth, and of having steered his way through the Gang of Four and recent upheavals. He was wearing the new, smart prototype uniform. With him was his male secretary, a junior lieutenant, who poured General Wang's tea as soon as the general sat down. At the same time Wang lit up a Red Pagoda Hill, blowing clouds of smoke into the air and prompting the Comprador to produce a small personal *guanxi* gift. He reached into his briefcase standing on the floor beside him, the one he used away from home. He found most convenient the sort of flight bag carried on board by airline flight crews: spacious, strong and with a sound combination lock. And it kept files upright. Slowly he took out six cartons of Dunhill International, the general's favourite, giftwrapped, pushing them towards the secretary whilst bowing slightly to the general. They knew each other well enough to talk about family.

"How is your dear wife and your household? How were the gifts from Hong Kong received?" asked the Comprador, with a slight smile and flicking on his CW.

Last time they had met was in Hong Kong where the general, on his first visit, had asked the Comprador to show him around. The Comprador had excused himself, asking two of his young secretaries to go instead. The eldest of the girls had reported the next day. They had met the general at his hotel, the Island Shangri-la. He had been wearing a suit and tie. Gone was the military uniform, but the ebullience was still there. She said that the highlight of the general's shopping had been in Pacific Place's Sheer Elegance where he had bought three costly ensembles in varying sizes and degrees of lusciousness. He had estimated the different sizes by walking round the store checking out the girls and calling out in stilted, broken English, "One this size…" and so on. In an aside to her he had cheekily said, "One for wife, one for mistress, one for daughter."

The Comprador, looking at the young lieutenant, started to think about his coming weekend with Jason, then stopped himself. It was one of his weaknesses, in common with many intelligent people: a short attention span. It had often got him into trouble during his time at the Sorbonne. Mostly he knew what people were going to say before they said it and his brain got bored. It didn't help that his IQ was one hundred and forty-five and that he was physically sharpened for speed by hourly sessions of Tai Chi Chuan. He brought his Sinbad Fuel Systems file out of his briefcase and untied the string. The secretary did the same. This was the last meeting before Tsui attended the big one on the island in The Straits. It had better go well.

"Sinbad Fuel Systems has been patented in all significant markets. So the main potential for you will be in supplying the narrow market of the PLA. As the figures show…" – and the Comprador waved a hand in the direction of the papers in front of the secretary – "…it's extremely profitable."

The general spoke abruptly and at a tangent.

"As you will have learnt, there is much talk of curtailing the PLA from making money, stopping all its businesses, and that the Great Steel Wall – the silence about our businesses between the military and the politicians – is rusting. This is nonsense. The orders have been issued and the orders have been ignored. We will proceed."

"Good. That leaves only Taiwan. The Nassau lawyers did not register in Taiwan within thirty days of the original registration in USA. So Taiwan is a question mark."

"Don't worry," countered the general, "Taiwan is no problem, you'll see. Our military capability will overtake theirs by twenty ten." He paused, then added an afterthought, as if the two were only tenuously connected, "Everything is not as it appears."

The Comprador decided not to push further. He began to talk in generalities.

"I am hearing about your new 'unrestricted warfare' with its emphasis on information dominance. Even now you follow *The Art of War*!"

General Wang said nothing. Instead he turned to his secretary. "Give the Comprador his gift." He said 'the Comprador' with a tinge of disrespect, as if the Comprador was only an intermediary, a go-between and a civilian to boot. He leant back in his chair, hands behind his head, in control. The secretary picked up a zippered basketball bag and passed it over.

"It's a uniform. We made you a brigadier! If you're coming here again, use the North Gate, as if you are coming from the interior. Your UN get-up is wearing thin!"

The Comprador pulled the bag towards him, cradling it in his arms. This could be dangerous, very dangerous. He heard the general's sociable voice again.

"Have a look! It's not a bomb!" The Comprador thought he better do as requested. He pulled back the zip: one of the old style uniforms with the right insignia. He closed the bag.

"Thank you, General Wang."

"Sorry, only generals…" As he spoke the Comprador saw two soldiers running silently past the steel-framed windows. Instantly he slung the bag across the table at the secretary. It landed in his lap along with some of his papers. As it did the door was kicked open and armed soldiers came charging in. They waved their assault rifles in their direction, yelling at them to sit as three soldiers handcuffed them. Why weren't they using more force, thought the Comprador. He glanced across the table. The secretary was nervous, but not alarmed. General Wang was outraged, beginning to swear in street Cantonese. The Comprador turned slightly to look at the smashed door, knowing that the chances of escape were best the nearer to capture. As he did, a sergeant marched in, closely followed by the major-general, who smartly saluted General Wang.

"A training exercise, Sir. To show how good my men are in a realistic way! Dismiss, Sergeant." The handcuffs were taken off. The soldiers left at a jog, their rifles at port arms. The sergeant saluted smartly as he followed them.

General Wang said nothing, steepling his fingers, elbows on the table. After a long time he smiled, laughed heartily and clapped his hands.

* * *

The car took him through the gates on the way back to Macau. This time there was no captain. The bag with the uniform was on the seat beside him. In the empty mess hall they had had a well-prepared seven-course lunch with the major-general, full of false bonhomie and military raucousness. The Comprador realised the military men wanted a personal share of the Sinbad project. He was playing a dangerous game.

The driver kept a steady pace, which made the short trip comfortable. The Comprador, relaxing, let his mind wander to the weekend ahead, with the anticipation of a younger man. As he always did, he had booked into the Landmark; a junior suite. He didn't want to be ostentatious and flamboyant, attracting the attention of the 'occupiers'. Even in the smaller rooms the hotel gave absolute five-star luxury and understated, discreet and outstanding service. Just what he needed, he thought.

The Comprador had met Jason through one of his contacts, an Indian lady who at the time had been a senior executive at Swires. Jason was twenty-five and extraordinarily handsome, a mix of Portuguese, Indian and Chinese, his body always trim and taut, muscles rippling from a dedication to yoga. They would have some fun this evening trying on his new uniform, almost golden, a 'Golden Fleece'. Used correctly, it could open lots of doors. So could Jason. He might make him a member of his Beta Cell.

'Of All The Bars' Piano Bar, Wanchai 2002

Iain and Bruce were back at the Fire-Fly club, on their second San Miguel. Friday night and the 'happy hour' crowd was in. They had the same waitress, who had come to them as soon as they came in, taking them to one of her tables. She was back again, this time with a Fire-Fly flyer, which she laid on the table beside Bruce. She had written down her name, Catherine, and her phone number. She squatted down beside him, glancing furtively back at the bar.

"On Sunday come to Statue Square. Some friend's picnic. The fountain nearest the bank." And she was gone.

"That'll be the Hong Kong Bank," said Iain, teasing.

"She seemed very nervous." Bruce, as always, concerned.

"They don't treat them well…" As he spoke he saw four policemen coming in the main entrance. Others appeared at the exits and at the bar. The music stopped and a young Chinese police officer took the microphone. He spoke good English.

"Do not be concerned. We will not be long. We are here to help the Immigration Department." As if on cue, blue-uniformed immigration inspectors filed in. "Please place your ID cards or passports on the table in front of you." He said the same thing in Tagalog, though not in the same polite tone.

Some of the staff tried to slip away but were firmly restrained and made to sit with the customers. Some started sobbing. Catherine quickly sat down with them, giggling nervously and patting Bruce on the knee. Her papers must be in order or perhaps she needed their support, thought Iain, as Sebastian sat down on the fourth chair.

"They're checking Filipinas' paperwork. Do as they ask. Leave quietly ten minutes after they're gone. I know the officer." There was no doubt he was good. He already had sound contacts with the new people. It was the command voice that was annoying, and the omnipresence, thought Iain. Bugger.

"All right, Sebastian. Agreed," said Iain, holding up his hand. Catherine's big eyes opened wider as she watched the burly Maori giving orders.

Iain turned to Bruce. "Have you been to the new place in the Tsui building?" That would please Sebastian: it was only five minutes' walk, and secure. "A piano bar called 'Of All The Bars'. It'll be quieter there. We can talk better…" As he spoke, Immigration checked their IDs and moved on, hardly looking at Catherine's.

* * *

They jogged side by side along the pavement in the steady drizzle, ignoring the stream of splashing traffic until they reached the covered walkway into the Tsui building. They were brushing the rain off their shoulders as they walked through the sliding doors into the vast atrium of glass, steel and marble. Iain lead the way to the two customer lifts that went to the seventh floor only. At the back of the building three service lifts looked after deliveries to the restaurants.

"K. K. Chen has leased the whole of the seventh floor," Iain explained to Bruce as they walked. His father had told him to tell Bruce more about the workings of OSM. "Then they've sublet to six restaurants – a sort of food plaza – but this is a gourmets' one." The ornate lift doors opened and closed. Going up, Iain continued, "There's one Chinese, one Indian, a Japanese, a Thai, a French, and an Italian one. It's a good idea. The bar acts as a rendezvous place, somewhere to have a drink before and after eating and a 'watering hole' for it's own clientele. It's all going well. They've settled in now after ten weeks, so they're going to start promoting the concept soon. Probably in your old rag!"

* * *

It was as he said. The bar was extravagantly designed to a 'Casablanca' theme, with subdued colours and lights and with luxurious armchairs, sofas and futons. The walls were hung with black-and-white pictures from the movie. Yet another Filipina was playing at the piano-cum-bar, where customers sat around drinking, making requests and putting notes in the brandy balloon on top of the piano. She had been asked by the manager to call herself Samantha so she could respond when the customers asked, "Play it again, Sam!" It was a misquote, as the picture of Ingrid Bergman and the real quote behind the piano showed, "Play it, Sam. Play 'As time goes by'." It was a movie he and Bruce knew well, having studied it for Arts at Melrose College, and the misquote aggravated him. As did the name of the piano bar. It wasn't 'Of All The Bars' but 'Of All The Gin Joints'.

They found a quiet corner away from the piano and tucked away behind a bank of palms. The staff followed them over and put down a fresh selection of nuts and a plate of zacusca on small pieces of rye bread. They ordered two more beers. The body language of the waiters did not turn negative as it normally would when customers ordered beer. They knew that Iain was getting into the habit of bringing free-spending OSM junior executives in after work.

"It makes good business to come in here!" said Iain, laughing. "You know I've got shares in OSM from my mother?"

Bruce nodded. Iain seemed to want to talk. Do him good. Yes, he did know Iain had shares in OSM but he didn't know how many.

"Well, my uncle, you know, Wai Kwok, advised me to tell my stockbroker to buy up five per cent of K. K. Chen. I checked it out. He's got five per cent himself. They're doing very well, for some reason. So, drink up. I get five per cent!" Iain laughed again as he raised his glass. Bruce smiled and kept listening. He'd been reading his copy of *The Art of War*, which Tsui had given him along with *5BX*, the Canadian Air Force exercise book.

"I've been asked to keep you posted about what's happening in OSM." Iain didn't mention Tsui. "Do you mind? Before we get pissed!"

"Sure. As Bill would say – no worries," replied Bruce, leaning back, relaxing, with his lager in his hand. Bill was the Australian bar manager at the Foreign Correspondents' Club.

"Asiaway is way ahead of its five-year plan. But there's been some shifting around of people. Ian Ross has gone. For good measure Susan Tang divorced him as well! There's all kind of gossip! But, as we're taught, gossip should be ignored. I'm not so sure. Anyway Ms Tang's two Shanghainese brothers have come on board. These guys are sharp. The Comprador says they may use the network for distribution after all. If they do, we will have leverage to use them as 'safe houses'..." – Iain glanced around to make sure no one could hear – "...for the China Deal."

"Let's see, what else...? The Floor is taking a strong position on the Yuan Renminbi. They're betting on a revaluation and the authorities are allowing limited trading in Yen, Euros and HK and US dollars. But the Yuan will still be pegged at the new rate."

Iain paused and took a drink. He looked worried, old for his age, figuring out how to tell Bruce the next piece of news. He looked around again then leant closer, confidingly.

"About Li Kai Sing, the Defence Secretary. He's been caught out by our people in Taiwan. He's looking at the... venture as a way of satisfying his personal greed without thought for the moral issues. Put simply, he's been stealing from us. He seems to think his power has no limit. He has to go..."

He didn't finish the sentence, leaning back in his chair, hands behind his head, gazing at the ceiling. They sat for a while until Bruce started talking about his magazine and the plans for the radio station.

Whilst they were talking, some customers came to sit near them, joking and laughing loudly. The bar was filling up. One of the new group, a gorgeous Chinese girl in a perfectly fitting high-cut office suit, broke away and came languidly towards them, smiling broadly. Iain recognised; one of the Comprador's 'secretaries'. She sat down on the sofa next to Iain, pulling herself across to him, putting her arm around his shoulder, still smiling. She continued to smile but when she spoke her voice was hard and cold, glacial.

"I have a message. Mr Chen says do not speak about China business in public." She leant across, kissed him on the cheek and left them, laughing.

Iain looked grim. Raising his voice, he turned to Bruce. "Let's go to the Japanese restaurant. We can talk about your Norwegian and my Korean," and raising his voice further, "beautiful Pak Suk Soon."

Club Marina Cove, Hiram's Highway 2002

Bruce and Katla were driving out into the New Territories on their way to a Saturday lunch poolside party given by Ogilvy and Mather, who had begun buying bulk space in *Trance*.

Bruce had been surprised at the freedom he'd been given in running the business and now, since he was being moved sideways to head up the new OSM radio station, the freedom of recruiting the executive to take over management. He'd chosen a local.

Katla was silent in the passenger seat.

"A penny for your thoughts!" he joked, squeezing her thigh.

"Later! I'm still thinking. How much further?"

"We're here," he replied, turning right into Marina Cove opposite the soya factory, as the map on the back of the invitation had shown. Bruce slowed down as he drove around to the clubhouse, the private road flanked by spacious Spanish style villas with terracotta-tiled roofs, yachts and cruisers moored at the bottom of the garden. More yachts, their masts bobbing in the water, were moored at floating jetties.

He parked in the club car park, which was nearly full: they were late. Grabbing their sports bags off the back seat, they headed for the main entrance. Last time he was here Bruce remembered seeing the Hong Kong British flag of the Crown Colony flying from their flagpole. It had gone, replaced with the attractive red SAR flag bearing the white flower of the Hong Kong orchid tree. Small but significant changes everywhere, he thought.

At reception they asked for the Ogilvy and Mather party, signed in, and were casually pointed in the direction of the swimming pool.

* * *

Bruce was enjoying the last of the Thai curry, glad that the club catering had provided Asian food instead of western. They had swum when they arrived, afterwards changing into 'smart casual', Bruce wearing his old cricket blazer from Melrose. Now they had settled at a large round table with their friends, mainly from the FCC, in a palm-filled corner away from the splashing of the pool. The champagne was still flowing as the short twilight approached and the swimming pool lights came on. The group around him were talking about the retirement of Anson Chan. Katla was talking earnestly to Vimana. She looked across at Bruce, her blue eyes sparkling, animated. “We’re going to have a sauna, then one last dip.”

Bruce noticed Tony Parker, drink in hand, watching Katla hungrily.

“OK. Don’t be too long; we’ve got a fair drive home,” Bruce replied.

Vimana appeared to be happy, and alone.

Without notice Bruce heard Tony slouch down on the seat beside him. “How are we, dear fellow?” Not really wanting an answer, Tony continued, “How’s Katla? I hear she’s being posted to the mainland. Shanghai, I think.”

* * *

Katla and Vimana had persuaded Bruce to go back to Vimana’s place, Greenview Villas, only five minutes away up in the hills across the highway for ‘one for the road’. Katla had gone with Vimana, and he was following their bouncing tail lights on the rough country road. They climbed through a small village, reflecting eyes of stray cats and dogs dashing across in front of them. The streetlights were dim and few before they came out on the well-lit terrace of the villas, each light a swarm of night-time insects. The ground floor apartment was cool. An air-conditioner had been left on; he could hear it humming in another room.

“The maids are out for the night,” Vimana said to no one in particular, gently kicking the heavy ornate front door shut behind her, and then walking across the scatter rugs to flick on two brass table lamps. Katla walked silently behind her. As Vimana turned, smiling, moist lips apart, Katla took the final step that separated them, kissing her passionately and running her hands down her arched back.

Bruce became an interested spectator. No need to worry about how to start this threesome, he thought, as Vimana broke their kiss. She held Katla’s hand and pulled her after her, trotting towards the master bedroom.

“Let’s have a shower,” she said breathlessly. “Bruce. The bar’s over there. There’s some champers in the fridge.”

* * *

Their loving was erotic and Vimana amazingly supple. She was in a deep sleep now, under the silk sheet. Katla and Bruce were talking quietly. Now was a hard time for Katla, yearning a smoke. He’d gone naked to find the kitchen to make her a sandwich:

cheese and ham. She leant back in the pillows, nibbling and grinning while he poured champagne. They had a rule not to analyse performance afterwards, but this felt like an exception to her.

"That was fun, yes?" she said.

"Yes, it was," but, it seemed to him, much more fun for her. He'd better not talk about it. Talk about something else.

"My new job at the radio station," and he glanced at the sleeping Vimana, "seems to be mainly passing on editorial comment for the old man. 'Editor' he calls it, compared with the UN 'Under-Secretary for Communications and Public Relations United Nations Secretariat'. He's very sarcastic about the 'useless UN'."

No response from Katla, who continued eating. Becoming more sober, he remembered what Tony Parker had said. "What were you thinking about in the car? Got any news for me?"

"Well, yes," she said, putting down her drink and empty plate, reaching across the bed to hold his hand. "Yes. The paper wants me to do more about China. They've posted me to Shanghai. I'm sorry."

She was assuming they were finished. So be it but he was irked to find out that Parker knew first. So what? he thought. Must be the wine.

"Never mind. I'll probably be up in the 'Pearl of the Orient' often enough."

Katla wriggled more upright, covering her breasts with the sheet.

"By the way. Since we're talking shop," she said, laughing lightly, "there's all kind of rumour with Tsui – have you any comment?"

"None," Bruce answered, laughing lightly. This might become a conflict of interests. Just as well it was ending.

Vimana stirred in the bed and turned to Katla.

"Let's play," she said, giggling. She didn't sound too sleepy, thought Bruce.

Vimana rolled over to the drawer in her bedside table. As she did the silk sheet slipped off her tight dark buttocks. She rolled back across the bed, holding some short satin ropes. Without talking, she quickly put the slipknot around Katla's left wrist and tied the other end to the bedpost. She threw two of the ropes at Bruce as she moved down to Katla's ankle.

The Peninsula Suite, Kowloon
2002

The businessman got onto the crowded 'down' elevator of Tower One of the Koala Building in Admiralty. He was dressed like most of the men in the lift – in a suit and tie – but in some way he was unusual. Old Hong Kong hands could tell the difference. He was from Taiwan. The name was contrary, too. He was in government, so referred to his country as ROC, the Republic of China. The popular conception was that mainland China considered Taiwan an offshore island, a wayward province, an integral part of China itself; the United Nations and others sitting on the fence, as Chinese Taipei. The office he had left was called Chung Hwa Travel, a front for a Taiwanese consulate or embassy.

He strode out across the lobby with a military bearing: back straight, shoulders back, chin up, carrying a Damiro laptop briefcase. He looked full of confidence and self-importance, going straight to the MTR knowing that, with a change at Central, he could catch the Airport Express, which would get him to Chek Lap Kok in half an hour.

He was going to meet his superior. He had left two hours early, telling his people that he never liked to be rushed. In fact he was taking a helicopter from the airport heliport directly to the roof of the Peninsula Hotel in Kowloon for a meeting with Tsui. He'd easily have a spare hour.

* * *

Tsui was waiting. He was looking out of the Peninsula Suite across the harbour at the office towers of Central and Wanchai. With satisfaction he picked out the Tsui Centre, with its distinctive modern architecture topped off with a world globe. He turned away and went back to refill his coffee at the kitchen's breakfast counter. He glanced at the wall clock. Half an hour. He pressed the button for his butler.

In less than a minute he heard the subdued doorbell. Putting down his cup he went over to the door, not wanting to shout. He checked the video monitor. Sebastian insisted. Trained him well. Sebastian would be on the roof by now in the helipad reception, waiting to check out their visitor.

There was no peephole in the Peninsula Suite front door. Tsui swung it open.

"Sir?"

"My guest will be here by eleven. Please replace the coffee, and bring some Jasmine tea as well just in case. Ring down for some Scottish shortbread and some chocolate éclairs…" Tsui was going to add "with fresh cream" but didn't. He knew that at 'the Pen' it wouldn't be anything else.

"And please, once my guest has arrived, absolutely no interruptions. My head of security, Sebastian, will be in the corridor during the meeting."

"I understand completely, Sir," the butler said with a slight bow.

"Thank you, Liu Jianguo."

The butler had introduced himself when Tsui arrived. He had memorised his name. There were no vulgar name tags for those giving personal service. Liu closed the door discreetly and went into the butler's pantry. Tsui wandered through the suite, counting the rooms: two large lounges; five bathrooms, one with a full harbour view; a mini-gym; office; and conference room, which would be the only space he'd use for business. Exorbitant luxury to impress the Taiwanese and Iain at lunchtime.

* * *

Iain and his father were enjoying smoked salmon on rye, salade nicoise and a light house white, watching the shipping moving in the harbour.

"Bit over the top taking this place for the day, don't you think?" laughed Iain, gently challenging his father.

"Not really! I wanted to impress our new man and you see it worked. But I agree it is expensive. I calculate it costs seven cents a second, that's US cents! That's why Cheng Cheng is coming over this evening!" And bringing your overnight bag and Mary-Lou, I'll bet, thought Iain.

"What will happen to Li Kai Sing?" Iain asked, more aggressively.

His father hesitated, then turned away from the window, locking eyes with his son. When he spoke his voice was quieter, measured.

"We have finished with him." It was obvious to Iain that the topic was closed, like a steel trap. He said nothing. Tsui got up, throwing his napkin on his chair and, in a rare show of affection, patting Iain on the shoulder on his way to the washroom. Iain drank more wine, waiting. He wondered why he was here.

* * *

Tsui came back, talking about business in Shanghai.

"Have you heard we won the court case over the ownership of the apartment block in Luwan?"

"Yes. The Comprador told me yesterday," replied Iain, though he got the impression his father had wanted to tell him himself.

"Lot of good it will do us. Our lawyers there told your uncle that 'You may win now; enforcing legal judgement is a different matter!' It may take five, ten years. The Party needs to sort out their property law quickly if they want to keep their foreign investment and their fantastic growth rates."

They had moved into the first lounge, settling down in two of the relaxing armchairs, facing each other across a heavy Chinese rug. No coffee table. Good, thought Tsui, it made the space seem larger, uncluttered. They had chosen a good port to mellow the afternoon as they watched the rain teeming down and streaming across the window.

"What time are you leaving?" Tsui asked, his tone more businesslike.

An old trap, thought Iain.

"Whenever we are finished," he replied without hesitation. Next question.

"What do you know about the Ninjas?"

Not what he expected. He was certain that the Comprador would have reported to Tsui. Careful.

"Only what I've seen at the movies. And what you've told me. Which is incredible."

"Would you say… unbelievable?" asked his father.

Beware, Iain said to himself, never challenge his word. "Well, you've been there, so it must be true. But for outsiders it would seem impossible."

"Exactly my thoughts. That's excellent," Tsui said, taking a sip of port and savouring its after-lunch sweetness as he leant further back in his chair. He carried on spreading his hands expansively. "I want you to learn about the Ninjas. I myself am training in the OSM gym when it is closed. A Ninja is teaching me. He's attached to Sebastian's security department. Takji Yoshida is our contact. I happened to be at Cambridge with him. He's a good man. He organises the ryu, the school, and the nine Ninja training halls, which are all complementary."

Iain began to ask a question. Tsui remonstrated with his son and held up his hand. "Questions at the end! Sometimes I wonder how your teachers at Melrose coped." Tsui laughed without humour.

"Complementary because they teach one way of physical attack, ten ways of attacking their adversary's mind. That's from Buddha: 'Your greatest weapon is your enemy's mind.'

"These Ninjas are from the Fuma Ninja, who specialise in espionage and chemistry, meaning poisons. They did not join the peace accord in sixteen thirty-seven; they carried on.

"Their physical dimension is best covered by Sun Tzu." Tsui looked up at the ceiling, recalling the quotation: "'Ethereal and subtle, the master strategist passes by without leaving a trace. Mysterious like the Way of Heaven, he passes by without a sound. In this way he masters his enemy's fate.'

"Ninjas plan their exit strategy from their pre-emptive strikes with great care, meticulously. More than half their planning goes to their exit strategy. Unlike Pearl Harbor, the Six Day War and, of course, now Iraq. History, for those who want to learn, will teach so much.

"And last but not least, the Ninjas are not handicapped by the samurai's bushido, code of honour. This means, among other things, that Ninjas have no loyalty outside their clan. So they will give their services to the highest bidder. Takji may give you the opportunity to match a third-party offer; he may not."

* * *

The afternoon was moving on. They had moved to green tea.

"The Comprador tells me that you are in touch with Pak Suk Soon?" Tsui said, getting up and going to the window, his back to his son. Surprise attack, thought Iain. The question hung in the stillness of the suite. Iain decided on simplicity.

"Yes."

Tsui decided to tell him the story of the *Swallow*. He paused in reverie, then told his son the memory.

"I still have feelings for that girl today, though I will never see her. At the time I hated my father. Now I understand, and I wish I had provided the same experience for you..." He paused again, feeling the years go by. "Let us consider Ms Pak a personal matter. It will not interfere with OSM or the China Deal. Though her nationality might be a challenge.... Let's shake on it in the Scots way," said Tsui, walking across the carpet, hand outstretched. Iain knew that in Scotland a handshake makes a contract. Tsui held onto his son's hand firmly. Unusually, they stared deep into each other's eyes, unwavering.

"One last thing. As future taipan, if you are going to disobey me, tell me first. Agreed?"

"Agreed."

Tsui started walking to the hallway. They were finished for the day. He started talking in what appeared to be a casual manner. Iain thought his father wanted to unwind the tension of what might have been confrontation. It wasn't so.

"I read in *The Economist* that the Yank's B2 stealth bombers cost US dollars one point three billion each, three times their weight in gold! They've made twenty-one so far, for themselves and their client countries."

As Iain left, puzzled, they shook hands again.

* * *

Soon after, Cheng Cheng arrived with Mary-Lou and a porter carrying Tsui's and her Gucci overnight bags. She had told Mary-Lou to pack her things in her holdall. Sa had her own card key. "Have you had a good day?" she said to Tsui as they kissed and hugged. Sebastian was hovering in the background.

"Yes, thanks, and it will only get better! Actually, I had a good talk with your favourite 'step-son'."

"Don't bully him!" she laughed. "You know he's more relaxed and confident, manly, when you're not in the room, when you're not around!"

Mary-Lou had wandered off with the porter, 'oohing' and 'aahing' as she went through the suite. Cheng Cheng had told her to shower and jump in the sauna. She was not to work while they were here.

LIN KUAN-YIN'S FLAT, TAIPEI 2003

At dawn the block of flats was silent. The morning call was beginning in the park across the road. The local traffic hadn't started.

He sat motionless, reading yesterday's *Taipei Times*, specifically the Defence Ministry's press release, which had given out some hardnosed facts: three hundred thousand Taiwanese armed forces facing over two million PLA across the Taiwan Straits. Over seven hundred ballistic missiles pointing at Taiwan. He laid the paper on his lap, considering. Odd, he thought. Why now?

The Ninja started his mental review of the past months and yesterday, looking for errors and ways to improve.

He had flown into Kaohsiung from Manila six months ago, carrying a Taiwanese passport and ID in the name of Lin Kuan-Yin and using a cheap downtown hotel for an address in Taipei.

Later he had taken this flat on a one-year lease. He had taken it because he had found out that one of the staff who worked at 'Happy Delivery' lived alone next door. Happy Delivery was an upmarket flower and fruit shop in the Far East Department Store near a gaggle of government offices.

His neighbour was from a rich Chinese family living in San Juan, Manila. He was studying for an MBA at Chengchi University. Being an older student he had opted out of dorm life, preferring to live alone. Lin Kuan-Yin had got to know him weekend carwashing and dealing with their flats' potted plants. He was called Bobby Hwang. Now Lin worked with him part-time at the store.

Yesterday had been Lin's 'birthday'. In the evening they had gone to a local bar to drink and talk to the gorgeous girls. No uniforms, just simple designer street clothes. They were tall, graceful, moving like hungry tigers ambling across the veldt. After a few quick drinks he ordered some bar foods. He wanted Hwang to eat.

The place was filling up. The piano player was joined by a singer wearing a sequin dress and a cowgirl hat, matching the bar's western theme: lots of timber and harness, with sawdust on the floor. When Hwang went to the toilet and the girls were gossiping amongst themselves, he easily dropped the Fuma rapid-dissolve pill in Hwang's drink. He had brought it through customs with half a bottle of well-known aspirin. This one pill was a slightly darker shade of white.

The Ninja had suggested finishing their beer and moving to cognac for his birthday toast. They made their way to a table near the piano, the girls following along behind. Gradually Bobby seemed to everyone to be getting more and more drunk. Eventually, and so he would remember, Lin asked the manager to help him get Bobby to his car. The girls had walked off, gently swearing at Bobby for getting drunk too early.

Lin drove carefully to the flat, parking in Hwang's spot. He took the keys from the car to open the front door. Easily he pulled Hwang out of the car, throwing him over his shoulder and carrying him inside. He took him into the bedroom and laid him comfortably on the bed, his head sideways on the pillow.

Later in the evening he had reconstituted from tablets in his vitamin containers, another drug. He had bought a syringe, and some other pharmacy items, including some wipes, off the shelf at a large discount chemist. He filled the syringe and went back to the bedroom. His neighbour was snoring heavily. Gently the Ninja rolled him over further, and dexterously injected him at the top of the spine. Takji Yoshida had told him that it would disable him for twenty-four hours, if he came round at all. It would be more convenient if he did.

* * *

The workday noises were beginning to drift through the windows. The drone of rush-hour traffic, the noise of local scooters making deliveries, schoolchildren calling out to each other on their way to school. Lin stood up, stretching like a cat. He looked at his watch. Eight twenty. Time to call the store. He walked over to Hwang's phone on the wall in the kitchenette.

"Hullo, Manager Kwan, this is Lin Kuan-yin."

"Good morning, Mr Lin." The tone of his voice sounded as if he expected bad news. Good, it made things easier.

"Mr Hwang sick this morning. He asked if I could take his place. Would that be OK?"

"Yes, that will be good. We are going to be busy." Relief sounded in the manager's voice. "Thank you, Mr Lin."

"That's no trouble, Mr Manager. But I only heard now. Will it be all right if I get in at ten?"

"Yes, that's all right." The manager hung up.

* * *

Five past nine. This time he'd be using his Jamaican accent, which was one of the things he had to learn, training in one of the soundproof study rooms at the shrine. He dialled the Happy Delivery number again. As he had expected, one of the girls answered.

"Happy Delivery – how can we help?"

"I would like to order a large fruit basket," he said in his singsong rapper's voice. The girl was nervous dealing with a foreigner so he went slowly, making sure there were out-of-season mangoes to impress and some of his favourite: bananas. He gave the details of his Jamaican visa card, expiry date and the name on the card, Deonte, P for Penn, Williams; the Ninja's support section was thorough. "Delivery should be for late afternoon today, so he has time to appreciate it before our meeting tomorrow! And the greeting should read, 'From the Jamaican Delegation'." The girl read back the order, as she had been taught, without a mistake.

"And the delivery address, please?"

"Minister Li Kai Sing, Ministry of National Defence."

* * *

His third and last call was to the Ministry's Public Relations Office, as a journalist confirming the time of the Jamaican delegation's pre-lunch press conference tomorrow. Twelve noon.

* * *

Lin hung up and moved like a shadow into the bedroom. He looked down at his patient and took his pulse. All at peace with the world. He picked up Hwang's keys from the table by the front door and quickly walked along the concrete veranda to his own flat. Once inside he changed into his Happy Delivery uniform, checked and left on his answering machine. His voice was distorted to block voice recognition. Finally, he picked up the small bag he had prepared.

He drove carefully, taking the easier but longer route in by the Civic Boulevard. It was not unusual for him to drive Hwang's car; Hwang had lent it to him many times before. He was taut and alert, just as he should be. Everything looked and felt good.

The Ninja cruised into the car park of the Far East Department Store, took a ticket, threw it on the dashboard and went up to the fifth floor, parking away from the lifts and the foot traffic. His delivery motorbike was parked on the basement floor with all the other bikes.

* * *

At lunchtime he had spoken to the shipping florist to tell her that he would deliver the order for the MND last as it was on his way home. Now he was carrying the elaborate fruit bowl in the lift back up to the fifth floor. In the relative privacy of the car he carefully undid the silk ribbon which held the cellophane wrapping in place. He took out the bananas, breaking off the biggest. He put the rest on the floor in front of the passenger's seat; later he'd put them in one of the bins at the far end of the flats. He reached over for his bag and took out the full syringe. He released the catch and injected the banana three times. He knew that the target was greedy by nature and banana was his favourite fruit. As there was only one banana, and it on top of the fruit, he would grab it before anyone else could. Also Lin had a distraction for him, so his natural instincts would be uninhibited.

He took out a wipe and carefully rubbed away his fingerprints, wrapping up the cleaned syringe and putting it back in the bag. After pulling on his light cotton driving gloves, he took out an antique-looking silver bowl. He turned it over and again read the inscription on the base etched in Old English scroll and dulled down to make it look at least a few years old. On the first line: *Authenticated Pirate Treasure* and underneath, *c.1680 Jamaica.* Beautiful work. That will be distraction enough for the target's instincts to take over, thought Lin.

He slipped his own note into the envelope, replacing the card filled in at the Happy Delivery. Printed out on a computer at the department store's internet café, it read: *From the Jamaican Delegation – don't throw away the bowl*!

He stopped briefly, slipping slowly down in his seat as two women with trolley loads of shopping got into the Toyota seven cars away and drove off.

Nimbly he changed the silver bowl with the bamboo basket from the store and rewrapped the fruit, with the banana conspicuously on top and the card in easy reach. On the way down to the motorbike park he threw the bamboo basket in a rubbish bin as he passed.

* * *

He rode the Happy Delivery scooter the two blocks to the Ministry of National Defence building. The traffic was getting heavier. He arrived, as he had planned, at seventeen hundred hours, when the guards at the main gate were changing. The guards knew him by now, helped by his uniform and the signwriting on the bike, and very often waved him through, writing him in the book themselves. They did today, which avoided any repartee about the silver bowl.

The Ninja had made two deliveries previously so knew the layout. He quickly reached the outer office, where the target's personal secretary worked. He walked directly to the heavy doors of the inner office, extending his stride and accelerating his pace so that he was imperceptibly moving at surprising speed. At the same time he called over his shoulder in a happy and almost cheeky voice, "A personal delivery for the Minister."

"You can't go in! He's on the phone…"

But Lin was halfway through the door. He stopped, but the Minister had seen the gift and waved Lin in. Leaving the door open, Lin crossed the large office and reached over the ornate Chinese desk, placing the fruit in the centre of the leather ink blotter, with the card facing him. The Minister was still talking on the phone when he waved his chubby hand in dismissal. Lin gave a fake American salute and a vacant grin as he left the room.

* * *

He had parked the bike and was wiping the car clean of most of his prints. He had kept on his white woollen delivery gloves. He drove out of the car park into the rush-hour crush. The traffic moved more quickly once he had made it to the freeway. To distract the driver behind him he swung into the fast lane. At the same time he dropped the syringe out of the top of the window. With satisfaction he saw it smash as one of the following cars ran over it.

* * *

Back in his flat he put on his suit and tie and finished his final packing. He had checked Hwang, who was still out. His breathing seemed laboured, which wasn't good. He had left some water by the bed; if he did wake up he'd be thirsty.

He'd wiped Hwang's flat, even the keys, which he had put in their place. He'd left a note for Hwang to tell their manager that he'd be off for a week. In a 'post script' he told Hwang that he'd taken one of the bar girls up to the mountains. He had one last look around his flat. Nothing. He picked up his shoulder bag and briefcase, locked up and began walking to the small hotel round the corner. From the bar he'd phone for a taxi to the airport. Hwang had been all right. He hoped he would not be in too much trouble if he lived. He didn't expect the Jamaican delegation would meet the Minister of National Defence.

* * *

The Ninja was beginning to relax, like a released steel spring. He was on a Qantas flight to Hong Kong and drinking a Crown Lager to fit in with the heavy-drinking Aussies. This was the second leg of his 'itinerary' and his second passport, with a visa in it for the PRC. First, Taipei–Manila on one passport, then Manila–Hong Kong on another, both with matching entry visas. At Manila airport he had used one of their cubicles to change into more informal clothes and to shave off his straggly moustache.

In Hong Kong he was to take two taxis on his way to the ferry terminal and a catamaran to Canton, Guangzhou, where he'd be met by a vehicle from Zhu Hai garrison. Finally a drive to Macau, using the military gate. The driver would drop him off at the Hotel Lisboa, where he would walk through reception to get another taxi to the villa in Coloane. Later he would burn his extra passports. He would be 'off the radar' in Macau.

He was to stay in Macau for two years before returning to Japan. He didn't mind: first because he would be a rich man and, second, he would be living with one of the miko. She would be waiting for him at the villa. He would be 'working' at the local OSM office.

The Villa, Coloane 2003

The villa was silent except for the early night sounds: cicadas and the distant rumble of the waves of the South China Sea at the bottom of the cliffs. She lay on her back, totally in tune with the darkness. Never total darkness, she thought. She was on low watch, a state between sleep and wake. She was to protect him. The Ninja was at last in a deep sleep. She had been warned that she would need to make him rest after such a long solo mission.

When she had heard him arriving she had waited for him inside the front door – his servant but not subservient. She welcomed him without fuss then served him hot sake and kimchi udon: thick noodle soup with sliced pork and Korean chilli-preserved cabbage. It was rumoured that his mother was Korean. His entrance to the clan had been difficult.

She turned her head on the pillow to see him better. Involuntarily her muscles contracted. She grinned to herself in the dark. She had done a good job. But so had he. It was true what the girls said: he had golden fingers.

Suddenly she tensed, becoming fully alert in an instant, half sitting up and straining her ears. Over the other recognised sounds she heard a repeated scuffing noise. Someone was trying to force the window to the small office above the kitchen further along their corridor. Only the downstairs windows had security bars. She swung her legs out of bed and started for the door. She had oiled all the hinges, except two for strategic reasons, and had memorised any squeaking upstairs floorboards and steps. She wore black long-sleeved and long-legged underwear and black cotton slippers. She was nearly invisible, moving with catlike stealth. As she reached the door she heard the quiet, strong and steady voice of the Ninja behind her.

"It's OK. It's one of those Macau rats trying to raid the pantry downstairs. We'll get some poison in the morning."

The miko said nothing but turned round and started moving towards his bed, slipping off her clothes as she did. She needed to put him back to sleep. Maybe a massage this time.

* * *

Fusion was swinging at anchor in the gentle waves of Ham Tin Bay. The rugged hills of the New Territories surrounded the bay and the long sandy beach, totally deserted in midweek without surfers, walking tours and family picnics. Sebastian stood in the bows, leaning on the rail, looking at the wildness and the peace. It reminded him of the Bay of Islands and home. Why was he here? Another economic migrant. Right now he was waiting for twenty minutes with Tsui, which he had asked for. Like it or not, he had to talk with him. The rumours were getting too loud.

He turned as the Comprador's houseboy came towards him. "Tsui, please." His English was not too good.

Sebastian followed followed the boy down to the main cabin. On the way they passed the crew playing mah-jong in the galley. Sebastian had learnt to play, though slowly. Very popular with the Cantonese in Hong Kong, it was a game of skill and calculation. But also a game of chance. Sebastian had asked all his men to learn how to play when they first arrived as part of their acclimatisation programme. But Iain argued with him, saying they should have learnt the aristocratic Go, in which there was no chance, only strategy and calculation.

Tsui was alone, standing, looking out to sea. In silhouette he seemed more strongly built and taller, straight-backed and imposing. He didn't move. No sign of the Comprador as Sebastian had expected. No doubt taking one of his characteristic catnaps. Like Churchill, he thought.

"Good afternoon, Tsui. It's Sebastian," he said to Tsui's back in his deep Maori voice.

"Come in and sit down," came the unfamiliar and abrupt reply. "What's all this about?" Tsui hated rumour and gossip, but had decided to make himself listen.

"It's the rumour mill; it's moved up a gear. I thought I should let you know. After all…" – and here Sebastian thought he would gain a few points by quoting *The Art of War* – "…is it not good to hear what your enemy is hearing?"

"Very good, Sebastian," said Tsui, beginning to relax and pace up and down. "Go on."

"Well, the word is, something very big is going on in OSM. That's been going around for some time but now they appear to be piecing things together. The China Deal is common parlance, though no one appears to know what it is. Some say it's linked to the Sinbad Fuel deal. Now there's gossip about OSM exposing the Taiwanese minister of defence. It's getting messy."

How much did he know about Li? He couldn't ask. But there was no doubt that Sebastian was an outstanding operator. Tsui decided to encourage him rather than slough him off with brusque words.

"Don't worry. We're going through a phase. It's happened before." That wasn't exactly true, but it was near enough. "Thanks, Sebastian, for bringing it to my attention. If there is any more you consider significant please let me know. You're right, no memos. Like this, face to face." Tsui held out his hand, smiling, for the dismissive handshake. Sebastian shook Tsui's hand, looking him in the eye as he continued to speak.

"There is one other thing."

"What's that?" said Tsui, his voice preoccupied already with other thoughts.

"Our workload in security and the increasing sophistication of that workload requires more manpower."

"How many people in your department?"

"Twelve, and me, thirteen." Sebastian knew to keep answers brief and to the point.

"How many more do you need?"

"Six." He might explode and he might not. It was a real need.

"Done." Their meeting ended.

* * *

The Ninja had a different name: an Anglicized one to make it easier for the expats he'd be dealing with. Jimmy Kwan. He'd been given the Macau Ferry account. OSM supplied their hydrofoils from Kawasaki Heavy Industries. He was working in the small conference room, marine design maps spread out on the table. He had to become a semi-competent go-between.

There was a soft knock at the door.

"Come in," he called.

The Eurasian secretary came in.

"A message for you, Mr Kwan. A messenger just dropped it in." He took it from her and thanked her as she turned to go. Very few people knew where he was. As the girl closed the door behind her he held the note in front of the powerful desk light. There was a single page inside. It looked like hotel stationery. Nothing else. Nevertheless he opened it cautiously with his knife and pulled out the page.

It was on Holiday Inn paper. The note was handwritten in capitals, written with the left hand by a right-handed person.

NOON, ROOM FIFTEEN FIFTEEN.

There was a chop mark in the bottom right-hand corner. He read the mark 'Orchid'. Takji's adjutant was in town.

He put the note in his pocket. He would burn it when he got back to the villa.

He decided to walk to the hotel. It was a beautiful sunny day and not too hot.

* * *

It was a small room. The adjutant sat on the bed, Kwan on the one chair. To Kwan he looked unfamiliar in a blue suit and tie. No flowing kimonos. He seemed shorter, more like a Hong Kong businessman. The adjutant did not explain himself but started right away with business, not Japanese at all.

"I don't expect you've heard – there's been nothing in the media – your sojourn was a success." The adjutant was a euphemist. Neither man spoke for a while. The adjutant continued. No praise or congratulations – that wasn't his job.

"Our client has some business in North Korea. Did you know that one of the sons lives here? He has some agents with him. Thugs really. That's about all we have on them. There are some funny things going on at their local bank, Banco Delta Asia. We need more information. You are to infiltrate his entourage. You have a free hand."

And keep me out of mischief, Kwan thought. "What sort of information?" He regretted the question as soon as he said it.

The adjutant frowned. "For example, the client heard from his own sources that two US senators and a CIA operative paid the North a visit. Our client would like to know about these sort of things before they happen." He paused, looking in his briefcase. He passed the Go piece to Kwan. "I've to give you this Chinese Whistle. They've not been compromised yet!"

Treetops, Singapore 2003

Tsui had returned today from Beijing. Cheng Cheng had been sorting his mail and dealing with as much of it as she could herself. That still left more than a dozen for him to deal with. She put them in the embossed leather mail folder and headed for his office. The door was open so she went right in. Tsui was sitting at his large desk, half spun round in his chair, gazing out of the window. He was doing nothing. It always amazed her. Compared with her hyperactive secretarial world his life seemed idle.

"Here's the mail, Tsui," she said, breaking his reverie. She had a question for him, and needed to know his mood. "Coffee?"

"Yes. And bring one for yourself."

Good, she thought. A few minutes. Efficiently she poured the coffee, which was in her anteroom, at the same time telling Jane to hold calls till she got back. She handed him his coffee and sat down in one of the leather chairs in front of the desk. She came straight to the point, as she knew he preferred.

"Julia is going to be out of Singapore for a month. She says we can use the apartment if we want a break. I'll bet she just wants somebody to keep an eye on her Cartier franchise and to make a few sales, knowing her! Can I take Ina this weekend? I've been promising her for ages."

Tsui looked at her steadily, his eyes sparkling and a smile playing around at the corners of his lips.

"Sure. Make it a long weekend. Jane can stand in for you. That's odd, though. I'm meeting her husband on Friday, with the Comprador, on *Fusion*."

"It's Mary-Lou's weekend off. Will you be all right?"

"Of course. The staff can look after me. Besides, I think Antonia will be around. She's got to revise for some exams and there's too much noise in her flat."

"Good." She got up to leave. On the way to the door she stopped. "Oh! That computer guy in security is reimaging computers this afternoon."

Tsui frowned. "Have the Comprador's nephew work alongside him today, and always from now on."

* * *

Cheng Cheng and Ina had checked into Julia's well-appointed apartment early yesterday evening. She had taken her to Neptune's for the show. With fifteen hundred seats it was the biggest Chinese restaurant in Singapore. OSM had a substantial cross-share with OUE, the ultimate owner, so they always ate there when in town. They had been given the 'quick tour' of the premises and the huge kitchen with the head chef's office six foot in the air and surrounded by glass. Ina had whispered, giggling, that she felt like a fish in a fishbowl. The food had been wonderful – unusual for such a big nightclub restaurant. The show had been colourful and the topless girls titillating at close quarters. Now Bugis Street had been closed down, night-time venues for visitors were fewer and The Island State was ever more staid: even Neptune's was closing down, but for the other Singapore reason: this building was being demolished.

When they came back to the apartment at Treetops they put mosquito lotion on each other before going down for a drink by the pool in the relative cool of the evening, surrounded by dense tropical vegetation and tall tropical trees. Their bamboo lounges close together, and on their own, they casually held hands and relaxed. They sat through two Honolulu Coolers, talking little, in tune with the insect chorus and themselves. There was no hurry; they had all weekend. They would go up to the apartment when they were both ready.

* * *

They were beginning to wake up, naked and curled sleepily around each other, when the phone rang.

"You take it! It's on your side!" Cheng Cheng said.

Ina made a cheeky face as she picked up the phone.

"Hullo."

Ina signalled that it was for her and touched her wedding ring. Ivan.

"You got the job? That's wonderful!" and she winked at Cheng Cheng. Suddenly her expression changed. First perplexed, then worried and finally agitated. She tried to warn Cheng Cheng.

"You came down on the first flight? You're downstairs now?"

She looked imploringly at Cheng Cheng. Ivan didn't know she was bisexual. Cheng Cheng was pointing at her wristwatch, then holding up ten fingers. Ina was nodding.

"OK. Come up in ten minutes. I'll have to wake up Cheng Cheng to warn her. She's in the other room."

Cheng Cheng was running her forefinger across her throat. Cut now, don't say too much. She ran into the bathroom and began collecting up her things. Ina followed her, putting on one of the bathrobes.

"OK, Ina, don't panic! We'll shift all my things into the other en suite. You can say you woke me up and I decided to take a shower, in my bathroom, of course. Later, tell him I'm going to look in on the Cartier outlet at the Hilton so that you can have this place this morning." Sa was racing around as she spoke, not bothering with a robe. She still looked good: tight and supple and brown, like a girl fifteen years younger. Ina stopped to watch her.

"Come on, keep going," said Cheng Cheng, giggling.

"Oh yes! Ivan said it was Tsui's idea to come down with the good news to surprise me. He said we should have a break before we have to move next week."

So it was Tsui's idea, thought Cheng Cheng. She would deal with him later…

Five minutes gone. She went back to Ina's room for a last check. Ina was putting on some make-up and some splashes of perfume.

"God, where's my vibrator, Ina?"

"It's under my pillow, I think."

Cheng Cheng reached across the bed, showing herself to Ina, who bit her lip.

* * *

When Sa came out of her room, showered and dressed, they were sitting in the dining alcove with a view of the treetops, nursing coffee and eating croissants with Swiss black cherry jam.

"Hullo, Ivan. Good trip down?" said Cheng Cheng, in her business voice.

"Yes thanks — "

"Coffee, Cheng Cheng?" Ina interrupted.

"Is there any green tea?"

"In teabags in the kitchen, if that's all right?" asked Ina, getting up to make it.

"That would be fine, thanks."

"I hope you don't mind me barging in on your shopping weekend. It's just that I got the job and I start in ten days. We thought – I thought we…" Ivan apologised.

"Not at all," said Cheng Cheng easily. "It's great news. Where will you be living? Shanghai?"

"No such luck. Beijing."

"Then you'll have to let Ina escape to HK each month!" and she smiled her thanks to Ina, crossing her strong legs as Ina handed her her tea. Ivan smiled and said nothing.

"I'm going to 'inspect' the Cartier outlet at the Hilton Shopping Gallery, so you can have the apartment this morning. You'll have everything you need. There's a broadband connection over there, Ivan, and a business centre next to reception should you need it, and the huge pool for the dolphin," and she grinned at Ina. "And there's a gym if you want a workout, Ivan." Cheng Cheng paused. "We could meet for lunch, if you'd like. Say at 'Sakai Sushi' in Orchard Road, the one in Wheelock Place? You can just tell the taxi driver…" Cheng Cheng stopped, sipping her tea. Steady, she thought. Sound too much like the boss.

"That's fine," replied Ivan coolly. "We'll meet you there." He turned to Ina. "We'll need to get some Singapore dollars—"

"Don't worry," butted in Sa. "Get some after lunch. Whatever you do, don't get them downstairs: their rate is lousy."

He knew that the Chinese loved to deal on 'forex', travelling an hour to get a two-cent better rate. But he felt uncomfortable with Cheng Cheng's intrusive bossiness. She felt it and got up to leave.

"I'll just get my briefcase, then I'll be off."

* * *

"My god! She likes to play the leader!" exclaimed Ivan, once the door had thudded closed behind her. "It must be interesting when she's with Tsui."

"She never leads Tsui."

How does she know that? wondered Ivan. And how does Cheng Cheng know 'Ina' means 'dolphin'? They were becoming close friends.

"Do you want to make love?"

He'd been away in China three weeks, getting close to their limit. "Let's talk first." Give her a bit more time. Then she could wash first.

"OK by me."

He sounded aggrieved. "There are actually two things, but I couldn't talk in front of Cheng Cheng. The first one is about the job with the PBC. You know all about that already, really. I'm sorry it had to be Beijing in the end; but the expat life is getting better there, they say. The specific job is developing their Sovereign Wealth Funds. I've also to give 'guidance' for their anti-money-laundering legislation."

Ina sat in the big armchair, coffee in hand, long legs curled up under her. She didn't interrupt, knowing that he would lose his single-minded train of thought.

"Tsui is all right. He seems interested in us. Sort of father figure even though he's probably younger than me." She knew but said nothing. Talking about securing the job, he started patting himself on the back, quoting Gary Player's 'The harder you work the luckier you get!' She'd heard it all before.

"But the real thing we have to discuss: you know what it's been like without any proper income and all that debt we've taken on since the Barings collapse? Well I, for one don't want to be in that position again."

Ina unsuccessfully stifled a yawn and stood up to stretch her legs, going to the window. She saw Cheng Cheng getting into a taxi. She felt happiness and yearning at the same time.

"Anyway," continued Ivan irritably, "cutting a long story short to fit your attention span," – Ina looked at him sharply – "Tsui wants me to be a consultant for him, which means…" He looked round the room furtively. Ina thought he looked absurd. "… Which means passing on information, particularly insider information, of which I'll have plenty. As a consultant he'll pay me one and a half million Hong Kong dollars per annum. He always uses Hong Kong dollars when 'buying': it sounds more! That's about—"

"I know how much US dollars that is," cut in Ina. He always treated her like some dumb blonde, which she wasn't.

"All right. All right. There'll be times you can act as courier. If you're going up and down to Honkers you might as well."

He wouldn't tell her about the payout per transaction, which would depend on the quality of the information. Sometimes, at Tsui's discretion, Tsui would place a bet on his behalf and payments would be by TCI Bearer Bonds.

"What do you think? For a rainy day?"

"How do you know we'd be paid?"

"Oh! I think we can trust Tsui; everyone does!"

"And how?"

"That's in the detail. Don't worry."

Never mind. She'd find out later.

"He wants to know by nine o'clock Monday. That's the real reason I had to come down. Don't tell Sa. In fact Tsui specifically said not to tell Sa. Doesn't want her involved, 'entangled' was his word. So is it 'Aye' or 'Nay'?"

He was a pompous ass sometimes. She wondered what the Chinese would make of him.

"Yes," Ina said, firmly and decisively.

"OK then! Damn it! You're in a bit of a mood." He changed the subject. "Tsui's good company, good value and very astute. He was warning me about corruption. He was saying that near the bottom of the food chain a favourite lead-in is 'The man with the key is not here'! But he warned that the face of corruption is changing, with over three billion new and hungry capitalists."

Mei Foo Sun Chuen, Lai Chi Kok 2004

Iain was going to be late. He should make the five-minute 'grace' period. He had taken the crowded air-conditioned express KMB from Tsim Sha Tsui to the company flats in Mei Foo: the first high-rise housing in Hong Kong, with a population of seventy thousand. About the same as a good Saturday race crowd at Shatin, he thought.

The bus was approaching the terminus. He caught a glimpse of the tree-lined pedestrian malls above the traffic, awash with people. The walkways connected all the residents to every amenity imaginable, from restaurants to schools, supermarkets, shops and doctors; from basketball courts to noodle hawkers.

OSM had bought, off the plans, the first ten floors in one of the Stage One blocks on Nassau Street. They leased nine of the floors to regular tenants. The seventh floor they had gutted on the inside to make into an odd-shaped office, to which the management company for the Stage had been persuaded to turn a blind eye. Tsui used the office space for his own personal research department. He had kept one flat as it was, as a pied-a-terre and as a secure meeting place.

They cruised into the custom-built underground terminal, the buses moving in regimented order. The noise volume of the Cantonese passengers dropped momentarily. The rumbustious locals annoyed many of his non-Asian friends, but he loved the noise. He pushed and jostled his way to the front, being sworn at light-heartedly as he went, so he could jump out as soon as the hissing door swung open. He ran for Nassau Street, no one taking any notice of another rushing *guilo*.

* * *

They were waiting for Iain while the ceiling fan circled and Tsui paced up and down, watching the clock. The flat was many dismal shades of brown, looking more like a lodging house than a home.

Tsui stopped and sat down at the round table opposite Bruce and facing the door.

"Did you see Bellatrix in her Group A race, Bruce?"

Small talk from Tsui? That must be a first. Perhaps horse-racing wasn't small talk. Luckily Iain had tipped him off.

"Yes. It was a close race." What else could he say? She'd come in second.

"Damn jockey's fault. That O'Brien thinks he knows it all. Should have brought her in 'arms and legs'. Once you show Bellatrix the whip, you're finished. She'll never take a beating like he gave her. Then there was the second place steward's enquiry into 'bumping and boring'. No, we'll let him go next year. Use one of the Australians; at least they'll ride to instructions." Tsui was still angry about the incident, which had had extensive press coverage with graphic photos. Bruce could see him control his anger, looking out at the fading light and breathing deeply. "Ah well, that's racing. How many passions can a man have, Bruce? There is loving, making money and horse-racing; and not necessarily in that order!"

* * *

The bell rang and Bruce got up to open the inside door and the steel security door on the outside to let Iain in. Tane hovered on the landing. The two young men smiled acknowledgement, moved to the table and sat down, nearer each other than to Tsui.

"Sorry I'm late," said Iain, even though he really felt he wasn't.

"You'll be late for your own funeral one day," growled Tsui, and without pausing, carried on. "I have some tangible and intangible information today. I think the efficient way is to treat this like a tutorial. Does that work for you?"

They both nodded submissively. No point in disagreeing, thought Bruce, following Iain's lead.

"First, about Asiaway. Susan Tang was in town last weekend." Iain knew that, but said nothing. He had put two agents on his payroll now. "She is recently divorced. Ian Ross – spelt the Sassenach way – is paid out. She has two Shanghainese brothers – accountants – joining her, which is satisfactory. Presently we are in twenty-two countries: sufficient critical mass to start our distribution network and to use the outlets as safe house in CD: Susan is happy with both those developments."

Tsui stopped and took a drink from his small bottle of Evian put out by the office girl before they arrived. He took out a couple of Go pieces from his pocket and played with them in his palm. Like *The Caine Mutiny*, thought Iain.

"And now, Gentlemen, a little bit of history. See what you two learnt at Melrose! Who said, 'The world will little note, nor long remember what we say here.'?"

Bruce nearly put his hand up but answered anyway.

"That's part of the Gettysburg address. Eighteen sixty-three. November nineteenth. Abe Lincoln."

"Very good. I'm impressed. Abraham, I think. Did you do American history?! An unexpectedly short and brilliant address. Though he got it wrong in three areas, one of them vital. First, the world never forgot. It is one of the most quoted historical tracts. Second, 'that this nation, under God' is clearly illogical; but we can talk of religion another day. And third, the vital one, 'government of the people, by the people, for the people' should simply read 'government for the people'. Why is that so?"

Tsui barked the question at the younger men. This time Iain answered, knowing full well the answer his father was looking for.

"In some cases the nation state will not be, will never be, ready for democracy."

"Correct." For some reason Tsui never thought it necessary to praise his son. "Which brings us neatly around to the raison d'etre of the China Deal, to which you have subscribed and which you should already know." Tsui paused for effect then growled the single word, "Governance."

Iain leant forward in his chair. Perhaps at last there would be some detail, some meat on the bones. Bruce watched his friend closely while biting a fingernail.

"We are executing a small handbook—"

"Who is the 'we'?" asked Iain aggressively. Bruce was surprised. Yet Tsui allowed the interruption. He looked exasperated, but answered evenly enough.

"A professor of International Law and National Governance."

"Would that be Professor Ewan McDonald?" asked Iain again.

"Yes, that's right. You met him once. It's a few years ago now." Tsui turned to Bruce. "He and I were at Cambridge together. At present he's in residence at the Murdoch School of Law in Perth. We're writing it together. Of course it will be published and distributed totally anonymously. It will be called *Good National Governance*. Physically it will be bound in imitation gold leather with heavily embossed red lettering, colloquially referred to as 'The Gold Book'.

"In our cells only Takji Yoshida and the Comprador will have copies supplied. Otherwise it will be sent out to all heads of states and leaders of the opposition or equivalent; and to the chiefs of the national bureaucracies, the most important mandarins. Production and distribution will be done in secrecy in Geneva. The Comprador's nephew will be responsible for putting the work on the Internet and covering his tracks. The web address 'worldwidegoldbook.com' will be printed in The Gold Book.

"That's about it for the mechanics. But what of the content? The content is absolutely critical. I am tired, and I expect most people around the world are tired, of the 'word-fests' which are the United Nations, UNESCO, the Copenhagen Consensus, the 'think tanks' of the West, G Seven, Eight, Twenty and so on *ad nauseam*. I would like your input. To give you some idea of the format we have decided on, here are the sections. When you've finished with them, carefully destroy them. Make no copies of your work."

From his inside pocket Tsui produced two four-by-six cards, neatly printed, and handed them to his young associates, who read them silently and searchingly, as a good lawyer would.

Principles of Good Governance Scorecard	
1. Free Speech	*16*
2. Property Rights	*15*
3. Rule of Law	*15*
4 .Corruption	*12*
5. Equal Opportunity (Education)	*12*
6. Micro-Credit	*10*
7. Single Flat Tax	*8*
8. Minimal Regulation	*6*
9. Small Government	*6*
	100%
Nation State's Result	*_%*

"Ewan and I worked this up when I was in Sydney last month after years of debate," said Tsui, breaking the silence in the small apartment. "I came back by Perth. We ran it for the UK and Burma, Myanmar. Very interesting: UK scored sixty-eight per cent and Myanmar nine per cent. We think that any score under twenty per cent is cause for immediate… alarm."

Bruce spoke first.

"Will it, The Gold Book, be translated into languages other than English?"

"No," replied Tsui firmly, "the recipients will be asked to do that as required. Good question. That's it. Thank you," said Tsui, standing up and looking out at the darkened balcony and the night watchman's laundry hanging on a bamboo pole.

"Please keep a check of the time you devote to TGB. Get back to me with your ideas after the weekend by noon Monday. Bruce, you go first, if you don't mind. Please take a taxi to Central. Iain, you wait a while and then go on the MTR from Mei Foo. I've got to go next door for a meeting with my research department."

Man Fat Monastery, Shatin 2004

In the calm stillness of early morning in the anteroom off the main temple Tsui sat on the highly polished wooden floor, legs crossed, arms outstretched, his hands resting on his knees, palms pointing upwards. He was meditating as he waited for the abbot.

He had arrived at daybreak with Sebastian after again climbing the steps. The temples, built in traditional Chinese way with their floating tiled roofs, broad red-painted eaves and great high doors, were surrounded by stone-paved courts and overshadowed by the sentinel and magnificent pagoda, whose top they could hardly see in the mountain-hugging early-morning mist. A monk had offered them two bowls of vegetable congee, which they accepted gratefully. Now Sebastian was outside, slowly looking round the compound.

Tsui heard some soft footfalls behind, then silence. That would be the abbot waiting for him to finish his devotions. Tsui bowed, palms clasped together, towards the hall's lesser Buddha. He stood up, turned slowly and bowed to the abbot, who bowed in return, smiling. The abbot felt no need to apologise for keeping him waiting. He knew Tsui was aware of the first rite of the day, where each monk unreservedly committed to the abbot's teaching for the day, and conversely the abbot committed to serve each monk.

The abbot had known Tsui since he was a boy and he had been his teacher. He had tried to make him understand, as a future taipan, the obligations of his position of leadership, expressed in a fundamental tenet of the religion: 'To lead is to serve'.

For now he shook Tsui by the hand, western style, and led him across the courtyard to his sparse office. The abbot wondered what was on Tsui's mind. He rarely came up to the monastery and when he did he seldom, in recent years, asked to see him. Any administrative tasks were handled by his secretarial staff on Hong Kongside. They settled on stools either side of a plain wooden desk, their drinks in antique Chinese bowls.

Tsui respected his teacher, from whom he had learnt a great deal. He respected him even more when he did not allow significant differences of opinion to interfere with their friendship, their relationship. As Tsui sipped his steaming mountain tea, watching the abbot, he realised for the first time that most of his best mainland Chinese contacts had come through the abbot and his network of secular part-time monks.

For a while they sat without talking, relaxed in each other's company, no need for pretence. Each man respected the other's authority, though in worlds apart. Tsui thought of talking about the monastery's finances, but decided against it. Besides, the office was handling that. He decided, more or less, to start at the beginning.

"My good Abbot, I am embarking on a wild enterprise!" he began.

"When was it not so?" responded the abbot in his deep, resonant voice, chuckling.

"Yes," replied Tsui, smiling unusually broadly, other ventures flashing through his mind. "But this one is the most ambitious by far. So much so that I cannot discuss it with you for your own good. But I still need your help."

The abbot did not speak. His tranquil large eyes studied Tsui's face and then moved away to gaze at the hillside trees that surrounded the temples and the pagoda. The sun was beginning to break through. After a long pause and a glance down into his half full teacup the abbot looked up into Tsui's eyes.

"Let me ask two questions. First, how will this 'enterprise' affect the people closest to you?"

"Only the ones who have volunteered of their own free will."

"And subject, as they would be, to your own considerable persuasive power," said the abbot, not smiling now.

"Yes, I suppose so…. Anyway, those people will be affected by having to work in considerable secrecy and at considerable personal risk. But that will be limited to the restricted knowledge each one has of the venture, apart from the Comprador. Each individual will be handsomely rewarded." He was going to add "or their heirs if needs be", but decided against it in case he alarmed the abbot.

"How is the Comprador?" mused the abbot, speaking quietly, gently like a horse whisperer. He continued in his normal voice, not waiting for a reply. "Secondly, how might it affect the larger OSM family?"

"Absolutely in no way at all."

The abbot was surprised and said so. "That's unusual. Look back. I think the only time you went on your own was with your elder brother when you were lads: the infamous 'Quail Egg Company'. You two nearly got it listed! So you're sure OSM is not involved?"

"No. In fact Tsui Wai Kwok is handling nearly all the day-to-day business already," Tsui said emphatically.

The abbot sipped his warm tea. "How can I help?"

"If things go wrong, terribly wrong, I will need a sanctuary, a place to hide. I am arranging this now so I have an exit even in the worst situation. Once arranged, I will only aim for a positive outcome."

The abbot did not hesitate.

"Of course that is possible because, if Tsui is involved, the endeavour will not be evil. You are a good and generous man. However Man Fat is no longer a place of sanctuary. Since the takeover, the government is much more interested in our activities and pushes tourism more and more. No, much better to go to Pat Sin Leng, where there is a hamlet with a forgotten retreat and loyal people."

* * *

As a courtesy as much as anything else Tsui went to the main temple on the way out and prayed, though his thoughts kept wandering. Someone behind him started to use the Daoist fortune sticks, the rhythmic sound of the modified incense sticks in a bamboo cylinder filling the hall. He smiled to himself as he recalled his amah, a devout believer, teaching him how to use them: "Hold the cylinder with both hands at a slight angle and shake them till one falls out." She showed him how to do it, and when one fell to the ground she hurried to her favourite monk, who connected the numbered stick to one of the poems, which he interpreted. It was the most ancient method of fortune telling which, in spite of his western ways, Tsui followed with one small change: he asked his interpreter to tell him only the good news.

Tsui decided to use them today. After shaking the cylinder and retrieving his single stick, number eleven, he turned to find the abbot waiting for him. He had always been their family fortune-teller, respected as a management consultant in the East, the risk of decision making being taken outside family or company. Tsui bowed and handed the bamboo stick to him. As he did so, he thought he saw a flicker of concern in the abbot's eyes.

LAIRD HOUSE, THE PEAK
2004

Tsui was working on Sunday on a fax to the Comprador in his second office at Laird House. He paused to think, looking out of the window at the glorious autumn sunshine. His thoughts drifted to Kawhia and his brood mares and freer, happy times.

His office looked out at the heavy wrought iron gate set in a high cream stone wall and the guard house euphemistically called 'Reception'. From his vantage point he could see all the comings and goings.

Takji should arrive in half an hour. He returned to his draft. The Comprador had voiced concern that NGOs and the like, with their vast lobbying power, would object to their omission in The Gold Book of health and nutrition. Tsui was saying that when the nine points were implemented, good nutrition and good health would follow automatically and in direct proportion to their effective execution. Satisfied, Tsui encrypted his plain text and sent the fax to the the Comprador in Sai Kung. He had the key.

Tsui had started to shred his notes and the originals, secure in the knowledge that shredded material was incinerated twice a day, when there was a confident knock on the oak door.

"Just a minute…. Come in."

Antonia came bursting in. She was dressed for squash in white with a white headband. She dropped her bag and racquet by the door and crossed the small room to peck Tsui on the cheek. She smelt fresh and young.

"I'm off up to the cricket club to play squash. Want to come and watch us?" she said, smiling her happy smile. "We could have lunch afterwards?" Before he could reply Antonia added cheekily, "My shout!"

He smiled. "I'd love to, but I've got a meeting." He'd have to get her to leave quickly. He didn't want her to meet Takji.

"You work too hard, Tsui."

"Another time," he said patting her forearm. "You'd better get going; you'll miss your start time. Who are you playing?"

"One of my flatmates."

"Take one of the cars; there's one at the front door. I'll call down. Play well."

"Thanks, Tsui. Bye."

She spun around, spinning her miniskirt. At the door she bent over to pick up her things, showing off her white sports briefs. M&S probably, he thought.

* * *

At the Hong Kong MTR station the train stopped imperceptibly and the doors slid open. Takji allowed himself to be swept along with the surge of passengers arriving from the airport. Shaking free of the crush he headed for his exit; he was meeting Tane, who would be Takji's minder on this short trip. Thoughtful of Tsui, but of course it worked both ways.

Takji was in his marketing-executive-of-their-sweet-factory role. He wore a blue suit, white shirt and maroon tie. Scuffed black shoes. He carried his cheap briefcase and a large leather shoulder bag. Being fit and agile for his age the bags did not slow him down as he strode across the concourse on his way to the Exchange Square's Starbucks franchise. Tsui had told him that in Hong Kong Starbucks was in a joint venture with Maxim's, and OSM had a part of Maxim's. He slowed down as he came in the wide entrance so he wasn't noticed and had more time to observe.

He saw Tane hold up his hand and get up to leave. They weren't going to eat together. Tane would have paid and tipped already so they could leave at once. They acknowledged each other with eye contact, starting to walk together towards the General Post Office, chatting, as other expats, about the weather. At the post office they took a taxi to the Peak tram terminus, catching a departing tram. Starting the steep ascent, they were pushed back into the wooden seats, laughing. They talked loudly about the spectacular views of Central and Hong Kong like any other businessman-tourists. They passed close to tropical vegetation and the waistline of tall buildings. Reaching its destination, the funicular railway stopped with a slight judder and the girls on a school trip squealed.

The two businessmen avoided the Peak shopping malls and crowds and began walking along Lugard Road till they had gone round the first two bends. Tane looked around and, seeing no one, disappeared down an overgrown track. Takji followed without a word. The track ran down the hillside at a steep angle. About ten yards in there were two signs which had been kept clear of undergrowth which said, in Chinese and English, 'Private Road, No Entry' and 'Danger, Falling Rocks'. After about two hundred yards they came to a sharp right turn and the end of the track, which was straddled by an old and narrow garage painted in peeling grey paint. This was where they kept the armoured Land Rover, ordered by Tsui's father during the Sixty-seven Riots. Tane unlocked the small pedestrian door, stepped over the entrance, ducking his head and beckoning Takji to follow. He locked the door behind them and switched on the strip lights. Unlike its surroundings, the Land Rover was perfectly maintained and washed.

The two men remained silent, squeezing quietly between vehicle and wall. At the far end of the garage Tane opened a hidden panel leading them into a dimly lit corridor which echoed their quiet footfalls. Their way was blocked again by a false wall. Tane walked over to it and used a concealed wide-angle peephole to make sure that the billiard room next door was empty. As they came out into relatively fresh air Takji took a few deep breaths and brushed down his suit, as Tane reached back inside and switched off the lights, closing the partition behind him. He smiled at Takji.

"Are you all right?"

"Fine. Thanks," replied Takji.

Tane had a lot of respect for Takji and liked him. For example, he had insisted on carrying his own bags today. But he knew he didn't talk much so he simply kept on leading him, out of the spacious basement billiard room, and up the servants' staircase to Tsui's office door. He knocked and waited.

"Come in."

As they went in Tsui was walking towards them, hand outstretched to Takji. They shook hands and bowed, Tsui looking slightly incongruous in his loose-fitting tracksuit and sneakers.

"Welcome, Takji. Good morning," and, looking over Takji's shoulder, "that will be all, Tane, thank you."

Tsui waved his hand to the upright chair on the other side of his weekend desk. "Have a seat. Tea?" He filled two colourful highly glazed Japanese cups from the tall vacuum jug of green tea on the desk extension beside him. Tsui had already adjusted the blinds to cut out the glare and any prying eyes or cameras.

"What did you think of our taipan's clandestine entrance, Takji?" Tsui asked, grinning like a schoolboy.

"Interesting," said the Ninja, sitting upright but relaxed in his chair.

"It's seen some fun and games in its time! It's not intended for any serious subterfuge, but it can be useful, like today. It's a very well-kept and forgotten secret. My great-grandfather had it made for his paramours at the suggestion of the comprador of the day, so the tale goes."

Yoshida smiled understandingly. Next he cleared his throat, a mannerism Tsui had learnt meant he was ready to talk business. Always surprising, thought Tsui. Usually the Japanese preferred a long preamble and once in negotiations, lengthy debate of the smallest detail. He smiled as he recalled once talking about one US cent on a warehouse in-and-out charge in Osaka for three days and through one small earthquake.

"I thought it best to report face to face," Takji began.

"I agree," replied Tsui.

"Your new man has been groomed, since passing the highest level set by the Examination Yuan, for the Defence Ministry. As you know, he is now in the upper echelons, in a position of extreme influence. He is noticeable for being inconspicuous, a conformist, which makes him ideal for your purpose. He has a regulation four-member family, with a standard house with a standard mortgage and a modest departmental car. Even his secretary is plain and unassuming.

"After a month of observation, nothing. Except one day, in a conversation with his secretary, his only confidante if even she was that, he mentioned the delivery of one B-2 Spirit and how the air force mechanics, after the handover, had found a sophisticated homing device. Apparently the Americans wanted to know where their plane was heading."

"Excellent, Takji."

They talked about strategy for the first two jobs till the light was fading. Yoshida was staying the night, using the anteroom in Tsui's suite. Tane would be working as their butler tonight. As they stood to go upstairs for their evening meal Tsui reached into a desk drawer and brought out a small giftwrapped package. He handed it to Takji.

"Your copy of The Gold Book. Some bedtime reading for you. It's being distributed now. In Myanmar it will be sent to the senior general and to Aung San Suu Kyi."

Shiga Heights, Japan 2005 Onwards

"Good morning!" Takji addressed the small group. They were sitting at a large round table, more practical than on the floor, with maps and plans to look at, facing a podium and a stage surrounded by modern audiovisual equipment. The conference room was hidden in the training basement of the shrine, soundproof and windowless, with its own air-conditioning unit. Because there were no windows they were unable to enjoy, as they they might through Shintoism, the beauty of spring in the valley with everything coming to life, the streams running and gurgling again, the sacred waterfall crashing to the ground and the birds nesting in budding shrubs and trees. Their environment was for security and concentration.

Takji felt like their instructor. He was standing a little away from the table so they could all see him easily. Six specialists had joined him for the morning meeting: the head of research; two young monks who were sub-contractors at Microsoft; two from the lab – one a microbiologist trained at Tokyo University of Science; and one of his own Ninjas, Kazuki Ichikawa, the team leader.

"Good Morning," he said again as they settled down, files and papers in front of them. No drinks on the table. They all wore their working full-length red robes. "Let's get started. We have a lot to cover this morning. You will have gathered that our client has work for us in Burma. You have all had for a week the comprehensive six-hundred-page 'Country Report' prepared by Research. Makes the EIU's country profiles seem like a high school thesis! Thank you," and Takji bowed to the head of research. "Particularly interesting are the bits on the ethnic groups; we need that information.

"Kazuki Ichikawa is to be the team leader for this project. He and I will go to my office…" – he waved his hand imperially to his door at the end of the room – "…and talk with you, speciality by speciality. Please come back here when we have finished, and wait so that, if there are any more questions, we can recall you. Finally, as usual, no discussion amongst yourselves. Let us begin."

Takji beckoned Ichikawa and started walking to his office. He opened the door, standing back with a small bow and letting the handsome young Ninja go in first. This small gesture elevated the team leader in the eyes of the watchers.

Yoshida's office was frugal, the furnishings contemporary. Everything was neat and in its place. The dominant colour was grey, even in the well-lit picture of the shrine in winter. The only colour came from the focal point: a bright yellow-and-green jasmine ikebana arranged by a miko in an alcove in the wall next to the desk. Wherever you sat you could see it. The office was filled with its gently pervading scent.

* * *

The others had left, having made their reports and having answered questions. They had had a late lunch served at the round table, with a little sake. Now Takji and Kazuki were back in the office to formalise their strategies and outline plans.

"Our client wants to improve state governance, you know, 'government *for* the people'. We don't have to agree with our clients to work for them, but in this case I do. So much easier when it's like that. And Burma, with its fifty-million persecuted population is a prime example. Military rule by the generals since nineteen sixty-two has steadily become worse, with suppression of all kinds, depriving the people of even basic human needs and rights. Even the Buddhist monks are now claiming that 'the government is the enemy of the people'. The people themselves are distraught and humiliated. I read of one taxi driver talking to an undercover BBC correspondent: 'I hate the people who run my country. My hatred of the government knows no bounds.' Even the opposition leader Aung San Sun Kyi, 'The Lady', is impotent. So there it is. One of our client's mantras sums it up: 'To have peace you must have positive force.'

"We have contacts..." – through the Comprador, thought Takji – "...with the Karen National Union, or KNU, in the mountainous refugee camps in Thailand, a few miles from the border with Burma. The generals have been targeting the ethnic minorities, even in the camps in Thailand, but the KNU refuses to sign a peace accord which ties them in to trafficking in heroin for the government. At any rate two young women have been recruited as mercenaries for us: Burmese nationals who joined the ethnic minority group KNU from university as their only hope for freedom. You will train them.

"But first things first. Let's look at your exits." Ichikawa said nothing but sat up and adjusted his spiral notebook, pencil in hand. Takji cleared his throat and took a drink of tea before continuing. "The client and I have agreed that you will not enter Burma. You will work out of Chiang Mai."

"With respect, Yoshida-san, I don't agree. I always —"

"Ichikawa," interrupted Takji vigorously, "this is not a discussion but a final decision. I am aware that you consider it possible to move around northern Burma as one of the North Korean refugees. The risks are too great. So for your exit you will take an ordinary commercial flight, business class, to Hong Kong, then the ferry down to Macau for a three-month cooling off period at the villa. Minimal risk.

"For the girls it will be more challenging. Fortunately they are already active in clandestine operations. After they have been to see you in Chiang Mai for briefing about the product and the plan – they are totally dedicated to success – they will return to the camps before crossing back over the border." Takji was glad of the CW in his pocket. Even so he tried to be as vague as he could. "The eldest girl has a special general already. During the move of the government from Rangoon north to a remote greenfield site near Pyinmana, surrounded by mountain jungle and startled locals, her general told her to 'get lost' for a few months till things settled down. When she goes back she will officially join the entertainment department on the base. From there she will encourage her general to help get her young cousin into, not entertainment, but mess catering. She may have to offer her cousin to him personally to swing the deal. Then the cousin will have to work her way in, to become accepted.

"The exit begins. First, and critically important, they will have to get a weekend pass to Rangoon through their general. Once they have that they can go active. You'll recall the liquid biological agent has a twelve-hour minimum incubation period. In effect that gives them twelve hours to exit. That leaves them two hours at the Pyinmana end, eight hours on the train and two hours in Rangoon. Probably much longer: incubation is more usually twenty-four hours or longer and the early symptoms are the same as a cold. They will rendezvous with some KNU backers, who will take them to the fishing fleet, where one has been bribed handsomely: quarter now, three-quarters on his return, and fuel. Once in international waters they'll be met by a speed launch…" – one of OSM's, thought Takji, manned by some of the Comprador's pirates – "…which will head south-west to Port Blair on the Andaman Islands. Our man will meet them and escort the girls to the small airport and a private jet…" – OSM again – "…which has clearance to fly direct to Chiang Mai. The young ladies…" – Takji used the words intentionally – "… want to get back to the camps and action as soon as possible.

"Their alternate exit is more challenging. Now the government has moved up to Pyinmana it is two hundred miles of hilly jungle to their usual crossing point near the Thai multiracial border town of Mae Sot. With the military active in the area and few of the villagers of their ethnic group there whom they can absolutely trust, that exit would be much more testing. Another reason why the weekend pass is so critical. From Yangon it is much easier and quicker to reach Mae Sot, if they have to use their alternate.

"You will only have contact with our man who is working as a Japanese tour guide. Use our supplied sat phones minimally, and our latest codes. This Ninja is our contact with the KNU." Takji stopped talking. He had been talking for a long time, which was unusual for him, but always necessary at the planning stage. "Let's take a break, Ishikawa-san." Again he showed him respect. "We've been at it all day. We'll walk through the garden; it is beautiful this time of year and full of life. When we come back we can attend to any questions you might have…"

* * *

The grey river gravel crunched under their feet as the two tall men, in flowing robes teased by the spring breeze, strolled through the manicured gardens.

Takji still had his CW on in his pocket. He was always careful. *In Cavendum Salus*. One small lapse in attention to detail could mean the end. He spoke again, quietly.

"Kazuki. Our microbiologist, like his peers, tends to convolute his presentations! Let me recap what he had to say. The liquid biological agent, which is clear and odourless, is made from the virulent Ames strain and presented in aerosol form. A respiratory attack has an eighty-per-cent fatality rate, and the vaccine has a ninety-point-two-five efficacy rate. The girls have been vaccinated and they know the risks. They are proud to take them. The incubation period is at least twelve hours and it is not contagious.

"Personnel working in a sprayed room do not notice the fine aerosol hanging in the room around them. Most satisfactory."

Holiday Inn, Chiang Mai, Thailand

He had taken the flight direct from Japan to Bangkok and then on to Chiang Mai. At the airport he had picked up a taxi in to the city centre and on to the Holiday Inn close by, a crowded, mid-range hotel where no one would pay them any attention. Ichikawa was travelling for their wagashi confectionery factory. It was an excellent cover. He had actual appointments set up with retailers, the product was first-rate and there was absolutely no contact with the shrine, apart from the occasional work of part-time reps.

He had the first evening to himself except for a brief meeting with a leader of a Japanese tour group who phoned from the lobby and came up to the room to deliver a small giftwrapped package. The next day he made some successful calls. He came back to the hotel, childishly pleased with the orders.

In his small room he went through his training and meditation regime before washing and ordering his evening meal through room service. The girls would be here at nine thirty.

* * *

The phone rang on time.

"This is Mary. I have Susan."

"Is it raining outside?"

"Of course. It's the monsoon season, you know, Sir." The right answer, down to the 'Sir'.

"Good. Make sure you let one of the bell-boys know you're entertaining me tonight. Something so normal, they'll lose interest in us. Come on up. Room four twenty. The door will be open."

"Five minutes."

He pushed his meal trolley out into the corridor. No one about. Coming back in, he arranged the two small armchairs and the deskchair around the coffee table. The green tea he had made up and some of his samples he had arranged on the narrow dressing table in front of the smoked-glass wall mirror, which he had checked. He went into the bathroom and sprayed himself with 'Allure', something he would never do at the shrine. He heard the door handle and turned round to see it turning. Slowly the door opened and the two girls slipped into the room, smiling.

They looked younger than he expected. Perhaps it was the full-length colourful sarongs they both wore, accentuating their height, their seductiveness and their appearance of innocence. By contrast they wore plain-coloured blouses down to the waist, one fawn and one blue. They were slim and petite, almost too thin, Kazuki thought. Yet they moved effortlessly to the armchairs he pointed out and sat down, gracefully crossing their legs and putting their large rattan shoulder bags on the floor beside them.

"Some tea?" Kazuki spoke softly; he knew where these girls had come from.

"Oh! no," said the young one, getting up and going to the tea. "Me do!"

He sat down, his dark eyes smiling. For once he was a little lost for words. Normal pleasantries: "Was the trip good?", "How's the weather back home?" and so on seemed frivolous when he knew that the girls had struggled north for a week from their refugee camp near Mae Sot avoiding police, Thai military and Burmese spies; with little money for food, water and buses. They had changed near the hotel in a dirty public toilet, using their guide as a lookout.

"Would you like to eat something?" He had noticed that his wagashi had gone.

"Yes please," the elder said without hesitation, "a double serve each of Singapore rice." More an order than a request, thought Kazuki, smiling to himself. No doubt who the boss was here! He rang room service again, then turned back to the girls.

"You must be Mary?"

"I am," said the eldest, "and this is Susan. We're cousins."

"Fine." He knew that part already. "Listen; when room service comes we'll have to pretend. You know, a 'love nest', a threesome."

"All right, we understand. I'll go into the shower room and come out when they here. Better get ready." She left them, closing the bathroom door quietly behind her.

Her younger cousin did not hesitate, sitting easily on his lap, her hard, firm buttocks pressing down on him. With assurance and a smile she began to unbutton her blouse. He noticed her brown breasts and black nipples peeking out and looked away.

"It's all right," Susan reassured him. "It's all in the day's work," and she added in a more subdued manner, "you know, it's for our cause."

Kazuki felt himself becoming aroused so started asking questions, any questions, to keep his mind on business. Control of the mind, he scolded himself.

"Where do you cross the border?" She may not tell him, thought Yazuki.

"Like most people, unless they want to go to China, near Mae Sot. You know, where the Friendship Bridge is. A few go over the bridge during the day, but the busy place is the river underneath at night. Upstream and downstream there is smuggling and illegal crossings in makeshift ferries. The Thai soldiers try to send them back in a half-hearted way; the Burmese don't worry about people coming in, unless they think they are Ethnic Revolutionaries."

Susan was talking now. She had said little before with Mary around. She obviously trusted him; too quickly, he thought.

"We were in the hill camp called Huay Kaloke at first. Cut out of the jungle. Seven thousand women and children. Little water. The Burmese military raided the place. Rape and murder. They burnt all the huts down. The KNU got us out fifteen minutes before enemy arrived."

"How do the generals keep control?" Though he had a fair idea.

"They have a stranglehold on the economy. Cronyism, monopolies and corruption. They have a murderous military backed up by a brutish paramilitary and local thugs. They rule by fear, and by fortune-tellers. Evil government."

She was smart. She knew a thing or two about the enemy, reflected Kazuki.

There was a hurried knock on the door; the monsoon rains always made room service busy. Susan jumped and turned to the door, startled. Then he felt her body relax as if by conscious effort.

"Come in!" he called out, projecting his voice like a military commander.

The waiter fixed the door open and wheeled in the trolley with the Singapore rice, a large dish of bok choy, some fresh fruit and tea.

"Good evening, Sir, Ma'am."

Susan leant forward to take a banana. The waiter was so distracted he nearly forgot to wait for his tip. As he did so Mary came dripping naked out of the bathroom, a towel in her hand. She stopped in the hallway.

"Oops! Sorry!" Slowly she covered herself. "Good evening; that's quick!"

The waiter had to get past her on his way to the door.

"Excuse me, Ma'am." As she moved aside the towel fell apart, up to her hip.

"See we're not disturbed!" Kazuki called after him. As he closed the door the waiter hung up the snooze sign, smiling to himself as he decided that there wouldn't be much sleep in that room tonight.

"Well done," said Kazuki, standing up, picking Susan up as he did so. "Maybe a bit too much, Mary."

"Not at all," she retorted. "In a hotel like this that's how it is if you want to make an impression." She walked off to the bathroom and returned, wrapped up in one of the hotel's cotton bathrobes.

"Please eat." The waiter had uncovered the dishes. "It will get cold."

"You sound like my mother, Mr Ishikawa," Susan giggled. So she knew his name, well, his name for this venture. Mary gave her a sharp look. They sat down on the end of one of the double beds and pulled the trolley towards them, starting hungrily to eat their rice. Kazuki helped himself to some tea before Susan could protest.

"I ate earlier," he said. "Enjoy your meal. I'll talk a little. No planning or training tonight. You need to rest up. Tomorrow is Saturday. I have the weekend off from my 'selling job'. Morning we'll work in the room here; housekeeping will leave us alone. In late afternoon we'll pick up your Thai passports after they've had time to sort out your photos."

Kazuki went to his wardrobe and brought out an unopened bottle of Remy Martin. He had brought it at duty free when he arrived. He poured three generous shots into the hotel glasses.

"Here, have a nightcap. No balloons, sorry."

* * *

He watched the local news as the girls showered. They were happy and sleepy after the cognac. Mary, more relaxed now, had told him, "We haven't had such comfort since we left Rangoon nearly two years ago. It's lovely. I almost feel guilty."

It was getting late. They took one of the double beds, leaving the one he'd been using for him. As he got into bed, Kazuki told himself again that there was no way he would become emotionally involved on such a mission: that was rule number one. Eventually he dozed, then woke again to the secretive sounds of the girls caressing each other. In the dark his training made it easy for him to pick out the gentle rhythmic movement of their bodies. Suddenly there came a stifled orgasmic squeal. That was Susan, thought Kazuki, smiling and falling asleep to the hum of the air-conditioning.

* * *

At dawn, as the girls woke up, they watched from their bed as Kazuki went through his vigorous exercise. Later they joined him and he taught them some simple Shinto meditation derived from Taoism.

Once the hotel had become alive again the girls had ordered full English breakfast while Kazuki had plain porridge, the nearest to his usual congee. The waiter, a different one on a different shift, was disappointed to only hear the girls washing through the half-open bathroom door.

Unnoticed, Kazuki watched them as they ate, now in denim shorts and T-shirts, Susan's of Che Guevara, and barefoot. Their file, which Yoshida had suggested he leave in Japan, had told him they had been lucky enough to go to Yangon University, unhappily a shadow of its former self. There they had studied geology because the department had taken research trips out of the city up to the rivers and the mountains. The more he was with them the more he realised, sometimes contrary to outward appearances, how smart they were, and experienced. After breakfast he pushed the trolley out, checked the 'Do Not Disturb' sign and, automatically, the empty corridor. Back inside he called housekeeping and told them that they were sleeping in and did not need their room done today; they were always glad to hear that. Kazuki settled down at the desk, leaving the armchairs for the girls. Surreptitiously he reached into his kimono sleeve and switched on his CW.

"Let's begin."

* * *

It had gone well. There had been little disagreement about the operation and the Burmese had added some important detail. They would go back across the border and report their return to the Karen, but not the operation. They would go back to Yangon in the usual way, where Mary would contact her general and head back to the new capital to join the new entertainment department. Once settled in she would persuade her general – who was married with children – to get her sister into officer catering and probably into a threesome.

"How about the aerosol?" Susan asked, serious at last.

"The yuppie room freshener that 'lasts all day and is a disinfectant as well' is new in Thailand. It will be imported through Mae Sot by the KNU and deviously sold on to the military Q Department. Susan, you have the job of getting your supervisor to order some as a 'must have' for the senior officers' meeting rooms, and his kickback. After that it is a matter of you spraying each morning in your rubber gloves – they all wear them – for a long enough time for others to get used to the routine. And enough time for you, both of you, to prearrange your exits. We'll cover your exits after lunch."

They had been sitting forwards in their chairs, listening, attentive. Mary asked the main question.

"What about the 'real' aerosol?"

Kazuki nodded but did not answer, instead getting up and going to the drawer under the TV. He brought out the giftwrapped parcel which had been delivered to him. Undoing the ribbon and pushing off the paper, he spoke severely to get their full attention.

"This is a scrious weapon. Don't be fooled by its appearance," and Kazuki pulled out of the tissue paper a large pink dildo. The girls giggled, particularly Susan, holding their hands over their mouths, feigning embarrassment. Kazuki continued, ignoring their reaction, as if he were talking about an AK-47. "You press the tip firmly and at the same time turn the head clockwise, like this. You see, the joining seam is all but invisible to the naked eye." He gently shook out the contents, an aerosol identical to the Thai deodorizer, onto the bed. There is a safety catch right here," and he showed them both. Kazuki had also had the vaccine.

Mary reached over and picked it up and put it together again. She smiled. "Very good."

"Susan, you will have to carry the complete dildo over the border and, on the day of the attack, into work in your usual shoulder sack. At all other times have the dildo with your other toys; don't hide it. If you don't have any toys with you now, we'll buy some this afternoon…"

Office of K. K. Chen Ltd, Tsim Sha Tsui

When it wasn't too hot he enjoyed the walk up from Star Ferry to the Comprador's office in Haiphong Road. He remembered first coming, when he was about seven, with his amah and their driver. She had insisted on walking, lecturing, "The exercise will do you good, Master Iain." He also remembered the meeting with the Comprador, this for the first time, how he had been frightened of the tall, imperious Chinaman, and initially half hiding behind his amah.

Today he passed the old, weatherbeaten man in Salisbury Road still making elegant bamboo grasshoppers, sheltering from the sun under a large black umbrella. He used his umbrella to display his work, the light-coloured bamboo contrasting against the black. Iain wondered if it could possibly be the same old man.

He cut down the side of the Peninsular into Hankow Road which, surprisingly, had hardly changed except for a few modest office blocks squeezed between the restaurants. The street was always busy with the ebb and flow of the customers to the well-priced Chinese and Malaysian establishments, some with tables on the footpath, some doing their butchery and dish washing there. As he strolled past one restaurant he stopped to watch a kitchen hand skin a snake alive. He walked on, looking, listening and smelling. He loved crowded Tsim Sha Tsui, which to him, before Central and all the other glitzy shopping areas, was the heart of Hong Kong.

He had arrived early for his appointment because he wanted to escape and think, away from phones, computers, secretaries and interruptions from Tsui. On purpose he had not asked Tane to walk with him; he was about fifty yards behind. He came out of Hankow Road at the T-intersection with Haiphong Road and all the street sellers, buying some stir-fried mein noodles and walking across the road up the steep entrance to Kowloon Park, memories flooding back. When he was young the thirty-acre park had been one huge adventure playground where his young trainee amah spent the hours chasing after him. In his teens he had walked his first 'girlfriend' through the winding wooded paths. He found his favourite bench underneath an arbour near the elderly men airing their parakeets and finches in elaborate bamboo cages. The birds' singing was beautiful but imprisoned. Sometimes it made him happy, and some days sad.

He sat down and, breaking apart the wooden disposable chopsticks, started eating his noodles. He felt happy with himself and with the world, more so since the family, with the help of Uncle Alexander, had accepted Suk Soon and he was able to see her frequently. Work too had improved. He had escaped from the frenetic dealing room to become what Tsui called 'ambassador-at-large' for OSM, going from company to company and country to country, sorting out challenges and motivating management. He knew he was mature for his age. He felt in control of his office, enjoying his work and getting results.

One thing puzzled him: the Comprador had become much more attentive. As well as OSM Iain now spent a lot of time on K. K. Chen business. In fact some days he wasn't sure who he worked for. The Comprador was giving him information in a most un-Chinese way. For instance, last week he had told him that each of the nine hundred workers at K. K. Chen produced for him five times the revenue of each OSM employee and with much less overheads. If this was accurate it was an incredible statistic and it could be argued that the Comprador was working more for his own benefit than for OSM's – a constant and historical fear of the hongs and their taipans. "Getting too big for their boots," they would mutter into their after-dinner drinks. But why had he told him?

* * *

He put his rubbish in the covered bin and started back to the K. K. Chen office. The contrast with OSM in Wanchai was remarkable. At OSM there was discreet opulence which, to those who knew, spoke of serious wealth. K. K. Chen, on the other hand, stood out as a working office of open plan floors with rows of plastic-topped desks and a common coffee station. The only nod towards the twenty-first century was the latest computer, with software to match, in front of each employee.

Reception was the only part that had been 'modernised'. To nineteen-seventy standards. Stone rampant lions stood either side of the automatic smoked glass doors. As Iain walked in he was struck by a blast of cold air from the overhead air-con unit. Straight ahead, as one would predict, was the main reception desk with two satellite desks on either side. The girl was getting up and smiling at him in recognition. Behind her, the company name stood out in bold gold letters set out on Chinese red. Her black cheongsam looked severe beside the bold colours.

"Good afternoon, Mr Iain. The Comprador is expecting you." She walked across to the lifts and pressed the 'up' button. As the door opened she ushered Iain in, then followed herself. Leisurely and noisily the lift climbed to the seventh floor – the top floor – the small but clean ceiling fan gyrating slowly. Iain had time to enjoy her perfume, her thighs and tight bottom. She simply smiled at him as the lift stopped, escorting him into the Comprador's office.

The Comprador was on the phone. He waved Iain in and to a pair of hardbacked court chairs. The receptionist bowed and left, closing the door quietly.

The Comprador's office was sparse and functional. Nothing unnecessary. He had all that he needed to run his organisation within reach of his desk. The Feng Shui expert had put his office at the east end of the building, with all the seventh floor in front of him and a view of the treetops of Kowloon Park through the window on his right. Before he had moved to Sai Kung he had used the seventh floor as his accommodation, and the simple roof garden for Tai Chi. Now, except for his office and a bedroom he had kept for when he worked late, the seventh floor had been made over to his executives and the roof into a driving range.

There was a restrained knock at the door and the Comprador's nephew came in. The phone call was ending. It had been in Fukien, not one of Iain's stronger dialects, or one of his favourites after all the teasing at Melrose.

Iain was surprised that the nephew was joining them; he thought he was exclusively a 'star' of IT.

"Good afternoon, Iain," said the Comprador. The nephew, who had settled down on the leather sofa against the wall, smiled briefly at Iain, saying nothing. "I expect you've already heard my nephew has become a vice-president." How the Chinese were taking up the American business model, thought Iain. "He has grown into my right-hand man, my heir apparent." Of course he hadn't heard. But why was he being told now? He was sure that Tsui didn't know either. That was more worrying.

Iain thought he should say something in reply.

"Congratulations," came out rather lamely.

The Comprador interrupted, taking control again. No time for tea and small talk like in the old days, or when on the mainland.

"We have heard that you are going to meet the Shanghai brothers and visit the Asiaway people in Europe."

"Yes. Next week actually," he added, probably unnecessarily.

"And you're seeing some of your old Melrose College friends."

How did he know that? He was in fact, at Tsui's request, making contact with a particular OMA, Hills-Bennett, who was in MI6. Iain didn't reply.

"Well, Iain," the Comprador continued after a long pause, "might I ask you to, in a subtle and circumspect way without drawing attention to yourself, check out the underlying distribution network provided by the Asiaway chain? It's been operative since June. The quality control of the product has proved it most successful."

Old hashish chocolate chip cookies, thought Iain.

Foreign Correspondents' Club, Central

Katla was down from Shanghai for a few days doing a bit on the democratisation or otherwise of Legco. She was fit and well, thought Bruce, looking at her long blond hair cascading down the back of her denim jacket. Friday early evening and they had met for a drink at the main bar of the Foreign Correspondents' Club. They had walked in together and were met almost at once by Vimana and Tony Parker. Being Friday they could only find seats for the girls as they settled down in their favourite corner, the men standing facing them, backs to the crowd, drinks in hand. Vimana started talking earnestly to Katla, bringing her up to date on local gossip, patting her knee for emphasis. No doubt part of the gossip would involve herself and Parker being an 'item', smiled Bruce; she was certainly spreading it around. She was overexcited and overdressed in one of her long Indian dresses, her conversation gushing. Katla leant back, a little defensively. Tony interrupted in his booming voice and usual banter.

"You know what the traders on the floor are saying beloved OSM stands for?" He asked Bruce and anyone else who could hear.

"No," said Bruce, without considering. Monosyllabic was best with Tony. Like Etonians he was fine one on one; but in a crowd of his peers he was obnoxious. Tony paused for effect.

"Omnipotent Sex Machine! A nod towards the old man!"

Some of the listeners smiled and giggled and went back to their drinks. They were used to Tony on Friday night.

"What's news?" Tony continued, using one of the club's well-worn greetings. He must have had a few before he got here, thought Bruce.

"There's talk that China's sort of 'Sovereign Wealth Fund' is going to be buying huge chunks of foreign assets," said Bruce, striking out for some middle ground.

"Oh, come on, Mr Bruce! That's boring old news! Give us something with a bit more bite. For instance, I've just got a new domestic helper; she's a sweetie. She's supposed to be thirty-nine from Cebu. Been up here for twelve years this year. Sending her money back home to feed and school the children. Sees them once a year, at Christmas, if she's lucky. An economic refugee. Now there's a human interest story. Of course you two don't have a deadline; it's only Katla and me." He laughed for no real reason and drank, the ice clinking in his near-empty glass.

"She's an interesting lady," Tony carried on, his sentences getting shorter. "She says the Chinese are the worst bosses. Yes, they give them one day off a week, Sunday. But they have to get breakfast first and be back in time to put the kids to bed. Australians and Brits are appreciated for their fairness. But the best are the Scandinavians. Take a bow, Katla. She knows one maid whose Finnish boss lets her go on Friday evening and come back late Sunday. And not to a full sink to return to; she says the place is always spotless. Maybe I'll do a story.... Ruffle a few feathers—"

He wanted to continue, but Katla butted in, changing the subject away from his nibs.

"I read in the *Toronto Star* a piece headed up 'Is a veto democratic?' The writer gave a very good case for the answer 'No', citing the case of the constipated and farcical UN Security Council."

"Oh I say! Steady on, old girl."

More drinks came, courtesy of Vimana's magic. Tony kept on talking as if he hadn't stopped.

"I love articles that headline a question. Maybe 'Are you employing an economic refugee?' Yes, I think so. 'A wise man – person – will make more opportunities than he finds'." He was talking to Vimana, who beamed back at him, as if proud at such erudition. Then he suddenly turned back to Bruce, wobbling a little.

"Bruce," he barked at him, "what is a Gamma cell?"

A thought went through Bruce's mind: perhaps Tony wasn't as drunk as he made out.

"I've no idea. In what context?" he replied, his mind clearing as he did.

"Oh come on, old fellah. There are rumours everywhere. What's up?"

"I don't know what you mean. Are you talking about the supposed terrorist group that's supposed to be in Hong Kong? Or that Tsui is going to be the next chief executive?"

"Come on now. If I didn't know you better, I'd say you were warning me off."

Vimana sensed an argument brewing. She smiled her friendly and sympathetic smile on Bruce, at the same time appealing to Katla to back her up, squeezing her arm to get her attention.

"But you're Tsui's PR, aren't you, Bruce?" she said.

He just shrugged in reply. He sometimes wondered himself. In his new job he'd never been in attack mode, only on defence. Tony had started muttering to himself again, but making sure that everyone heard.

"Something to do with China and Korea and Taiwan."

"Where are you hearing all this, Tony?"

Tony didn't honour the question with an answer. Bruce carried on looking at him. He would have to report him to Tsui, friend or not. He wondered what sort of friend he would be when the chips were down. He could be a pretentious ass; but he was nobody's fool. The tension grew within the group. Katla looked at Bruce with a worried expression, like a mother to a son when the son might make a major indiscretion. Vimana worried about a spoilt evening and her agenda. The men glared at one another, toe to toe.

The bar was packed, the noise making any sensible conversation impossible. Vimana, when she spoke again, trying to reach all three of them, had to raise her voice, standing on her tiptoes.

"Let's all go back to my place to eat. I've got a super vindaloo. It's been a couple of days now and it's red hot! We can go on to Soho afterwards if we want." She winked at Katla.

"I can't, Vimana, I'm sorry. I'm meeting up with Catherine," Bruce replied.

"Is that the hottie from the Fire-Fly?" Tony asked Bruce, sneering.

This time Bruce did not answer, kissing Katla on the cheek as he turned to go.

Tony called after him above the noise, "I hope your affair lasts longer than a firefly's life!"

NIYOGAN, THE PHILIPPINES

"Cerise!" called out Alexander from the office.

"Yes, Honey," she replied from the veranda, where she had been watering her plants in the coolness of the evening. He had never been able to cure her of her American influences. He didn't really mind. She came in, full of life, wearing a simple T-shirt, shorts and thongs, a wisp of hair falling across her forehead. She looked good, he thought.

"Let's sleep out at the nipa hut tonight. It's a perfect evening," he added soothingly.

She was still cross with him for giving all the staff the week off around All Saints Day so they could follow tradition by celebrating a visit to their families' graves. He did it every year and every year she argued with him.

Earlier he had seen two of the men, whose family grave was too far away to visit and who were staying on the farm, preparing a suspended dog carcass for pulutan by burning off the dog's hair with a blow torch, intermittently hitting it with a bamboo stick till the skin was a golden brown. Occasionally the stick caught fire by mistake and was put out by hitting it on the trunk of a nearby palm. Later the carcass would go on the spit. Some of Eddie's men from next door had joined them. Lots of Tuba tonight, Alexander thought.

* * *

They rode out in the twilight. He had collected the things for the barbeque and saddled up their horses. Before he mounted The Grey, frisky because of the evening ride, he slung his guitar across his shoulder. When they first came to Niyogan his driver had patiently taught him how to play. Now he enjoyed playing at the nipa hut, out in the open. After one or two quince brandies Cerise would sing along in her attractive deep and husky voice.

He was good with the barbeque and soon, after they had penned and watered the horses, he had their food cooking. It was simple like most good cooking: marinated pork with brown rice and pumpkin, followed by mangoes. He laid it out on fresh palm leaves on the trestle table and they ate with their fingers. They had 'Off' repellent on for the mosquitoes.

All was quiet and peaceful in the still warm night apart from the cicadas and the occasional bullfrog. After they had eaten and played some music they made gentle love on the bamboo floor inside the nets.

* * *

Alexander woke suddenly. The horses whinnied their alarm. The footsteps were louder now, closer. He could see light between the bamboo slats. Hurriedly he pulled on his trousers as Cerise woke up.

"What's up?"

"Don't know yet. Get dressed." He stood up and buckled his trousers as the flimsy door swung open, and the hut was bathed in dazzling light from a powerful hurricane lamp. When his eyes adjusted he could see three men in fatigues, two of them carrying Uzis. NPA. One was Chinese. They would know he didn't carry a gun. Cerise came to him and he made her stand behind him. There was no chance of escape.

"That's good, Cerise, don't panic."

"Quiet!" shouted one of the soldiers, probably the leader, he guessed. The soldier with the lamp put it down, taking handcuffs from his belt. Moving quickly he roughly wrenched the couple's arms behind their backs and clicked the cuffs on. Maybe Alexander could kick over the lamp. As if reading his mind, one of the armed rebels moved directly in front of him. The bamboo door squeaked open behind him and the men from Eddie's place and his stay-at-home two crept awkwardly in. He looked at them searchingly, but said nothing. They put ropes around the couple's necks so that they could be yanked and pulled along like mules. The lamp was doused. Outside in the dark they moved off in single file up into the hills. One of Alexander's men men jogged over to the horses' corral and let them out so they could graze. As The Grey went by she snorted, tossing her head and whisking her tail.

They were both fit, so the march would be little hardship. But he was concerned that all the men were unhooded and they had not been blindfolded.

* * *

Cheng Cheng took a call from Antonia. She seemed nearly hysterical.

"This is Antonia. I need to talk to Tsui."

"Antonia, are you all right? Tsui's in a meeting with the top forex people. He left strict instruct—"

"I don't care! It's my family. Put me through at once, Cheng Cheng."

This didn't sound like the usual polite and friendly Antonia.

"Hold on, I'll try."

There was a pause, then Tsui's irate voice.

"Yes?"

"It's Antonia. I've just heard from the Embassy that Mummy and Daddy have been kidnapped..."

For a moment Tsui did not reply.

"Antonia. He knew the risks when he went down there, living where he does. I have two huge deals coming up; I've been working on them for years. I am unable to help now. He's on his own." He hung up before she had time to control her emotions and reply.

After the meeting was over he went across to his favourite spot by the window and stood, legs astride, hands clasped behind back, looking out at the grey harbour, raindrops rolling down the window pane. He thought of the extended family, of his father and grandfather. What would they do? If he were honest with himself he knew the answer. When the chips were finally down, if it were family, they would help. He stabbed at the intercom on the conference table. Jane answered.

"Jane."

"Get me Cheng Cheng."

"Cheng Cheng speaking."

"Get a hold of Antonia. Tell her our people are on it. Whatever needs to be done will be done. Put me on the evening JAL flight into Osaka, transferring to Haneda. Forget Narita. I can take the monorail and be in downtown in twenty minutes. Palace Hotel as usual. Stop everything."

"Everything?"

"Yes, everything. Don't go stupid on me now!"

Not his best day, thought Cheng Cheng, as she phoned the house to pack his things.

* * *

Tsui had been up at six, doing his exercises and showering before room service brought him breakfast: steamed rice and miso soup with a side dish of grilled salmon, which he ate at the window overlooking the moat and gardens of the Imperial Palace. With his second cup of coffee in hand he was waiting for Takji's driver to take him out to the shrine's Tokyo house. Takji worked from there when he was in town. The driver would phone from the lobby at seven thirty. The phone rang.

"Yes?"

"Good morning, Sir. This is your driver. Please come down and meet me at the main entrance."

Tsui picked up his briefcase and left the room for the lift, which took him smoothly, silently and quickly to the lobby. He strode to the front waiting area and stopped.

"Taxi, Sir?" asked the doorman.

"No thank you."

Tsui waited a few minutes, becoming impatient. Suddenly the driver appeared out of the shadows from behind the pillars.

"Sorry to keep you waiting, Sir. Our protocol."

He walked Tsui over to a shining black Crown on the forecourt and opened the rear door. Tsui anticipated the white cover on the headrests and the 'fir tree' pine deodorant hanging from the roof, and the woollen white gloves of the driver. The door closed with a pleasant clunk as he settled back in the relaxing grey 'armchair' seats. He couldn't hear the engine as they headed for the freeway and Shibuya-ku.

The traffic was light as they sped smoothly along for about twenty minutes, sometimes in tunnels and through interchanges and a toll gate, with the driver casually but often checking the rear-view mirror. They took a minor exit and soon found themselves driving slowly through a maze of little streets which was Nanpeidaicho, an exclusive suburb, home to embassies, consulates and diplomats; and, for Tokyo, a surprising amount of greenery. The houses and apartments lining the narrow streets looked expensive, architect designed. Most roofs were made of heavy coloured tiles, fashionable and good in typhoons; not so good in earthquakes.

The Crown slowed to a crawl as the heavy, high black gates beyond the pavement opened automatically. They stopped in one of two car spaces, the driver jumping out and opening the door and touching his cap. He indicated that Tsui should take the outside stairs to the first floor.

As Tsui climbed up he noticed the people next door had a magnificent St Bernard and no garden. The dog was in a cage about his own length, lying down and looking back at him with sad brown eyes. Wicked. He wondered why Takji didn't fix it. He knew the answer as soon as he thought of the question. This was a good safe house in an outstanding location. The last thing Takji wanted was to disturb his neighbour. The driver came silently up the stairs behind him, two steps at a time. Ninja.

"Good morning, Tsui," said Takji briskly, opening the carved door wide himself and ushering in his friend. Two miko in the background bowed towards Tsui, one of them handing him some slippers. He stopped and bowed in reply.

"Thank you."

The whole of the first floor had been made over to a large European style living room with soft leather sofas and armchairs in muted colours on a highly polished wooden floor. The low coffee table was surrounded with large green silk cushions. On the walls hung some fine Japanese charcoal prints of old men fishing in the mountains. He looked at his watch: not yet eight o'clock.

"Tea or coffee?"

"Green tea, please."

Takji nodded at the miko.

"This sounds urgent, Tsui. What is the challenge?" He had come down from Shiga Heights whilst Tsui had come up from Hong Kong; this wasn't a social gathering.

"It's my elder brother, Alexander. He's been kidnapped with his wife in the Philippines."

Takji knew that; he had anticipated an attack on the flank. He was only surprised that it had come so soon. Tsui's reaction was exactly as he'd expected. Takji stroked his chin, as if considering the news. Otherwise his face showed no expression.

Tsui continued, "I've stopped everything until this nonsense is sorted. Can you go down to PI with two or three of your people?"

"No, Tsui, I'm sorry, I will not go. I'm most useful at base. I will send three. Shall we make this operation part of the overall plan? The finances we will work out later."

"Agreed," said Tsui. "There are seven of them, we think. Might I suggest your people go in as industrial machinery salesmen? That way they have a reason to contact my brother's factory manager; he's Japanese. He'll have a good idea where they're holed up."

"It's a distraction. Or an unhappy coincident," interposed Takji. Tsui wondered: did he mean that the kidnapping itself was a distraction, or that the kidnapping was a fabricated distraction? Coincident?

North Island, New Zealand

They sat out on the spacious veranda at Kawhia. Cerise, still recovering, had taken a siesta after lunch. Gavin McLeod, the stud manager, had gone back to work. Apart from the staff tidying up in the kitchen they had the place to themselves.

They were both drinking a light port from Hawkes Bay. Tsui had come down to New Zealand to debrief his brother for the company. He also wanted to give Alexander the chance to talk to someone in the family. Without being told, the older brother knew that he should talk.

"They took us up into the hills the first night to a deserted field camp. At first I thought there was one Chinese but I'm sure all three 'soldiers' were Chinese. They spoke to each other in Cantonese. There's no doubt they were in charge: they had the guns and gave the orders. The others seemed to be going along for the ride.

"It was that night the Chinese raped Cerise. They took turns. All I could do was to try to use my eyes to tell her not to fight." His voice broke and he paused.

"Their demands were simple. They wanted OSM out of the Philippines because of their rice trading on the Manila market, and they wanted us to 'understand the local tax laws'. No demand for money; it all seemed political. It felt as if our people wanted land rights.

"When your people did come, they were incredibly efficient. They were in black with hoods and struck in the small hours with speed…. In the first seconds they seemed to ignore the Filipinos; most of them were asleep anyway. They took out the armed 'soldiers', crippling two and killing one, the leader. Then the biggest of them picked up Cerise; the other two half carried, half ran with me to their jeep hidden off a mountain track.

"We drove hectically for about half an hour before we came out into open land and I thought I recognised bits of our place in the dawn light. I was right. We soon stopped outside the farmhouse. They had taken our handcuffs off in transit and now hurriedly helped us out. One of them handed me a mobile, and they had gone. They had not spoken once.

"Cerise was shivering as she clung to me. We started for the house and then I stopped, pulling Cerise towards me. The grey mare lay dead on the front step, her brains all over our front door. Cerise stared in silence for a while, then looked up at me. 'Let's go to New Zealand.' And I think I said, 'Yes let's.'"

It was very quiet now in late afternoon, the sun set over the green paddocks and trees of the stud.

"You're lucky you have the option," Tsui said softly.

"Yes," he replied, as he watched the mares grazing, tails swishing against the evening flies. "You know, as I was made to watch those bastards rape Cerise, I became aroused. Isn't that a terrible thing…?"

HEAD OFFICE, TSUI CENTRE, WANCHAI

Before he had left to see Alexander he had had an evening call from Ivan Isaacson on his encrypted mobile phone. The encryption had been done by the Comprador's nephew, based on Siemens's hardware cryptology, to military level. It had been explained to Tsui that they had created two-hundred-and-fifty-bit encryption strength, which would take a few years of even the best computers to break. He hoped they were wise to so completely trust the nephew.

They never used encryption on the mainland because of the risk of it being illegal. That meant Isaacson was probably in Hong Kong. He should have arranged a meeting face to face. Low-tech old-fashioned couriers were still the best. Tsui put on his CW to make doubly sure his end was secure. Then he picked up the phone and pressed the flashing key marked 'crypto'.

"Osprey?"

"*J'ecoute*."

"I have some news for you."

"Good. It's been a long time coming," replied Tsui. In fact Isaacson had been in Beijing for more than three months without a sound. Isaacson didn't respond but carried on directly, wanting to keep the conversation short.

"K. K. Chen shares are going to be bought by CICC and CITC Pacific, starting the first of next month; up to twenty-five per cent. K. K. Chen shares will go through the roof."

"Thank you."

"*Sayonara*."

Good, thought Tsui. They had three weeks; they should make a killing. He still had time to talk to Wai Kwok, if he was still in. He glanced at his computer clock: nearly eight thirty. He dialled his direct line.

"Tsui Wai Kwok."

"Tsui here. You're working late."

"It's that time of year."

"Can you come up for ten minutes."

Tsui hung up. He walked over to the drinks cabinet and poured a couple of Grant's. While he waited he sipped his, looking out at the bright Wanchai lights and the shipping lights on the harbour.

Even his younger brother knocked and waited at his door.

"Come in!"

Wai Kwok looked the part: perfectly cut dark blue pinstripe Saville Row suit, blue shirt with white collar and matching blue tie, all probably from Burlington Arcade, all speaking of the legal profession, a lawyer. He was shorter than Tsui.

"Have a seat," Tsui said, kindly enough. He often thought this brother worked the hardest of the lot. "Drink?"

"Yes. Thanks." He slumped down in one of the Falcons, leatherbound notebook in hand, and raised his glass silently to the taipan.

"Before the first of next month I want to buy, with stealth, into K. K. Chen. As you know, they are listed here, in Shanghai and in New York. Spread it about a bit as deviously as possible. Use five of our most opaque companies…" He paused to give Wai Kwok time to make his notes. "Each company to buy a two point five per cent holding. There are rumours, and we don't want OSM to be vulnerable."

Tsui looked at his watch. His brother noticed and stood up, putting his notebook away in his inside jacket pocket and picking up his half-full drink.

"All divisions appear to be on target since the management changeover," said Wai Kwok, sounding pleased and satisfied.

"Well done," said Tsui, enthusiastically remembering his use of *The One-Minute Manager*. "Do you need any more help?"

As he asked the question there was another knock on the door, louder than before. Whoever it was wasn't waiting for his reply.

Antonia came bursting in. She did not stop to acknowledge Wai Kwok but rushed impulsively towards Tsui, talking excitably as she did.

"I just heard. They've landed safely in Auckland."

"I know. Now calm down," said Tsui, smiling kindly. "And say good evening to your uncle and sit down. We're finishing up anyway. I've got to leave in twenty minutes."

He turned to the security guard, who remained waiting nervously at the door.

"Never mind. Next time stop whoever it is, no exceptions. I'll phone down when Miss Antonia is on her way. Escort her off the premises." He finished, waving his hand in dismissal. As the guard left, Wai Kwok followed.

"Have a good trip, Tsui. Goodnight." And he smiled at Antonia, who was dishevelled but as radiant as ever.

Tsui nodded to his brother and went back to his deskchair, swivelling back to face Antonia.

"Yes, it is good news. I hear they're going to stay in New Zealand, build a house on the stud."

"Thank you, Uncle, thank you," she said, tears coming to her eyes as she stood up, coming round the desk and perching herself on the corner next to him. She wiped away her tears and smiled cheekily at Tsui.

"I couldn't think how I could thank you. Then there seemed to be only one way…"

She had crossed her pretty legs demurely, but now began to swing her foot provocatively, her shoe balanced loosely on her sheer stockinged toes.

Tsui looked at her openly; he never thought of the other nieces in the same way. He looked at his watch again. Antonia noticed and giggled huskily.

"Come on, Tsui, they say you only take eleven minutes!"

Nay Pyi Taw, Burma

During their afternoon break the two cousins met in the Entertainment Zone canteen. It was a large impersonal building full of chrome tables and chairs, looking new but not modern. There was always a long well-regimented queue at the cafeteria even for a pot of tea. Those in the queue kept to themselves, intermittently talking with their immediate companion in subdued tones. There was an uneasy feeling in the air. No one knew who was an informer for the army and who was not so they assumed that everyone was. Even some dressed in monk's robes were spies. Two military police patrolled around the building in opposite directions. The new capital hadn't settled in.

Mary and Susan took a table by the window, away from the crowd. The window was sheltered from the sun by a wooden shutter which served as protection when put down during typhoons. It looked out on to a huge open space criss-crossed with wide defensive roads. The buildings had been constructed in clusters, with large open areas between, discouraging any spontaneous gatherings. About a quarter of a mile away they could see the Hotel Zone, with its pastel colours making it look incongruous in its mosquito-infested jungle environment. The Hotel Zone was where Mary entertained her general. He had a permanent reservation at the most expensive hotel, the Royal Kumudra, for their best accommodation: their executive villas. They had five. One of them did not show on the inventory.

They drank their tea, not talking much. Mary looked smart and attractive in a long black silk dress and a crisp white blouse. She could be working in reception. By contrast Susan had tried hard to make herself look drab, fitting in with the other mess kitchen staff, not wanting to attract attention. As the group nearest to them moved away Mary spoke sharply enough to get her cousin's attention.

"Susan, I have our passes for this weekend."

"That's good," she replied without any emotion, as if they went every month. But Mary saw her eyes flashing. She looked down at her bowl of tea.

Temple Street, Mongkok

Catherine and Bruce were browsing through the open market. He had bought from a hawker a frangipani lei which he had hung around her neck, with a gentle kiss. In the evening air the fragrance was strong and refreshing. She wore an old torn T-shirt and frayed and faded denim shorts. She looked stunning, he thought.

"Let's eat," said Bruce, beginning to unwind away from the office and the operative China Deal. As they sat down at a noodle stall his phone rang.

"Bugger," he said as he reached into his pocket and flipped open his mobile. "Sorry, Darling…. Hullo." She turned back to the dirty menu, not wanting to eavesdrop on his conversation. The voice on the other end seemed to be talking urgently. She didn't think they'd be eating now.

"It's Katla," said Bruce, putting away his phone. "She sounds excited. She's got some breaking news I must hear and so…. Sorry, I'd better go."

"That's OK. But when can we talk to immigration? It's ending soon."

"I know. Next week, I promise." Standing up, he waved his apologies to the stall owner, who swore at them in Cantonese. Lucky she doesn't understand, Bruce thought. "I've got to get off at Admiralty. You can go on to Wanchai. OK?" She just smiled and took his arm.

* * *

Katla, wearing the hotel dressing gown, put down the phone and turned to Tony Parker, who was leaning back on the pillows of the other single bed. She had asked him over for back-up and as a witness, she supposed. It could be a huge story.

"He's coming over; about half an hour. Don't drink too much."

"All right, Madam!" he replied, not smiling. He put down his G and T with a thump on the small bedside table.

Katla always stayed at the Central Hotel. It wasn't in Central but next door at Admiralty, which suited her fine. She liked the hotel. It had a spacious marble reception and the required piano bar. There were no in-house restaurants, only room service; every kind of restaurant abounded outside the front door. And once you left the elegant public rooms for your own room you would find it well appointed but tiny. That way they could keep their prices well below other four-and-a-half-star hotels. That pleased Bergens Tidende.

As she waited she worked on her computer whilst talking to Tony to amuse him and keep him sober. The English-speaking media was an easy-going group though professionally ruthless and jealous.

She had given Bruce her room number so he could come straight up from the basement, avoiding reception. There was a crisp knock on the door and Bruce came busily in. Katla got up and gave him a hug and the one chair in the room, in front of the dressing table-cum-desk, sitting herself down on the other bed.

"Hullo, Katla," said Bruce; and turning to shake Tony by the hand, "Tony." He was not surprised to see the older man in yet another safari suit.

"Drink, Bruce?" The way she said his name still stirred him.

"No thanks. What's the panic?" No messing about. Straight to the point. She liked that.

"It's a story. Could be big. Could affect you." She leant over and hit a few keys on her laptop. A dim photo came up. She turned the computer round so that Bruce could see better.

"Looks like a hospital ward," he said.

"Right. But not just any old hospital ward. It's in the Military Hospital in Nay Pyi Taw." Tony, lounging back on the pillows, noticed Bruce's reflex reaction, his sitting up straighter. "It's from our big friend's library archive photos. We have a friend. We reckon that seven of the patients are from the senior general's elite corp. Of course there's talk of conspiracies. Most interesting for you – Tsui's name has been mentioned."

"That's absolutely ridiculous. For one thing, OSM has an absolute embargo on any trade with Burma." Except for some marijuana, Bruce thought. "We even have partial embargoes on countries that do trade with the junta."

He'd have to go up to Laird House – the locals called it Laid House – once they broke up. Tsui had come back in this evening. Unusually, Tony spoke for only the first time.

"Mr Einstein says, as opposed to Mr Confucius, 'The difference between stupidity and genius is that genius knows its limits.' I hope Tsui is not proving himself stupid!"

* * *

The phone kept ringing. Shouldn't be a problem mid-afternoon. The unmistakable thin, reedy voice of the Comprador came on the line.

"Merlin."

Peter Maynard often wondered why the Comprador bothered to use his codename with a voice so recognizable.

"Pigeon," Maynard replied, using one of his. "Scramble now."

There was a pause. He had to report to the Comprador now because of that meddling Cheng Cheng. At least he returned his calls, unlike Tsui.

"Yes, what is it?" asked the Comprador.

"We've had another hotel room break-in. Central Hotel. Neat job. They got everything: cash, cards, passports and, the bell-boy says, a laptop. They were strangled in their sleep. Must have been two assailants. They were friends of Harrier, so I thought you ought to know. The Norwegian girl and Tony Parker. We'll try and close the case quickly but it may be difficult with the media involved.... One unusual thing I noticed... the contusions round the neck didn't seem heavy enough for strangulation." There was a long pause. All right, he thought, don't speak.

"Thank you." There was a click and Maynard had dial tone.

* * *

The Comprador's air-conditioned Crown moved steadily through the evening traffic on his way to his meeting with the taipan. They had a rule that they kept to their schedule even on the most dramatic news: Hong Kong was a rumour mill. The Comprador sat erect, austere even, when alone with his driver. He was debating the news from Maynard with himself.

Ever since Tsui had told him about the Ninjas he had been doing his own extensive research. He had learnt a great deal, both myth and reality. He was recalling now a book he'd been sent from London: *The Real Ninja: Tactics and Weaponry*. He had a good memory and something was nagging at it now. Then it came to him as they began winding up Peak Road.

Kakute were usually used by kunoichi, female Ninjas. They were custom-made rings with two protruding minuscule needles coated with natural poisons. The Ninjas quietly began to strangle the victim, making sure the needles pierced the neck, causing paralysis within seconds and death soon after. It was clean and simple, leaving very little evidence or cause of death.

The Comprador sighed. His information would not be news to the taipan.

* * *

Whilst he waited for the Comprador in his small office Tsui was reading again the part in *The Art of War* about 'The Use of Spies'. The house was peaceful in the lull before the dinner gong.

If a secret piece of news is divulged by a spy before the time is ripe, they must be put to death together with the person to whom the secret was told.

Wittingly or unwittingly, Tsui reflected. Certainly, intelligence, or lack of it, won or lost wars. He closed the book and waited, thinking: *On such a full sea are we now afloat...*

Taiwan Straits

They were waiting in transit at Songshan International for a flight down to Kaohsiung. They could have flown direct from Hong Kong but the times from Singapore were no good. He'd had a meeting with Ina. More news from the North.

Sebastian was with him, walking steadily around the long transit lounge looking fit, imposing and alert. He should have been an All Black. Tsui needed him this trip. This was the big one, and not without its physical risk. He needed someone to watch his back, be his second eyes and ears. Sebastian had worked hard at his Mandarin. They'd decided not to let the Chinese know. They wouldn't expect it of a Maori. Let their racism work against them.

Tsui had bought a copy of the *Taipei Times* and was smiling as he read a leading article about defence. Two point two million PLA against three hundred thousand Taiwanese armed forces. More than seven hundred ballistic missiles aimed at Taiwan at any one time. A navy which is planned to include seventy-five surface ships, fifty-three submarines – one executive one, thought Tsui – fifty landing ships and seven hundred patrol vessels. The Chinese defence budget had double-digit increases annually during the past fifteen years.

This will mean that the balance of power will tip towards China in two thousand and ten. It is because of these intelligence reports that the Taiwanese legislator continues to approve multi-billion-dollar arms purchases from the US.

What a bluff, admired Tsui, as Sebastian came back from walking and their flight was called.

* * *

They were met by a civilian driver in a plain unmarked jeep. They drove steadily north through the city, not speeding, obeying the traffic laws and the waving police. Noisy but well-disciplined motor bikes were everywhere. Yet there were few delays. The road ahead was a shimmering mirage and pollution hung in the air. It was going to be hot. He turned and spoke to Sebastian, who hadn't been on this trip before. They used English.

"Not long now." They had wound up their windows and asked the driver to put on the air-con. There wasn't any, so they wound down the windows again. Sebastian seemed unusually quiet.

"Are you all right?"

"Yes thanks, Tsui. Just going over your briefing on the plane." Actually he had been thinking about the two journalists back in Hong Kong, particularly the young and lovely Katla, whom he had got to know.

The jeep swung off the main road and started down towards the naval dockyard. They were stopped at three gatehouses manned by smartly turned out ratings. Their searches and identification checks were brisk and efficient, cross checked on their activity schedule by walkie-talkie.

The years rolled back as Tsui looked out on the dockyard, immaculate with everything in its place, as it had been when his father called in a few favours to get him seconded for a year from Mons to one of six tank regiments. They had come through Kaohsiung on an amphibious exercise, 'invading' Tungyin Command Island. Now at midday all was oddly silent. It seemed that every blade of grass was in place and every marker stone was sparkling white. He remembered his sergeant-majors at officer cadet school always shouting at them, "If it moves salute it; if it doesn't, paint it white, you horrible men!" He still had contacts in the Officer Corps.

They stopped outside a nondescript wooden hut. The driver took their bags out of the back and led the way inside. At one of the long tables with wooden benches they were served a simple meal: stir fried vegetables with rice, followed by fresh fruit. As they ate, more officers arrived, some of them very high ranking. When they had finished eating one of his old friends and now his main contact, Lieutenant-General Wang, sat down opposite them, smiling and stretching out his hand. Tsui introduced Sebastian, wondering what rank he would have reached if he'd stayed in the forces. Wang was talking in his good American English.

"It's beginning to blow hard out in the Straits, but that won't bug us." He sounded confident and in charge. "Your kitbags are on board; we'll be going down soon. Excuse me." And he left at the summons of the vice-chief of staff. Everyone had arrived and there was a general exodus towards the back door, Tsui and Sebastian being escorted by a young ensign. Once through the door they began a gentle descent in a covered gangway similar to the loading tube of a commercial airline. As they came round the bend Sebastian caught his first glimpse of the grey executive submarine. Tsui glanced across at him. He had warned him of their mode of transport; but seeing it in reality was a different thing. His Maori features gave nothing away. He had been well briefed; no surprises. The submarine was twenty metres, and took ten passengers at an average speed of twelve knots. Mission time was thirteen hundred hours. It had a price tag of around fifteen million US dollars. It was a perk of senior politicians but worked for the navy as well; carousing parties were legendary. As they came on board Sebastian grunted as he saw the luxurious cabin.

"It's like first class."

Tsui leant towards Sebastian unobserved, and spoke softly.

"About the only thing not 'Made in China'; it's 'Made in Florida'! And the safest way to travel. Never been a fatality in commercial submarining!"

* * *

They could have no significant conversation because of the submarine's resonance. Tiring of looking out the large porthole, Sebastian had asked his leave to nap. He was now in a shallow sleep, almost alert, like a well-trained guard dog. Tsui was reading his BlackBerry from the research department in Lai Chi Kok: the message had been encrypted using Izemail. They were becoming verbose again. He'd have to talk to them. Still, they had the information he wanted. Best estimate was that nine hundred vessels sailed through the Taiwan Straits each day. Most were Japanese and foreign-registered ships, mostly carrying oil. Risk of piracy was minimised because of the heavy military presence. The prevailing wind over North Korea was from the north: not good news.

He turned to look at Sebastian. They had been told that their passage time would be two and a half hours. The Chinese group was coming down from Zhoushan near Shanghai: a much longer trip. But they had the next executive sub up the list, with much more comfort and luxury: en suite cabins, conference room, a large self-contained galley and separate crew quarters. It had a submerged cruising speed of thirty knots. Not even the Taiwanese politicians could swing all that.

They were about an hour out. He woke Sebastian.

"Wakey-Wakey! My turn," Tsui said, smiling.

"Sure," said the Maori, fully alert and upright immediately, scanning the cabin.

* * *

They surfaced, seawater running down the portholes like rainy-season rain, in a similar covered docking pool looking like a large version of his college boathouse at

Cambridge. He had never seen outside but Wang had told him that, on the outside, the docks had been made to look like camouflaged ground-to-air missile launchers. He also learnt that the island was uninhabited except for a small Chinese and Taiwanese hidden military presence. As they stepped out they were hit by the humidity. Tsui remembered from before that they would be walking up a tunnel for about a hundred yards before reaching a heavily guarded gate and entrance to air-conditioned underground quarters for a company of commandos; no women.

Everyone was frisked again, without exception. He hoped they wouldn't find Sebastian's listening device. It was very slim, all parts made of plastic. When static it could beat the Chinese CW. Once through the guard post they were led by their assigned batman to one of the meeting rooms, which had been converted into a buffet for lunch. Their batman took their overnight bags, saluted and left. Must be American-trained, saluting inside and without a hat, thought Tsui. The buffet arrangement allowed everyone to mingle, though Sebastian kept close to Tsui.

Before they had left Hong Kong Tsui had briefed Sebastian under oath about the Chinese and about the PLA in particular; about how in the nineties the politicians had encouraged the military to go into business to make money for themselves and the army budget; about how they came to realise that this encouraged corruption. The politicians ordered the military to hand over their businesses to civilian control. So the PLA were desperate to find other sources of 'income'. That's why Sinbad Fuel had been so timely. Now they were nervous. There were rumours that a deputy chief of the Navy was in trouble for corruption. Much worse, the PLA should be put under state control and not the Party's.

But the real reason for making Sebastian swear to secrecy still astounded Tsui. In the nineteen fifties they, old members of the Party and the KMT, created the Joint Liaison Pact: they were allies. In the pact they agreed to share all technical knowledge and physical equipment whilst continuing to act as antagonists. It had worked well playing America against Russia and some other suppliers. It gave them both access to the American and Russian arsenals. None of the five people on each side were members of the Executive Yuan Council or the Politburo Standing Committee. But they were all here, with the raw power in their hands.

They had taken Tsui on as a 'consultant' when he had helped procure some military software. They had even made him an honorary general. They greatly admired his business acumen and valued him as their 'ideas man'. Leasing military equipment to friendly nations had been his idea and OSM Financials did well out of it. They had asked him to give his ideas about controlling religion and cults, their latest paranoia, at the meeting this afternoon. In return he had asked for a meeting with the vice-chief of staff and Wang this evening.

* * *

"General Tsui, your thoughts on control of religion and cults. Please."

Tsui walked steadily to the dais and the whiteboard. He sensed a change of attitudes in the room; perhaps he was becoming paranoid.

"Grant absolute freedom of religious expression." There was an audible sucking in of breath around the table. "By banning religion outright you will make it stronger. We want no martyrs. Look at the UK's Church of England; almost asleep, in terminal decline. Look what happened, is happening, with Falun Gong.... No, there must be freedom of expression.

"However, there needs to be some restrictions. Groups gathering for religious or cultic reasons may only do so in groups of twelve or less. The gatherings may only be held in the private home of one of the group's members. The religion or cult may own no property, either directly or indirectly."

Tsui turned to the whiteboard and wrote down his summation before returning to his seat amid a murmur of voices.

* * *

The meeting with the diminutive vice-chief of staff, the dapper General Wang and Tsui was held in the otherwise deserted lecture room. Sebastian was asked to wait outside in the anteroom. The chief was brusque and abrasive so Tsui was not surprised when he started without the usual Asian pleasantries, drumming his fingers on the table.

"What is so important, General? Our time is short." What did that mean? Time on this mission or our natural time. Innuendo, always innuendo. All right, he could be direct as well, but he didn't need innuendo.

"I have a job, which does not involve China," he hoped. "I need to hire one of the joint force's two B-2 Spirits and its crew for a month, and to buy a 2NW."

All Tsui could see in the chief's hardened face was an enlargement of his pupils; this would be a good pay day for the PLA – about forty million US dollars. The chief replied at once, as if the answer was prepared.

"We will let you know tomorrow," giving himself face when, no doubt, he knew the answer already.

* * *

Sebastian had stuck it to the base of the vice-chief of staff's briefcase when his batman was looking after it. You could hardly see it with the naked eye, particularly as it was made of transparent plastic, tinged grey to match the briefcase. Tsui was lying back on his bed in their billet, listening to a discussion next door about his execution. He could recognise Wang's voice and occasionally the chief's in the animated group. It sounded as if Wang was summarising:

"We have heard from our people that OSM is in turmoil. Their *guanxi* is labyrinthine and extremely valuable. It would be premature to terminate Tsui and his Maori. That can be done at any time, when the signs and times are right, which is not now."

Turmoil at OSM? What did they know that he didn't? Execution? He'd have to act first.

SEOUL, SOUTH KOREA

Suk Soon used the family apartment in the Kangbok, north of the river. Her mother had used it when she was in business. Even though it had a western layout it had some unusual amenities which Suk Soon enjoyed and which she had persuaded her mother to leave behind.

She had come home for her birthday and had brought Iain to meet her parents. They didn't meet. Instead Iain had been met at the airport by the manager of the OSM Seoul office. At first she had thought he had come to give them a courtesy lift into town.

"Mr Iain, Miss Suk Soon," he said with a slight bow, looking every bit the managerial executive, "I'm sorry to be the one to mess up your plans." He addressed Iain. "I have a message from Tsui's office. You are needed back in Hong Kong immediately."

"Damn! Damn!" He took Suk Soon by both hands, moving away from the manager and looking into her eyes. "I'm getting fed up with this!"

"I'm sure it must be very important, Sir," he heard the manager say.

"You must go," she said, fighting down her annoyance and irritation.

"I've got you a ticket on the return flight, Sir. If we hurry you might just make it. Miss, my driver will take you wherever you want to go," and he waved towards the crowd waiting for arrivals.

Iain was holding Suk Soon and kissing her on the cheek.

"So sorry. Please give my apologies to your mother and father."

"What can it be, do you think?"

"I've no idea," he lied

* * *

Neither his wife nor his daughter knew he had been a double agent since the end of the fighting along the thirty-eighth parallel. His payments from South Korea went to Tokyo; those from North Korea, to Macau.

He kept his crewcut and military bearing. His dark blue quilted jacket and black trousers were neat but not flashy. His questionable border trading activities gave useful cover. He had assumed the common surname Pak.

Over the years he had built up a group of five dependable agents – three women and two men – with similar goals, motivated by money. Their cell was difficult to crack as they had no need of people beyond their immediate group. Also, because of his contact with the South and thus the Americans, his agents had US military radios using frequency-hopping spread spectrum, good at preventing adversary jamming. Their security was further enhanced by being engineered with the portable voice encryption, KY-57, and by using a word-of-day key.

Recently, shortly after the furore surrounding Iain and Suk Soon's departure from Hong Kong, and OSM research accidentally finding out about Pak when looking into Suk Soon's 'history', the Comprador had sent Peter Maynard to Seoul to interview Pak. After ten days of clandestine meetings around the capital, Maynard was ready to outline his mission: that OSM would buy 'solid' information 'not in the public domain' about any facet of North Korea's nuclear programme. Since then there had been some beneficial exchanges, particularly about the North's centrifuge-based enrichment programme. Pak now reported directly to the Comprador.

His last report had covered his asked-for opinion of the IAEA. It had been brief: 'The IAEA would never be able or allowed to conduct a full inspection of North Korea's nuclear facilities.' The request had come back without hesitation: 'please explain'. And he had, talking rapidly but clearly into the microphone. "For example, they will not find the hot cells where, in compact shielded rooms, small amounts of spent fuel are secretly being reprocessed. My agents have so far identified nine locations."

The Comprador's Place, Sai Kung

In the early evening the Comprador was relaxing in bed with his young houseboy. The boy's head was resting on his shoulder, the Comprador's arm around him. He was breathing steadily, almost asleep. The Comprador shook him gently and started talking.

"As I've told you, you take the second car and driver and pick up Fitzgibbon and Vimana at two o'clock at reception at the Luk Kwok Hotel in Wanchai. It is convenient for them as they were at the annual cricket club dinner and they stayed overnight at the hotel. Fitzgibbon will just be surfacing by then, so treat him gently."

The houseboy was sitting up, now paying careful attention. He grinned cheekily at the hint of the taipan's well-known disposition. The Comprador took no notice of the impertinence, continuing, "You will only be five minutes from the Tsui Centre – they know the meeting is there – as do the others." After a pause he added quietly, "I know what strings to pull." Then in his peremptory manner, "You may go now."

The boy got up obediently, walking naked across the living room. The Comprador watched him go, gently smiling in appreciation. He leant back in his down pillows, reviewing his plans. Tomorrow was the *coup de grace*. He had decided to use his nephew's money, not his or K. K. Chen's. It was cleaner that way: besides, he always preferred to use other people's money than his own. And his nephew was well connected in a shadowy sort of way, being a son 'on the outside' of one of Hong Kong's richest men.

Later, looking out at the sea and the junks and the people, tea mug in hand, wearing his flowing silk housecoat, he smiled to himself, recalling how he had chosen his codename 'Merlin'. Most appropriate! The bird of prey, not the magician. For the Merlin flies slowly after its prey, simulating the flight of a pigeon, before the surprise attack.

Bruce's Flat, Broadcast Drive

They had played a very early eighteen at Kau Sai Chau to beat the heat and to make the meeting. Summer was coming to Hong Kong.

After the game, Iain wining four and three, they had called in at Bruce's flat to clean up and have a cold Tsingtao before going on to the twelve-o'clock meeting-cum-lunch at Tsui's. The flat looked as if it had been furnished by an expat – mostly black, from Dairy Farm's Ikea in Kowloon Bay.

Bruce took his mail through to the bedroom which he used as a second office. He called over his shoulder to Iain.

"There's beer in the fridge and some decent cheddar and French bread on the table. I've got a new maid. She's fantastic." He sat down at his desk, put on his computer and flicked through the envelopes. One stood out from the rest: the Hong Kong Police. He tore it open.

"Would you believe it? A courtesy letter from the police. They said it was a burglary gone wrong, case closed."

No reply from Iain. All Bruce heard was the fizz from two crown caps. He swung round to his computer, clicked on his bookmarks and went straight to the 'Weather Underground' web site. He raced through various Asian forecasts, eventually stopping briefly at North Korea. South-east, fifteen mph. He checked some other countries before logging off. He'd take his laptop to the meeting.

Iain came in to give him his Tsingtao, wrapped in a tissue to catch the condensation.

Head Office, Tsui Centre, Wanchai

This morning there was a certain tension in Tsui's conference room. Bruce, wearing a smart suit with an open neck as usual, was fiddling with his laptop on the conference table in front of him. Iain was staring out at the harbour, still in his golf clothes: a yellow Pringle with dark brown trousers and Hush Puppies.

Tsui was talking quietly to Takji. The Comprador was there today in his black high-collared Chinese robe. It made him more austere, appearing to give him extra height and accentuating his long wispy beard, grown back again. This robe, with its long-life symbol interlaced, was the houseboy's favourite. The Comprador had his slimline stainless steel briefcase with him: a sure sign, thought Iain, that there was some serious business ahead. Finally there was Sebastian, discreetly in the background, existing as an unsuspecting threat.

"Apologies from the nephew. He has been delayed," said the Comprador softly as the meeting settled down. Tsui nodded in acknowledgement. Takji remained standing, his back to the artificial fireplace. The miniature Jardine's noonday gun would not be used today. They were to have a sandwich-and-soup lunch: Gentleman's Relish thin white bread sandwiches and clear game soup.

"A word before we start." Takji spoke with confidence, in command of the situation, standing erect, hands hanging loosely at his side, looking smart today. "We have seventeen exits – about what we expected. Three of the remainder have swung behind the 'true' democracy banner. We are getting daily reports. Our people are ex-theatre, as I speak." Inviting no questions, he sat down at Tsui's right hand. All heads turned to the Comprador, seated at the bottom of the table, as he began to speak.

"I have called for this meeting," and he bowed slightly to Tsui. Standing up, he stood behind his chair, hands resting on its back. His voice had become high pitched and imperious. He was a proud man, always mindful of his duties to his ancestors, mandarins to emperors.

"We are obliged to debate our grandiose ideas. There are others, a few, who have similar goals. For example, the World Economic Forum, an organisation, and I quote: 'committed to improving the state of the world', and very little to show for it." The Comprador paused and took out his little Gold Book, holding it up high, as Mao Tse-Tung. The symbolism was not lost on Tsui.

"Good governance for all, Tsui. Yet this good governance is always linked to your favourite maxim, 'To have peace you must have force.' Is that so? There are some weaknesses in the philosophy. You must ask some questions. Is good governance dependant on force? Is it exclusive to democracy? And if it is, what is democracy? Does good governance allow for a veto?"

"Excuse me, Comprador. I have critical information," said Bruce, pointing at his laptop screen. "The wind has changed to the prevailing north-west."

Iain was on his feet. "That takes it right over Seoul, and Seoul is less than one hundred miles from the target!" Frantically he looked at his watch. "Tsui, you have to abort."

"Sit down, boy!" shouted Tsui angrily and pointing at his chair. "I always thought so. When push comes to shove, you're weak like your grandfather." Too much, Tsui thought. Calm down. "They say the fallout is contained and if there is some…"

"You bastard," shouted Iain. "You know Suk Soon is there!" He was moving quickly towards his father, jaw set, clenched fists raised. With astonishing speed Takji attacked from behind, an open-hand chop felling Iain. The Ninja caught Tsui's would-be assailant as he crumpled, and laid him gently on the carpet. No one else had moved, not even Sebastian.

Bruce was the first to react. He knelt down beside his friend, feeling his neck pulse and checking his airways before putting him in the recovery position. He looked up at Tsui still sitting in the chairman's armchair.

"He's OK."

"Of course he is!" Takji interjected forcefully.

The Comprador was sipping his tea and stroking his beard, not perturbed by the wind change or the reaction it had caused.

"Let me continue." The words were spoken with a sergeant-major's high-pitched bark to regain their attention. "Simply put, you have to save the environment first before the people, or you will have no people. We need to swing our resources behind the politics of saving the environment."

"Absolute nonsense," challenged Tsui. "It's been tried, is being tried. It doesn't work."

He wanted to upset Tsui more before the battle.

"At least we will not be putting One Sun Moon," he used the old name intentionally, "and all the work that's gone before, at risk as we are at present. We should slow down. That's why I ordered the diversion in the Philippines, nowadays the triads' backyard, to slow things down. I'm sorry about the rape; that wasn't in my plan, though I hear some enjoyed it."

Tsui had stood up and was pacing, hands clasped behind his back, a sure sign of fury and frustration. The sandwiches were being served with a silver tureen of soup on the side. Iain had dragged himself up into his chair, dazed. There was a uneasy pause until the servants left.

The nephew came in with Tsui's brother Wai Kwok, who was looking extremely nervous. Wai Kwok sat on the left of the Comprador, the nephew on the right. As his nephew sat down the Comprador leant over to him, speaking softly in French.

"Good work." His hacking into the Weather Underground site would last a few more hours.

"Master Iain, Mr Bruce," continued the Comprador, with authority, "sit tight; we have important business today." He watched Tsui still pacing and not talking. Now he spoke in a gentler tone, as if they were at one of their regular Laird House meetings. "At any rate, Tsui, where are you leading us? I see an ocean whipped up by typhoons…" As he waited for Tsui to reply, he unlocked and opened his briefcase and took out a sealed manila envelope. No one spoke. Tsui stopped pacing. The only noise was the ticking of the Victorian mantle clock and the hum of the computers. Tsui recognised his father's seal but continued to keep his own counsel. The Comprador continued. "I have here a document from your ancestors, your father. The instructions are that it is to be opened when certain preconditions are met, in the presence of any and all of the original and surviving witnesses. The preconditions are met."

The Comprador handed the paper to Wai Kwok. It was passed around the table in silence until it reached Tsui, who had returned to his carving chair. It was short – one page, five paragraphs. Tsui settled back to read.

This is the last will and testament…. Surprise number one. Next, he was terminated as taipan. The Comprador was to take over until Iain was twenty-five, the minimum age for an OSM taipan; or until the Comprador judged him able, whichever came latest. In the meantime a figurehead European taipan. In closing, the detail. United States dollars twenty million to be lodged at their HSBC bank in Covent Garden to be paid to Tsui once he had agreed not to influence OSM or its people or acquire any of its assets, including bullion. Living outside Hong Kong. The witnesses to his father's signature were the Comprador, Tsui Wai Kwok and Shelagh Tsui. As he laid the page upside down in front of him he looked down the table at his younger brother, rubbing his hands together like some latter day Pontius Pilate washing. In his officer-and-a-gentleman's voice Tsui turned to the Comprador, holding him with his steely gaze.

"What are the preconditions?"

The Comprador bowed and took another page, which again went hand to hand around the boardroom table. This one was only one paragraph, signed as before. Whilst referring to his last will in a broad and open-ended statement his father had instructed the Comprador to take over the company if he felt it under threat, for the benefit of the family. Tsui considered. This was a source of attack he had not anticipated. He could see possible ways of legal defence, which would mean a legal fight against his forebears. His foreigner side said fight through the courts. His Chinese side said no, do not go against the ancestors. As usual the Chinese side won. As he thought, a strange thought came back to him. He remembered his grandfather telling him once that when a scorpion was surrounded by fire, it fatally stung itself. The circle of fire was not complete.

"What threat?" Tsui asked, though he knew the answer.

"The China Deal. One Sun Moon is too close."

Tsui was pacing again. He came close to the family's comprador, stopping by the window.

"I'm not finished yet," Tsui said.

"Right," replied the Comprador, in his silkiest and most dangerous tone. "But you are finished in Hong Kong."

As he spoke, Sebastian's mobile rang. The Comprador smiled faintly, as though welcoming the interruption.

"Excuse me, Tsui. Tane has some unregistered visitors at reception."

"Who?" Tsui snapped.

Sebastian leant forward, talking softly. "Peter Maynard, Vimana, their two 'drivers'," then, hesitating, "…and Mr Fitzgibbon."

"Tell Tane to send them up. All welcome!" he said sarcastically. "Tell Tane to come up with them." Tane had been a good double agent. He couldn't have foreseen this.

Sebastian relayed the message and added, "Bring Bill with you." Bill was on duty with Tane. He was the largest and meanest of the Maori detail.

"Your guests, I presume, Comprador," Tsui shouted down the table. The Comprador smiled again and lowered his head, infuriating Tsui more. "What the hell do you want with Fitzgibbon?"

"He will be acting taipan," the Comprador said calmly, "until Master Iain is ready…. We need a European, a white man. What you call a 'figurehead', I think."

Is that what you thought of me? supposed Tsui, incensed. The door opened and the 'palace coup' members filed in, standing behind the Comprador: Peter Maynard, three triads from the boat people in Sai Kung, Fitzgibbon and Vimana. Tsui got up to go to his office but his way was blocked by one of the Comprador's triads. The Maori and Takji moved towards him, but Tsui shook his head.

"Not now…"

As he passed Sebastian on his way back to his seat he spoke to Sebastian in the broken Maori he had learnt from him. "Go back to South Auckland and the impenetrable security of your Iwi."

Cheng Cheng had followed Vimana, surprised by the unusual shouting and the number of people at the meeting. She stood silently by the door. The Comprador noticed her and turned to Vimana, speaking in a voice loud enough for all to hear, "Please escort Ms Cheng Cheng to the house. You will be able to help her pack two suitcases. Allow her to pack Tsui's small bag. She always includes his condoms. Take a taxi."

Tsui's eyes now smouldered with hatred. Good, thought the Comprador – control would be easier.

Vimana had started for the door at once, as if she had expected the order. She was followed by one of the Comprador's men. Sa looked anxiously at Tsui, who simply nodded his head.

Iain sat stunned, regretting the fight with his father. He'd have to talk with Uncle Alex.

* * *

The Mercedes taxi powered its way up the snake-like Peak Road on its way to Laird House. The three passengers did not speak, doing a good job of ignoring each other by staring straight ahead. Their driver was unusually young, wearing a grey HKU T-shirt and jeans. His radio was tuned to the BBC, which was broadcasting the local time one-thirty *Asian Business News*, read in the expected clipped Oxford English.

"Unsubstantiated reports from Hong Kong say that the day-to-day running of leading conglomerate OSM has been taken over by their Chinese manager – the Comprador – in the surprise resignation and absence from Hong Kong of the chairman and chief executive officer – taipan. Being a private company, OSM is not quoted on the Hang Seng, nor is it subject to the Stock Exchange's regulations, its checks and balances…"

Damn, thought Cheng Cheng, that K. K. Chen organisation was efficient.

* * *

The helicopter taking them to the airport had taken off from the helipad on top of the Tsui building. The Comprador was bound to change the name, thought Tsui. Iain would be too weak to stand up to him. Sa and Tsui were up front. She clung to his arm tightly as he stared out of the window. Behind them sat their escort Peter Maynard, and two of the Comprador's Chinese. In the wind they were flying across the harbour like a crab.

Tsui thought briefly of his father. He had never really trusted his father. He'd called Tsui 'tempestuous', but in the end he had decided he was the best he'd had. Now he had left him in a precarious position. The Comprador had moved with speed and rapier precision. Once Wai Kwok had confirmed the will authentic the battle was over, but… the Comprador had told his smart-alec nephew to abort the mission, communicating with the pilot by encrypted radio from a different site, and having their new contact in Taiwan confirm the order and its execution in person as a bona fide courier. In those first few minutes the Comprador put out a 'cease and desist' order to the principals in the China Deal. He had politely asked for Tsui's chop. Maynard had given him their tickets to London with Singapore Airlines – Economy. He'd upgrade at the airport.

As they approached, a squall cleared. Across the water, in the distance, he could see the Kowloon Hills. He felt the tug of his ancestors and all of Hong Kong.

Changi Airport, Singapore

The transit lounge at Changi was well set up for business, children and tourists. Sa and Tsui were wandering aimlessly about, in limbo. Eventually they stopped for a coffee near the swimming pool. Tsui looked at his watch.

"I need to go to the loo…. They'll be calling the flight soon." He stood up, leaning over and kissing her on the forehead. "Won't be long."

He left his hand luggage with her and strode off in his usual fashion, nearly pushing other passengers out of his way, walking in a more-or-less straight line forward. Sa smiled to herself as she watched him go.

Takji had said two young Ninjas he would recognise from training would meet him at the toilets next to the Rainforest Lounge. He picked them out in casual clothes for travelling, drinking gin and tonics, which would be Perrier with a slice of lemon and ice. He kept going towards the toilets as one of the Ninjas got up to follow him.

When they came into the toilets they used the urinals as a bossy German father was admonishing his nervous young son while he finished the boy's ablutions. As soon as they left, the Ninja and Tsui went into the end cubicle. Quickly the Ninja took a wig, long haired and grey, from his shoulder bag, shook it out and put it on Tsui. Next came a pair of heavy-framed clear-lensed glasses. Almost in one movement he took off Tsui's tie and jacket and hung it on the cubicle, miming that they should be left behind. They both heard someone come in as he handed Tsui a Canadian passport and a ticket. The Ninja opened the passport and pointed to his name 'Eldon Robert Oliver' and his birthplace. Tsui noticed that his new date of birth was the same as his real one except for one digit. The photo looked good. The Ninja pointed to the door, smiling broadly.

"Please smile."

They came out of the cubicle together, to the surprise of two men in the stalls. The Ninja was giggling.

"I hope that will keep you going for ten days!"

Tsui was so amazed he could think of nothing to say.

They began walking back to the bar. The Ninja tapped him on the arm.

"Don't walk so fast – and meander!"

What good English, thought Tsui as he slowed down. Out of the corner of his eye he saw the other Ninja leaving a 'sensible' tip on his way to joining them. Only one thing gave them away. If you looked closely with trained eyes you would notice that the Ninjas were supremely fit.

Tsui had decided against using the potential perjury and secrecy of the masonic network in China. Instead their exit would take them to Okinawa, a far-off southern province of Tokyo, whose authority Okinawans detested and whose rules and regulations were consequently more lax.

They were flying up on Air Canada, business class. From Okinawa they were going on a well-armed fishing vessel through the East China Sea and the Sea of Japan to Kanazawa castle city on the coast below the Japanese Alps. From there they would wear Shinto robes as they worked their way back to Shiga Heights.

Tsui settled back in his seat. Cheng Cheng would be all right; she'd be well taken care of. He had to find sanctuary before the Chinese picked up his trail. He thought of his Japanese connections, and of Cheng Cheng's lineage. In her soul she thought of herself as a Daughter of The Emperor, colouring her judgement. She still didn't realise that a Ninja was a Ninja. They would go to the highest bidder. Their loyalty lasted only as long as the money. He might easily become a dead-on-delivery hostage. Maybe Man Fat…

The Ninja next to him broke into his reverie.

"Well, Eldon," the young man said, "we'll be back in time for Shogatsu. Time for a fresh start."

* * *

What's taking him so long, thought Cheng Cheng. As she did so Ina sat down beside her.

"Hullo, Darling, isn't all this terrible? Tsui wanted me to go with you to London and help you settle in."

"Where's Tsui, Ina?" Sa interrupted her monologue.

"He's gone away for a bit. He doesn't want you to…"

* * *

Somehow Tsui had got them First Class seats. They were on their third glass of Moet.

Ina squeezed Cheng Cheng's hand.

"Now we're well on our way, I've got something for you."

From an inside pocket of her business suit Ina pulled out an envelope. Sa recognised Tsui's bold handwriting as tears came to her eyes. He had written on a Laird House letterhead: *Rather light a candle…*

GLOSSARY

2NW	Neighbourhood Nuclear Weapon
A	
All Black	A past or present member of the New Zealand rugby team
AIT	American Institute in Taiwan
ANZ	Australia and New Zealand Bank
B	
BBC	British Broadcasting Corporation
BVI	British Virgin Isles
C	
CD	China Deal
CEO	Chief Executive Officer
CIA	Central Intelligence Agency
CICC	China International Capital Corporation
CIM	Coffin Intercept Missile
CITICp	China International Trust & Investment Corporation (Pacific)
CKS	Chiang Kai Shek International Airport (Taiwan)
Comprador	Manager of and go-between for a hong
CW	Chinese Whistle
E	
EIU	*Economist* Intelligence Unit
EPA	Environmental Protection Agency
G	
Gaijin	Foreigner, often derogatory
Genbuku	Celebration which showed a Ninja was considered adult
Getas	Japanese wooden clogs worn with warm one-toed socks
Godown	Warehouse in Asia

Guanxi	Contacts, relations: relationships with people
Guilo	Red-faced and round-eyed stinking foreigner: ghost

H

HKU	University of Hong Kong
Hong	Mercantile house of foreign trade in China and overseas

I

IAEA	International Atomic Energy Agency
ICAC	Independent Commission Against Corruption, Hong Kong
Inchek	Uncomplimentary slang for Chinese
IPOA	International Peace Operations Association
IRA	Irish Republican Army
Iwi	Maori clan

K

Kami	Gods, Shinto
KCR	Kowloon–Canton Railway, Hong Kong
KMB	Kowloon Motor Bus Company, Hong Kong
KMT	Kuomintang Nationalist Party, Taiwan
KNU	Karen National Party, Burma

L

LEGCO	Legislative Council, Hong Kong

M

MI6	Military Intelligence Six, a now informal title for Secret Intelligence Service UK
Miko	Young lady, Shinto, Japan
MND	Ministry of National Defence, Taiwan
Mossad	The Institute for International & Special Tasks, Israel
M&S	Marks and Spencer
MTR	Mass Transit Railway, Hong Kong

N

Nipa	Palm, whose leaves are used for thatch
Niyogan	An abundance of coconut
NPA	New People's Army, the Philippines

NSB	National Security Bureau, Taiwan

O

OMA	Old Melrosian Association
Onsen	Japanese hot spring bath
OSM	One Sun Moon Company
OUE	Overseas Union Enterprise Limited

P

PBC	People's Bank of China, Central Bank
PFIAB	President's Foreign Intelligence Advisory Board, United States
PLA	People's Liberation Army, China
PRC	People's Republic of China
POTUS	President of the United States
Pulutan	Beer snacks, the Philippines

Q

Quing Ming	Tomb Sweeping Festival

R

R&R	Rest and recreation
ROC	Republic of China

S

SAR	Special Administrative Region, China
SAS(i)	South Auckland Security, New Zealand
SAS(ii)	Special Air Service, United Kingdom
SFS	Sinbad Fuel Systems
Shogatsu	Purification ceremony for New Year, Shinto
SIS	Secret Intelligence Service, United Kingdom
Snakeheads	People smugglers
SOCOM	Special Ops (operations) Command

T

Taipan	Autocratic chairman and chief executive officer of a hong
TCI	Turks and Caicos Islands: overseas territory of United Kingdom
Technion IIT	Israel Institute of Technology
TECRO	Taipei Economic & Cultural Representative Office

Tuba	Spirit made from coconut
U	
UCLA	University of California and Los Angeles
UK	United Kingdom
UN	United Nations
UNESCO	United Nations Educational, Scientific & Cultural Organisation
US	United States
USA	United States of America
W	
Wagashi	Traditional Japanese sweets
WJB	Water Jet Boat
X	
XHT	Cross-Harbour Tunnel
Y	
Yakuza	Japanese mafia
Yasukuni	Shrine for Japanese war dead including those executed by the Pacific War Tribunal
Yukata	Unlined kimono for informal use

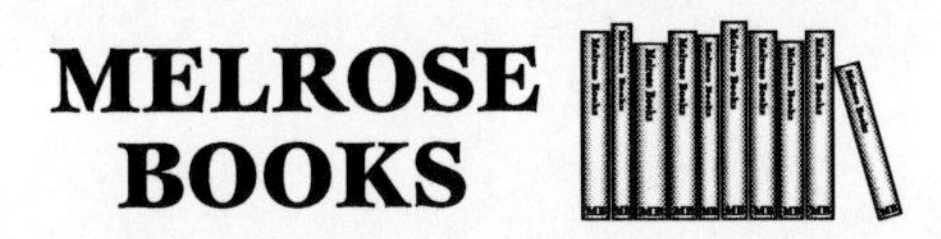

If you enjoyed this book you may also like:

The Grey Scale, Devil's Game

Claire Shearwood

Charlotte Fletcher has been surrounded by darkness for too long. Due to the extreme training techniques and torturous childhood that she has endured she has become the epitome of fear and is virtually indestructible. When she awakes to the lies which she was fed by her creator, Victor Fletcher, she sets forth against him seeking revenge. With the aid of Sam Matthews, a young Central Intelligence Agent, they discover the only way to defeat the devil is to play his game. Only one question looms, will she win and reach the white horizons which before seemed out of reach? Or will she fail, and be forever caught in the midst of grey.

Size: 198 mm x 129 mm
Binding: B Format Paperback
Pages: 128
ISBN: 978-1-907040-10-8
£9.99

Lucifer Rising

Nigel Hogge

Max Krueger's girlfriend has disappeared, and the tough ex-mercenary is angry. Very angry.
What Max and Manaha's crafty Chief of Police, Colonel "Diablo" Fernandez, don't know is that the beautiful woman has fallen into the hands of a fiendish religious sex cult and the dreaded grip of the Yakuza, the centuries-old Japanese mafia, who have come to the turbulent south-east Asian island nation of Verubia to expand their empire and feed their insatiable appetite for helpless, delectable young women.
But the Yakuza and the strange, charismatic leader of the cult have made one mistake: they've pissed off Krueger - big time!
Heart stopping excitement, weird and wonderful characters and lovely yet vulnerable women, *Lucifer Rising* takes a wild ride down the violent paths of Asia

Size: 234 mm x 156 mm
Binding: Royal Octavo Paperback
Pages: 224
ISBN: 978-1-906561-43-7
£9.99

Day of the Komodo

J. H Ainsworth

Nick Forbes, the young surgeon volunteers as an aid worker following a tsunami in Sumatra, Indonesia. Entering a disaster zone that is rife with dishonesty and deceit, his moral code would not accept the awful reality set before him. He risks his life to expose a child prostitution ring which involves a tangled web of corruption at the highest level of power.
Having embarked on a personal crusade, he must draw on all his ingenuity and courage to survive. Once more, he fought with the demons within him, knowing his mental reserves had started to run low. Survival was nothing more than a mind game.

Size: 198 mm x 129 mm
Binding: B Format Paperback
Pages: 306
ISBN: 978-1-907040-11-5
£9.99